PRAISE FOR BARBAI

"A stunner of a thriller. From the first page to the last, *Blood on the Tracks* weaves a spell that only a natural storyteller can master. And a guarantee: you'll fall in love with one of the best characters to come along in modern thriller fiction, Sydney Rose Parnell."

—Jeffery Deaver, #1 international bestselling author

"Beautifully written and heartbreakingly intense, this terrific and original debut is unforgettable. Please do not miss *Blood on the Tracks*. It fearlessly explores our darkest and most vulnerable places—and is devastatingly good. Barbara Nickless is a star."

—Hank Phillippi Ryan, winner of Anthony, Agatha, and Mary Higgins Clark awards and author of *Say No More*

"Both evocative and self-assured, Barbara Nickless's debut novel is an outstanding, hard-hitting story so gritty and real you feel it in your teeth. Do yourself a favor and give this bright talent a read."

—John Hart, multiple Edgar Award winner and *New York Times* bestselling author of *Redemption Road*

"Fast-paced and intense, *Blood on the Tracks* is an absorbing thriller that is both beautifully written and absolutely unique in character and setting. Barbara Nickless has written a twisting, tortured novel that speaks with brutal honesty of the lingering traumas of war, including and especially those wounds we cannot see. I fell hard for Parnell and her four-legged partner and can't wait to read more."

—Vicki Pettersson, *New York Times* and *USA Today* bestselling author of *Swerve*

"The aptly titled *Blood on the Tracks* offers a fresh and starkly original take on the mystery genre. Barbara Nickless has fashioned a beautifully drawn hero in take-charge, take-no-prisoners Sydney Parnell, former Marine and now a railway cop battling a deadly gang as she investigates their purported connection to a recent murder. Nickless proves a master of both form and function in establishing herself every bit the equal of Nevada Barr and Linda Fairstein. A major debut that is not to be missed."

—Jon Land, *USA Today* bestselling author

"*Blood on the Tracks* is a bullet train of action. It's one part mystery and two parts thriller with a compelling protagonist leading the charge toward a knockout finish. The internal demons of one Sydney Rose Parnell are as gripping as the external monster she's chasing around Colorado. You will long remember this spectacular debut novel."

—Mark Stevens, author of the award-winning Allison Coil Mystery series

"Nickless captures you from the first sentence. Her series features Sydney Rose Parnell, a young woman haunted by the ghosts of her past. In *Blood on the Tracks*, she doggedly pursues a killer, seeking truth even in the face of her own destruction. The true mark of a heroine. Skilled in evoking emotion from the reader, Nickless is a master of the craft, a writer to keep your eyes on."

—Chris Goff, author of *Dark Waters*

"Barbara Nickless's *Blood on the Tracks* is raw and authentic, plunging readers into the fascinating world of tough railroad cop Special Agent Sydney Rose Parnell and her Malinois sidekick, Clyde. Haunted by her military service in Iraq, Sydney Rose is brought in by the Denver Major Crimes unit to help solve a particularly brutal murder, leading her into a snake pit of hate and betrayal. Meticulously plotted and intelligently written, *Blood on the Tracks* is a superb debut novel."

—M.L. Rowland, author of the Search and Rescue Mystery novels

"*Blood on the Tracks* is a must-read debut. A suspenseful crime thriller with propulsive action, masterful writing, and a tough-as-nails cop, Sydney Rose Parnell. Readers will want more."

—Robert K. Tanenbaum, *New York Times* bestselling author of the Butch Karp-Marlene Ciampi legal thrillers

"*Blood on the Tracks* is a superb story that rises above the genre of mystery . . . It is a first-class read."

—*Denver Post*

"Nickless's writing admirably captures the fallout from a war where even survivors are trapped, forever reliving their trauma."

—*Kirkus Reviews*

"Part mystery, part antiwar story, Nickless's engrossing first novel, a series launch, introduces Sydney Rose Parnell . . . Nickless skillfully explores the dehumanizing effects resulting from the unspeakable cruelties of wartime as well as the part played by the loyalty soldiers owe to family and each other under stressful circumstances."

—*Publishers Weekly*

"An interesting tale . . . The fast pace will leave you finished in no time. Nickless seamlessly ties everything together with a shocking ending."

—*RT Book Reviews*

"If you enjoy suspense and thrillers then you will [want] *Blood on the Tracks* for your library. Full of the suspense that holds you on the edge of your seat, it's also replete with acts of bravery, moments of hope, and a host of feelings that keep the story's intensity level high. This would be a great work for a book club or reading group with a great deal of information that would create robust dialogue and debate."

—*Blogcritics*

"In *Blood on the Tracks*, Barbara Nickless delivers a thriller with the force of a speeding locomotive and the subtlety of a surgeon's knife. Sydney and Clyde are both great characters with flaws and virtues to see them through a plot thick with menace. One for contemporary thriller lovers everywhere."

—Authorlink

DEAD STOP

ALSO BY
BARBARA NICKLESS

Blood on the Tracks

DEAD STOP

BARBARA NICKLESS

THOMAS & MERCER

Text copyright © 2017 by Barbara Nickless
All rights reserved.

Published by Thomas & Mercer, Seattle

www.apub.com

Amazon, the Amazon logo, and Thomas & Mercer are trademarks of Amazon.com, Inc., or its affiliates.

ISBN-13: 9781503943384
ISBN-10: 1503943380

Cover design by Cyanotype Book Architects

Printed in the United States of America

To Nelle Anderson Stafford,
who gave me her love of words.

WHAT CAME HOME WITH HIM

Her husband brought home little from the war.

His rucksack, worn to a pale softness by desert winds. A Silver Star. Two Bronzes for valor. A promotion. A set of white creases etched around his eyes from squinting into an unforgiving sun. He came home with a slight drag in his right foot that on bad days required a cane.

But he came home.

And that, along with his newfound joy in his wife and children, made Samantha Davenport feel like the luckiest woman alive.

But there was a darker side to what Ben Davenport brought home from the war.

Nightmares. A tendency to startle. A fixed determination to drive more slowly than traffic or road conditions warranted. The occasional flare of temper followed by a long evening drinking whiskey and then a silence sharp as a suicide's knife.

Now and again he had such a faraway look in his eyes that she didn't know how to reach him.

At those times, Samantha wondered if her husband had really come home at all.

◆ ◆ ◆

Ben Davenport's youngest child didn't care about any of this. Daddy was Daddy, and eight-year-old Lucy loved him with her entire being.

That Friday, at five minutes till seven, Lucy went into the kitchen where her mother stood browning meat at the stove. In the Davenport household, family dinner was nonnegotiable. No matter how crazy things were. No matter how much Lucy's brothers grumbled about having to eat late or eat early or eat fast—whatever the night's schedule required. No matter how tired their dad was or if the dog had been sick or if one of the kids had a project due for school. Their mom traveled a lot, but when she was in town, they ate together.

Precisely as the big hand on the clock ticked onto the twelve, the garage door rattled open outside and an engine rumbled as a car pulled in.

"Daddy's home!" Lucy cried and went to crouch behind a chair at the dining table. It was part of the game.

A minute later, her father came through the kitchen door on a wave of heat, carrying with him the smell of sun-crisped grass and baked asphalt. He tossed his briefcase on a chair, set his sunglasses on the counter, and grinned at his wife.

He was a big man—six feet three and wide across his chest. His hair was military short, his face kind but serious—even, Lucy had noticed, at birthday parties and barbecues.

"Like an oven out there," he said.

Her mother leaned away from the stove to kiss him. "They're saying more rain tonight."

"Thank God."

His fingers brushed her shoulder before he turned away to rummage through the refrigerator. He emerged with a green bottle, popped off the top, and took a long drink.

"How was work today?" Lucy's mother asked. She asked the same question every night. Sometimes Lucy heard something in her mother's voice. Something sharp but hidden, like a needle lying forgotten in the carpet.

"Let's see. We got in an order of office supplies. The Internet went down for two hours. Emily brought kimchi for lunch. You ever smell that shi—stuff? Makes your eyes water. All the usual excitement."

She set down the spoon. "Dull as a butter knife, is what you mean."

Her father took a long drink. "It's fine, Sam."

"Fighting is part of you. I know you miss it."

Those words, Lucy somehow knew, were the needle sliding in.

Her father put down his beer and touched her mother's cheek. "Not half as much as I missed you guys while I was over there. I'm good, Sam."

Samantha Davenport turned her face into her husband's palm, and he pulled her close. They stayed like that for a moment, their skin flush in the evening light. They made Lucy think of the statue in France, the one they'd seen last summer at the museum. *The Kiss.* As if nothing existed but the two of them. As if that was the way it should be.

Then her father stepped back. Smiled. "And your day, my beloved?"

Her mother picked up the spoon again. She was tall, with long, dark hair and brown eyes a magazine writer had called soulful. She was a famous photographer who took pictures of mothers and children. Her photos of Lucy and her brothers hung all over the house.

"Cranky babies," her mother said. "Fretting mothers. I did get up to the factory, took more shots for next month's gallery opening."

"And no weird guy lurking in the background?"

Her eyebrows came together in that way that made Lucy think of bird's wings. "Nothing. Jack didn't see anything, either. Maybe I'm just paranoid."

Her dad nodded, but not like he agreed with her. Lucy thought her mom's assistant was mostly okay, but she was pretty sure her dad didn't like him at all. "You packed and ready to go?"

"Pretty much. Four a.m. is going to come too early." She gathered her hair in a fist and lifted it off her neck. "I'm going to miss you, Ben Davenport."

He took her hands in his, freeing her hair, and pressed his nose into the long strands. "Where are the boys?"

"Upstairs, doing their homework."

"Then it's just us." He put his arm around her.

"Daddy!" Lucy cried.

Her father winked at her mother. "Did you hear a mouse?"

"Daddy!"

"There it is again. That little field mouse. I thought we shooed it away."

"I didn't hear anything," her mother said, smiling.

"Dad-dy!" This time Lucy stomped her foot.

Her dad lowered his gaze until his eyes met Lucy's.

He winked.

Lucy lifted her chin and held up her book. "It's time, Daddy."

Her mother folded her arms, but not in an angry-mom way. "You two have twenty minutes until dinner."

In the library—it was really the family room, but Lucy and her father called it the library—Lucy grabbed Bobo and waited until her dad had turned on the lamp and seated himself in his favorite chair. Then she clambered into his lap and curled against his chest, her stuffed monkey tucked into her own lap. Her father carried the heat of the day, like a stray bit of sun in the air-conditioned house. He smelled of the office—papers and stale air but also cigarette smoke and a whiff of grease. The grease said he'd been in the yard with the trains that day.

"You had peanut butter for lunch," she said.

"Satay," he answered as he opened the book. "Chicken with peanut sauce. Much better than kimchi. Now where were we?"

His chest rumbled beneath her ear as he read. *The Lion, the Witch, and the Wardrobe.* Her favorite. Not least because her mother had named her after the little girl in the book, Lucy Pevensie. Lucy, who was brave and honest and good.

Outside, through the western windows, clouds gathered. July was the time for thunderstorms in Colorado, her mother had told her. "It might storm while I'm in New York," she'd said. "But don't be afraid. It's just God rearranging the clouds."

Lucy watched the sky darken while her father read aloud about the white witch. She could see their reflection floating in the glass. The window was a magic world; it held both the inside of the house where she and her father sat and the outside where the trees had begun to lash. Far away, a train whistle blew. Her father loved the trains. That's where he worked now that he wasn't a soldier anymore, writing a book about the railroads. But the sound of the whistle always opened up something in Lucy that was far away and sad.

A silver thread of lightning shot down from the sky. Lucy shivered.

Her dad paused in his reading. "The train?"

"No," she said, wanting to be brave. "And not the lightning, neither."

She sat on the shiver, squeezed it until it went away. Then she lifted her head and pointed toward the window. "Could we go there?"

Her father followed her gaze. "Outside? Sure, after dinner. We can go for a walk once the storm has passed."

She shook her head. "No. Look. See us in the window?"

Her dad sat up, shifting her on his lap, and squinted toward the glass. "I do, Lucy."

"And you see the trees, too?"

"I do," he answered gravely. He always took her ideas seriously. But she could feel his smile.

"It's a magic place," she said. "An in-between place. Like the wardrobe."

"What would we do there in the window, Lucy Goose?"

At the use of her nickname, she looked into his face. Her father hadn't called her Lucy Goose since she started kindergarten. Now she was a big third grader.

"We'd find things," she said. "Special things. Like Lucy did in Narnia."

"I'd like that, Lucy Goose."

She looked back down, hugged Bobo. "Does Mommy have to go?"

"Only for a few days." He tilted her chin up. "What's bothering you?"

But Lucy shook her head. She was always seeing things. That's what her teachers said. "I'm not afraid."

A shadow cut the light from the kitchen.

"The spaghetti is ready, you two," her mother said. "Come and eat." She went to the bottom of the stairs and called up for the boys to come to dinner.

Her dad eased her off his lap, set her on her feet. "Shall we dine together, milady?"

She took the arm he offered. "Of course, milord."

Dinner was the usual rambunctious affair. Noisy in the bright kitchen as rain slapped the windows, her brothers talking over each other in their eagerness to tell their parents everything that had happened that day in their summer science camp. They were big kids, twins who would be starting middle school next year.

Brian was halfway through a story about making balloon rockets with straws and string when his flailing hand caught the pitcher and sent it flying.

Juice went everywhere. Her mother stood to grab rags while her dad
and Brian knelt and began gathering the broken shards. Her parents
didn't get mad about stuff like this. They just took care of it. Lucy had
been to friends' houses, seen how different it was.

In the midst of all this, the doorbell rang.

"One of you kids get that," her mother said.

But now the boys were arguing over who had knocked over the
pitcher. Lucy stood and walked out of the kitchen toward the hall. As
she rounded the corner, the light from the kitchen fell away and the
front door emerged from the darkness. Through the window next to
the door, evening light fell soft. The storm was gone, and a single star
shone in the sky.

Far away, another train blew its whistle. Lucy paused in the hall,
one hand pressed flat against the cool texture of the wall, one foot lifted
as if afraid to touch down.

The doorbell rang again.

"Lucy!" called her mom. "It's Carla. She needs to borrow the mixer.
Can you let her in?"

The hallway grew longer. Darker. The door loomed, its brass handle
gleaming in the dying light.

Lucy glanced back into the library where her book and Bobo lay
in the chair.

Whoever had rung the bell began to knock.

"It's like the wardrobe," Lucy whispered. "Don't be afraid. It's Aslan
waiting."

Or the white witch, said a voice from somewhere.

Lucy's hand found the door handle.

Don't open it, said the same voice.

"Lucy!" called her mom.

Her thumb squeezed down on the latch and she pulled open the
door.

DAY ONE

DAY ONE

CHAPTER 1

Every chance you get, remember: hang on to the living.
Don't take up with the dead.

—*Sydney Parnell. Personal journal.*

Death did not become her.

Standing near the tracks in the cool of predawn, I ran my flashlight along the dark spaces between the wheels of the coal car and carried out as much of an assessment as I could, given the condition of the body. The jumper—railroad slang for a suicide—was an adult white female, probably in her late thirties. She had a lovely face, arresting despite her age and the blood spatter and bruising.

There wasn't anything beautiful about the rest of her.

I flicked off the flashlight, dropped it through the ring in my duty belt, and shoved my hands in the pockets of my railway police uniform, letting the velvety gray predawn air wrap around me. Sitting beside me and pressed against me, my K9 partner, Clyde, looked up into my face. His faint shivering traveled up my leg.

The death fear.

It was a gift from the war, like the ghosts.

I untucked my hands and squatted so Clyde and I were eye to eye. I tilted his muzzle up gently with my fingers.

"We're still good," I told him.

He studied my face, and after a moment his shivering stopped. I released him, and we pressed our heads together.

Somewhere on the other side of the train, a meadowlark spilled its morning song into the darkness. Something small rustled through the grasses. A couple hundred yards away, just visible between the cars, the water of the South Platte River lapped at its banks. So early in the morning, the city seemed far away, more promise than substance, the headlights on the highway like stars burning in another galaxy. For Clyde and me, this was the time when the membrane between the possible and the impossible was at a gossamer thinness.

Dawn was the time for ghosts. For we can least bear our guilt in the long, low hours of near dark, when the sun is a rumor that might never blossom.

I'd been haunted since my return from the war. My therapist talked about referential delusions and post-traumatic stress and a refusal to let go of the past. But I put my faith in a fellow Marine who told me that our ghosts are our guilt. A lot of soldiers and Marines are haunted. Eventually, my friend promised, we move on.

Now, I warily brought my gaze back to the tracks where a slick, shadowy mess of shattered bones and destroyed flesh were all that remained of a once-beautiful woman. Nothing stirred but a stray strand of her dark hair.

"No ghosts, Clyde. See?"

Clyde huffed.

I wondered if the jumper had left a note for her family. Then I wondered if she had a family. And if they would have been able to save her if they'd known what she intended.

In metropolitan Denver, an area covering forty-five hundred square miles and holding more than three million souls, how had she found this lonely place? Was it luck or planning that sent her here where there wasn't a chance in hell that someone would wander by in the middle of the night and stop her? Luck or planning that made her choose a place where the tracks curved just enough to hide her, right up until the locomotive cleared the overpass and came around the bend?

"You wanted death so badly?" I asked the corpse.

Clyde gave a small whine.

I scrubbed behind his ears. "Yeah, I know."

Clyde and I had reached the tracks half an hour earlier. I'd spotted the body—in pieces—and taken a single step toward the tracks. In an instant, I was halfway around the world, in the dust and heat of Iraq, loading parts of dead Marines into the back of a refrigerated truck.

It was Clyde's persistent nudging that had brought me back—crouched to the ground and hyperventilating—near this quiet stretch of track.

I'd been in work-mandated counseling for five months, ever since Clyde and I had helped the Denver police hunt for a killer in an investigation that led to a horrifying pileup of bodies—victims and perpetrators alike. If the therapy hadn't helped with the flashbacks and the nightmares and the ghosts, at least I'd weaned myself off the pain meds and the Ativan, off the cigarettes and the self-reproach, working hard to find my way back to a clear head and a clean conscience. Back to who I'd been before first the war and then the investigation had undermined everything I believed in.

But the past, of course, never goes away.

Clyde was doing even better. He was the most agile and fit he'd been since Iraq, his black-and-tan Belgian Malinois coat glossy, his eyes bright. The injuries he'd sustained during the manhunt were just a bad memory.

He nudged me again. Get to work, Marine.

"By all means," I told him, "don't let me slow you down."

Red-and-blue lights pulsed through the dark behind me, and a car pulled to the side of the road at the top of a small rise. A door opened and closed, and the voices of two men came softly through the gloom. The cop who'd answered my call-in, presumably, and the engineer who'd been driving this train. I'd sent the engineer up to the road to flag down the patrolman. And to get him away from the death he'd unintentionally caused.

I turned at the sound of footsteps coming down the hill. A flashlight bobbed and weaved, the beam flickering over Clyde and me, then to the ground before it came to rest on the side of the train looming against the fading stars.

"You the rent-a-cop that called it in?" asked a young male voice.

"I'm Special Agent Parnell."

I didn't take offense at his choice of words. Often, even other cops didn't understand what my job entailed. A railroad cop worked for a private company but was also a Level 1 POST-certified peace officer, just like any cop employed by the government. We had state and federal mandates to patrol, investigate, and make arrests, on and off railroad property.

I waited while Thornton PD's first responder made his way toward me. In the back glow from his flashlight, he looked no more than twenty-two or twenty-three; this was probably his first jumper. I felt a flash of pity.

His light came to settle on my face a beat too long before he lowered it. I blinked away the afterimage.

"I'm Officer Ketz," he said. "You found it?"

"Her. Yes." We shook hands. He ignored Clyde, who returned the favor.

"Detectives are on their way," he said. "Why don't we take a look-see?"

"I were you, I'd leave that to the others."

As we spoke, the sun nudged up toward the horizon and a thin glow seeped into the gray. I could make out more of his features. Ruddy skin and blue eyes. Blond hair beneath his uniform cap. I caught the faintest whiff of cologne. Officer Ketz was handsome, athletic. Confident.

He frowned at my words.

"Your first body?" he asked.

"Well, I—"

He almost patted me on the head. "First one's always the worst."

"True," I said. "Just treat it as a crime scene. And watch out for her leg. It's ten yards to your right."

He paused at that but then climbed the slight rise toward the tracks, his boots crunching on the ballast. He squatted on his haunches and panned the flashlight beneath the coal car and along the tracks.

"What the—" he started. Then, "Fuck."

I lifted my face to the cool, moist air. The stars had disappeared. From the other side of the train, the rising sun sent stabs of light in our direction, a bold promise that this July day would come on hard. Denver was suffering a record heat wave along with torrential nightly thunderstorms that had soaked the ground, overloaded the storm drains, and turned the city into a swamp. People remarked that between the weather and the uptick in crime, Denver might as well be the Congo.

Behind me came the sweep of headlights as another car pulled to a stop. More doors, then voices. Men, chatty and grumpy. The detectives.

Another sound disturbed the morning quiet. The patrol officer had managed to make it thirty feet from the tracks before he heaved his breakfast into the weeds.

"First one's always the worst," I said.

The detectives were bleary-eyed old-timers. Frank Wilson—five-eleven, overweight, and balding, his face as off-color and wrinkled as crumpled newsprint. And Al Gresino—a few years younger, six-four, red-faced and beefy, with a puffiness that hinted at heart problems.

They flashed their badges, shook my hand, and Wilson asked if Clyde would offer a paw. Clyde obliged.

"Aren't you gorgeous," Wilson said to him. "Malinois, right? Smart buggers."

Clyde preened.

"What's with the rookie?" Gresino jerked a thumb toward Ketz, who still stood bent at the waist in the weeds. He raised his voice. "Hey, this jumper pop your cherry?"

Ketz didn't turn around. But he lifted his middle finger.

"Something he ate," I said. I liked his moxie.

Gresino snorted.

I filled them in on what I knew. My engineer had observed the woman standing on the tracks while heading south at 0358. He'd been running the train at a legal fifty miles an hour and had seen her in the glare of his ditch lights. He was approximately two hundred yards out from her as he came out of the curve. He blew the whistle and put the train into an emergency stop, but the woman hadn't moved and he had no hope of avoiding a collision. Nearly a mile further on, the train finally squealed to a halt. He called dispatch, who notified me as the duty officer.

I then picked up the engineer where he was stopped and ran a quick sobriety test even as I phoned in the accident to Thornton PD and alerted an ambulance. I'd removed the train image-recorder and event-recorder hard drives, then left the conductor with the train. The engineer and I had come here. I'd found the woman, then walked up and down the towpath a hundred feet in both directions, making sure there weren't any other bodies. Standard procedure.

I left out the part about the flashback.

Wilson nodded up the hill toward the vehicles. "You run the Lexus?"

"It's registered to Samantha Davenport, over in Washington Park. Age thirty-eight. No wants or violations. The description I received fits with what I can see of the body."

"What can you make out of that mess?" Gresino asked.

"Her face," I said gently.

He turned to look.

"Wash Park?" Wilson raised an eyebrow.

Washington Park was one of the tonier neighborhoods of Denver and a forty-minute drive away in zero traffic. Wash Park citizens didn't usually end up under the wheels of trains. When the wealthy chose to die, they did it discreetly, behind closed doors.

"The Lexus's doors are locked," I said. "Interior's clean. My flashlight showed nothing inside other than a pair of sunglasses, a woman's rain jacket, and a sock monkey."

"A what?"

"A stuffed animal. It's a child's toy." Clyde had one, too, which I didn't mention. Clyde and I kept our secrets.

Gresino turned to me. "Why drive forty minutes to throw yourself under a train?"

"If that's how you mean to go," I said, "this place is as good as it gets. No one to talk you down."

Wilson nodded as though some part of him understood. "It *is* kinda peaceful here. Nice place for a picnic. Down by the river, there."

"Are you shitting me?" Gresino glared at his partner. "You some kind of nature Buddhist granola nut? It's a goddamn awful way to go. Here or anywhere."

Goddamn awful, indeed.

"Let me know when you guys are ready to break the train and get her out of there," I said. "I'll call a crew in."

◆ ◆ ◆

The train's engineer, Deke Willsby, stood by my railway-issued Ford Explorer, one foot propped on the running board. A cigarette dangled from his mouth, the ash long and soft, forgotten. His brown Denver Pacific Continental jacket hung from his shoulders like loose skin.

"Gonna be another hot one," I said as Clyde and I approached. Trying for normal.

Deke startled. His fingers found the cigarette, pulled it from his mouth. He tapped the ash free and cleared his throat.

"What's that, you say?" he asked.

I gave up on normal. "Suck of a day."

He raised his cigarette and dragged in a lungful of smoke.

"And it's just getting started," he said. His eyes were hollow.

Deke was tall and balding, his arms ropy coils of muscle from working the trains. The creases of his hands were permanently black with oil, his knuckles knotty, the skin around his eyes webbed with wrinkles from forty years staring out the windows of a locomotive. I'd seen Deke laugh until he cried, seen him red in the face with anger. Found him drunk once at a retirement party. And caught him bone weary after a long haul.

But I'd never seen him like this, as raw as the dismembered woman on the tracks.

"I'm sorry, Deke," I said.

"Oh, God, the *sound*." Deke swiped his arm across his eyes. "You can't never forget the sound. Like a meat grinder."

I'd heard this from other engineers. And it had surprised me—that one frail human body could make any protest at all against a locomotive.

"The care team is assembling back at headquarters," I said. "They'll help."

"Sure. I . . ." His lips found the cigarette again.

"What is it?"

He shook his head, blew smoke. But there was a lot going on behind his eyes.

"Your shift," I said. "How many hours in?"

He snapped into himself, pulled up a look that could have drilled pavement. "I wasn't asleep. Wasn't even tired."

"I have to ask, Deke."

That was partially a lie—neither the railroad industry nor the federal government tracked fatigue-related crashes, so there was no requirement as such. But having a potentially exhausted crew at the controls of a ten-thousand-ton train wasn't something I could ignore. And if anyone decided to sue Denver Pacific Continental over Samantha's death—a likely event—the soundness of the crew was one of the first things the lawyers would look at.

"I was ten hours in," Deke admitted. "Supposed to come off before the Joint Line, but that didn't happen."

"How many days on?"

"Six. Today's my Friday, then I got four off." His eyes met mine. "I'm not new at this. I was a little tired. What do you think Red Bull is for? But I wasn't asleep at the wheel. Watch the LocoCAM. You'll see."

Most DPC locomotives were equipped with a train image recorder—a small camera mounted on the inside window that recorded the engineer's eye-view of the track. It also tracked sound—conversation in the cab as well as horns and brakes. I'd look at it as soon as I was back in the office.

"What about Sethmeyer?" I asked. The conductor.

"He might have been a bit tired."

Meaning lights out and probably snoring.

"We run solo all the time, you know," Deke said softly, the frown still in his eyes. "No other way to manage the shifts with the railroad cutting crews."

He took another drag, then let smoke billow out like an embrace. I grabbed the chance to enjoy the nicotine secondhand and said nothing. Sympathy could be interpreted as approval.

When he fell silent, I switched tactics. "You called Betsy yet?" Betsy and Deke had been married since Christ was a corporal. This would be her third call-out.

He finished the cigarette, ground it under his boot heel. "She's on her way. Just getting off her shift at the diner."

Below us, Wilson was jotting notes while Gresino took photographs. They looked accustomed to the routine.

Jumpers weren't as rare as you might wish. Five Marines from my platoon had succumbed to the siren call of suicide. I'd stared down that monster myself. But those who used the trains to make it happen either forgot, or didn't care, that they were forcing another man or woman to kill them.

Gresino's voice floated up. "That is *not* her other leg. Is it?"

Deke looked at the ground. "I didn't . . . I couldn't . . ."

"I know, Deke."

Better to keep him busy. The Thornton cops would want the details, as would the Federal Railroad Administration. It was my job to get them. The local detectives would process the scene and determine if there was reason to believe a crime had occurred. If the coroner ruled the death accidental or a suicide, the detectives' work would be complete. Once forensics had what they needed, I'd clear the tracks and everyone would get on with their day.

Everyone except Samantha Davenport. And whoever she'd left behind.

Reluctantly, I reached in the Explorer and pulled out a clipboard with the Death and Dismemberment form.

"You ready to talk about it?" I asked.

"It's my third."

"I know."

"But—" His haunted face turned animated; the shock was wearing off. "This one was different."

"How so?"

"I been going over it in my mind. Figured maybe I wasn't thinking straight. But I'm sure. This wasn't right."

I started shaking my head. As if I'd already guessed where he was headed and didn't want to follow. "Tell me."

"It was dark. I'd just hit the overpass and come out of that curve. But, I'd swear"—his eyes found mine—"I'd swear she was hurt before I hit her. You tell those cops. I saw her in my lights before I—before it happened. She was hurt."

The nausea that had come with the flashback tried to crawl up my throat. "What did you see exactly?"

"I—" Now he was shaking, the protection of shock completely gone. "She was bloody. Eyes wide, looking right at me. Standing straight up and, I don't know, *squirming* like she wanted to get away, but she"— he was crying now—"I don't think she could move. Her mouth was open. Probably she was screaming, but I couldn't hear her over the engine. And then—and then I—"

I laid a hand on his shoulder. "Okay. Let's get the detectives up here."

He sucked in air.

"Just give me a moment," I told him.

As Clyde and I headed toward the edge of the rise so I could flag the detectives, my headset buzzed. I glanced at the number. Detective Michael Walker Cohen. A murder cop for Denver PD. Last night we'd been in his bed—*our* bed, he insisted, since I'd all but moved in with him five months ago—our bodies curled together, skin to skin, warm in the summer night. He'd told me he loved me. I'd told him that was crazy shit.

It had gone downhill from there.

We'd still been awake when, in the early hours of the morning, he'd gotten a call, thirty minutes before my own call came in. "It's bad," he'd told me after he hung up. He had rolled out of bed, splashed water on his face, stepped into his suit, grabbed a tie, and been out the door before I had time to pour coffee. He hadn't said good-bye. I hadn't expected him to. He was already with the dead.

Now I figured he was just checking in after our fight and I let it go to voice mail. I'd call him back when I was done here.

Then he sent a text.

Multiple homicide. Vics are two kids. Father also shot. Railroad link. Call me.

Kids. I lowered my phone. Closed my eyes. Planted my feet and started the slow breathing my VA counselor had taught me.

One . . . I'd been doing well. Exercising. Eating healthy. *Two* . . . maybe drinking too much. Okay, definitely drinking too much. But . . . *three* . . . nothing worse. Not even cigarettes. Going to every brutal therapy session and doing as I was told . . . *four* . . . with the faith that eventually it would make things better instead of worse.

Five. I opened my eyes.

"We're still good," I whispered.

Say it till it's true.

Down by the tracks, Wilson was on his haunches. He had his head cocked sideways as he peered under the train. He scratched at his chin with his knuckles, as if puzzled by something.

I thought of the electrical wire I'd noticed when I first approached the body. I'd figured it had dropped off one of the maintenance-of-way trucks.

She was bloody. She wanted to get away.

I punched Cohen's number.

CHAPTER 2

Mortality check.

In war, one of the first things you learn is that you don't get over finding someone who died violently. You can't spend the day in combat, then waltz through the evening swapping jokes and telling stories like any other day. Instead, the moments leading up to finding the body—and the body itself—replay in your mind like a movie. You are hung up by the suddenness of it, the senselessness. Your relief that it wasn't you, then the survivor's guilt that follows. And the horror of that what-if line that separates each corpse you recover from those you love. Mortality? Check.

—Sydney Parnell. Personal journal.

Cohen answered on the second ring. Without preamble he said, "I need you to check something for me."

My mouth was so dry I had to gather spit to speak. "Go ahead."

"I've got an alphanumeric code I have to identify. I'm thinking it's a train classification number."

Shack up with a railroad cop, you learn a few things. "Okay. Read it to me."

"*U-N-M-A-C-W-A-T,*" he spelled out. "Then the numbers *2-1*. Am I right? Is it a train ID?"

As distinctly as if someone stood behind me with a pistol, I felt a cold jab at the nape of my neck.

"Read it again," I said. Stalling.

"UNMACWAT21," Cohen said. "What is it?"

Down by the tracks, Wilson was waving Gresino over to look at whatever had caught his attention. I could read Gresino's lips. *You're shitting me.*

"It's one of ours," I said to Cohen. "But it's not a normal run. It's a regulated tanker train carrying hazardous materials. Chlorine gas."

"Damn," Cohen said. "When?"

"Give me a sec."

I ran through a mental list of the train consists I'd viewed on my laptop the day before—recalling the type and number of cars on each train along with schedules and manifests. I had a photographic memory for some things. Numbers. Maps. Anything spatial. When I joined the Marines and volunteered for Mortuary Affairs, the skill had endeared me to my CO because I could effortlessly recall serial numbers, locations, and other details for the casualty reports. I kept a catalogue of the dead more efficiently than any computer.

Now I locked onto the listing for UNMACWAT21.

"That consist doesn't actually exist yet," I said. "But once the train is assembled, it will leave the CP Eider chemical company in Macdona, Texas, on Monday at 1640," I said. "If there aren't any delays or mechanical problems, she's scheduled to come through Denver thirty hours later."

"What happens then?"

"She'll undergo a safety check then continue on her way. Fifty hours after that, she'll arrive at a waste treatment facility in Watertown, South Dakota. Denver isn't her only stop. There will be a fuel stop, seven crew changes, and nine safety and security checks along the route with a dozen regulatory agencies involved."

"What happens in Watertown?"

"Once she drops her load, she'll turn around and make the journey back, hauling the empty tankers back to Texas, along with anything else the linker needs to add along the way. She'll be back in play within twelve hours. But she'll be a junk train then. With a different designation."

"Meaning it will be a different train."

"Right."

"Okay. Hold on."

Cohen's voice was a flat line, the result of an astonishing ability to focus combined with the compartmentalization common to homicide cops. I pictured him in his expensive suit and his cheap haircut, his face tight as he jotted down everything I'd said in his spiral-bound notebook.

Sensing we were in for a wait, Clyde stretched out on the dusty ground, tongue lolling as a warm wind lifted with the rising day. Wilson and Gresino conferred near the tracks, their voices tight.

Cops are trained to never assume a call-out is a suicide—treat every unattended death as if you have no idea what happened so you don't get careless with the scene. But in a case like this one, you figure you're going through the motions. The deliberateness of the locale, the presence of the victim's car, and the fact that Samantha Davenport had been facing the train when it struck made suicide likely.

Now, though, my thoughts went down a dozen paths as I tried to understand what a hazardous materials train had to do with murdered children. "Cohen—" I began.

"Hold on."

I closed my fists.

Sometimes, in the middle of the night, while Cohen slept and I did my best not to, I studied the notebooks he used, a new one for each case. I'd take the latest book into the kitchen where I'd pour myself a finger of whiskey, then sit at the table and use the flashlight app on my phone to read his notes about whatever case he was working. It wasn't the investigation I was scrutinizing, but what he chose to say about it.

I read everything in the hope that I could understand the man who'd coaxed me into his life and who now claimed to love me.

Love, I'd told him, hadn't been part of the deal. Which sounded suitably honest. Even pious. But what I'd really meant was that I didn't know if I could ever love anyone or anything other than the man I'd fallen in love with in Iraq before he died there. And his dog, who'd come home with me.

I shook myself and bounced on my toes. Clyde's sides rose and fell gently as he snored. A true Marine, grabbing any opportunity between missions to doze. Gresino had lowered himself to a squat and was peering under the train. Wilson called Ketz over. They talked, and Wilson pointed up the hill.

Cohen came back on the line. "I need the names of the crews for that train. The names of the people who arranged the transport, and the companies and regulatory agencies involved. I also need a detailed map of the run. The tracks and everything around them. And any stops the train makes for a crew change or for those security checks or refueling. Throw in anything else you can think of. The more detail, the better. Can you get that for me?"

"Of course. Now can you tell me why you're asking about a hazmat run?"

"Also, we need to notify the Feds, and I need you to stop that train."

"You think?" I snapped, my nerves getting the better of me.

Ketz reached the top of the rise and ignored me as he headed toward his black-and-white.

"This morning's call-out," Cohen said. "The killer left us a couple of messages. Wrote one in the master bedroom, the other in the living room. That train ID and—" He stopped. His voice turned dark, pooling with anger like blood filling a sudden wound, compartmentalization gone. "In the living room, he wrote the train ID and below it the words 'If you must break the law, do it to seize power.'"

I opened my mouth to speak, then found myself speechless.

Hazmat trains were vulnerable to extremists. They were most exposed when schedules and track sharing left the cars unattended. If a terrorist managed to hack into a database of shipment types and schedules, he or she would know exactly where a hazmat train would be at any given time. He could place a bomb on a train while it sat in the windswept wilds of Wyoming, then detonate it as soon as the train reached a densely populated area.

"Then," Cohen went on, "in the bedroom he wrote something about how he'd keep killing until he's paid everyone back. The exact words were—hold on." There came the sound of pages turning. "He wrote, 'There will be killing till the score is paid.'"

"Homer," I said.

"Simpson?"

I rolled my eyes. "*The Odyssey*. 'Nor would I yet stay my hands from slaughter that way, until the suitors pay for every transgression.' After returning from Greece, Odysseus promises to murder all of Penelope's suitors. Which he then proceeds to do. I wrote a paper about it. Your killer used a translation by Robert Fitzgerald. Not quite as poetic."

"The hell," Cohen said. "I keep forgetting you're an educated railroad cop. So what about the first line, the one about power?"

"If you're asking who wrote it, my education hasn't gone that far. But jealousy and power and explosive materials—that's a dangerous cocktail."

We fell silent, thinking on that.

"Suitors?" Cohen said after a moment. "So this might be about infidelity instead of terrorism?"

"If the killer actually knows the context of the quote."

"Given that he wrote it in the master bedroom, maybe he does. The attack was personal. The father and sons shot, the mother and daughter taken. Could be the wife has a lover. Maybe she broke it off and this is his way of feeling powerful again."

"But what would a love affair have to do with a train carrying hazardous materials? Unless—"

"Unless it wasn't enough for him to kill the family," Cohen said, knowing where I was going. "Maybe he wants everyone to suffer. That whole 'killing till the score is paid.'"

Ketz opened the trunk of his unit and leaned in. Beyond him, the day lay heavy and still as the sun climbed. The river had turned from gray to green, the water an unfurled bolt of faded velvet.

"So our educated suspect killed two of the kids," Cohen said. "Father's heading to surgery. Doubtful he'll pull through. And now I find out the mother and daughter are missing. So if—" He sucked in air. "If the mother isn't the guilty party, what are the chances we'll find them alive?"

My face went hot. "A child is missing?"

"An eight-year-old girl."

Ketz emerged with a roll of crime-scene tape, a hammer, and a bag of wooden stakes.

Sweat popped on my skin. "Who are they, Cohen? The family. What is their name?"

"Davenport. Parents are Benjamin and Samantha. The missing girl is Lucy. Why?"

"I . . . fuck."

A flare of wind swooped across the nearby road and flattened the field grass. Wilson's comb-over lifted in a white salute and Gresino's maroon tie fluttered sideways. A haze of dust filled the air, and Clyde startled awake, coming to his feet as if on a premonition. I looked down the hill again to where Samantha Davenport's crushed body lay pinned beneath an incomprehensible weight.

"Parnell?" Cohen said. "What's going on? You got something?"

I thought of the sock monkey shoved halfway under the back seat. Inevitability closed like a fist around my heart.

"I don't know where the little girl is," I said. "Somewhere close, maybe."

"The hell—?"

"But he killed her mother."

CHAPTER 3

*Iraq. It was the best of times, it was the worst of times, the
age of camaraderie and the age of loathing, the epoch of belief,
and the epoch of cynicism. The season of light, and the season
of the darkest things you hope to never see. It was the spring
of our patriotism, and the winter of our disillusionment. We
were all going to heaven.*

Or so they said.

We just had to pass through hell first.

—*Sydney Parnell. Personal journal.*

Cohen and I talked quickly through our next steps, both knowing how
critical the following few hours were. We outlined what I would do
at this crime scene while I waited for him to arrive from the first one.

If Lucy had been abducted by a stranger, then hers would be the
rarest form of child kidnapping. Of the eight hundred thousand child
abductions reported each year by the National Center for Missing and
Exploited Children, only a hundred of those children were taken by
strangers.

But stranger abduction was the kind most likely to end in tragedy.
Some of these children were held in exchange for ransom, or kidnapped

by someone who wanted to raise them as their own. Many of the children were stolen for trafficking purposes—to work in fields or sweat shops or as sex slaves.

What Cohen and I both knew was that, given what someone had done to Lucy's family, she seemed likely to belong to the smallest subset of abduction victims. A child taken for the express purpose of being tortured and killed.

Most kids taken like that die within the first hour. After three hours, we could start assuming the worst. After three days, we'd almost certainly locate her body in a shallow grave. Or a dumpster. Or not at all.

Judging by when Samantha Davenport died, the first two windows had already closed.

I'd never heard of a case like this, a child taken during a home invasion while the rest of the family was slaughtered. And I didn't need so much as a single finger to count the times that an abducted child had been linked to a hazmat run. Or that the child's mother had been killed by a train.

After Cohen and I hung up, Clyde and I hurried down the hill toward the detectives, my bad knee complaining at the haste. Tendons shredded five months ago had still not completely healed. Two surgeries and hours of physical therapy had made things better. But the doctor cautioned it might never be what it was. Kind of like me.

Wilson and Gresino straightened and watched us approach with narrowed eyes. Ketz, hard at work hammering stakes into the ground, noticed the detectives' stillness, followed their gaze toward me and stopped.

The flies had found Samantha's body, and in the silence that fell after Ketz laid off his work, their whine hit like a buzz saw. The odor of death, little more than a promise when I'd arrived, had worsened, rising with the warmth seeping into the day. Why did death have to offer the parallel wound of indignity?

I stopped a safe distance away and kept a firm grip on Clyde's lead.

Wilson and Gresino watched me. There wasn't any surprise in their eyes. Whatever they'd noticed under the tracks had set them up for anything I had to tell them.

Up above, gravel crunched as a car arrived. I heard Deke's wife telling him to get in the car, that everything would be fine.

"She isn't a suicide," Wilson said. "Am I right?"

"Her name is Samantha Davenport. Her husband was critically injured and two of her children were shot dead last night in their home. A third child, eight-year-old Lucy Davenport, is missing."

I left out the part about the hazmat train due to run in two days. I didn't know where to slot that information.

"Fuck me," Gresino said. He hitched up his pant legs one at a time, like he was preparing for a sprint.

Wilson's gaze went far away. He patted his shirt pocket beneath his sports coat.

"When I woke up this morning," he said, "I thought it was going to be a beautiful day. That's what my wife said. A beautiful day." He pulled out his hand, stared at the pack of cigarettes he'd retrieved then stuffed them back in his pocket. He met my eyes. "She was tied up, looks like. Electrical wire. There's the remains of what looks like a hefty chunk of wood."

"Like the crossbar on a crucifix," Gresino put in.

Wilson glared at him. "We don't know that."

"She was cru—"

"Stop. For God's sake, stop. We don't know anything yet."

I looked away from the darkness in the detectives' eyes, put aside how their words made me feel. "Denver and Thornton's crime scene units and the lead detective from the Denver crime scene unit are en route. Right now, our focus is on the little girl."

Ketz had joined us, restlessly swinging the hammer between his second and third fingers, its steel head cupped in his palm. "They think the girl's around here?"

"She hasn't shown up yet with any friends or neighbors," I said. "They're operating under the assumption she left the house with her mother, who initially was the top suspect. Our discovery puts a different spin on things. An Amber Alert has gone out. The FBI is putting together a rapid-response team and the media's been put on notice. In an hour, the entire world will be looking for her. But right now we're all she's got."

"Goddammit," Wilson said. "She could be anywhere."

As if suddenly aware of how big "anywhere" was, the four of us took in the fields and the road, the warehouses and suburbs and the distant ruins of a former industrial site. We ended up looking between the train cars toward the river.

Ketz said, "We'll need divers."

"There's a child's toy in the Lexus," I said. "The lead detective wants us to do a quick process of the vehicle then break a window and grab that toy, see if my dog can pick up a scent trail."

"Your dog any good?" Gresino asked.

I gave him a cool stare. "Former Marine."

"Let's do it then." Wilson turned to the other men. "Al, stay on the body. Keep doing the dance. Ketz, call in additional units and have them set up a roadblock in both directions and reroute traffic off Potters. Get someone to block the bike path by the river before a bunch of exercise nuts wander in."

He rubbed his right eye with the heel of his hand and looked at the river again.

"A missing kid," he said. "Goddammit."

◆ ◆ ◆

Wilson went by the book as he did an exterior examination of the Lexus. No doubt he shared my gut-churning need to hurry. But if Clyde couldn't pick up a trail for Lucy, the SUV might be the only link we had to her. He had to do it right.

While he snapped photos of the vehicle and the surrounding area, I dialed my boss. Captain Mauer had transferred to Denver from Chicago two years ago and proved himself as worthy as any of the home-grown brass. When he picked up, I gave him a quick rundown of what I knew. The murders. The child. And the tanker train, UNMACWAT21. A train he now needed to cancel.

"I'll be damned," he said softly. "I'll jump on that data the detective asked for. And I'll cover the train. You and Clyde find that little girl."

"Yes, sir."

From the back of my Ford, I removed the tools I'd need to get inside the Lexus. I gave Clyde some water and downed him in the shade, then shucked off my jacket and pulled on sunglasses. I swung the strap of my small duffel over my shoulder and made a wide circle of my own around the Lexus, careful not to disturb the immediate area.

Samantha Davenport's car was a late-model mint-condition black SUV with tan leather interior. Vanity plates showed a stretch of green prairie with a mountain range in the distance and the word *Madonna*. An impressive ego. Or maybe a business name. I walked around to the front of the car. Grass blades and thistle stems bristled from the front grill, shoved through the grate by the speed of her passage through the field. A spatter of mud clung to the wheel wells and along the running boards.

Samantha Davenport—or whoever had been driving—had come off the road in a hurry. And, judging by the mud, she'd arrived here during or shortly after the late-night thunderstorm. With luck, the crime scene guys would manage to pull some footprints. In the thick tangle of weeds, all I could make out were a few broken stalks.

I walked to the road and looked north, the direction she'd come from. There were no rubber burns on the asphalt. If she'd hit the brakes before veering off, she hadn't braked hard. A quarter mile beyond the railroad overpass, she'd swerved, plowed through the brush by the road, and come to a stop a few feet short of the embankment that dropped steeply toward the railroad tracks.

"What were you looking for?" I asked softly. "Or was this simply your only chance? Did you run off the road hoping your daughter could escape?"

Or—an even uglier thought—had the engineer been wrong about what he thought he'd seen? Had Samantha shot her family then killed her daughter somewhere else before climbing onto the tracks? Maybe the blood hadn't been hers.

That was a path I didn't want to go down.

Assuming the killer had taken Lucy somewhere nearby, I did a three-sixty. Half a mile to the north lay a two-acre sprawl of warehouses and industrial buildings. Two miles southeast, a new housing development. Directly east, a pair of silos were just visible behind the ridgeline of a hill—an abandoned cement factory that sat slowly decaying on DPC property from the days when trains had hauled material to and from the plant on a T&W short line.

I glanced at my watch. Ten minutes had gone by. Wilson was now talking into a small voice recorder. I used my forearm to wipe sweat from my face and fumbled in my pocket for cigarettes I didn't have. Agitation burned in my stomach with the delicate touch of a welding torch.

"Day's wasting," I said to Wilson.

"Yeah, I know." He dropped his recorder in the pocket of his suit jacket. "Let's do it."

I pulled on latex gloves then walked around to the rear driver's-side door. I wedged a strip of hard plastic into the narrow gap between the top of the door and the frame, then used my fist to pound it in until the gap was wide enough to allow me to squeeze an air bladder into the opening. I inflated the bladder until the gap widened, then slid a metal rod inside and hit the unlock button. I opened the door and got out of Wilson's way.

The detective took photos of the car's interior, then leaned in with gloved hands and dislodged the stuffed animal.

"One brown stuffed animal, a monkey," he noted into his recorder. He looked around the back seat area. "The only other items visible in the car are an adult's blue rain jacket, also in the back seat. And a pair of sunglasses hanging from a clip on the driver's sun visor. We are not touching the glove box or the console between the front seats."

He emerged from the car and backed away to where I waited.

There was no way of knowing if the monkey belonged to Lucy. It could be hers or belong to one of her siblings or even the family dog. But it had a pink lace ribbon pinned to the top of its head. And a single long, light-brown hair caught around one of the shiny black buttons.

Wilson used tweezers to remove and bag the hair. Then he dropped the toy in a paper bag and handed it to me. I turned my attention to Clyde, who came to his feet, tail swishing.

"Ready to get to work, boy?"

I showed him his Kong, a bright-red chew toy that he adored. His ears came up and his tail wagged faster. For Clyde, like other military working dogs and K9s, work was play. More than that—work was joy.

I opened the bag to give him a good whiff of the sock monkey, then waited until his eyes returned to mine.

"Seek!" I said, giving him the search command.

Clyde made a beeline for the Lexus and thrust his head through the open doorway. I called him back, then gave the command again, indicating he needed to look for the scent elsewhere. He circled the SUV, found Lucy's scent on the far side and trotted down the embankment toward the train. I followed him, my heart in my throat.

"Dear God," Wilson said.

Deke was sure that only Samantha Davenport had been on the tracks. But if Deke had struck an eight-year-old child with a four-hundred-ton locomotive churning out more than ninety-seven thousand pounds of force, a glancing blow wouldn't make a sound or cause a ripple.

Then, fifteen feet from the tracks, Clyde did a ninety-degree turn and headed away from the tracks and the silent train. I found my breath again. He trotted briskly, tail straight out, hips swaying with confidence.

Where would a terrified eight-year-old go in the darkness? Storm clouds. No moon. She would have run anywhere that was *away*, I figured, her mother's voice in her ears. Maybe the train tracks—empty then—had given her a faint path in the dark.

Clyde stayed steady.

"It's a good scent," I told Wilson, who was jogging behind me.

"How will we know we're getting close?"

"Clyde will tell us."

Up above, a car drove past going the opposite direction. I glimpsed the gawking face of a woman through the driver's window and the flash of brake lights as the driver slowed before resuming speed.

"Ketz, get that roadblock up, *now*," Wilson snapped into the radio.

Clyde and I fell into the familiar rhythm we'd developed when we came back from Iraq and joined the railway police, our emotions moving back and forth along the lead as if it were an umbilical cord. Although Clyde and I hadn't been a team during the war, we'd since created a cadence born of trust, a rhythm we'd been improving the last two months through rigorous instruction and hours of practice with a man who'd trained canines for the Israeli intelligence agency Mossad, before moving to the United States. In many ways, Clyde knew me better than anyone. Likewise, I understood his needs and moods more intimately than my own.

Now my partner confidently struck due east, heading in the direction of the cement factory. Morning sun settled our shadows behind us. Larks sang in the meadow and swallows swirled up from the trees along the river, darting like arrows into the brightening sky. Beneath thistles and tuft grass, water pooled in tiny hollows, evidence of the rare Colorado monsoon. On our right, falling further behind as we walked, the train sat quietly, waiting for velocity with the patient heft of iron. The smell of oil and coal and creosote wafted in the air, a discordant note against the dusty burn of sage and the faint, sweet notes of wild primrose.

"Were you a Marine?" Wilson asked as we walked. "Like Clyde?"

"First Expeditionary Force."

"Iraq, then."

"Yes."

"You and Clyde worked together there?"

"I wasn't a handler then. Just a—" I stopped and started again. "When I was over there, Clyde's handler and I were close. After he died, someone arranged for me to take his dog."

"Your friend die in combat?"

"He was kidnapped and tortured."

"Dear God. I'm sorry."

For a moment, I had no words. Not a day went by that I didn't miss Doug Ayers. Dougie, with his wit and his booming laugh and his seemingly indefatigable optimism. Clyde, I was certain, missed him just as much.

"Sometimes," I said, "I speak before I think."

Wilson waved a forget-about-it hand. "I have a son in Afghanistan. Kandahar. He's on his third tour."

Why did you let him go? I wanted to ask. "He like it okay?"

"He must. When he's home between deployments and comes for a visit, he stays in his room playing video games. Comes out to eat. Says pretty much nothing. Grunts if we ask him questions. Then goes back to his room. Only time he seems happy is when he's heading back."

"You ever serve?" I asked.

"No."

Which meant he didn't understand that being in a war zone with your buddies was easier than trying to fit in at home. A friend of mine, a fellow Marine named Gonzo, once said that while the Marines went off to war, Americans went to the mall. Some Marines found that willful ignorance hard to forgive. And even harder to fit back into.

A lone hill now loomed above us, high enough that the tops of the silos vanished behind it as we approached. Clyde led us straight up the rise, through the last of the morning's coolness still clinging to the shadows on this western slope. My bad knee popped and creaked, and Wilson's breathing turned raspy; it would have been a steep scramble even for an eight-year-old.

And with that thought, my hope that Lucy had fled on her own dropped away like a fall from a cliff. In its place came a cold, certain fear. The killer had—for whatever reason—abandoned the Lexus and taken her to the cement factory. A grim ruin filled with broken machinery and empty windows and floors that yawned into darkness. A haunt used by tweakers and junkies and boozers. Sometimes by the insane.

The kidnapper could not mean any good from this. An abandoned factory wasn't where you stashed someone while you waited for a ransom payment.

It was where you did much worse things.

We crested the rise and emerged back into sunlight. I snugged my ball cap lower to shield my eyes as I halted Clyde and stared down at the decaying complex. Wilson straggled up alongside me. He bent at the waist and placed his hands on his thighs, sucking air. His radio buzzed with static, a back-and-forth chatter between dispatch and Thornton police.

"You got kids?" he asked when he could talk.

"No."

He straightened and stared down the hill. "Cripes. The hell *is* that place?"

"Edison Cement Works," I said. "Went under in the early nineteen hundreds."

But I knew that wasn't what he was asking. What he wanted to know was what kind of wasteland we had stumbled on.

The sprawl of buildings covered probably twenty acres. The morning light picked out every blemish and defect in a place filled with them. Unknowable structures thrust skyward, scaly with age and black with soot from long-gone furnaces. Vegetation, rarely running wild in a place as dry as Colorado, was rampant here, the roots sucking water from the South Platte to create snarled thickets of bramble and low, scraggly trees. Cacti clustered in places where the sun pooled. A deep silence hung about the landscape, as if the tweakers had fled and even the animals avoided trespassing. Above all of it, the three silos glared like baleful sentries.

"She's down there somewhere," Wilson said.

"I think so, yes."

I'd been here five or six times, sent to roust trespassers. A Sisyphean task during which I handed out protein bars and water bottles and directions to the local shelter. The last time was three months earlier, when there'd still been snow on the ground, and I'd been hobbling around with a cane and a heart monitor. So I knew the factory's baseline—the bleak melancholy of a place where humans came to hide from other humans. But now I imagined something had shifted toward venomous—as if a snake had coiled.

"It just me," Wilson said, "or does that look like a place where the devil would go to ground?"

"Let's just hope he hasn't gone too deep."

I raised my hand to motion us forward, then froze as six silent figures emerged from the ruins far below and scowled up at me. Six dead men, made that way by my hand months ago. Never mind that they had been men who practiced the worst kind of brutality—torture and murder and rape. Because however much cops and Marines don't talk about it, killing someone destroys who you thought you were. Our ghosts are our guilt, and these six had hounded me for five months, a howling chorus of retribution.

I dropped my hand. Seeing them now turned me cold.

"You okay?" Wilson asked.

The dead men turned and disappeared into the shattered stones of a warehouse, morphing into nothing more than a trick of light and shadow.

"Parnell?"

I blinked. *Lucy.* "Let's go."

I gave Clyde the seek command again and we headed down the hill, watching for cacti and prairie-dog holes. Silence descended as Wilson lowered the volume on his radio. I followed suit, adjusting my earpiece so I couldn't hear the railroad chatter.

When we were halfway down, Wilson said, "You feel like we're being watched?"

"No." *Only by the dead.*

But in truth, my skin crawled with the worry that somewhere down there, a killer observed us coming. It was just like my days rolling into some hellhole to collect the dead after a battle or an IED. Heart in your throat and eyes everywhere.

At the bottom of the hill, we closed a fifty-yard gap to reach an eight-foot-high chain-link fence angled out at the top to make scaling it difficult. The fence hadn't been here on my last visit. Along its length, signs were bolted on at regular intervals.

FUTURE HOME OF MOMA-D
MUSEUM OF MODERN ART—DENVER

"Moma Dee," Wilson said. "That some kind of art humor? Sounds like a jazz player."

Whatever it was, the sign was news to me. If DPC's board had decided to sell this stretch of land, they hadn't bothered to tell the grunts. I was scheduled to do a walk-through here next week.

Clyde turned and trotted alongside the fence. Just as Lucy or her kidnapper must have done. A dozen yards down, he stopped and pressed his nose to the fence. He gave a low whine, waiting for me to solve the puzzle of how to get him to the other side.

"They crossed here?" Wilson asked.

"Must have."

"How the hell did they do that?"

I pulled back the weeds and studied the fence, spotting a place where the links didn't quite line up. Someone had cut the metal to create a flap, which they'd then snugged back into place and fastened with wire. This kind of opening wasn't something you created in the dark of night with a hostage on your hands. Nor was it the work of casual trespassers. The killer had made the opening before the events of this morning. And he'd been calm enough in the dead of night—and had Lucy enough in his control—to take the time to open and close the gap, rewiring it shut.

The location of the gap bothered me. It was nowhere near the road that led into the cement factory; if someone came here by car, they'd have to walk half a mile in to reach this improvised gate.

Another puzzle in a day filled with them.

I dropped Clyde's lead and untwisted the wire without bothering with gloves—it was too thin to hold a print. Then Wilson and I grabbed the edge of the flap, yanking it open enough for Clyde to squeeze through. I ordered him to wait. He stopped, his eyes on mine, ready for the next command.

"You're next," I said to Wilson.

"You're kidding. I'm twice his size."

"Optimist," I said. "You can walk around to the gate, if you'd rather. Assuming you can get in there."

41

"I've been dieting, you know. Doesn't do a damn thing."

I tugged the fence open as far as it would go and waited.

"I'm wearing my best suit," he muttered. But he lowered himself to his belly and wriggled through. While he gripped the flap from the other side, I crawled in after him.

As soon as we were clear of the fence I grabbed Clyde's lead, and he took off again.

◆ ◆ ◆

The first two buildings rose quickly around us, dropping shadows so deep it was like walking into an eclipse. It was ten degrees cooler here. I tucked my sunglasses into my shirt pocket and let my eyes adjust to the gloom as I scanned the buildings. Warehouses or offices, I assumed. Graffiti festooned the old brick walls. Broken windows glared as we passed. Small creatures skittered away in the tall grass, ignored by Clyde. Mica or a similar stone glittered in the dirt. Dew-bejeweled cobwebs guarded gaping doorways.

Near the end of the passageway between the warehouses, Clyde stopped, just as he'd been trained. I gestured for him to back down as I approached the corner and pressed my back to the wall. Wilson drew his gun and followed my lead, standing against the opposite wall.

I squinted into the brilliant splash of sunlight. Nothing stirred save the whir of grasshoppers rising and falling in the weeds. An immense cogwheel lay rusting in the open. A cluster of beer bottles twinkled brightly. I swiveled and checked the area around the immediate corner. All clear. Which didn't mean anything except that Lucy's abductor wasn't waiting for us in the open with an M16 and an invitation to tea.

"See anything?" Wilson asked.

"Nothing. You?"

"Empty as a confessional in prison. But it doesn't feel right. The hair is up on the back of my neck."

"Wait here. If the killer circles around, you'll have our backs."

"Ah, hell." Wilson holstered his weapon. "Wife's always telling me I've turned into a desk jockey. You lead, I'll follow."

I unclipped Clyde's lead, giving him more range, then gave him the go ahead. He jogged north and then turned east again as he pursued Lucy's trail through the complex.

We followed him at a fast walk through shadow and sunlight as he led us past a factory and another warehouse and unnamable, cylindrical structures. Our path threaded between fallen concrete and unidentifiable slabs of metal and other chunks of debris. In one place, someone had made a campfire. The ground around the cold, charred wood was littered with empty crack vials and crumpled foil.

At each corner, Clyde stopped and waited for me to clear the next space. It was a beautiful demonstration of the drills he and I had been running under the guidance of the former Mossad K9 trainer I'd hired.

Your dog is one of the best I've seen, Avi Harel had told me. *With good training, he will amaze you. But you've become lazy, and so has he.*

Not lazy, I'd considered saying. *Afraid.*

Then, nearly a quarter mile into the complex, Clyde's behavior shifted. He was twenty feet ahead, but a sudden alertness showed in his tense posture and the prick of his ears. It was different from the reaction he'd give if we were getting close to Lucy—he was uneasy, not jubilant. If Clyde was a human Marine on guard duty, this would be when he'd put out his cigarette and go quiet.

"Clyde's got something he doesn't like," I said softly.

"What?"

"Don't know yet."

As I approached Clyde, he kept his gaze focused forward. Once I reached him, I touched his back and felt a faint shivering.

The death fear. Damn.

He'd stopped next to a half-fallen wall framing a set of stairs. The steps led down to an immense, sagging floor—a former basement-level room now completely open to the sky. The half wall, the stairs, and the floor were all that remained of whatever structure this had once been. At our feet, the ancient railroad spur that had served the factory curved through the tall grass.

But whatever interested Clyde was fifty yards away, across a meadow where five immense, beehive-shaped structures squatted in a field crisscrossed with concrete pathways. Twenty feet tall and the same distance apart, the domes were completely enclosed save for a single rounded doorway at the base of each. The railroad tracks swung behind the domes and disappeared. Beyond the buildings, a dirt road angled north.

I strained my ears, listening. Just the wind through the grass. High above, a hawk flew past, its shadow rippling along the ground.

"Kilns," Wilson whispered. "It's where they heated the raw materials to make cement. Back before someone designed rotary kilns."

I gave him a look. He grinned and tapped his forehead. "They don't make brains like this anymore."

Impatient, Clyde started forward.

"*Bleib,*" I told him. *Stay.* To Wilson, I said, "There's something dead. Up ahead."

"Dear Jesus, tell me it's not the girl." His gaze followed mine toward the domes. "What are you looking at?"

"Nothing yet."

I swung my duffel to the ground, removed my binoculars, and glassed the kilns. A swarm of flies moved in and out of one area in front of one of the domes. Whatever had attracted them was hidden by the tall grass. I handed the glasses to Wilson.

"There's something outside the second dome from the left," I said. Wilson raised the binoculars.

"Could be an animal," he said after a moment.

"Could be." I took the binoculars back and gave the area a final scan but saw nothing else. I replaced the glasses in my bag and hoisted it back onto my shoulder.

"Seek!" I said.

As we moved into the meadow, the place felt empty in a way it had not before. Save for the distant flies, the malevolence was gone as suddenly as if a spell had broken. All of nature seemed to sense it. A flock of starlings swooped in suddenly, settling on a nearby stand of cottonwood trees. A few feet in front of us, a bull snake whipped through the grass and disappeared down a hole.

As we reached the far side of the field, I halted Clyde and the three of us stopped twenty paces away from whatever the flies had been feasting on. Clyde pressed hard against my legs. I gently eased around him and took a few more steps until I could see what had drawn the insects.

A man lay sprawled on his back, his arms and legs flung wide, eyes open and empty toward the heavens. He'd been shot in the gut and left to bleed out, his face a rictus of agony.

He looked to be in his midforties, with closely trimmed blond hair and a strong, angular face, blue eyes turning opaque. He wore blue jeans, a button-down denim shirt, and a rain jacket. Even in death and with a face filled with pain, he looked cruel. The kind of man who kicked dogs and shot squirrels.

"Our killer?" Wilson whispered.

"Gut shot by an eight-year-old?" But I was wondering what kind of weapon had been used in the Davenport killings. "Maybe a security guard."

"Where's his uniform and radio?" Wilson frowned. "Nothing says the killer was working alone. Maybe they had an argument."

I took a quick glance around the open space and the other kilns, at the buildings of the cement factory. I ordered Clyde down; no need to expose us both. Then I said to Wilson, "Keep watch. I'm going closer."

I heard the scrape of Wilson's weapon leaving the holster.

As I approached the body, the flies lifted, buzzing angrily. When I was close to the dead man, I slipped my phone out of my pocket and took a few quick shots. I did it without thinking. In Iraq, it had been my job to catalog the dead. Maybe that would never leave me.

As soon as I stepped back, the flies dropped onto the body again.

"Large caliber," I said to Wilson when we were together again. "GSR and stippling suggests it was at close range."

His eyes met mine. Both of us no doubt asking ourselves what we were walking into.

Leaving the dead man for now, I again gave Clyde the seek command. He skirted the corpse and went straight to the rutted dirt track. There, he hesitated for the first time since picking up Lucy's scent at the Lexus. He sampled the air then dropped his nose to the ground. After a moment, he turned back in the direction we'd come, ignoring the body and trotting in a snakelike back-and-forth pattern around the kiln and through the surrounding vegetation. Finally, he returned to the dirt track and lifted his head to again taste the air. Then he looked at me as if to say, "I got nothin'."

Together, Wilson and I turned north, to where the road curved toward the gate.

"She's gone," Wilson said. "He must have had a car stashed and took her away. Maybe you're right—maybe the dead guy was a security guard. Saw them and tried to help Lucy."

But I was still watching Clyde. He was moving back along the track, toward the kilns. He had his nose up—whatever he'd caught wasn't a ground scent.

"Wilson," I said. "Clyde's got something."

We hurried after him. At the farthest kiln, Clyde lowered his head and nosed his way toward the entrance. Just outside the doorway, his ears lifted with an expression of high alert and he lay down. Clyde was trained to detect explosives, contraband, and trespassers. This was his signal that he had something.

"Lucy?" Wilson breathed.

I shook my head. "Something else."

Wilson and I drew our weapons and placed ourselves on either side of the entrance. I pressed my back against the sun-warmed bricks, listening.

Whether Lucy was dead or alive, I knew that she wasn't in the kiln. If she had been, Clyde would have gone straight in. But someone or something was in there. Clyde's behavior was both anxious and supremely confident. Whatever he'd found, he knew I'd be interested.

A trace of cool air wafted out of the kiln, carrying with it a mustiness of soil and old things and—it took me a moment to place it—leather. I strained my ears, but the only sounds were the flies at the body and Wilson's labored breathing from the other side of the opening.

I slid my flashlight free of its loop on my duty belt, squatted to minimize myself as a target, then leaned into the doorway and shone the light inside.

The beam flicked over a large wooden chair, then a shovel. I sent the beam higher. Beyond the chair, the light picked out words painted on the wall in red, a quote I recognized from my classics class. My breath caught as I read the words and realized the killer had been here.

STRONGER THAN LOVER'S LOVE IS LOVER'S HATE. INCURABLE, IN EACH, THE WOUNDS THEY MAKE.

Euripides, I was pretty sure. Below that was written a single line of alphanumeric code—02xx56xx15xp.

I moved the beam back toward the floor. The large, circular space was pitted with holes, and—neatly arranged on one side of the room—two long forms lay wrapped in heavy plastic. Red paint spattered the inside of the plastic.

I thought, for just a moment, that I was looking at someone's attempt to make a home. Haul in a little furniture, splash on some cheery red paint.

I flicked my beam over one of the plastic forms and saw a face peering through. Someone had taken a knife to it—there were only sockets where the eyes had been and the nose was split down the middle. The lips had been carved away, creating a morbid grin.

"No!" I shouted, coming to my feet.

Before I could step into the doorway, Clyde came up fast and pushed me back. My arms went up as I struggled for balance and my flashlight flew from my hand and sailed into the room. It landed and spun, the light winking in and out as it rotated, with each gyration shining on a thin line of copper wire running across the door. A wire as thin and delicate as a garrote.

Iraq. Heading one fine morning toward the mess tent as the sun rose. Exhausted and still filthy from the night's work. My commanding officer, the Sir, beside me, nodding at something I'd said. Something about what I'd found in the pocket of one of the dead. From up ahead came the sound of Usher on someone's boom box.

Then a deep-throated boom.

The flashlight beam hit the copper wire again. That's when I noticed the bag on the floor. And the other wires.

"Parnell?" Wilson was saying.

"Run!" I shouted, giving Wilson a push. "Go! Go! Go!"

The flies soared into the air as we sped past the dead man and raced toward the farthest kiln. My mind flashed to the thought that we should try to bring the man with us. So we'd know who he was. So there would be something left to bury.

The explosion came with a sharp staccato crack and the world broke open.

CHAPTER 4

Ghosts are the persistence of guilt. The persistence of memory.
They are the dark, drowning persistence of grief.

—Sydney Parnell. Personal journal.

Something struck my face.

In the seat next to me, Gonzo shot me a grin.

"Put on some music, Lady Hawk!" he whooped. We were all using call signs by then. "Scare the shit out of them crazy raghead motherfuckers."

"You're the crazy motherfucker," Robo muttered from the back seat.

Gonzo winked at me. "Gotta be crazy to stay sane."

I steered the seven-ton with the refrigeration unit, following the line of Humvees along the wide, flat road. Behind us came the explosives ordnance disposal team in their specially equipped vehicle. The military police brought up the rear in an armored security vehicle. Through the windshield, beyond rows of cinder-block houses, a smudge of smoke was just visible on the horizon.

Another IED. Another group of dead troops. Another broken day.

"Steady," said the Sir over the radio. "We're okay."

At precisely that instant, we blew up.

The truck hurtled into the air, pitched, then smashed like an anvil into the desert. The sky disappeared behind a wall of dust. The truck went sideways and my arms flailed for a hold, my knees slamming into the gear shift, my head striking the window, the seatbelt biting deep.

Then a long, slow silence.

Dust sprinkling into the cab like snow. Robo talking soundlessly in the back seat.

I sucked for air and found none. My lungs were clotted with debris; I was drowning in earth.

Another boom, and something wet spattered my face and chest.

Gonzo.

◆   ◆   ◆

The first sound I heard through the ringing in my ears was a deep, ragged coughing.

I lay on my back, a sharp pain in my leg and another in my shoulder. Grit cracked between my teeth. I turned my head and spat then coughed again. My eyes burned with dust and I kept them closed. Something nudged my ribs; I swatted weakly with my hands.

I rolled into a fetal position, then, with a nauseating surge of dizziness, made my way to my hands and knees. My entire body screamed in protest. My face burned. I coughed again, drooling dust onto the ground. The world spun.

"Gonzo," I whispered.

Not Habbaniyah, I told myself. Denver.

I rocked back on my heels.

Edison Cement Works. Kiln. Bodies.

Bomb.

My eyes shot open. "Clyde!"

A bark and another push against my ribs. Blinded by dust, I scrabbled for my partner. I felt his tongue warm and rough on my face and hugged him tightly before gently pushing him away. I pulled my shirt-tail free and wiped my eyes clear—blood made a Rorschach blot on the white fabric.

Clyde's nose touched mine.

Frantically, I ran my hands over his head and back, down his rib cage and then along each leg. My hands came away thick with dust but otherwise clean.

"You're okay, Clyde. *Brav*! Good boy." My voice sounded like it came from half a mile away. I gathered spit and yelled, "Wilson!"

"I'm . . . okay!" His voice was faint. Maybe he was a faster runner than I was.

"I'm over here!" I called.

Done with Clyde, I checked myself. As I'd been taught in the Marines, I patted my legs, then squeezed my groin, armpits and neck, looking for arterial bleeding. When I lifted my fingers to my face, they came back bloody. Gently, I ran my fingers over my face and skull—the wounds seemed superficial. I rotated every joint. My knee felt like someone had taken it out with a sledgehammer. My leg and shoulder still hurt. But nothing was broken.

"We're all right," I whispered to Clyde.

I felt around on the ground until I found my earpiece and shoved it into my pocket next to my phone. Nearby was my hat. My sunglasses—an expensive pair of Ray-Ban aviators from Cohen—were shattered. He should know better than to give good gear to a railroad cop. I leaned on Clyde and staggered to my feet, stumbling away from the kiln and into the open.

The structure Clyde had kept me from entering was vaporized. In its place was a deep, gaping hole rimmed with debris. The explosion had sent the bricks flying out in all directions and raised a cloud of dust I couldn't see the end of. The chair, the bodies, the message in red paint, all were gone. As was the body of the dead man. When I saw a foot and ankle, severed from the rest of the body, I closed my eyes, picturing the red flags we'd used in Iraq to mark remains.

Just like Samantha Davenport.

Breathe. Stay here.

Please stay here.

When the ground stayed steady under my feet, I opened my eyes again, well aware that only distance and the intervening structures had saved Clyde and me from being blown apart.

"Wilson?" I ran my tongue along my dust-furred teeth and tried again. "Wilson!"

"Can't . . . get up."

I turned in a circle. Through the haze, I could just make out a form lying on the ground a dozen yards away. Clyde and I stumbled across the ruined landscape and found the detective sprawled on his back. His eyes were closed, his face awash with blood.

"Wilson! Dammit, you said you were okay."

He groaned.

I dropped next to him and studied the gash running across his forehead. Wide and shallow. A bleeder. I did a quick check of the rest of him. He'd suffered a lot of superficial cuts on his arms and he had a painful-looking wound on his thigh. His left arm lay awkwardly across his stomach, the wrist turned at a bad angle and clearly broken. When I looked more closely, I saw a growing stain of blood beneath his hand. Gently I moved the arm aside, ignoring his groan, and lifted his suit jacket. Blinked. Put it back. I reached for my radio.

"First responders are inbound," dispatch told me.

I touched Wilson's shoulder. "Can you hear me?"

He opened his eyes, squeezed them shut. "The hell?" he croaked.

I forced a smile. "You look like shit."

His smile was more a grimace, his teeth red. When he tried to open his eyes again, I told him to wait. I wiped his eyes as I had mine, using my shirt to clear away the worst of the dirt and blood.

"Florence Nightingale," he said when I'd finished. "Clyde okay?"

"Yes. He's good."

Wilson coughed. "You look like a fucking dust mop."

"An improvement, then."

His eyes found mine. "Lucy?"

"She wasn't in there. Clyde would have known."

"What did you see? Before the bomb?"

"Bodies," I said, picturing the destroyed face that had stared at me through the heavy plastic. "Two of them."

Approaching sirens wailed. A long string of vehicles sped along the road toward the gate, their lights dulled by the miasma of dust and smoke.

"Cavalry's coming," I said. As if they could fix what had happened here.

"Damn chest hurts like a son of a bitch."

"I know, I know," I soothed. "They'll take care of you."

"Asshole got my best suit." Wilson's gaze drifted away, turned distant. "Wife always said I'd be buried in it."

"Stop." I caught his fingers with mine and held tight. Because I'd seen the ruin underneath his coat and knew: some things you couldn't fix.

"My son," he said. "You should talk to him."

"I'm going to bring the EMTs to you," I told him. "Five minutes. Promise you won't move until I come back."

"We gotta find Lucy."

"We will. But for now, I need you to stay here while I get the paramedics. Okay? Promise?"

"Lucy."

"Try to be a hero, you'll just slow us down."

He closed his eyes. Color leeched from his face as I watched.

"Wilson? Frank! Damn it, answer me."

His cough came wet and deep.

"I'm thinking it's not so bad," he said. "Being a desk jockey."

◆ ◆ ◆

Thirty minutes later, I stood with Lieutenant Engel of the Denver PD and watched as the paramedics loaded Detective Frank Wilson, pale and sedated but still alive, into the back of an ambulance.

"We'll take good care of him," said one of the EMTs. A woman with dark curls and kind eyes.

"He has a boy," I told her. "A son in Afghanistan."

Sympathy surfaced in her eyes behind the professional calm. She gave my arm a squeeze, then climbed into the back.

The driver closed the doors and headed toward the cab.

"Wait," I said. "Where are you taking him?"

"The K and G. He's a cop, right?"

Denver Health Medical Center. Otherwise known as the Knife and Gun Club because they had the best trauma center. If you were a cop and the paramedics took you anywhere else, the first thing you did when you got there was look around for a priest.

The driver opened the door. "You need to go, too. You need a chest X-ray. And an MRI. You don't want to be one of the walking wounded. A bomb can—"

"I know. I got it."

Clyde and I waited by the gate with the lieutenant as the ambulance pulled away, a feathery plume of dust rising in its wake. When the driver reached the road, he hit the lights and siren and amped up the speed. I watched until the strobe of lights blended into the rush of traffic on the interstate.

"He'll be all right," Engel said. He didn't meet my eyes.

"Sure," I agreed.

"How about you? You gonna be—"

"I'm fine." I shoved my hands in my pockets so he wouldn't see them shaking.

"You'll go to the hospital later?"

"Of course."

But I wouldn't. I'd been outdoors when the bomb detonated and I'd found shelter behind multiple structures before it blew. Which meant I was probably fine. And anyway, the kinds of brain injuries created from a bomb blast are generally subtle, long-lasting, and untreatable. At the hospital, they'd give me aspirin and a rabbit's foot—equally effective.

Engel cleared his throat. "Get you some water?"

"And some for my dog. Thank you."

Engel left, heading down the line of vehicles toward a canopy tent where paramedics were setting up a first aid station for what was likely to become command central in the search for Lucy Davenport. I found an empty patrol car and steadied myself against the driver's door. My eyes burned hot and for a moment I worried my own terror would drive me down. It had been a long time since I'd had to face the aftermath of a bomb. I'd planned on making it forever.

No panty waists, Gonzo whispered in my ear. *No fucking girlie yellow-bellied ninnies.*

"Shove off," I said. I'd handled myself just fine in Iraq. But maybe I didn't have it anymore. I pushed away from the car and stood straight, ignoring the way my knees shook.

During the time the paramedics had been taking care of Wilson, motes of dust had begun drifting back to earth like startled birds returning to roost. In the thinning haze, law enforcement continued to arrive in a cacophony of noise. Flashing lights, blaring horns, the wail of sirens and the screech of tires. Doors and trunks opened, then slammed shut. Feet pounded, men shouted, radios squalled like abandoned children. All around were cops from Thornton and Denver, sheriff's deputies from Adams and Weld Counties, a handful of departmental brass, and the requisite PR people. On the far side of the gate, the morgue guys chatted with a man I recognized as a forensics photographer—they stood near a series of folding tables where evidence would be collected. The Denver crime scene detectives were busy around their mobile-lab vehicle, and a hostage negotiation team wearing headsets and Kevlar waited on standby. A three-person bomb crew in heavy blast suits conferred a safe distance from the kilns, watching their bomb-disposal robot roll toward the door of one of the structures. Parked along the road was the GPR engineer—he'd be using ground-penetrating radar to scan the area near the kilns for Lucy or any other victims.

Further away, Thornton SWAT and their bomb-detecting K9s had spread through the complex, checking and clearing each space. Their voices, strong and masculine and confidence-inspiring, echoed among the structures as they called to each other.

All of this manpower, all of this investigative and forensic talent and sheer show of strength, should have made me feel better. But I looked at the silent, indifferent silos looming overhead and I thought about what I'd seen in that kiln. Thought about what Cohen had found in the Davenport home and the severity of Wilson's wounds and the knowledge that all of us had arrived too late to save Samantha Davenport and maybe her daughter. And I ran hard into a truth I'd known since Iraq. You could throw everything you had at a problem—firepower, manpower, logistical support. You could get a lot of really smart people working on it. You could even get a lot of people to sacrifice their lives for it.

And, in the end, might be all you've got is the same problem and a higher body count.

Forget saving the world. Sometimes you can't even save one small child.

I swiped at my eyes as Lieutenant Engel reappeared with a large bottle of water. He looked at my sweat-sheened face, and I could see the debate raging behind his eyes. Let her do her job or insist she go to the hospital? And from there take a quick hop over to the psych ward.

He passed me the bottle. "I tried to find a bowl for your partner there. They didn't have anything."

"I have a bowl in my bag. We're good."

"If you want to get to the hospital straightaway, we can get your full story later."

Anger flared like the strike of a match. I looked down so he wouldn't see the heat in my face. Staying near the bomb crater now would keep me from developing avoidance behaviors. Familiarity bred contempt— or at least acceptance. No different—I told myself—from getting back on a bicycle after a fall.

"I'll wait," I said.

"Okay. Good. Detective Cohen is on his way. And the Feds are sending in specialists. A terrorist task force and an abduction team. You okay to wait for them to arrive? Say, thirty minutes?"

"Of course." *Suck it up, Marine.* "I'm just going to bum a cigarette from someone and let my dog stretch his legs. I'll be back."

"Here." Engel pulled out a pack of cigarettes and a book of matches. "Keep them. I got a stash in my car. Wife tells me we should be buying stock."

I took the pack and forced a smile. "Thanks."

But his wary look remained. I felt his gaze on me as Clyde and I headed out into the field.

I shook out a cigarette and lit it as we walked, sucking in the sweet burn. Five months of restraint up in smoke. The morning sun drilled through us as if focused by a magnifying lens. Spots danced before my eyes in the white light, and Clyde's tongue unfurled like a roll of carpet. The voices of the police and the chatter of their radios faded as we walked; closer by, insects droned, and the tall grass whispered against our legs. The smell of concrete dust hung in the air along with the wet-dirt odor of weeds. Overlaying that, the chemical burn of the bomb swirled in the wind's eddies like a vortex, trying to suck me into the past.

I pulled a tennis ball out of my bag and threw it hard, giving Clyde some exercise in a space newly cleared by SWAT. He didn't seem to be suffering any emotional fallout from the blast. But just in case, I hoped a game of fetch would shake him out of it. And it gave me a chance to check him for any injuries I might have missed.

I threw the ball a few times, and Clyde gamely ran it down. He looked good—no break in his stride, no hesitation. But the day was climbing toward the upper nineties; I whistled him back and found a wedge of shade next to a ruined wall thick with vine. Clyde and I shared the lieutenant's water, then Clyde circled and made a place for himself among the weeds. I snugged in next to him on the damp ground, leaned against the wall, and enjoyed another cigarette. A few minutes was all I needed, I told myself. Just long enough to gather myself.

But it was a lie. My hands shook, my knees trembled, and my thoughts were so scrambled it was like a second bomb had gone off inside my head.

I startled when Clyde came to his feet.

The Sir walked toward us from the crowd of first responders, his body a shimmer of light, his stride smooth despite the ruin of his legs. For months, the only place I'd seen him had been in my nightmares. Now he crossed the field, gave Clyde and me a nod, then hunkered down next to us, spectral hands dangling between ghostly thighs.

Our ghosts were our guilt. Nothing more. I pulled in my feet and hugged my knees.

Through my two tours in Iraq working Mortuary Affairs, the Sir had been my everything—commander, mentor, confidant. Then one night he'd asked for my help covering up an atrocity. At the time, I'd been certain we were doing the right thing. That the ends justified the means. But everything had gone to hell after that, and a lot of people had died. Loyalty and betrayal had become so knotted up inside me that I didn't know where one ended and the other began.

"Why are you here?" I whispered.

"I'm wondering what you're going to do about this child."

"I'm a railroad cop," I reminded him. "I'm going to tell people what happened, then go on with my day."

The Sir worked out a crick in his neck as if he could actually feel it. "You going to let a bomb stop you from doing the right thing?"

"Survival is not without its appeal." I pulled on the cigarette, enjoying the irony.

"Survival is a short-term strategy. Don't confuse it with living. Life isn't about whether you live or die. Because we're all gonna die—not a damn thing any of us can do about that."

"Right," I snapped. "The war didn't help me figure that out."

"Rather," he went on, "life is about the grace. About making sure that while you *are* alive, you're living for something bigger than yourself. Frankly, Corporal, you've had your head up your ass, thinking these last few months have been a life."

"You're wrong. I've been working, training Clyde. Going to community college. Maybe falling in love. That *is* living."

For a dead man, his look was penetrating. "What you've been doing is eating, shitting, watching crap on TV, and pretending to fall in love when you're too scared to actually do it. Even your damn job is all about hiding from yourself. You can give that bullshit to your counselor, Corporal, but not to me. It's time to go outside the wire."

Clyde's ears flicked. In the field, the Six drifted into view. Dead men with tattoos and shattered skulls and eyes of flint. They'd fought ferociously for their lives. And I'd killed them anyway.

I kept my eyes on them. My earlier uncertainty about this investigation had hardened into miserable resolve. "Clyde and I are done with death investigations. We left that in Iraq."

The Sir snorted. "You want to spend your life as a damn *fobbit*, shaking in your boots while someone else does what needs doing?"

A fobbit—a Marine who hides inside the wire while his buddies go out and do the tough work. My anger rose like a slap.

"I'm no fobbit, sir. In Iraq, I went out every single time. But the thing is, if I step into this, I'm not sure I'll find my way back. I'm—" I sucked in air. "I'm tired of killing."

He shook his head at me. "We do what we have to do. And we learn to live with it later."

"Easy for you to say," I sniped. "You're dead."

The Sir pressed. "You let a child down before. How you going to feel if you stay inside the wire while all of this is going down?"

That one hurt. I drew on the cigarette, sucked heat into my lungs, stared off at the bomb techs in the distance. "Alive, for starters."

"You believe that?"

I smashed the cigarette against the wall. "I liked you better when you didn't talk much."

"My wife used to say the same thing."

We were both quiet then, stung by life's small moments.

After a time I said, "Truth is, sir, I think I'm turning certifiable."

He shrugged. "If you're hell-bent on going crazy, Corporal, be my guest. But right now we need every boot on the ground, so I suggest you take the slow train getting there."

"No offense, sir, but it's a bit late for that. I *am* talking to a dead man."

Was that a hint of a smile? "Crazy isn't all bad." He stood. "Ooh rah, Marine."

He strode off into the field, his desert uniform stiff with dust and blood. He walked through the six men, who turned and followed him. Halfway across the field, they disappeared.

Clyde and I looked at each other. "You think I'm a fobbit?" I asked.

Clyde stayed silent.

"Thanks, partner."

Cohen's sedan pulled in between a pair of patrol units. He parked, threw open the driver's door, and leapt out. He mouthed my name as he took in the dust and the bomb unit and the SWAT vehicles. Was that how I'd looked when I found the Sir lying dead—my eyes wide with horror?

I rose and walked toward him, an arm raised to catch his attention.

He spotted me and took three steps in my direction, then stopped and braced himself as Clyde surged toward him with full dog-on zeal.

Belgian Malinois may not be as hefty as their German shepherd cousins. But they made up for it with a level of enthusiasm shown by two-year-olds at Christmas. And the detective was someone Clyde had a lot of enthusiasm for.

Cohen had cared for my partner when I'd been in the hospital the previous winter. He'd earned Clyde's undying love through shameless bribery—daily treats of T-bone steak. Probably lobster and caviar, too, given Cohen's faith in food. I counted myself lucky my partner hadn't developed a Scotch habit while I was laid up.

Cohen knelt in the weeds as Clyde reached him and roughed Clyde's fur with equal zeal. It *had* been hours since they'd seen each other.

When I caught up, Cohen let go of my partner and stood. He opened his arms to hug me, and without intending it, I flinched. Something faded in his eyes, but after a beat, he hugged me anyway.

"Sorry," I whispered into his shoulder as the warmth and weight of his presence brought me back. "I'm not myself."

His lips brushed mine, then he stepped away, giving me space.

Cohen was a tall man, lean beneath his suit. He laughed a lot, despite his job, and carried a soft spot for strays like Clyde and me. But this morning, any laughter was far away. His gray eyes were dark as wells and deep lines bracketed his mouth. He looked exactly like a man who'd been up much of the night, most of it for nothing good.

He frowned. "You're hurt."

"I'm fine."

"You're bleeding." He tipped his head toward my forehead. "In case you hadn't noticed."

I pushed back my cap and touched two fingers to my scalp, stared at the wetness that had leaked through the bandage taped on by the paramedic. "I'll take care of it."

"Did an EMT look at you?"

"All checked out."

"They said you're good?"

"I'm good." I directed Clyde into the shade of Cohen's car. "Tell me what we've got."

Cohen considered me, wondering how far sideways the bomb had knocked me. And how much to trust me about it. But after a moment he pulled sunglasses out of his shirt pocket and slid them over his eyes. Debate over.

"I know you'll go through everything when the Feds get here," he said. "But give me the morning's highlights."

I lit a cigarette and filled him in on the last couple of hours, telling him about the man we'd found gut shot and about the two bodies in the kiln, at least one of which showed signs of torture. I texted him my pictures of the dead man and sent another text with the alphanumeric code that had been written in the kiln. I ended with the fact that although Clyde and I were all right, Wilson was badly injured. And it didn't look good.

Cohen listened in silence. When I was done, he borrowed my cigarette and took a single puff before handing it back. "The father, Ben Davenport, works for DPC."

I jerked in surprise. I hadn't made the connection when I ran Samantha Davenport's plate. "Ben is Hiram Davenport's son?"

"His only child."

My chest ached with that. "How did he take the news?"

Cohen leaned back against his car and shrugged. "The victim's advocate said he calmly asked her a few questions, then kicked her out. A man like him, I'd figure he needs all the friends he can get."

We watched as the bomb techs sent their robot trundling toward the next kiln. The bot's double-track tread rumbled over the debris, its armlike manipulator bouncing. Grasshoppers ping-ponged out of the way.

Hiram Davenport was the owner and CEO of Denver Pacific Continental. A poor kid from Ohio, he'd scrabbled his way into Harvard and an MBA, married the daughter of DPC's owner, then steered his father-in-law's railroad from its nineteenth-century gold mining roots into one of the country's top freights. Under his leadership, DPC grew to thirty-five thousand miles of track and forty-five thousand employees.

It had been years since Hiram had anything to do with day-to-day operations. But six months earlier he'd proposed building a high-speed train to run from a hub in Denver to the surrounding states. This Gold Line Express would be his crowning glory. But the project wasn't yet his; he was in an all-out battle with the west's other big railroad, SFCO, for billions in federal funding. Pundits and corporate watchdogs considered him the likely winner. But whether it was Hiram who won or the owners of SFCO—Alfred Tate and his son, Lancing—the bullet train would make Colorado a model of modernity and environmental soundness.

Or the owner of the country's priciest white elephant.

I crossed my arms and tucked my chin, thinking. "Tell me what you're looking at."

"We've got four angles that I can see. One, someone doesn't want that bullet train and is attacking the man most likely to build it. If so, that means Lancing Tate is also vulnerable. Tate mentioned that someone has been sabotaging his trains, which could be linked. So we've got men with him."

"What else?"

"This is the first volley by terrorists who are targeting the railroad infrastructure. That theory could, of course, tie in with the first possibility. Or"—he shoved his hands in his pockets—"it's more personal. Either the lover angle or the business rivalry. You've seen the shots Hiram and Tate have fired at each other?"

I nodded. Every day brought a new video clip or sound bite from one side or the other in this clash of the titans. It was pure bank for the media; when the gods fight, people pay to watch.

"Ben Davenport was hired six months ago to write a history of his father's railroad," Cohen said. "He's published an article every few weeks."

"Puff pieces?"

"Pretty much. No question they're designed to convince investors and the Feds that Hiram, not Lancing Tate, is the man to take American railroading into the twenty-first century. Ben's status as a decorated war hero gives his stories weight."

"Bet the Tates love that."

"Tate, single. Just found out that Tate senior had a stroke six months ago. He's alive, but he can't even go to the bathroom by himself."

"What about Lancing, then? How's he taking Ben's articles?"

"Oh, he's angry. But something this savage . . ." Cohen's voice trailed off.

"Don't they say one in five American CEOs is a psychopath?"

He gave a half laugh, the sound harsh. "That's why we're talking to Tate as well as protecting him. But his alibi is solid. Did your train have a video recorder?"

I nodded. "I pulled the TIR's hard drive, but you need special software to view it. As soon as we finish here with the Feds and I'm back in my office, I'll burn the relevant segment to a CD."

In the distance, the SWAT team and their dogs appeared, heading back toward the command area. They moved slowly, the dogs dragging tongue and tail, the men carrying their helmets, their faces sheened with sweat.

"No more bombs," I said, too softly for Cohen to hear.

Cohen checked his watch. "Feds said they'd be here by now. We're burning up daylight."

We fell quiet. I settled with my back against his car and closed my eyes. The heat danced spots on the other side of my eyelids and I swayed, still carrying the events of the morning like a live wire in my hands.

"Sydney." Cohen cleared his throat. "You don't have to pretend. Not with me."

My eyes shot open. "Would you shut up? I'm fine."

"You forget I'm the one who listens to you talk in your sleep."

"You *eavesdrop*?"

"Shamelessly. Mostly you mutter. Makes it damn hard to work out what you're going on about. Bombs and guns. Lethal hand-to-hand. Normal girlfriend shit like that."

I reached for a joke about how *all* Marines talk about bombs and guns. But instead I was thinking I'd never be able to keep my secrets if I needed a muzzle at night.

"Your job," I said, "is to make me feel better. And you suck at it."

"I'm just doing a little reality check. You got that denial thing going."

I looked at him full-on. "You talk in your sleep, too."

"Don't change the subject."

I love you, he'd said to me in the dark hours of early morning. And he'd been fully awake when he said it. But love had to be built on mutual understanding, and Cohen and I were still groping our way toward that. I didn't have a lot of confidence we'd get there. We'd grown up in worlds so far apart that one of us might as well have been raised by wolves. That, of course, would be me.

Plus there was the fact that at least one of us carried secrets that could get you killed. Five months earlier, a man claiming to work for the CIA had come to kill me. I'd spared his life and sent him back to his superiors with a message: Despite what they believed, my beloved in Iraq hadn't given me anything before he died beyond a few personal effects and his dog. No list of spies, no secret plans, no map to Saddam Hussein's gold. I had nothing they could possibly want and I had no idea how to find the little Iraqi boy they were also searching for. I hoped that by sparing their man, I'd proven myself credible. They were now free to crawl back into their respective holes and leave me alone.

But I'd have to be crazier than I am to count on that. So I'd taken the few things my beloved had given me and locked them away, then spent the last five months watching over my shoulder. Watching over Cohen's shoulder, too, although he had no idea. Five months, and nothing but silence. Except for the scar at my hairline and the hole in my kitchen drywall, I could almost chalk everything up to paranoid delusion.

Now, in the droning summer warmth, I crossed my ankles, letting the car take most of my weight. Heat radiated from the metal.

"About this morning," I said. "When you told me you—"

"Don't worry about it." He gave me a lopsided grin, all the more poignant for being so hard to manufacture on a day like this. "I just didn't want it to be obvious that it's all about the sex."

"The sex is pretty good," I admitted.

"Not too shabby," Cohen agreed.

The wind gave a little kick, and the last of the dust from the bomb swirled away. Overhead, the sky was as wide and untroubled as a clear conscience. Smoke from my cigarette vanished with the breeze. A red-winged blackbird lit on the fence erected by MoMA-D and gave a single, lonely trill.

"I *am* sorry about this morning," I said. Glutton for punishment. "I shouldn't rush you."

"But I didn't need to be an ass about it."

"Half an ass."

I elbowed him.

"Okay," he said. "Total ass."

I couldn't help it. I laughed. He smiled. For just a moment, God was in his heaven.

Behind us, engines rumbled. We turned and watched as a pair of Ford pickups threaded their way around the other vehicles and pulled to a stop near the gate. A woman stepped out from the first truck. Tall, early fifties, dressed in slacks and a navy blazer, her thick, brown hair cut short to frame her face, a badge on a lanyard around her neck. She wore sunglasses and looked as composed as if she were glancing over a wine menu.

Two men got out of the second truck. They wore navy-blue jackets stenciled with bright yellow lettering: FBI. Then below that, JTTF.

"The woman must be our SAC," Cohen said. "Madeline McConnell. She's in charge of the CARD."

My bomb-addled brain hurried to catch up with Cohen's alphabet soup. SAC. Special Agent in Charge. And CARD. The FBI's Child Abduction Rapid Deployment team. At least I knew the other string of letters. The JTTF was the Joint Terrorism Task Force.

Lieutenant Engel had seen the three agents and was heading toward them. He waved at Cohen and me, gesturing for us to join them.

I dropped the cigarette, stepped on it, and retrieved the butt. I pulled my earpiece from my pocket. "Time to roll."

Special Agent in Charge McConnell's poise was even more striking up close. I wondered if she'd ever been drunk or lost her temper, said something she regretted or smoked her way through a pack of cigarettes before she even got out of bed. I'd bet my bank account she'd never had Jack Daniel's on her morning cereal.

I wondered how it was possible to reach your fifties and be so self-possessed. Today, even thirty felt out of reach.

The JTTF agents had the erect bearing and tight haircuts of former military. John Ritland was midthirties, five-ten, a weight lifter, with an old scar at his temple and another along his jaw. He was all economy of motion, but the spark in his eye suggested he was prepared to kick ass before his target saw it coming. His partner, Bob Wyman, looked ten years older and was five inches taller, but he had the same look in his eye. I liked them both immediately.

We shook hands all around.

"I heard about you," McConnell said when I introduced myself. Her eyes were invisible behind the shades. "You took down that white supremacist gang last February. Excellent investigation. The papers called you a hero. You're still working the rails?"

"Even heroes need gainful employment."

She regarded me a moment longer, and I got the distinct impression she was disappointed with my decision.

"There a problem?" I asked.

A beat of silence. Then she said, "Of course not."

Her gaze shifted to my partner and she squatted so she was eye level with Clyde. "This must be former Staff Sergeant Clyde."

I nodded, surprised at her use of his rank.

"Belgian Malinois," she said. "Best breed there is. Loyal. And smart as hell."

Clyde preened, clearly smitten. Pushover.

McConnell straightened. "You were a sergeant," she said.

So she knew the tradition of ranking military working dogs one level higher than their handlers as a way of showing respect and ensuring discipline.

I shook my head. "A lowly corporal. I inherited Clyde from his second handler."

She seemed about to ask more but read the warning in my eyes. There were lines no one was allowed to cross.

Engel cleared his throat. "We're happy to have your help, Agent McConnell. You'll be leading CARD?"

She rose. "Call me Mac, please. And yes, I'm the lead on CARD, at least for the moment. If we don't find Lucy within twenty-four hours, they'll send someone from LA." At our expressions, she added, "It's about protocol, not experience. I spent six years working CARD in Alabama and Texas. Had a ninety-five percent recovery rate. So I'm not unfamiliar with the process. Just tell me what assistance you would like. My team is at your disposal."

"Appreciate it," Cohen said. "Right now I want the door-to-door manpower. Checking the registered sex offenders, looking at other potential suspects, running backgrounds. We're setting up a hotline and could use some bodies on that. And we'll take whatever specific suggestions your team can offer on how to conduct our search."

"We're happy to follow through on the RSOs. Although, as I'm sure you know, that's usually a dead end. We can help with your tip line and we'll handle any leads from the Amber Alert hotline—we'll let you know about the ones that aren't obviously cranks." Her phone buzzed. She glanced at it, then slid it back in her pocket. "We can also craft the media announcements, since that's usually considered a shit job the police are happy to hand over."

Engel swallowed a smile. "Good."

"What about a cell phone? Did Lucy have one?"

Cohen shook his head. "We're still working to pull phone records, but according to friends of the family, she didn't have her own."

McConnell turned to me. "Give us a rundown of this morning?"

I went through what I'd told Cohen. All three agents asked a lot of questions; Ritland and Wyman were especially interested in what I'd seen before the bomb went off. They asked about the wire and whether I'd seen any kind of timer. I told them about the bag and the other wires.

"Trip wire *and* a remote?" Ritland said to Wyman.

"Or a delay of some kind," Wyman said.

"So no chance Lucy was in that kiln?" McConnell asked.

"Clyde would have let me know."

She nodded, her gaze going to the vast sweep of the cement factory. "Then unless forensics tells us otherwise, we'll proceed under the assumption that Lucy was taken away from the site."

Ritland was watching the bomb techs. "We brought a digital fingerprint scanner. As long as the bodies weren't atomized, we can probably get enough of a print to run an immediate check."

"Let's talk to the crime scene guys," Engel said. "See what we've got."

Static burst in my ear. Dispatch. I excused myself and walked a short distance away.

"Parnell," I said. "Go ahead."

"The police are almost ready to unhook the fouled train. The operating crew is standing by for your go-ahead."

"Roger that," I said. "Tell them I'll be there in twenty."

I walked back to where the others were still talking. "I've got to return to the first scene."

"I'll radio one of the units to drive you back," Engel said.

"Since this is train related, I assume you'll be part of the interagency task force," McConnell said to me.

For just a second, I hesitated. I'd lost something important when that bomb went off and maybe walking away wasn't how I'd get it back. Then again, walking away might be the smartest thing I could do. For me *and* the investigation. A good Marine knows when one man's weakness can bring down the entire team.

"You want my boss," I said. "Deputy John Mauer. He's collecting information now."

McConnell nodded as if she expected no different. I thought I saw a flicker of disappointment in Ritland's eyes. Well, one thing you could say about fobbits—our survival rate didn't suck. We shook hands again and I headed toward the line of patrol cars to catch a ride back to the first crime scene. Then, at a thought, I spun back around.

"Agent McConnell," I said. "What do you think the chances are we'll find her?"

McConnell removed her sunglasses. Her left eye was severely bruised, a ring of blue and purple that went all the way around, turning the socket into a deep pool. Seeing her injury was like finding a crack in a perfect piece of glass. But I guess you never know anyone's story.

"This one will be tough," she said. "Our killer is organized. Thorough."

To the west, the sky had turned black with threat, smaller clouds churning fast across a gray canopy. The air crackled with the tang of ozone and spats of rain slapped the ground. A sudden wind whipped through the grasses and I caught my cap before the wind could take it.

I said, "But still, ninety-five percent likely, right? Like you said."

She looked at me a moment longer. "Right." She turned away as if to say something to Ritland.

A cold and frightened voice inside me made me call her back, even though I knew better than to ask. "Of that ninety-five percent, how many of the kids were still alive?"

Something dark swam into her eyes—something I recognized from my own gaze when I looked in the mirror. Madeline McConnell was haunted. I'd bet on it.

"How many were alive?" I asked again.

Her eyes stayed steady on mine. "Most," she said, "were not."

The wind pulled up the dust in the road, gathered it in a fist, and hurled it at the world.

CHAPTER 5

Some cultures believe true wisdom is attained only through suffering—that our pain allows us to cross the void between the living and the dead and bring back knowledge. Thus, veterans are lauded as having special insight.

But in other times and places, warriors fresh from combat are named unclean and kept from society until ritual can make them pure again.

In America, I don't think we've decided which of these two views we hold. Most often we see the traumatized as merely weak. When our veterans struggle, they are pitied. Or ignored.

—Sydney Parnell, ENGL 2008, *Psychology of Combat.*

I stepped out of the patrol car into the bucketing rain. I opened the rear door for Clyde, then leaned back in. A sheet of rain came with me.

"Sorry about the mud," I said to the officer.

"Been worse back there." His eyes met mine through the steel-mesh barrier. "Try not to drown in the storm."

I closed the door and snugged down my ball cap. I put Clyde in the Explorer to get him out of the rain, then turned and looked for the operating personnel who would break the train.

Just as at the cement factory, law enforcement was everywhere. Crime scene detectives—now joined by the medical examiner and a crew from forensics—were crouched half-under the train, still working around Samantha's body. Despite the rain, uniformed cops and K9s had started a sweep of the area on both sides of the road; they walked a red rover line, each man an arm's length from the next so they didn't miss anything. A second crew of forensics detectives had set up portable lights around the Lexus as they searched for trace evidence. Nearby, a flatbed tow truck waited with flashing yellow lights for the go-ahead to take the vehicle back to the police garage.

The storm had made a mess of everything. The tarps the forensics guys had erected to protect the scene billowed in the wind, straining at their ropes. People shouted to make themselves heard, their voices faint against the squall. The cops and detectives in their long rain jackets and snugged-up hoods, and the forensics team in their water-logged Tyvek suits, looked blocky and inhuman. With the eerie shadows cast by the rigged-up lights, the scene was otherworldly.

Usually there would be people standing around smoking or taking a coffee break. Not today. Partly it was the weather. Mostly it was the dreadfulness of the crime.

I spotted the operating personnel standing by a DPC truck, their clothes heavy with water and grease, work gloves tucked into the pockets of their rain jackets. They hadn't bothered to zip their coats or seek the shelter of their truck. They were out-toughing the cops as they waited for the go-ahead to unhitch the coal cars.

A short distance from where the ME and forensics worked, Detective Gresino stood in the rain next to a woman holding a clipboard.

The detective's hair was plastered to his head, his suit soaked. But he seemed oblivious to the wet. By now his lieutenant would have told him what had happened to his partner, and even from here I could tell something had gone from his eyes. The woman, partially concealed by her hooded trench, was probably a claim rep sent by the railroad.

Unable to use a laptop due to the weather, she'd turned her back to the wind and flipped up the clipboard's protective sheet of plastic in order to write. When she leaned over to ask Gresino a question her hood fell back, and I recognized Veronica Stern, one of DPC's litigation lawyers.

Trains collided with cars and human flesh with depressing regularity. Lawsuits followed 90 percent of the time. With millions sometimes riding on the outcome, litigation was a high-pressure job, and Stern, only in her midthirties, was considered among the best in the business. In her time at DPC, Stern had earned a reputation as a coldly competent bulldog. The operating personnel hated her—in cases where they were hurt, she represented the railroad. And when those cases went to trial, she was known for destroying the plaintiff.

I'd read in the company paper that Hiram Davenport had hired her away from Alfred Tate's SFCO railroad only six months ago. More bad blood between the two men.

My earpiece buzzed. Captain Mauer.

"I've been following the reports," Mauer said, not bothering to be angry that I hadn't called in sooner. "But I'd like to hear your side of things."

I walked away from the crewmen and went through the morning again. Mauer asked a lot of questions when I got to the part about the bodies and the bomb. I finished by telling him that the police and the Feds needed a point of contact.

"It'll have to be Fisher until Monday," he said. "If I don't want my wife and daughter to put a hit out on me. I'm heading to Estes Park first thing tomorrow."

My heart sank. I'd forgotten. "Your daughter's wedding."

"Break Kimmy's heart if I back out. And Dot would call my murder justifiable. I'll get Fisher to come in. Starting tomorrow, whatever else they need, direct them his way. You can bring him up to speed in the morning."

Heat rose in my face, despite the fact that this was what I wanted. Or at least, what I needed.

"Fisher," I said. "Yes, sir."

"Oh, *that* was convincing. Tell me you're good with this, Parnell."

"I am good with it, sir."

"You don't have some crazy white-knight thing going, right?"

"No, sir."

"Okay. Good. Diane in HR is pulling the DPC employee records for the hazmat train. CP Eider and Falston Water Treatment are collecting data on their end. I'll light a fire under them. In the meantime, I'll keep working to pull up maps of the route and surrounding area. And obtaining files on everyone involved from the regulatory agencies. That piece alone is going to take hours. The cops need anything else?"

"I'll let you know."

"Okay, then. Come see me in my office once you're done there."

I signed in with the officer manning the inside cordon and made my way down the hill. Stern was now taking pictures and ignored my approach. But Gresino turned on me as soon as I got close enough to join them under the tarp.

"Tell me how bad Frank is," he said, his eyes jittering like a pinball. "No bullshit. Straight up, how bad? No one will talk to me."

I picked my words carefully. All I could offer Gresino was a careful version of the truth and a side of sympathy. And sympathy wouldn't get up and go to work with him in the morning.

"He was conscious after the bomb," I said. "Aware and talking."

"They took him to K and G, right?"

"You bet."

He thrust his head forward. "You're holding out on me."

"He got hit hard, Gresino. But he's a fighter."

"Three years to retirement." His gaze went off to some middle distance. "Then he was going to be all done with fighting. Wants to take up gardening. Tulips and roses and fuck-all what else. Can you see a murder cop being happy with that?"

"Sure," I whispered.

Gresino's regard came back to me in the form of a hard stare. "How is it he's hurt so bad and you—look at you. Barely a scratch."

Veronica Stern lifted her head from her camera. I sensed her steady regard on me—Stern the human polygraph, watching for shades of untruth.

But I would not look away from the crazy in Gresino's eyes. "The three of us were together. Clyde alerted on the bomb, and we all ran. I was behind one of the kilns with Clyde. Wilson was in the field. Maybe he was . . ." My voice trailed off—I'd been asking myself how it was that Clyde and I had zigged and Wilson had zagged. "I don't know why he wasn't with us."

"He's got bad knees. Did you know that? Maybe he needed help."

I thought back. Shook my head. "No. He was good."

"But you. *You* made it."

I recognized the misplaced anger and kept my voice calm. "It's not like running from a bear, Gresino. I wasn't trying to outpace him. And he didn't put himself between me and the bomb. Sometimes shit happens."

"But not to you."

"I suggest," Stern interjected in a voice like an ice cube down the back, "the two of you finish your playground fight later. We have work to do."

Gresino muttered something and looked away.

"You find anything else?" I asked him.

His jaw worked. "The keys to the Lexus, dropped or tossed a hundred yards from the vehicle. I'm thinking she and Lucy bolted, then she threw the keys away so their abductor couldn't take them anywhere else."

"Why didn't she try circling back and driving away?"

"Maybe she couldn't. Maybe he had Lucy." His eyes met mine again. "Maybe she had bad knees."

"Gresino—"

"I gotta talk to my lieutenant." He strode off toward the cars at the top of the hill.

Stern let her camera dangle on its strap and turned her glacier-blue gaze on me. The gale had tugged her bright hair loose from the coil at her neck; the golden tumble softened features that carried all the beauty and warmth of alabaster.

"Murder or suicide?" she asked.

"I don't have all the facts yet," I said.

"Just your opinion, Special Agent Parnell. A consensus helps at the outset of a case. Murder or suicide?"

"Murder."

She nodded, seemingly satisfied. "Good."

I narrowed my eyes. "Good for a consensus, you mean?"

Her look suggested I was a little slow. "Good because if this is murder, it won't score with the Federal Railroad Administration as a trespasser. Not the way a suicide would. Which means it won't impact our safety numbers."

I recoiled. "That's what matters to you?"

"That's my job. Where's the TIR?"

I bit down on what I wanted to say. "The hard drive is in my truck. I'll get you a copy."

"You've looked at it?"

"Not yet. For your record, the engineer says he was traveling at a safe speed and sounded the horn appropriately. It will be on the recorders."

"I'll take a look as soon as you send it. Don't give it to any plaintiff lawyers that might show up. Where's the crew? Deke Willsby and"—she flipped through her paperwork—"John Sethmeyer."

"They're with the Care Team. You can interview them upstairs at headquarters."

"I prefer to conduct interviews in my office. They'll need to come by before the end of the day. Make sure they know that." She pulled out a sheaf of papers and tucked them into a plastic slipcover. "And I'll need you to fill these out. Digital or hard copy, your choice. Have them back to me no later than close of business tomorrow."

The ME, Dr. Emma Bell, had been steadfastly ignoring everything but her work. Now she stood and walked over to join us under the tarp. I'd worked with her on a few jumpers. She was pleasant but distant. Maybe it came from keeping company with the dead.

"Special Agent Parnell." She stripped off her gloves and pushed back the hood on her mud-spattered Tyvek suit; her broad face was flushed despite the chill. "It would be nice to stop meeting like this."

I resisted the obvious pun about a dead relationship and merely nodded.

"I'm ready to get the body out," she said. "Then you can move the train and we'll finish up."

I looked at Stern. "All right with you?"

"I'm done for the moment." She tapped the papers she'd handed me. "Tomorrow by five." She spun on her boots and headed for the incline.

"You piss in her Wheaties this morning?" Bell asked me.

I watched Stern navigate the slick hillside. "I think she pisses in her own."

Fifteen minutes later, the rain had slacked off to a soft drizzle. Emma Bell and her crew finished removing what they could of the body while the train was still in place. They took pieces of Samantha Davenport and placed them in a black body bag and carried them up the hill. Watching was too much like being back in Mortuary Affairs, and I found myself blinking up into the sky. To the west, the dark clouds thinned and streaks of blue glimmered in the gaps.

"Special Agent Parnell?"

I brought my gaze back to earth.

"We ready to break the train?" asked one of the conductors I'd spotted earlier.

"Let's do it."

The two men stepped through the gore and began the uncoupling process while I made sure everyone was clear of the tracks. When the men were done, they stepped back and one of the crew got on the walkie-talkie. I listened in while he informed the engineers at each end of the train that we were good to go.

A hum started as the coal cars quivered to life. The air in the brake hoses hissed and a sonorous clanking echoed as, far down the line, the locomotives on each end began moving. The slack disappeared and, with a groan that seemed to rise from the depths of the earth, the train broke apart.

I closed my eyes and pictured Samantha Davenport as she had looked on her driver's license photo. The luminous dark hair falling behind her shoulders. The high curve of her brows. The knowing look in her eyes that spoke more of inborn wisdom than vast experience.

I pressed my hand to my heart and, in my mind, I made her whole. I gathered what the train had scattered and washed away the blood. I smoothed her hair, brought the life back to her eyes, and restored a pulse beneath her skin.

This habit of mine—morbid or life-affirming, I wasn't sure which—had started in Iraq. The body of a young PFC had come in— Private First Class Hart. Hart had been at the epicenter of an explosion loosed by a suicide bomber. Among his belongings I'd found a photo of him with his girlfriend and taped it to the wall of the bunker where we worked. And then I couldn't let it go—what he'd been, what he was now.

I opened my eyes. The rain stopped. Thunder rumbled in the distance as the storm washed past. Moments later, the sun came out, and steam rose from the damp ground. Far out in the meadow, a bird let loose a warbling song. The wind turned from violent to brisk, and everything sparkled, new and fresh.

I slogged back up the hill, ignoring Gresino's eyes on me. Ignoring everyone. At the truck, I let Clyde out but kept him close. We stood on the hill together while Emma Bell and her crew returned to the tracks to finish their work.

We had a saying in Iraq. *Embrace the suck.* My beloved, Dougie, had used it every time the going got rough. *Parnell, you've got to embrace the suck,* he'd tell me with a wink. *You gotta learn to be uncomfortable, and then you can conquer anything.*

The last of the clouds scattered to reveal a bright blue sky. Yellow flowers nodded in the damp and bees reemerged, droning contentedly. But Clyde had eyes only for the body bag and the gore. He looked as unhappy as I felt. I rested a hand on his head.

"Embrace the suck, buddy," I said. "You know the drill."

I scrubbed his head, roughed his ears, and gave him a treat from the stash in my pocket. We climbed into my truck and I started the engine and eased my way through the crowd of people and vehicles. All I wanted was to flee, to put this behind me, to pretend it was a normal day on the rails. That was all I'd *ever* wanted since I'd come home.

Just before I reached the road, I looked in my rearview mirror. Samantha walked along the tracks, a child on either side of her—eleven-year-old boys with wheat-blond hair and green eyes and knobby wrists. Her sons. She had an arm around the shoulders of each boy, her head bent toward one child, who rushed out a staccato string of words while his brother kicked a rock as if it were a soccer ball.

They walked through the throng of police, past the coroner and her assistants, and headed toward the cement factory where the Edison silos brooded against the brightening sky.

The dead are a load you can't set down.

They weigh nothing. And everything.

CHAPTER 6

Today, in Habbaniyah, we found a little boy. An orphan,
eight or nine years old. He was crying next to the body of his
mother—she was one of our interpreters.
She'd been beaten to death by insurgents for helping the
Americans. And for falling in love with one of them.

—Sydney Parnell. Private correspondence.

At Cohen's house, I gave myself fifteen minutes to get over the flashbacks and the bomb. I sat halfway up the stairs leading to the front door,
removed my duty belt, and stripped off my bloody blouse to let the sun
bake into my aching muscles. I removed my boots and scraped off the
dirt on the stair where I sat, then slid my fingers under the straps of my
sports bra and rubbed away the indentations the straps had carved into
my shoulders. When I rolled my head, trying to work out the kinks,
the bones popped like an old woman's.

In front of the house, Clyde nosed through a thicket of trees, hunting rabbits. Puffs of clouds drifted noiselessly overhead against the rain-
washed sky. Far away, a lawn mower sputtered and died. Cohen's swank
neighborhood was quiet as a tomb.

When Clyde gave up his pursuit and flopped down beside me, I
removed his gear and laid it out on the stairs to dry, then gave him a

rough scratching all over, mussing his vest-flattened fur. He smelled of earth and fur and the perspiration coming off his paws and hair follicles. I breathed it in, then closed my eyes and let his nearness and the heat dissolve me.

After a time, I sat up and shook out a cigarette from the pack the lieutenant had given me. I eyeballed it for all of five seconds before I stuck it in my mouth and lit up. How easily we fall.

"What do we do with this case, Clyde?" I asked.

Clyde let loose a gentle snore.

Homeland Security, TSA, and my boss would handle the hazmat train. Denver and Thornton police had the bodies. McConnell's CARD team was on Lucy. But now that I had time to think, my mind kept going back to the alphanumeric code written in the kiln. Why was it significant to the killer? And why did it seem familiar?

I blew a cloud of smoke into the clear sky. No doubt the Feds or Denver PD would figure it out. They had code breakers and analysts. The last thing they needed was a bomb-rattled, nutcase railway cop with post-traumatic stress, trust issues, and a strong penchant for whiskey.

But I couldn't let it go.

The question every Marine asks herself is whether she's got what it takes. Same with cops and EMTs and social workers. Hell, all of us. Every person on this planet. After my mother died, my grams taught me that God will give us only what we can handle. My twelve-year-old self pictured God with a notebook and a scale, measuring the strength of every heart and deciding whether we could cope with what was coming down the pike.

The question we each ask ourselves is, can I hack it?

From my back pocket, I pulled out the photo I carry everywhere like a talisman. I ran my thumb over its worn, silky softness. Malik. The orphan I'd left behind in Iraq two years earlier. We'd found him near the body of his murdered mother, Haifa, who had made the mistake of falling in love with a Marine; the Marine had returned the favor.

Retribution by the insurgents against them both had been swift and brutal.

When we found their bodies and Haifa's weeping, terrified son, I could not leave him alone, waiting for the insurgents to come back and finish the job. I'd bundled him in a blanket and brought him with me to the forward operating base.

In the photo, Malik is standing near my barracks on the FOB, grinning and holding a soccer ball one of the Marines had given him. I cupped my hands around the picture, shielding it from the sun, and marveled at the depths in Malik's young eyes. God must have figured Malik could handle a lot.

I'd tried to bring him home with me when I redeployed, working to get his application through the State Department. But then he vanished from the base in Iraq. At the time, I'd hoped he'd found his family. But later I learned he'd been brought to America by men who wanted to train him and send him back to Iraq as a spy—the same men I feared would pay me another visit.

Malik had escaped. And that was as much as I knew.

I slid the picture back in my pocket, braced my elbows on my thighs, and smoked. I stared at the dirt I'd scraped off my shoes, noting how even that humble substance glittered in the sunlight. A metaphor for the potential goodness in all of us, if I were inclined to think that way.

After a few minutes, I pulled out my phone and punched in the number of a friend, a man named David Fuller. David ran an organization called the Hope Project, which aimed to reunite Iraqi refugees with their families, whether the families were here in the United States, living in Europe, or still in the Middle East. A lot of these men and women had worked for the US government and then been forced to flee their homes in response to death threats.

Three months earlier, I'd enlisted David's help in finding Malik. He had a network of people working throughout the United States,

Mexico, and Canada as well as overseas, some of whom were living in or watching the communities of exiled Muslims. He'd agreed to show Malik's picture around—cautiously—because unfriendlies were looking for him.

David didn't answer. I sent him a text.

Word?

A minute later he texted back. Nothing. Syd, can't keep resources on this. Too stretched as is.

We'd had this conversation before. The last time, I'd begged for another month.

One more month, I typed.

You said that
Please

A long minute rolled by. During that time I imagined thousands of children as flickering lights, each carried off on a dark sea of indifference, war, carelessness, greed.

My phone chimed. One month

I closed my eyes in relief. Opened them and typed Thank you

Call me sucker

I typed Saint and slid my phone back into my pocket.

"This whole thing with Lucy Davenport," I said to Clyde. "We have to help. Our boss won't like it because he thinks I can't handle it. But we don't have a choice, right? She's only a child."

Clyde opened one eye.

"Yeah, I know. That bomb kinda blew my shit apart, too. Okay, it totally blew my shit apart. My therapist would tell me to spend a month binge-watching Netflix before I reengage." I rubbed my palms on my pants to wipe away the sudden sweat. "But we can hold it together until she's found."

Clyde looked like he was having no trouble whatsoever holding it all together.

"Right," I said. "I'm the weak link. Thanks for the reminder."

I crushed out the cigarette, stood, and went inside to take a shower.

◆　◆　◆

At work an hour later, I dropped my duffel at my desk and went hunting for my boss.

Clyde and I found Captain Mauer one floor up, staring forlornly at a coffee vending machine. The overhead fluorescents turned his gray hair yellow and carved canyons into his cheeks. He'd once had a gut you could rest a plate on. But lately his uniform was approaching baggy, draping over his six-foot-four frame and held in place with a belt and a prayer.

I'd asked him about the weight loss; he said that after his last visit to the doctor, his wife had put him on a diet. No processed foods. No sugar. Effing vegetables for breakfast, lunch, and dinner. Said he figured it was for the best, not having so much dead weight to haul around. But with all those damned vegetables, he did wonder how rabbits found the energy to hop.

As I watched, he reached out and smacked a fist against the side of the vending machine. The machine rattled into compliance, dropping a paper cup into the chute. Nothing wrong with his right hook.

He looked up when he heard us coming and his expression went soft. I was Mauer's youngest cop and the only female, and the paternalism he showed toward me was just a slightly weightier version of the one he extended to all his officers. After the pileup of bodies during the last murder investigation I'd been involved in, Mauer had accepted my side of things without reservation. He'd had my back in the follow-up investigation by the Colorado Bureau of Investigations and the DA's office and had never once lost confidence in me or my story.

Now as I approached, I worked to summon an expression that conveyed both a reasonable level of concern over what had happened and a quiet confidence that I was handling things just fine, so he'd let me keep handling them. Chin up. Shoulders squared.

His eyes narrowed as I approached. "You're doing it."

"Doing what?"

"Putting on your Marine face."

"Au contraire. This is my coolly competent face."

"Well, it looks like crap. And you didn't tell me you'd been hurt."

I waved a dismissive hand. "I've been hurt worse shaving my legs."

The machine stuttered and fell quiet. He stared at the empty cup, then grabbed the machine and shook it.

"People have died doing that," I offered.

"They're amateurs." A sudden spurt of coffee poured into the cup. He nodded with satisfaction and raised an eyebrow at me. "You look like you stepped into a wasp's nest and are mighty pissed off about it."

"Day in the life, right?"

"It would be normal to be angry."

Deep breath. Calm expression. "Might be I'm a little angry."

"Hm."

"The guy did try to blow us up."

"You got that going. What else you hiding behind that Marine facade?"

The best way to lie was to stick as close to the truth as possible. "What happened today was nothing more than a regular day in Iraq. Been there, done that, got the medal. It's not a problem for me. I want to stay on the case."

Mauer folded his arms. "Parnell—"

"Beyond this weekend, I mean. If we haven't found her by then."

"Patrolling getting a little dull for you? Look, Sydney, you have to understand my position. My first duty is to DPC. My second duty is to you. I'm not sure keeping you on the case is good for either of those."

"I'm already in. Let me help bring it home. Bring *her* home."

He scratched at his cheek. "You've already done more for your country than ninety-nine percent of us. It's okay to take a break and let others pick up some of the slack."

"Fobbit," I muttered.

"What?"

"Nothing."

"Didn't your counselor say you're supposed to avoid stressful situations and focus on healing?"

I folded my arms. "I'm a good dog for this fight."

"Uh-huh. 'Cause the Feds and Denver PD and Thornton PD and the Adams County Sheriff and the Colorado bureau, not to mention TSA and Homeland Security—all those guys, they ain't enough. They need a railroad cop, of all damn things."

"It's just for a few days. And if you sideline me and things go down badly, it will make me certifiable."

He closed his eyes and heaved a sigh. "You're already certifiable."

I waited.

He turned back to the machine. "Coffee? Black, right?"

I forced my shoulders down. "Yes."

He handed me the newly filled paper cup and fed more coins into the machine.

"What I wish," he said, "is that you'd take some time for yourself. A vacation, or something. Give yourself a chance to heal. You told me you took this job so you could get some distance from things."

"I am healed. And I don't like vacations. I don't know what to do with myself."

"You thought of getting a hobby?"

"I have one. Marksmanship."

He rolled his eyes at me. A cup dropped into place. The machine whirred. Apparently it had learned not to argue with John Mauer.

"Therapy has been good." I resisted the urge to cross my fingers and hide them behind my back. "I'm not saying it's all marshmallows and lite beer. But the therapist did tell me that I need to stay engaged. That I shouldn't back down from what upsets me." Now I did cross my fingers. "If you take me off this case, it could actually be a bad thing."

He handed me the coffee. "That sounds like a bunch of bullshit."

"A lot of psychotherapy sounds like bullshit. Doesn't make it wrong. And why insist I get counseling if you won't let me follow their advice?"

"Because I might have a better idea even than your counselor what price you'll pay if things go seriously south."

"What the hell does that mean?"

"I worked the railway bombing in Madrid," he said. "Back in 2004. A hundred and ninety-two dead. Nearly two thousand injured."

"That's not going to happen here."

"We hope it's not," he said. "But the point I want to make is that after I arrived, they were still cleaning up corpses. Still trying to figure out which heads went with which bodies. I was so shaken up those first days, I couldn't sleep. Every time I ate, I threw it back up."

"John," I said softly. He looked at me, his eyes both wary and tender. "It's not like this body was my first. Not the bomb, either."

"I know." He closed his eyes, opened them again. "I know that. Damn it, I know that. And I keep asking myself if that makes things better for you, or worse."

"It makes them what they are."

"Ah, hell." He mustered up a frown, which was sort of like having a teddy bear give you the evil eye. "You can do this. But on my terms. You're to tell your therapist exactly what is going on. You've got an appointment later today, right?"

I narrowed my eyes. "You know that how?"

"I pay attention. So you tell him every little thing. And if I see any sign you're coming apart, I'll yank you so fast you'll feel your stomach come out your eyeballs."

I resisted an urge to salute. Or hug him. "I appreciate it, sir."

"Damn it, Parnell. You could talk the hind leg off a horse."

◆ ◆ ◆

I picked up Clyde's lead and the three of us walked down the stairs to our department, two floors below the rail yard's control tower in a suite of rooms on the north end. Our area was empty. I was the only one on duty, other than the captain, which was the norm. DPC police work solo. I was itching to start trying to track down the alphanumeric from the kiln. But for the moment, the TIR video was more important.

I stopped by my cubicle long enough to pick up the TIR hard drive from my bag and to down Clyde near the windows where he could sprawl out and snooze. I hurried after Mauer toward his enclosed office at the end of the suite.

"You looked at the video?" he asked as he ushered me through the doorway.

"Not yet."

He set down his coffee, plugged in the drive, and pulled up the video on his computer. I used the software to search for the power cut-out switch—the moment when Deke applied the emergency brake. I backtracked three minutes before that and we watched as the nighttime tracks unspooled in front of us.

The picture was surprisingly clear, nothing like the graininess of CCTV footage, and the audio was sharp. Over the thrum of the engine, Deke whistled softly to himself, unaware of what waited ahead. No sound came from Sethmeyer, which meant my suspicion he'd been asleep was probably correct. The video itself was unremarkable in those final quiet moments. The train was passing through a mostly rural area, and there was little to see in the dark beyond the tracks—just the occa-sional telephone lines, a few trees, and sometimes a storage unit or piece of railroad equipment. Mile markers slipped serenely by.

"There!" Mauer said, just as Deke sounded his horn.

A figure appeared on the tracks as the train came out of the curve. At this distance, it was impossible to make out any details—identity and gender were lost in the combination of middle-of-the-night dark-ness and the over-wash of a two-hundred-thousand-candela headlamp and ditch lights. But it was clear that someone stood on the tracks. Deke began chanting, "Move! Move! Move!" like a prayer as he blew the horn and went into emergency stop, and a few seconds after that, Sethmeyer started shouting. As the train approached the figure and details emerged, I saw what Deke had meant—Samantha looked as if she was struggling. An instant later, the light hit her horrified face, then Samantha was under the wheels and gone.

"Son of a bitch," Mauer said.

I paused the recording. My heart had jumped into triple time as we watched. It wasn't the first time I'd had to view the recording of an accident. But it never got easier.

I thought of Stern's cold question from earlier and murmured, "Murder."

We went through the video ten more times, taking the critical moments frame by frame, trying to make out more of Samantha in the white flare of the headlights. Her clothes were splotched with some-thing dark, so Deke might be right that she was injured. As for whether she was trapped, there was no question. She'd worked frantically to free herself from what looked like some kind of wooden frame, right up until it was too late.

In the seconds immediately after the engine struck her, I caught movement on the right-hand side of the video—something stirring in the bushes. At the last second, whatever it was made a quick, sinewy leap away from the tracks and disappeared from the footage.

"You see that?" I asked.

"Yeah, but hell if I know what it was. Maybe a wolf?"

"Not in Colorado. And that close to a moving train?" Whatever it was, I thought of Lucy fleeing through the dark and shuddered.

Mauer copied the tape and edited it down to the fifteen minutes before the incident, right up to when the train came to a stop and Deke was talking to dispatch. He then pulled a stack of blank CDs from his desk and began burning copies for all the players involved.

"Print some stills, too," I said. "I want that animal, as well. If you'll distribute the CDs and stills to the team here, including Veronica Stern, then I'll get copies to the cops and the feebs."

"Yes'm."

"Where are we with the information Detective Cohen asked for?"

Mauer kept removing and inserting disks, building a stack on his desk.

"Diane has pulled up the employee files for everyone connected with the hazmat train," he said. "The assigned crews, dispatch, the schedulers. The linkers who were going to assemble the train in Macdona, Texas. That's the pile you see on the chair over there. Vic Macky yanked the maps for the route. I'll have copies made of everything for the cops and the Feds, including what we have on the vendors. In the meantime, the Homeland Security guys are trying to find the virtual fingerprints of anyone who might have hacked our database and gotten the schedule for that hazmat train."

I nodded. "The police are getting a subpoena for the personnel files. I'll run everything over to Cohen when the copies are ready."

"Speaking of Cohen, how are you two doing?"

I flushed. "Anyone ever tell you you're nosy?"

"My daughter. All the time. Here's the last CD. You need more, let me know." He pointed toward a stack of folders on the right side of his desk. "I've started going through the employee files, pulling out data from their personnel files and looking for any connections to either

Ben Davenport or his father. Or any indication we have a disgruntled employee." He pushed a piece of paper across the desk. "Here are the names of every DPC employee involved with that train. So far, the only connection any of them have with Hiram Davenport is that they work for his railroad."

"And on the disgruntled angle?"

"If they're unhappy, it hasn't come to the attention of the folks in personnel. I'll talk to them one-on-one, see if there's been anything HR didn't put in the file." Mauer steepled his fingers and bounced the tips against his teeth. "I'll talk to the union heads, too."

"Good. And while you're looking at the employee records, keep something in mind."

"What's that?"

"One theory is that either Ben or Samantha was having an affair. Given the train tie-in, seems like it might have been with someone who worked here."

"Joy," Mauer said. "Now get out of here and find the girl before I change my mind."

Back at my desk, I gave Clyde a chew toy and sat down. I took a legal pad out of a drawer and wrote down the alphanumeric code I'd seen in the kiln and burned into my memory right before the explosion.

02XX56XX15XP.

I frowned. Was this a unique kind of manifest number? Phone numbers with letters substituted for some of the numbers? A secret code to the location of the Holy Grail and the whereabouts of Lucy Davenport?

I was pretty sure I'd seen it before, or at least something like it. I drank my coffee and stared at the page until the characters started to swim.

All those *X*s.

In my mind, I heard the Sir's voice: *Shade it black.*

In the parlance of Mortuary Affairs, that meant to add what was missing. But if there was something missing here, I had no way to know what it was. Still, there was something familiar about the number, and the knot in my stomach said the feeling was more than wishful thinking. Sometimes you had to clear away the debris before you could see what mattered. I removed the *X*s and rewrote the number, then stared at the result while a chill needled its way down my spine.

025615P.

I was ashamed that it had taken me so long to see it. Maybe I could blame the bomb for rattling my brain. But when I finally realized what I was looking at, the number all but glowed with meaning.

The statistics varied, depending on where you got them. But every ninety minutes or so, a vehicle and a train collided in the United States. In order to track this data and determine where changes needed to be made, the US Department of Transportation assigned a number to every grade-level railroad crossing in the United States. More than 200,000 of them. Always six digits followed by a letter of the alphabet. The number could be cross-checked against a national database that contained the location, a description of the nearby road, all railroad and highway traffic data, and any traffic control devices in use at the crossing.

My fingers were tingling when I got on the computer and pulled up the database that contained the DPC crossings in Colorado and entered 025615P. Nothing. I broadened the search to all DPC crossings, then—when that failed—pulled up the Federal Railroad Administration's safety data website. The FRA's databank contained all known crossings for every railroad, but there were no hits. I switched back to DPC and searched our database of FRA accident forms, then hunted through an auxiliary system listing our own accident documents and Death and Dismemberment forms. When that failed, I switched tactics and scanned the numbers for the physical crossings north and south of where Samantha had died. No matches.

My hope turned to ash. I scowled at the computer screen. If the string wasn't a crossing number, then I had nowhere else to go with it. There were no other alphanumeric strings linked with trains, train consists, or their manifests that came even remotely close. Maybe the police or the Feds would have better luck.

But it wasn't quite time to throw in the towel.

I picked up the phone and called my contact at FRA. Margaret Ackerman's office was in DC, but news of the Davenport case had already hit there.

"Any word on that little girl?" she asked when I told her I was helping with the case.

"That's why I'm calling," I said. "And keep it under your hat. I've got a number associated with the crime that looks like a railroad crossing ID. But nothing is coming up when I run a search."

"Could be it's a defunct number, if the crossing is no longer grade level."

"That's what I'm hoping. Can you check your databases?"

"Of course. Hold on." I heard the sound of her keyboard as she typed. "What's the number?"

"025615P."

"Hm. Nothing. Let me check the discontinued numbers."

More tapping. I pulled a tennis ball out of my desk and started tossing it up and catching it one-handed. Clyde wandered over, his eyes following the ball.

"Nah," Margaret said. "Nothing in that database, either. If it's a crossing number, it's not only defunct, it's old. As in, phased out long ago."

Which might be a clue about the killer. "How old?"

I waited while she had a coughing fit.

"You still smoking, Mags?"

"Yes, thank God. You?"

"No," I said.

"You are such a liar."

"You talking old as in five years?"

She snorted. "I know you're barely out of diapers."

"Ten?"

"Better let this old girl teach you a thing or two."

She must have heard my eyes roll—she barked out a laugh that ended in another brutal cough. "Okay," she said when she could speak. "FRA developed the national crossing-number inventory back in the early seventies. But nothing was automated until the mid to late eighties. Which means your number falls somewhere in that fifteen-year black hole. And while I'm pretty sure we have physical records going back that far, I might have to search multiple archives."

"You're saying the number could be almost forty years old?"

"You say that like it was a long time ago. I was in my prime then."

"How long to search everything?"

"Honestly? It could take days."

"What about cross-referencing them with any 6180 accident-reporting forms?"

"Unless you have a date and a location, trying to track any accidents is a no-go."

"Mags, give me something."

"Seriously, Sydney. I know you're up against the clock. But even saying days might be optimistic. I may be able to find some of the forms on microfiche. But other inventory forms probably didn't make it past typewritten copies with carbons. I'm talking cardboard boxes in the basement, probably filed by gnomes who can't tell one number from another. Same with the 6180s."

"Did I mention we've got a missing child?"

"I'm on it," she said and signed off with another rattling cough.

The injury gouged into my forehead by the bomb burrowed through my skull. I took Clyde outside for a few throws of the tennis ball and thought of reasons why the killer would care about an old crossing. Accidents, I figured. The most significant thing about grade crossings was the people who were maimed or killed there.

I whistled to Clyde and we went back inside. The air conditioning raised bumps on my sweaty skin. Clyde plopped down in his usual corner. I called the Denver office of the National Transportation Safety Board and asked to speak with Mark Lapton, one of their investigators. Lapton and I had worked a handful of cases together.

"I'm investigating an old crossing," I said, "and I need to determine the location and if NTSB has any accidents associated with it. The number is defunct, which is why I can't find it on my end."

"This about the Davenport case?"

"Yes. But that's a close hold."

"So I'll only tell my close friends. How old is the number?"

"Twenty years," I said. "Maybe as much as forty."

"Then I can't help you. Or at least not quickly. That information won't be in any database."

"Don't tell me. Boxes in the basement."

"File cabinets, probably. But yes."

I squeezed my eyes closed, popped them open. "It's critical I find everything I can about that crossing. Tell me how I can do that."

"You tried FRA? They hold the—"

"They're looking for the initial request for the number and any accident reports. But it's going to take time."

"It's no better on this end. All our old forms are at headquarters, in DC. Plus, the whole thing could be a snipe hunt. You know we only handle the large-scale messes. Multiple fatalities, or cornfield meets where one train hits another. National news stuff. If none of those happened at your crossing, we won't have anything."

"Can we at least try? There's a little girl missing."

Lapton sighed. "What's the number?"

I told him.

"I'll call DC," he said. "Get someone there to start looking. But don't hold your breath. Our forms aren't filed by the crossing number, but by our own numbering system. There's probably a master log somewhere that cross references our number with the crossing ID. But that won't be digitized, either. If you can give me a location or the names associated with any accidents, that would help."

I balled my hands into fists. "I was hoping to get that from you."

"I'll do my best," Lapton said. "I'll be in touch."

Dead air. I flipped the world a double bird then opened a desk drawer for the sole purpose of slamming it shut. Clyde startled and gave me a narrow look. "Sorry, boy." I told him to stay, then went to Mauer's office and stuck my head in. "Death and Dismemberment."

He blinked.

"Where are the old forms?" I asked. "And the 6180s. Everything from before we started digitizing."

He gaped at me. "They're—it's not pretty."

I stepped into his office. "I'm almost certain that the alphanumeric written in the kiln is an old crossing number. But if so, it's discontinued, and there's nothing in the database. Margaret Ackerman with the FRA says she'll look, but right now she doesn't have anything. If I can find any D and D forms linked to that number, maybe it'll turn up something related to the case."

"Like what?"

"I'm not sure yet. Something that took place on or near that crossing. The number meant something to the killer."

"Show me what you've got."

I walked in and wrote down the number on the paper he offered, including the Xs. I handed the notepad back to him.

He pulled on his readers and studied it. Scratched his chin. "You took out the Xs."

I nodded.

"Okay. Could be you're right. But if you think something from the past drove our killer, then you're saying he held a grudge for twenty years or more."

"Anger burns a long time."

"You met my first wife. So if this really is a crossing number, why did he include all the Xs?"

"I don't know. We're not dealing with someone who thinks the way we do." I leaned against the doorjamb. "So what about the forms?"

"You heard of the vault?"

"The what?"

He propped his elbows on the desk, fisted his hands. "Years ago someone got the great idea to scan in all those old forms. And not just from Colorado. Across every line owned by DPC. The paper-pushers wanted the process centralized, so they brought the forms here. The 6180s, too. Boxes and boxes of them. Then the budget cuts came and the bosses put the kibosh on the entire plan. Now we have hundreds of forms here. Thousands. All stored in a closet the size of New Jersey. Unless you have a date, we can't narrow down the search to so much as a single box."

My right heel pistoned up and down. "There has to be a way."

"We'll see if FRA comes up with anything. And don't forget the Feds will be taking a whack at that number, in case it's something else entirely. In the meantime, I've been going through the employee files. And I talked to HR."

"And?"

He tilted his chair back and crossed his arms, tucking his fists in his armpits. "And there aren't issues with any of our people. Nine men, one woman. No flags, no performance problems, no record of any inter-employee discord. No unusually heavy absentee rates or sexual harassment charges or anyone who's complained at being passed over. They're all card-carrying members of their respective unions. Happy as clams. Union says the same thing."

"Which doesn't mean someone isn't deeply unhappy."

"Right. Police'll interview them." He twisted his watch around his wrist. "And I can't say any of them strike me as someone Ben or his wife would have an affair with, seeing as the men are all my age. Now, my kindhearted wife tells me I'm a real prize when I put the toilet seat down. But you see a woman half my age giving me the time of day?"

I stopped myself from reaching over and patting his hand. "And the woman?"

"She's a back-side-of-fifty grandmother. And you should—"

"Please don't say I should see her backside."

"Jesus, Parnell, you're taking all my good material."

"You call that good?"

His eyes looked bleary. "That's why I quit my stand-up career. So, that number. If you're right about it being a crossing ID, and if it's local, you could talk to Fred Zolner. He worked this territory for decades. For all I know, he's got that stuff in a file in his head."

"You're taking about Bull Zolner?"

"The same. He's retired now, but the bastard should be happy to talk to you. No family and I doubt he's got friends. Bit of a crank."

I knew Bull Zolner. "*Crank* is being generous."

"Okay, he's a racist, misogynist scumbag. Word is someone broke his heart once and it stayed that way. But he should be a font of knowledge if you can get him to crawl out of the bottle long enough to hold a conversation."

I'd met Bull once, when I was a kid. He had been one of DPC's old-school railroad bulls, an immense man with the attitude of a cornered badger on methamphetamines. He drank like tomorrow was something he didn't want to be around for and he'd patrolled his yards with a zest that bordered on pathological—he'd just as soon beat a tagger or tres-passer as look at them. He'd raised pit bulls just so he could bring one or two with him on his beat to terrorize the trespassers.

Now, sitting in Mauer's office, I remembered two things about Bull. His accent, which was soft and southern. And his eyes. One was blind—the result of an accident. The other was a flat sheet of gray from which anything human had long since packed up and left.

"You have a way to reach him?" I asked.

"Let's call him right now." Mauer tapped on his computer, found a number, then punched it into the landline on his desk. He passed the handset over to me. "Good luck."

"You're too kind."

The phone rang six times, then clicked over to an automated voice inviting me to leave a message after the beep. "Special Agent Zolner, this is Special Agent Parnell with DPC. I'm trying to track down a pos-sible crossing number, 025615P. I need to know where it's located and if you can remember anything significant about it. Please call me back. It's urgent." I left my cell number and hung up.

"I heard he hangs out at a bar," Mauer said.

I put a hand to my chest. "You don't say."

"Smart-ass. He likes some place called the Royal. Or maybe the Crown. Some old railroaders' bar, what I heard. My guess is it's within staggering distance of his house. If you can't get the information another way, you could try running him down there. Here's his address." Mauer scribbled on his notepad, then passed me the sheet. "If you go, take Clyde. And maybe a tank."

I stood.

Mauer rifled through the folders on his desk, pulled one free, and handed it to me. "Before you head out, you might want to look at this, too."

◆ ◆ ◆

Back at my desk, I opened the folder. It was DPC's file on Ben Davenport.

Davenport had been brought on board in 2009 as DPC's historian and archivist. He had an office downtown in the Colorado Historical Society building and reported directly to his father.

A photo clipped to the folder showed a dark-haired, athletic-looking man who hadn't bothered dredging up a smile for the camera. The flat wariness in his expression was one I recognized—I saw the same look in the mirror every morning. Combat will do that to you.

Ben had graduated in 2001 from CU Boulder with a bachelor of arts in philosophy, then started CU's law program. But something—presumably 9/11—had caused him to drop out and join the US Army. He'd attended Officer Candidate School and the Basic School, then deployed to Iraq. He'd served from 2002 to 2008. Three tours, starting as a second lieutenant and working his way up to captain. A lot of medals and commendations. With a record like that, he could have gone into any number of high-paying jobs. But maybe he loved being an archivist. Roaming through history and lost in the stacks. Maybe he loved trains.

Or maybe, like me, he needed to lie low for a while.

I flipped back to the photo.

Not everyone who served in war got PTSD. Far from it. The majority were fine, or seemed that way. But across all branches of the service, 20 percent of Iraq War veterans suffered post-traumatic stress, along with another 11 percent of veterans from Afghanistan. Every day, twenty vets—from wars dating from the current conflicts all the way back to Vietnam—killed themselves.

Ben Davenport's eyes said he knew all about flashbacks and nightmares.

I couldn't ignore the possibility that Ben might have come apart, suddenly and violently, the way half the vets I knew worried they would. Maybe his wife had been unfaithful, he'd learned of it, and her betrayal was the final straw. *There will be killing till the score is paid.* Was it possible that he'd murdered his sons, tied his wife to the tracks, then gone back home to kill himself?

And if so, what had he done with Lucy?

I closed the file. With nothing more to learn about Ben for the moment, I cyberstalked Samantha Davenport and found her company, Madonna Portraits.

Madonna Portraits' main business appeared to be taking pictures of babies. The website showed photos of smiling children along with glowing accolades from the parents. Samantha's whimsy—lots of oversize flower pots and puppies—along with a gift for getting the best out of her subjects, created a world that promised endless, joyous romps. Everyone—the children, the puppies, even the flower pots—looked happy. Her bio page revealed a long list of awards and credentials, along with those of her assistant, Jack Hurley. Hurley was about Samantha's age, handsome in a surfer-boy way, with an easy smile and bright-blond hair worn long. Probably great with the kids. And not bad with the mothers, either, I imagined.

Maybe his presence in Samantha's life provided a sunny counterpoint to Ben's dark brooding. Had his brightness been strong enough to lure her into his bed?

Next to the baby portfolios was a tab labeled NOIR GALLERY. I clicked on it and entered a different world.

Here, Samantha's work was beautiful, even wondrous. But eerie. Bleak landscapes. Corpses from what I guessed was a body farm, where forensic scientists study how the human body decays in different environments. Children appeared in some of the photos, but they were nothing like the smiling babies in the other gallery. I quickly noticed it was always the same three children and realized with a painful stab that these were Ben and Samantha's three. Two towheaded boys and a younger girl.

The boys, I realized with a shiver, looked exactly like the ghostly images I'd seen at the train tracks.

I found one of Lucy by herself. She sat on a tire swing, body stretched long, head tilted so she could look straight at the camera. Her soft brown hair nearly swept the ground.

I clicked to bring up an enlargement. A lively intelligence gleamed in her eyes and she had a certain boldness in the confident tilt of her chin. She looked like she'd been laughing just before the shutter clicked, her lips slightly parted and turned up.

Looking at her made me feel as though someone had reached in past my ribs to squeeze my heart.

"Lucy," I whispered. "Where are you?"

I printed her picture, then moved on. The next set of landscapes, shown in black and white, was in a locale I immediately recognized— the Edison Cement Works. The photos had been shot in low light during a snowstorm. The date on them was from last March. Samantha's children also appeared in some of these photos, mostly as tiny figures set against the colossal silos. In one, they stood before the kilns; their haughty expressions—something their mother must have worked hard to get from them—fit with the brooding presence of the kilns. The ovens, the snow, the children's arrogance—all conspired to make me think of photos I'd seen of Auschwitz. It was an unsettling comparison, and one I suspected Samantha was fully aware of.

Had the killer been busy inside that fifth kiln during the time Samantha and her children had been there? Had he seen them, maybe followed them, and chosen them as his victims? Samantha's familiarity with the cement factory could explain why she'd run off the road when she did. Maybe she'd known where the killer was taking them.

I texted Cohen and told him that the number in the kiln might be a crossing ID and that the video left little doubt that Samantha's death was an act of murder. When he shot a text back, asking why he was hearing from me instead of Mauer, I told him Mauer was leaving town, I was on the case, and that was where I wanted to be. A few minutes went by, then he sent me a thumbs-up.

Smart move. He wouldn't enjoy sleeping on his couch.

Next, I called Denver Health. I played the police card, identifying myself and asking to speak with a nurse regarding Detective Frank Wilson. While I waited, I went to stand by the window overlooking the parking lot. Sunlight glowed through the windows, a cool, white light. As if we'd leapt from July to January.

A nurse came on the line. "He's in surgery. Just started. The surgeon estimates five hours. We'll know more after that."

"What's his status?"

"Critical." Somewhere behind her, an alarm chimed incessantly. "We'll know more later."

I thanked her and hung up. I stared out at the white light, thinking about what the Sir had said about grace and acceptance. An old rage, as familiar as heartache, wrapped itself around me. There was no grace in Wilson's suffering, nor acceptance. His wasn't the kind of pain that forged you into a better person. It was needless torment.

I grabbed my bag and called Clyde just as Mauer came out of his office with a cardboard box holding the CDs, the video stills, and the information he'd collected for Cohen. I added Ben's personnel file to the box.

"Thanks for the intel," I told him. "I'm going by Zolner's now. Maybe I'll catch him sleeping off a drunk."

"Just be careful." At my look he added, "I know. Once a Marine, always a Marine. Come on, I'll walk you to your truck."

Outside, the sky was a chalk-gray dome. The temperature hovered around seventy—unseasonably mild. In the west, lightning flickered across the gray expanse.

Mauer frowned. "The meteorologists say floods are coming. Damnedest summer I've seen."

At my truck, I unlocked the doors and Mauer set the box on the floor in the back. I dug out my spare sunglasses from the glove box, then pointed for Clyde to hop into the passenger seat while I got in on the other side. I rolled down the window, and Mauer leaned in.

"Hell of a hornet's nest going on upstairs with that hazmat train indefinitely delayed."

I nodded. "All velocity, all the time."

"TSA. Homeland Security. It's gonna be more red, white, and blue around here than the flag. What if this guy really meant to blow up that train?"

"He can't now."

"Train's gotta run sometime. And I'm heading off to a wedding. I should stay. That little girl . . ."

"There's nothing more you can do here, John. And it really is priorities. Take care of your own daughter for a couple of days."

He ran a finger under his collar, like a man afraid of a hanging. "I know. But it doesn't mean I feel good about it. If you get a date for the Death and Dismemberment forms, let me know. I'm going to haul some of the boxes out of the vault and take them to Estes Park. Not like Kimmy and Dot will need me. Father of the bride is more about signing checks than anything else."

"You've got the wedding. And the dance."

"Yeah." His eyes misted. He drifted away for a moment, and I let him go. Finally he drew a deep breath. "You need anything, you call. I'm less than two hours away. You got Fisher, and we'll get backup from the other guys if you need it." He gave me a searching look. "Promise me if you find yourself in a jam or you aren't feeling good about this, you'll call."

"I will." I glanced at the clock on my dashboard. "Now let me get on this."

He slapped my truck. We were done.

I backed the truck out of the parking space and headed toward the gate. He was still standing there when I turned onto the street, and he and DPC headquarters fell from view.

CHAPTER 7

How well we think is the best edge we've got.

—*Sydney Parnell, ENGL 2008, Psychology of Combat.*

Bull Zolner lived in a part of town that made Korea's demilitarized zone look like a nice place for a family picnic. Years ago, Vietnamese gangs had turned three blocks into a turf war that landed more bodies on the autopsy table than most people had fingers and toes. Since then, Denver Metro Gang Task Force had gone in and cleaned it up. Now the killings only happened once a month or so. Progress.

Why, I asked myself, had a racist like Bull chosen to live there? Bull hated everyone, but according to what I'd heard, he especially hated Asians. Maybe he'd sunk so far into the bottle that gang turf was the only real estate he could afford. Or maybe he was one of those ornery types who preferred living in a war zone, especially one of his own making. Nothing like a purpose-driven life.

I turned onto his street. Halfway down the block, his house was immediately identifiable as the only one with an American flag and a colossal red F650 super truck parked in the driveway. I double-checked the address, then pulled up to the curb to take the lay of the land.

The truck, along with its fiberglass skirts and custom hubcaps, suggested where Bull's retirement money had gone. More than a hundred grand for a vehicle like that, I figured. It was clean, despite the recent rains, and freshly waxed and buffed. Clearly, Bull cared about something.

The house was a different story. Two stories, with curling shingles and broken gutters, the entire structure listed to the left as if preparing to lie down and rest. What was left of the paint was long past any hope of being assigned a color. The yard was packed dirt—indeed, the only spots of green were the weeds sprouting in the cracked driveway and the trash bin on the side of the house. With the drapes drawn, lights out, and the promise of rain in the air, the place gave off the gray-white pallor of something six feet under.

"Nice digs," I said to Clyde as we got out.

Clyde—ears perked—looked ready to rumble, regardless.

At the front step I pushed the bell, found it broken, and knocked on the aluminum screen door.

The house seemed to hunker into itself, brooding in silence.

I stepped back to the edge of the porch. Overhead, the sun broke free of the clouds with a blinding burst of light; the crumbling window sashes and every crack and fault in the clapboards popped in sudden relief. Hoping against hope that Bull would be passed out on a chaise lounge in the back, I walked with Clyde around the side of the house and let us into the back through a gate set in a chain-link fence. The packed-earth backyard was empty of anything except a length of chain hooked to a steel stake driven into the ground and surrounded by mounds of dog shit. Clyde sniffed the nearest pile disdainfully. None of it looked fresh—wherever Bull had gone, he'd taken his dog with him. The curtains were drawn on every window. Even the sliding glass doors were shrouded. My knocks on the glass also went unanswered.

Clyde and I looked at each other.

Somewhere on the drive over, my heart had begun to throb in my chest, as if it were a clock tracking each second Lucy had been gone. Now, in Bull's squalid, weedy yard, it gave an anxious hop, threatening to go into triple time. I sucked in air.

"The neighbors," I said to Clyde.

I picked the house to the east since someone had at least mowed the lawn in the last month. A curtain twitched and a minute later, a woman yanked open the door. She had a five-foot frame, gray-black hair cut sharply at the chin, and a wary squint. The scents of fish and ginger wafted out. She left the screen door closed and scowled up at me, taking in my badge and uniform with suspicion. Then her eyes lit on Clyde.

"Oh, isn't he precious!"

Former Marines don't aspire to be precious, but Clyde bore up well. He opened his mouth and let his tongue unfurl, which made him look happy. The woman beamed.

"He's such a beauty! My son has a dog just like that. Adopted him through some veterans program." She lifted her eyes to me and the glare came back. Clearly I ranked far below Clyde. "Rosco was a military working dog."

"Ma'am, I'm here about your neighbor, Fred Zolner. Have you seen him today?"

"That nasty old man." The screen door pixelated her sneer. "Left yesterday evening. I saw him loading stuff into his truck. I went and asked him if he wanted me to keep an eye on his place. Trying to be neighborly."

"His truck is in the driveway."

She pushed open the screen and stepped outside, shielding her eyes with her hand. "Not that one. He took off in his old black Dodge. Looks like a piece of shit, but I guess it runs okay."

"Did he tell you where he was going?"

"Up to Cheyenne to spend a few days with his daughter. Said he'd be back next week. Mind if I pet your dog?"

"Sorry. He's on duty." I remembered what Mauer had said, that Zolner didn't have any family. "A daughter? You're sure?"

She glowered. "You think I'm lying? That old man's so bitter I find it hard to believe any woman ever slept with him. Plus he's ugly as sin. But some people get desperate. And he's got a pension. Makes a certain kind of woman chase him."

Probably meaning her. I pulled out a business card. "If he comes back, can you let me know? Tell him I need to speak with him. It's urgent."

She took the card. I was halfway down the porch stairs when she said, "You want to know about the other fellow who came by? He said it was urgent, too."

I stopped, felt that staccato beat in my chest, and turned back. "Who was he?"

"Salesman, he told me. Said Fred called for a quote on siding. But"—she sidled over to the top of the stairs—"I saw that movie. The one about the mob. You know, the one with the horse's head."

"*The Godfather*?"

She nodded triumphantly. "That's the one. That's what he made me think of."

"He made you think of Italian mobsters?"

The glare came back. "Hit man. Not Italian. Just a bad . . . what do you young people say? Dude. A bad dude. He smiled and smiled, and all the time I'm telling myself that smile don't mean a thing. I didn't want to get Fred in trouble, but I didn't think it was a good idea to lie. So I told him the same thing I told you. Daughter in Cheyenne. You ask me, old Fred's got a real problem. I think"—her voice dropped—"it's his gambling. Probably borrowed from the wrong people. Don't they cut off people's fingers if they don't pay up?"

"Did they threaten you?"

A snort. "You heard of the Asian Pride gang? I got two nephews and a cousin. Nobody better threaten me."

Back in my truck, I frowned out the windshield. Maybe, probably, Zolner's disappearance and his threatening visitor had nothing to do with the Davenports. Maybe the man was a siding salesman, although I'd bet my own pension against it. But I wasn't big on coincidence. I called Mauer, confirmed that there was no family on record for Fred Zolner, then decided I'd try to run Zolner down another way before backing off.

I drove half a mile north toward Colfax Avenue and a long strip of bars. As I went, I crossed out of gang territory and into a place where the lifestyle tended more toward hookers and fifty-cent beers. Plenty of bars, but none with *Royal* or *Crown* in the name. I circled back and still came up with nothing. I pulled over and dialed Dan Albers.

"I'm not on shift, Parnell," he said by way of greeting.

"Consider it overtime." Albers was one of our engineers. He had a bad temper, and I'd had to rein him in now and again at employee barbeques. For Albers, beer and too much idle time were a deadly mix. But he was good at his job and showed up for work as reliably as a Monday-morning quarterback. "I need something."

"Which is different how?"

"I'm looking for a railroading bar near East Colfax. The Royal or the Crown, something like that."

"It's not five o'clock, Parnell. But I'm in."

"You're out. This is business. You know the place?"

"The Royal Tavern's what you want. But if you're going in to knock heads, be gentle. Nothing but old guys there, getting drunk while they wait for the last stop." He rattled off an address. "Now, about that drink?"

"I should be so lucky."

He snorted. "Story of my life. Kidding, anyway. I'm in Topeka. And listen, Parnell? Call me again before I'm back on shift and it's over between us."

"That's all it'd take?"

He chuckled and dropped off the line.

I glanced at Clyde as I put the engine in gear. "Did you doubt me?"

◆ ◆ ◆

The Royal Tavern looked like a good place to go when no one else would take you in.

A squat, gray-brick building with blacked-out windows, the bar sat back from the road and was surrounded on three sides by an army of dying poplars whose leaves clung like the last strands of hair on a balding pate. I pulled into a dirt lot littered with broken glass and rain-sodden trash. There were only two other vehicles, and neither was a Dodge pickup.

The Royal wasn't a typical working-class bar or a friendly neighborhood bar or even a convenient stopping-off place for a beer and some peanuts before you went home to the missus. This bar was exactly what Albers had said—the end of the line. The kind of place where you went to get thoroughly wasted before the bar closed and you had to go home and face whatever waited there. Maybe your personal demon in the form of a fifth of rotgut. Or maybe nothing more than the echo of empty rooms and your own reflection given back darkly.

It would be hard to fall farther than this.

I got out of the truck and waited as Clyde hopped down.

"The sooner we're in, the sooner we can leave," I told him.

Inside was a gloomy cavern reeking of spilled beer and burned popcorn. A haze of cigarette smoke—illegal since Denver's ban on public smoking—obscured the air, and most of the light came from a television screen mounted in a corner behind the bar; the TV emitted a steady stream of shouts and organ music from a baseball game. The only other sounds were the crack of slamming balls from a pool table and an occasional slurred shout from one of the players.

I stood in the entryway until my eyes adjusted. Five middle-aged and elderly men sat at the farthest end of the bar from the door, their shoulders hunched, their hands wrapped around their drinks. Professionals in the drinking game, they gave off the desolate air of having long ago pulled off the highway of life, then found themselves stranded when their off-ramp led here. Two of them watched the television. The other three appeared to watch nothing but the approach of death. None of them glanced at me.

In the back, a pair of twenty-something toughs in leather vests played pool, their faces festering under long, greasy hair and a junkyard of piercings. They didn't fit in—but maybe they figured any port in a storm. The man bending over the table had his back turned, giving me an eyeful of his skull-head boxers. The one waiting his turn sent his gaze flickering over me; the look put me in mind of a dying bulb of questionable wattage. He said something to the other man, who glanced over his shoulder at me. They brayed like a pair of donkeys until their eyes lit on Clyde. Then they went back to their game.

I touched Clyde's head. Better than having my own SWAT team.

The only real motion in the place came from a woman who looked to be on the far side of sixty with a dusty blond ponytail, heavy eyeliner, and a black T-shirt pulled over a denim blouse. The T-shirt had a picture of a green alien and the words CLOSE ENCOUNTERS OF THE 3RD KIND. She moved slowly around the room wiping tables and collecting empty glasses. She carried a set of empties behind the bar, grabbed a fresh towel, then made her way toward me, wiping down the bar as she came. I slid between two bar stools and gave her a smile—two women in a place that reeked of dying testosterone. Clyde kept an eye on the patrons.

"Not that I want to turn away a customer," the woman said, "but you sure you're in the right place, sugar?"

"I'm looking for a man named Fred Zolner. I heard he hangs out here."

She puffed her long bangs out of her eyes. "I don't know any Fred, but if you're looking for Bull, he took off last night. Headed up to Cheyenne to spend a few days with his daughter. Left me shorthanded, the bastard."

"He works here?"

"It pays for his beer and most of his whiskey tab. He was supposed to be on tonight, when we actually get some business." She yawned. "Sorry. Every night's a long one. And every day I ask myself why I went into this business. Now I gotta find someone to cover Bull or work his shifts by myself."

"It's important I talk to him. You have a number for his daughter?"

She shook her head. But I caught something guarded in her eyes. I braced my arms on the bar and said, "If he wasn't really going to visit his daughter, you know where else he might go?"

"Now why would he lie about visiting his daughter?"

"He doesn't have one."

"Hm." She got busy wiping down the counter in front of me, forcing me to lift my arms. I noticed a leftover clear plastic sticker on her T-shirt indicating it was size L. "Well, it don't surprise me much, Bull lying. Sometimes him and the truth don't see eye to eye."

"He's lied to you?"

"Honey." Her voice carried the weight of centuries. "He's a *man*."

"I see." I offered my hand. "I'm Sydney, by the way."

She shook it. "Delia. Nice to make yours."

"So, Delia, you know where he hangs out when he's not here?"

"Inside a bottle, I suspect. Far as I know, the man does three things: drinks, sleeps most of it off, then pisses out what's left." She pointed at the DPC logo on my uniform. "That's one logo I recognize. We see a lot of that in here. You a railroad cop like Bull?"

"Special Agent Parnell. Bull worked with my father years ago."

"That so? A lady cop. 'Bout time." She screwed up her lips, thinking. "Parnell. You Jake Parnell's girl?"

The walls of the bar seemed to draw a breath and close in. The memory of my father and the fact he had walked out when I was little wasn't a door I'd expected anyone to open. I'd spent years working to push his memory into a crevice deep enough he couldn't crawl out. And here he was, smack out of nowhere.

I touched Clyde and managed a nod.

"Don't say a word, sugar," Delia said. "I can see it on your face. Jake seemed like an all right sort to me. More a talker than a drinker. Usually in here just to see his friends get home safe. But I know he took off and left you and that beautiful wife of his. You must have been, what, six or seven?"

"Eight." Eight and skinny and scrape-kneed and generally happy and then all of a sudden broken-hearted with a hurt that was like having the world crack open.

Exactly, I realized in that moment, the same age as Lucy.

Delia patted my arm. "What's your mom's name?"

I didn't correct her tense. "Isabel."

"That's right. Isabel. She always made the rest of us jealous with her movie star glamour. You look a lot like her." A wan smile. "But I expect you know that. How is she?"

"She passed away."

"Oh, I'm—"

"No, it's okay. It was years ago." I pushed away from the bar. "I need to get going."

"Wait. If you're looking for Bull, maybe Ronny knows something." She turned in the direction of the men hunched at the end of the bar. "Hey, Ronny. Ronny! Got another railroad cop here."

One of the men who was staring down death blinked and stirred, like a robot coming to life after someone flipped a switch. His head creaked in my direction and soupy eyes took in my face and then my breasts. They stayed on my breasts.

"A girl cop?" he said.

Delia flicked the bar rag in his direction. "Stop it, you old lech. She's a lady. Not that you'd know one if she bit you on the ass. You know where Bull is?"

The head creaked left, then right. "Ain't he here?"

Delia rolled her eyes. "Forget it, Ronny. Go back to your drink."

But Clyde and I moved down the bar to the old man.

"Where'd you work?" I asked him as I reached inside my pocket for the crossing number.

"Forty-seven years with the CWP," he said. "Now here I sit, drinking up my pension like those tramps I used to chase. What do they call that?"

Irony, I wanted to say.

"If I had a man with a pension," Delia said, "and I wish to God I did, I sure wouldn't let him piss it away in here."

I set the paper on the bar in front of Ronny. 025615P. "This number mean anything to you?"

He squinted. "I win the goddamn lottery?" He began patting his pockets.

"No, sir. It's a crossing ID. I'm trying to find where it's located."

"I lost my ticket." His hands were slapping at his pockets now. "Can't find my damn ticket."

Delia had followed me down. Now she grabbed one of his flailing hands and held it tight. "Ronny, Ronny, it's all right. No winners this week. Maybe next week."

He quieted like a lost child who'd just found his mom. "I didn't lose it?"

"No, sugar. We'll buy another one tomorrow. But look here." She picked up the piece of paper with the number on it and held it up in front of Ronny's face. "This is a—" A glance at me. "What'd you call it?"

"A crossing ID. For a grade-level train crossing."

"What she said, Ronny. You recognize this number?"

"Nah, I don't remember numbers," he said to me. Or actually to my breasts. "Ask Bull."

Ronny sank back to his beer. I retrieved my paper.

"Sorry, hon," Delia said.

But Ronny had given me an idea. Anyone other than a railroad cop wasn't likely to remember a crossing number, but at least it was another avenue to try if Mags Ackerman or Lapton didn't come through. "Any other railroad folk here?"

"Not today. And not usually. Don't get 'em like we used to." She folded the bar rag. "All I done now is make you feel bad. How about I pour you something?"

The longing that hit with her words blindsided me. The bad case of nerves that had been with me since the flashbacks and then the bomb would be quieted with a drink or six. My eyes darted to the bottles behind her. Delia gave a sad, knowing smile. She'd seen my kind before. She reached for a glass, but I shook my head.

I put my business card on the bar, turned it over and wrote the crossing ID on the back, then handed it to Delia. "If Bull comes in, have him call me. Tell him it's about the number and that it's urgent. Tell him it's literally a matter of life and death."

"That serious?"

"As a heart attack."

She tucked the card in her pants pocket. "Well, if I hear from him, I'll let him know. But don't hold your breath. If he lied about his daughter, then my guess is he's gone off somewhere with a fishing pole and a case of Old Thompson. And no, I don't know where."

"Has anyone else been in, asking about him?"

"Like maybe the Queen of England?" She laughed. "You're the first person to come in and ask about Bull since I've known him. Going on fifteen years."

"Thanks for your help," I told her. I backed away from the bar and Clyde and I headed toward the door.

Overhead, the baseball game switched over to a news announcement. Two of the drinkers jeered, but the bartender shushed them. She and I watched as a man appeared behind a podium.

"Who the hell is that?" the bartender asked me.

"Hiram Davenport."

"Who? Wait, ain't Davenport the name of that family that was killed?"

"Yeah. Turn it up."

She pulled out a remote and cranked up the volume.

Hiram Davenport stood confidently at the podium, his large hands gripping the edge as he leaned forward, his face all smiles. I was horrified until a news ticker rolled across the bottom of the screen. The press conference was from the day before. Hours before most of his family would be slaughtered.

I'd seen plenty of photographs of Hiram in company bulletins, looking jovial and kind, a man you'd enjoy having over for dinner. But this was the first time I'd seen him in motion, despite the fact that he was my employer.

Judging by the men and women standing behind him, he wasn't tall, although his erect posture and air of confidence gave that impression. He was fit and trim, with a solid build and a tanned, handsome face that made him look every inch the professional businessman. But his most striking feature was his eyes, a pale blue the shade of arctic ice, so light as to be almost translucent.

On the screen, he beamed at the gathering, waiting to speak until the applause died down.

"This is just the beginning, folks," he said when only a spattering of claps remained. "A bullet train from Denver to Albuquerque and north to Cheyenne. And that's just the start. From there, well, the sky's the limit. Actually, two hundred miles an hour is the limit. You folks will be able to skip the security lines at the airport and leave the gas in the gas pump. My train will allow you and your family to zip from one city to another in comfort and even luxury, and for far less than the cost of a single airline ticket. Read, watch television, surf the Internet—hell, we'll have private cabins for whatever you're surfing." He gave a big wink and got a few laughs from the crowd. "It's the future, and the Denver Pacific Continental railroad and my corporation, Transco United, are going to bring it to you. Now, how about some questions?"

One of the journalists in the crowd raised a hand, and Hiram pointed.

"What about Lancing Tate?" the journalist asked. "He's also in the running for the federal funding. Do you know something the rest of us don't?"

Hiram's smile broadened. "Mr. Tate is a tough businessman, and he's putting up a good fight. I relish that. It's a clash of the titans, folks, a clash of the titans. But mark my words. Transco United and specifically Denver Pacific Continental are going to win this battle. We'll be the ones laying the new track. We'll be the ones building the cars and locomotives. We'll be the ones creating an infrastructure that will provide thousands of jobs to the people of Colorado. *We* will be the ones to make the West great again."

Hiram and the press conference disappeared, replaced by a news anchor who announced that they were about to get a live update from one of their reporters. The picture cut to an attractive woman standing outside police headquarters, and the background changed to a picture of Lucy in braids and a blue dress.

"While her father fights for his life in a local hospital, there are still no leads on little Lucy Davenport's whereabouts," the reporter said. "The police are holding a press conference here this afternoon. There is some speculation that by then we'll have an update on Lucy's father, Ben Davenport. He's been in surgery all morning. We're hoping for some good news."

"Thank you, Lisa," said the anchor. "We're all praying for Ben and for Lucy's safe return."

The baseball game came back on, and the men at the bar cheered. Delia gave me a shrug. I nodded my good-bye and pushed open the door, walking out into the sunshine. When my phone rang, I was standing with Clyde in the parking lot, inhaling the stink of heat-sticky tar and car exhaust and listening to someone's dog bark with weary monotony.

"How much do you like your job?" Cohen asked when I answered.

"Not a lot, at the moment."

"That's what I was hoping you'd say."

I unlocked the truck and let Clyde into the passenger seat. "Go on."

"Ben's office. DPC's lawyers are refusing us access. Not that going through them was my first choice. Bastards'd likely yell coercion later if we found something they didn't like. But it's worse than that. The judge is a pal of Hiram's and he's dragging his feet over the warrant."

"Ben's *father* doesn't want his office searched? Why would that be?"

"Now that," Cohen said, "is the question of the hour."

"I see."

I said nothing more as I got behind the wheel. Instead, I let Cohen read a message in my silence. Since I was an employee of DPC, in the eyes of the law it was as legal for me to search Ben's office as it was for me to rifle through my own bedroom. I just couldn't tell Cohen what I planned, or I'd be acting as his agent instead of as an employee of the railroad. And we'd be back to needing a warrant. He'd already skirted the limits of the law by bringing it up.

The only problem now, of course, was the fact that I'd be acting against the wishes of my own legal department. Against my own boss. I thought fleetingly of my pension then said, "We didn't have this conversation."

Cohen let loose a breath. "What conversation?"

CHAPTER 8

In war, going outside the wire means risking your life. But at home, the things that will kill us are often what we bring in ourselves. Alcohol. A violent spouse. Cigarettes and prescription meds. Anxiety and falls and carelessness and anger. There are plenty of dangers in this world. But the most dangerous thing of all is what we see in the mirror.

—*Sydney Parnell. Personal journal.*

"So tell me what else you've got going," I said to Cohen as I pulled into traffic.

"Bandoni's in with Hiram Davenport. He's taking Hiram's statement, but he's also trying to keep him from calling in his sharks or getting in our way. Meanwhile, I'm enjoying the dubious pleasure of interviewing Samantha's assistant, Jack Hurley. Guy's a real douchebag, only been in her employ for a few months. His alibi is so-so and he clearly had a crush on his boss."

"You think they were sleeping together?"

"I don't get that vibe. My guess is she hired him out of pity. Starving artist, and all that. But after I sweated him, he admitted to making copies of some of Samantha's artsier stuff and selling it online to support his weed habit. Maybe she called him out on it. We're getting ready to have another go at him. What about you—anything on that crossing number?"

"Not yet." I gave him a summary of my visit to Fred Zolner's house—the fact that the old man had hotfooted it to parts unknown the evening before and lied about where he was going. And that some guy with a passing resemblance to a mobster had dropped by to see him. "The neighbor mentioned gambling debts. Could you run a BOLO?"

"You think his disappearance might be related to our case?"

"I don't see how," I admitted. "All I wanted from him was to see if he could confirm that number from the kiln as a crossing number, assuming that's what it is. But the timing says something, right?"

"Grasping at straws?"

"He's the best straw I've got right now."

"It works. I'll make it happen."

"Tell them Zolner was driving an old Dodge pickup. His Ford is still in the driveway."

"You got the hazmat information I asked for?"

"I'll bring it by in an hour or so."

"When you get here, drop it off at the incident room—we've set up a command center in a meeting room on the fourth floor. A couple of the Feds will start going through it right away. Your boss find anything suspicious in the employee files?"

"Not a thing."

A silence. I could picture him rubbing his forehead, probably looking at the clock. "Give me something, Parnell."

As I drove across town, I rolled Clyde's window down partway then fished Engel's cigarettes from my breast pocket and lit up. Clyde gave me a look and stuck his nose out the window.

"Sorry, buddy. It's just until Lucy's back."

My mind was on what the bartender, Delia, had said about my parents. Her questions and the murky atmosphere of the bar had pushed me back to childhood memories that made me long for the simple kind of pain you get forcing splinters under your fingernails. I was practiced at shoving aside thoughts of my father. But my mom, Isabel . . . she was always closer and harder to vanquish.

I cracked my window and released a stream of smoke.

Isabel had developed a drinking problem around the time I was old enough to be embarrassed by it. Her choice to be drunk at three in the afternoon became a war of wills, and my nine-year-old self didn't have a chance. Although my mom did her best to keep it secret—pouring the vodka into glasses of juice, using breath mints, hiding the full bottles in the garage and the empties at the bottom of the trash—I gave up on having friends over. Later, I gave up on having a mom.

Try as she might, Isabel couldn't hide the slurred words, the flushed skin, or the angry, bleary look in her eyes. The occasional missed school event when I was in third grade slid into complete absence by the time I hit fourth; she missed school plays, intramural games, the open houses when she was supposed to meet my teacher and admire my art. What I hated most were the holiday parties when the other mothers made cookies and caramel popcorn and helped us with a gift exchange, and everyone felt sorry for me because my mother sent me with a half-eaten box of vanilla wafers.

None of which compared to her coup de grâce when I turned ten—arrest for manslaughter.

Hard to top that one.

◆ ◆ ◆

Ben's office was on the second floor of the Colorado Historical Society in the Capitol Hill district. If the receptionist noticed the nervous sweat that started as soon as I walked in the building, she didn't say anything. She unlocked and opened Ben's door for me, gave me the key, and asked me to lock up when I was done. I waited until she'd gotten onto the elevator before Clyde and I went in and I locked the door behind us.

The office was large and bright. Three of the walls were covered with a combination of bookshelves, maps, and framed photos. The fourth wall was a bank of windows, the southern light filtered by a row of maple trees just outside. An overstuffed armchair with an ottoman was angled so that its occupant could enjoy the view. At the center of the space, an immense desk anchored the room.

It was a clean, well-lit, and perfectly normal space. Something as ugly as a killer should never have slipped into this world.

I shook myself. "Move fast, Parnell."

I downed Clyde near the door then set down my duffel, snapped on latex gloves, and removed a camera. I started with the desk. It was wide and plain, its surface almost entirely obscured by papers, books, file folders, a stack of notepads, and a scattering of pens. Family photos marched across the back of the desktop; I recognized Ben and Samantha and their children from the pictures I'd seen online. One frame held a photograph of Hiram and Ben beaming into the camera—Ben was maybe nine or ten, lifting up a string of fish. Another shot showed Lucy in a sports uniform, holding a soccer ball. With a lurch of my heart, I thought of Malik.

There was one shot of Ben in Iraq. Armored up and standing in front of a Humvee, he appeared confident and serene. A man who knew exactly what his mission was and how to accomplish it. Looking at this, I would have thought he'd come home unscathed. Except that sitting on the desk in front of the photo was a jagged piece of metal. I picked it up—shrapnel from an IED. A trophy of sorts, I supposed, of how close things had come. Or a reminder of how quickly things could go south.

I set it down in haste.

I started on the left side of the desk and worked my way to the right, sorting quickly through the books and papers. Cohen would follow up with a warrant if he could find a more amenable judge. Right now I was looking for business cards, phone numbers, hate mail, or a calendar with appointments listed. I hoped for anything about that crossing number.

Or anything that DPC might want to hide.

There were books about the railroad industry along with trade magazines and business journals, many of them dating back to the 1960s and 70s. A 1980 US railroad map showed a sprawl of railroad networks—small railroads in green, short lines in red, and the giants spanning the continent in bright orange. I skimmed a recent piece in *Fortune* magazine with the headline FASTEST MAN IN THE WEST? The article discussed Hiram's effort to develop a bullet train, which he had already dubbed the Gold Line Express. With the potential influx of billions in federal funding, some people were calling the project the Gold *Mine* Express, at least for whoever got the go-ahead. Flipping through the stacks, I saw that other magazines had followed *Fortune*'s lead. There were a dozen articles covering the battle between Hiram's empire and that of his biggest rival, Tate Enterprises.

I'd met Alfred Tate only once. He'd been a speaker at a joint training session between Denver PD and the railway cops from both DPC and Tate's company, SFCO. We ended up standing at the dessert table together. I reached for the cheesecake, but he recommended the chocolate mousse. He'd been wrong about the mousse. But his kindly manner and the slightly lost look in his eyes had won me over.

The only other thing on Ben's desk was a stack of yellow legal pads. The top three were filled with notes written in small, tight handwriting, mostly bulleted dates and brief headlines—a history of DPC. The rest were blank.

There was no computer, although a power cord was plugged in at an outlet situated directly under the desk.

In the desk's center drawer I found notepads, more pens, and old railroad maps, along with a bunch of historical articles about the start of railroads in Colorado and their vital role in the gold rush.

The next three drawers contained office supplies, a bag of cookies, a plastic pouch of beef jerky, a folder labeled REIMBURSEMENTS filled with gas and restaurant receipts, and a carefully rolled child's drawing of a house with five people standing in front—Mommy, Daddy, the twins, and Lucy. At the bottom of the picture, written in red crayon, were the words *I love you, Daddy. Love, Your Lucy Goose.* Ben had attached a yellow sticky note with the name and address of a local frame company.

I blinked, closed my eyes.

Outside in the hall, the elevator pinged. My eyes shot open. Clyde lifted his head as footsteps approached the door. Clyde glanced at me, and I signaled him to stay silent while I waited for a knock or a key in the lock. A minute ticked by, then two. Outside, a flock of starlings screeched. After a moment, whoever was at the door went on down the hall.

I let out my breath.

Faster, Parnell.

The last drawer was locked. Railroad cops are good at a lot of things, but certain job requirements make us demigods when it comes to picking locks. I pulled a small kit from my duffel and had the drawer open almost immediately.

Inside were seven things. A manila folder bristling with papers. Two plain white envelopes. A bottle of whiskey. Ben's medals from the war. A color photograph. And a handgun.

I ignored the gun, the whiskey, and the medals for the moment and placed everything else on the desk. I started with the photograph.

It showed Samantha Davenport standing in front of the Denver Art Museum. Her assistant, Jack Hurley, stood beside her, his hands deep in his pockets, a boyish grin on his face. Both were squinting into the sun, Samantha's hand cupped over her eyes. She wore a sundress; he had on cargo shorts and a U2 T-shirt. There was nothing inappropriate in their posture or their attitudes. The sunny sidewalk where they posed was completely innocuous. But the picture made the hair rise on my neck for the simple reason that Ben had chosen to lock it away.

There will be killing till the score is paid.

I studied the picture a moment more, then, finding no answers, turned to the manila folder, which was labeled MoMA in thick black marker.

Most of the papers inside pertained to the donation of the Edison Cement factory land to the recently formed art museum. There was also information about the creation of a board of directors and the hiring of an architectural firm to convert the existing factory buildings into a unique space. At the back of the file were letters of petition from artists worldwide who wanted their work displayed when the museum opened, and letters from someone at MoMA-Denver requesting funding from potential donors—the funding requests had gone to everyone from local arts supporters to people in Paris, London, Madrid, and Frankfurt. MoMA was nothing if not ambitious.

In the very back of the folder was an article from the *Denver Business Journal*. The reporter talked about the valuable land that Hiram Davenport had donated to the museum and said that the remaining acreage would serve as a thruway for a bullet train, should the train actually come to be. The title of the article was ART RIDES INTO THE FUTURE.

A business card was paper clipped to the folder's inside flap. Tom O'Hara, the *Denver Post*.

I knew Tom—he'd interviewed me for an article about my work in Iraq. I still regretted giving that interview. But that wasn't Tom's fault. We're all a lot smarter in hindsight.

I went back to the papers detailing the donation. I didn't know anything about finance beyond balancing my checkbook. But there were clearly different numbers floating around on the estimated value of the land. And someone had hired a site investigator from a firm called Clinefeld Engineering to do a subsurface investigation. I figured that was normal during a deed transfer. But the form dated to after the transfer of the deed.

Maybe someone was asking questions. Maybe DPC had tried to deduct more on their taxes than the land was worth. If Ben's job was to write articles and a book praising his father and DPC, I wondered what his interest was in a possible fraud.

I closed the file and opened the first envelope.

Inside was a copy of an article dated August 1982. It was a feature piece describing the on-going war between the two big western railroads and highlighting the recent decision by the Interstate Commerce Commission to approve DPC's attempt to take over one of the lines belonging to Alfred Tate's SFCO railroad, including the land occupied by the Edison Cement factory. The article questioned whether this decision would be the beginning of the end for SFCO.

"These two have been fighting since 1982," I said to Clyde.

His ears pricked, but he stayed where I'd downed him.

The ICC had reviewed the merger for four years, with Tate protesting that the proposed deal violated antitrust laws. The commission had seemed poised to reject the proposal. Then Alfred Tate had abruptly reversed his stand and spoken out in favor of the takeover. He'd convinced his stockholders that it was more financially sound to let the short line go. The reporter went on to say that the new owner, Hiram Davenport, planned to immediately upgrade the track and all grade crossings. "Safety," according to Hiram, "was paramount." The reporter lavished praise on Hiram's determination to put safety above profits, implying that Tate's railroad, the SFCO, had done the inverse by refusing to upgrade the crossings or by not maintaining them properly. A sidebar mentioned that the first crossing Hiram would upgrade was in the middle of a lonely sprawl of wheat fields, on Potters Road. Locals had nicknamed it Deadman's Crossing. There had been multiple fatalities there, including a couple of teenagers who had died while racing a train to the crossing. The upgrade would happen within months, Hiram promised.

The reporter's source was DPC employee and railroad cop Fred "Bull" Zolner.

I lifted my head. Clyde's eyes were on me, sensing my sudden excitement.

Potters Road. Deadman's Crossing. The missing Zolner.

"We got something, Clyde," I said.

The location listed for the upgrade wasn't far from where Samantha had died. While there was no longer a crossing at Potters Road, the tracks went above the street on an overpass a quarter mile away from where she'd been struck. It was inside the area the Feds, the cops, and a crowd of volunteers had searched and were still searching. Maybe that overpass had once been a grade-level crossing. Maybe it had been 025615P.

I looked again at the date. Almost thirty years ago. Could there really be a connection? Had the current feud between the Tates and the Davenports over the bullet train raised the specter of the past? And was that reason enough for murder?

One thing I knew—what Hiram Davenport had told the journalist about the crossings was a lie. Money to upgrade a crossing came from the Feds, and it was the states, not the railroads, who decided which crossings got active warning systems or if any got converted to nongrade crossings. Hiram might have applied some pressure to get that crossing changed. And no doubt he had political pull. But neither he nor Tate could have signed on the line to make it happen.

Still, his public push for an overpass at Deadman's Crossing was a stroke of genius. By eliminating the crossing altogether, he'd managed to persuade the public to his side in the battle between DPC and SFCO.

I refolded the article and placed it back in the envelope. I added it to the stack of books and magazines I planned to take with me. Then

I opened the second envelope. Inside was a sun-faded photograph of a young woman; I removed it and set it on the desk.

The picture had been taken outdoors during either early morning or late afternoon—sunlight slanted past the woman and into a thick grove of pines. The woman looked to be in her late teens or early twenties, tall and slender, with long, dark hair caught in a single loose braid, and eyes the deep blue of sapphires. She wore a pink-flowered dress that looked like it had gone out of style a couple of decades earlier and her feet were bare. In her arms she held a black-and-white kitten. Spread out on the blanket at her feet were the remains of a picnic—sandwiches and fruit and a bottle of wine.

The picture looked years old, but there was something unsettling about it that I couldn't put my finger on. Maybe just that the kitten looked unhappy, in the way kittens do when held against their will.

I slid the photo back into the envelope and looked at the whiskey and the medals. Their proximity suggested an anger that I could all too well understand: Good job, sorry your life is fucked, have a medal.

I made a small sound in my throat, and Clyde stood, his tail wagging tentatively at my sudden anger.

"You're right," I told him. "Gotta keep going."

I picked up the gun with my gloved hands. A Ruger P-Series pistol. It was clean and unloaded. I wasn't surprised to see it. Most former military guys like to keep a weapon close by. But again, its proximity to the whiskey and the medals suggested a relationship that made me uneasy. I'd thought at first that Samantha was a suicide. Had her husband ever stared into that abyss?

I slid the Ruger and everything else from the drawer into evidence bags and placed them in my bag along with the books and magazines. So far, nothing I'd found suggested a reason for Hiram to forbid the police to search.

I glanced at my watch. I'd been in the office for almost thirty minutes. Lawyers from DPC could arrive at any time. I went hastily through the rest of the room and was finishing up my search of the bookshelves when Mags Ackerman called.

"I drink Dom Pérignon," she said when I answered. "I want you to know that."

"You found the crossing."

"I sort of found the crossing. Mostly I found nothing."

"Mags," I growled.

"Okay, okay. You were right about 025615P being a crossing number. No question. I went down into the dungeon and located the original inventory forms. They're filed numerically. Or at least they're mostly filed that way. Some people's idea of how to count from one to ten is a little scary."

"Mags!"

"Don't bite my head off. Your form was missing. I went through a lot of forms—almost a hundred numbers forward and back from yours. All of them were there. Except yours. But—before you have a fit, I did find something."

I realized I was holding my breath.

"There was a piece of notebook paper stuck in the box with your crossing number written on it. And under that, someone wrote 'Potters Road, Adams County, Colorado.' So there you go. Your crossing. Voila! You ready to take down my shipping address? A case of the bubbly should be sufficient."

025615P. Deadman's Crossing.

I abandoned the bookshelf and crossed to the window. Sunlight filtered through the leaves, scattering diamonds in soft wedges on the wooden floor. I could just make out clouds massing over the distant peaks—another storm headed our way.

"You have any idea why that form would be missing?" I asked.

"A hundred reasons, starting with the fact it might have never gotten filed. Or someone could have pulled it to cross-check something and then forgot to put it back. Or maybe whoever pulled it ended up losing it and put in that placeholder. I'll ask the other old-timers. But here's the bad news. Or the good news, depending on your perspective."

I waited.

"Once I got the confirmation on the ID and the location," Mags said, "I started going through the 6180s."

"And?"

"And nothing. There weren't any accidents at that crossing. So if that's what you were hoping to find, you are SOL."

I shook my head. "I just found an article written in 1982, Mags, before that crossing was converted. It said there had been multiple accidents at Potters Road."

"Well, someone screwed up somewhere, then. I'll see if I can find anything at all. You can wait on the bubbly for now." She hung up.

I frowned. There was only one railroad crossing on Potters Road. Had the accidents occurred somewhere else in the county? Maybe the reporter had gotten his facts wrong.

I stared out the window. On the other side of the glass, the world lay flat and hard, like something overcooked in the oven.

Directly across the street from Ben's office, just visible through the trees, a daycare center sat quietly in the early afternoon heat, sun bleached into a lifelessness that gave me pause. Blinds were drawn, the front door closed, the playground desolate. I leaned forward and pressed my forehead against the glass, and that's when I saw her—a little girl sitting alone on a swing, her back to me, her long, brown hair riffling in the breeze.

The hair rose on the back of my neck.

"Lucy," I whispered.

The swing rocked, a trail of dust swirled. The little girl's head was down. Her pink-and-white sneaker drew a line back and forth in the dirt.

Was she real?

My fingers went to my pocket, to the photograph of Malik.

Children have no choice but to pay whatever price the world demands. But not this child, please God. Not this one.

The door to the center opened and a woman rushed out, her expression frantic. She spotted the girl and ran across the playground to lift her into her arms. When she turned and headed back to the door, the girl looked up, and our eyes met over the woman's shoulder.

Not Lucy. I pressed my palms to the glass. Not Lucy.

I jumped when my earpiece buzzed. Cohen.

"We've got something," he said. "A child's bloodied clothing."

CHAPTER 9

When your job is cataloging the dead, you focus on the injuries. How they were caused, which was the mortal blow. The person behind the wound becomes an abstraction—work laid out on the table.

At some point, when you realize what you've lost, you know you have to step away. Go listen to the voices of the living. Walk outside and look up at the stars. Listen to music or read something that breaks your heart.

You cannot carry the dead. But you must honor them.

—Sydney Parnell. Personal journal.

"It started with a tip on the hotline," Cohen said. "Several hours after Samantha's death, a caller spotted a woman and a little girl standing near a red Audi sedan at Ridge Park."

A buzz built behind my eyes as I locked up Ben's office and Clyde and I headed toward the elevator. Ridge Park was ten minutes from where Samantha had been killed.

The elevator door opened and we got on.

"Caller said he was walking his dog when he noticed them," Cohen said, unspooling the story in his methodical way. "The woman was trying to get the girl in the car, and the girl was crying. Caller figured it was just a kid being a kid. But then he heard the news about Lucy. He told us the little girl he saw matches the description for Lucy Davenport."

"Damn," I said.

"Yeah."

When we reached the lobby, the elevator doors slid open. Two grim-faced men in expensive suits stood waiting to get on, the receptionist with them. I forced a smile at all three and dropped the keys into the receptionist's open palm.

"I kept watch," I told the suits. "No one came by."

I slipped past them before they could get over their surprise and Clyde and I pushed through the front door and into the heat of the cloud-dappled day.

"What was that?" Cohen asked.

"Nothing. Did the caller get a license plate?"

"That's why we're talking right now."

I unlocked my truck and opened the passenger door for Clyde. "Spill it."

"The Audi," Cohen said, "belongs to Veronica Stern. And the description the caller provided of the woman matches Stern's DMV photo."

A frisson of shock rippled through me. "Stern was at the site this morning."

"One reason we jumped on it."

The first drops of rain hit my skin as I walked to the driver's side. "You going to get to the bloodied clothing?"

"A uniform found Stern at home, asked if he could look in her car. First she said no, said it violated her civil rights. But the officer must have been convincing. She finally agreed. She also agreed to let him look around her house."

"And?"

"Nothing in the home. But he found girl's clothing under a box in the Audi's trunk. Pink shorts and a T-shirt."

His voice held a combination of misery and excitement that made my pulse leap.

"Bloodied," I said.

"Soaked. They're running a precipitin test now to confirm it's human before we wait nine hours or more for a DNA test. We're bringing Stern in. She denies any knowledge of how the clothes got into her trunk, but she's pretty damn calm."

I opened my door. The rain came down heavier.

"The Ice Queen," I said when I found my voice. "That's her rep."

"Since you've worked with her, it might be good to have you observe the interview."

Stern the litigation lawyer, who had left SFCO for DPC only six months earlier, just as the battle for the bullet train was heating up. I thought of her coldness that morning—it no longer seemed mildly humorous or even annoying.

Now it felt ominous.

The rain turned into a downpour as I drove. Traffic snarled, and pedestrians darted around the vehicles on their way toward shelter. Clyde watched warily out the window. To the east, dark clouds towered on the horizon like piles of dirty laundry, the gray shot through with a sickly yellow.

I'd learned a trick or two living with Cohen and now I channeled his ability to compartmentalize. I put aside all thought of Stern and the child's clothing and dialed Tom O'Hara, the journalist whose business card had been paper clipped to the MoMA file in Ben's office. Tom had moved from features to crime six months ago, but we'd stayed casually in touch. Meaning every couple of weeks he called and bugged me about doing a follow-up to my earlier interview with him. Especially, he said, since I was now a big hotshot investigator, having worked with Denver PD to solve a homicide.

"Tell me about Denver's Museum of Modern Art," I said when he answered.

"What, no foreplay?"

"I'm not that kind of girl."

"I can keep hoping, though."

I braked as a stoplight turned red and pedestrians poured into the crosswalk. I forced myself to put aside all the horrors of the day and kept my voice light. "Hope and four bucks will get you a latte at Starbucks."

"Ha! Does that mean I can buy you a coffee?"

"I'm not that kind of girl, either."

When Tom interviewed me more than a year and a half ago, he'd caught me when I still carried a burning need to tell Americans what was happening on the other side of the world. I hadn't told Tom everything, of course. But, for me, I'd been pretty talkative. It had worked out great for Tom; he got a national journalism award. But for me, not so much. My grandmother read it and said that turning the contents of your heart into a headline was not something a Parnell did.

No one can shame you like family.

At the moment, of course, all of that was beside the point. I needed Tom.

"So we talking trade, Sydney?" he asked. "Hold on. Don't answer that. Back in a sec."

"Wait—"

But he was gone. Elevator music piped drearily in my ear.

Rain pelted the roof, and I turned up the speaker volume. Clyde's window was completely fogged and now he was working on the windshield. I shook my head at him and hit the defroster. Thanks to Clyde's work in Iraq, my partner hated thunder even more than most dogs. But he loved the rain.

The traffic light turned green and I nudged the truck forward.

The music stopped and Tom said, "I'm back. So what's our deal?"

"We'll keep it simple," I said. "You're going to tell me everything you know. And in exchange, I will let you live."

"You always were a sweet-talker."

"Sweet talk is the only kind of bullshit Marines *don't* have to do. So tell me about MoMA."

"What makes you think I know anything about it?"

"You're Tom O'Hara."

"Well played. But c'mon, Sydney. You're killing me. You are cognizant of the fact that I'm off features and on crime, right? I know this is about the Davenport case. I saw you on media footage from that old cement factory. Talking it up with the Feds and the police. Give me something before my boss switches me to international and sends me to Nigeria."

I tried to remember if I'd heard a helicopter overhead. "There was media footage?"

"At least promise that you'll give me an exclusive when they're ready to let something go to the press. Denver PD's playing hardball on this one. They didn't even go through me with that sketch."

I was starting to feel like the last kid picked for the team. "What sketch?"

"Ha! You, either."

"Tell me."

"See, now you want me. Some dead guy they found at the cement factory. They're trying to use the media to get an ID on him."

I gave a satisfied nod—Cohen had jumped on the photo I'd taken. Power of the press. Maybe they'd shake something loose.

"Tell me about Ben Davenport," I said. "Did he contact you?"

Silence.

"Have I ever let you down, Tom?"

"There was that time we were in bed . . . no, wait. That was a dream." Neither of us laughed. "I *am* still waiting on that follow-up, Sydney. Now that our women are home from the war, people want to know how they're doing, what life is like after witnessing all that death and destruction. You remember that one?"

"You remember that I gave you my story last spring? The one about the skinheads and all the dead people?"

"So we're even for the moment. Just say those three little words I'm dying to hear and our journey will continue. Three little words. Quid pro quo."

"We're talking about a little girl."

"Quid. Pro. Quo."

I made a left-hand turn onto 13th Avenue. A gust of wind slapped the rain against the windshield, and for a moment water ran so thickly over the glass that it looked like the world had fallen into the sea. "Fine. Quid pro quo. You'll get your exclusive. But with your full awareness that all I am is a railroad cop, bound by the legalities of working for a private company. And I don't know who the Denver PD brass will talk to."

"What I hear is that you got some influence with someone in the Major Crimes unit."

"Now you're a gossip columnist? How the mighty have fallen. Look, you know you're going to get this. You're pretty much the only guy around who knows his ass from his elbow. So help me out here. What's at stake"—I dropped into my do-not-fuck-with-me Marine voice—"is a little girl's life. Do not make me waste time hunting you down."

"You know you scare me sometimes, right?"

"That's what I count on."

"Okay, fine. Ben Davenport called me two months ago, around the middle of May. He asked if I knew anything about a new museum going up in Thornton near the South Platte. Wanted to know if I'd be willing to do a puff piece on it—folks bringing culture to the Wild

West. Told him it wasn't my bailiwick anymore. But then he called back a couple of weeks after that, asked if I'd be more interested in MoMA if there *was* something illegal going on. Of course, I told him yes."

"And?"

"And, that's it. He said he'd get the ball rolling, but then I didn't hear anything more. Mention of the land popped up with all the talk of a bullet train—apparently that acreage has got great right-of-way. So I looked at the public records—title and deed of transfer. Denver Pacific donated a nice chunk of that parcel to the museum. But when I tried to dig deeper into things like the tax records and appraisals, they shut me down. I pleaded the Open Records Act, and they said that releasing that information was under the discretion of the custodian. But the custodian claimed there was an ongoing investigation. When I couldn't find anything about that, either, I called Davenport back a few times. But he never took my calls. You're thinking the Davenport murders are about a piece of land?" He paused. "Is this about the bullet train?"

I pulled to a stop in front of Denver PD headquarters and squeezed into a space that others had avoided—right next to a fire hydrant. I figured I had bigger problems.

"I'm not connecting anything at the moment," I said. "And if you print what we talked about, I will roast your *cojones*. Davenport had a copy of the deed in his office, with your business card clipped to it. That's as much as I know. If he found anything illegal, he didn't leave any paperwork that I could find."

Sometimes, especially when talking to the press, it's okay to lie. Quid pro quo.

"Therefore," Tom said, "it's time for me to work my journalistic superpowers." I could almost feel his smile—he would relish the battle now that he knew there was something to fight for. And despite our banter, I knew he was as worried about Lucy as the rest of us.

"Make it good," I said. "You owe me. And don't tell anyone what you're working on."

"What kind of journalist do you think I am?"

"A good one. Let me know what you find."

"Then maybe I'll be the man of your dreams?"

I shut off the engine. "You don't want to be the man of my dreams, Tom. Trust me."

◆ ◆ ◆

The lobby of the Denver PD headquarters was a madhouse.

The first thing I noticed was the din, a rumble of voices that pushed out into the rainy afternoon as soon as I opened the outer glass doors. Clyde and I stepped inside, helped by a slap of wind.

"Press is going nuts," said a voice.

I turned to see a twenty-something man in jeans and a hoodie standing in the small antechamber, dismally eyeballing the rain.

"Fucking zoo in there," he said to me, shaking his head. "I got things I gotta take care of. But ain't no business going on today."

I peered through the next set of doors where a throng of men and women milled about the large space. They wore suits and dress shoes, with damp raincoats slung over their shoulders. A lot of them carried cameras or held up smartphones. Reporters.

I glanced at my watch. The press conference was more than an hour away. Which explained why Tom O'Hara was still at his desk.

The man in the hoodie muttered something that sounded halfway between a curse and a prayer and launched himself into the storm. I wiped my boots on the damp carpet, took a firm grip on Clyde's lead, then, with Mauer's sealed cardboard box balanced on my hip, pulled open the next set of doors.

The din became a roar. The smell of perfume, hairspray, and wet clothes hit like the draft downwind of a shopping mall, the restless mood somewhere between a basketball game and a wake. Police headquarters was, for the moment, the epicenter of the tragedy that had exploded into the Davenports' lives. The rain and police barricades would have sent all but the most optimistic reporters away from the tracks where Samantha had died and the cement factory where Lucy had vanished. No doubt a few reporters were in Wash Park, filming the Davenport home from a distance and talking to any neighbors who were willing. Some might be at the ME's office, hoping for early word on the autopsies, or at the hospital, trying to ambush a nurse or surgeon about Ben.

But it looked like most of them had shown up here.

Off to my left, an anchorwoman with coiffed hair and a pale-pink suit stood in front of a camera, speaking into a microphone.

". . . in this developing tragedy. Eight-year-old Lucy Davenport has been missing for approximately twelve hours, according to a police spokesperson, who offered little additional information. We do know that police have been talking all morning to Lucy's grandfather, billionaire businessman Hiram Davenport."

I shifted the box against my hip. Clyde's eyes were everywhere, he and I equally uncomfortable in the throng. We spent most of our hours alone, often in the wild open spaces of northern Colorado and Wyoming, where the only evidence of humans were the train tracks we patrolled. Crowds were places where people hid guns and bombs and moved with murderous intent. Crowds were Iraq.

I pushed down my unease, knowing Clyde would read it through his lead and take his cue from me.

"No worries," I told him.

I spotted Special Agent McConnell on the far side of the room, standing against the windows. She'd geared up from composed to intense, maybe feeling the weight of minutes ticking by. Her eyes met mine and she waved for me to join her. Clyde and I pushed through the crowd.

"Special Agent McConnell," I said. "Are reporters usually so early for a press conference?"

"Please, call me Mac." Her face was pale in the dull afternoon light, her injured eye a smoky blue-black. Behind her, rain washed down the windows. "Word is they've finished getting a list of possible suspects from Hiram Davenport and he's on his way down."

I fished in my duffel, handed her a copy of the CD. "Video from the train recorder."

"Ah. Thank you."

I tipped my chin toward her face. "You tried bilberry for that?"

"What?"

"Your eye. Bilberry extract. It's got antioxidants that strengthen the capillaries. Reduces the bruising."

An eyebrow went up. "You have a lot of experience with black eyes?"

"I used to trip a lot."

"Ah."

"Yours?"

"Sometimes I trip, too."

Above the noise, the clear ping of an elevator sounded on the other side of the lobby.

"Speak of the devil," McConnell said.

The anchorwoman gestured to her cameraman. "It looks like he's coming down."

The din quieted to the rustle of clothing and an occasional cough, the mob tightly focused, everyone straining forward. The anchorwoman murmured something to her cameraman, and he jostled to move a few feet closer to the elevators. For a moment the mob—with their bright eyes and eager faces—made me think of a pack of hounds about to fall on a fox.

The moment broke into a buzz of voices as the elevator doors opened.

"Any word on your granddaughter, Mr. Davenport?"

"Is your son out of surgery?"

"What are you feeling right now, Mr. Davenport?"

"No questions," a man said. I recognized Lieutenant Engel's deep baritone. The crowd parted as Engel and three uniforms shouldered their way through, followed by Denver PD's media coordinator. Engel and the officers had surrounded a sixth man and were hustling him in the direction of the doors. Hiram Davenport. All I could see of him was his high forehead and wavy gray hair.

But I knew that if they'd wanted to keep Hiram away from the reporters, they could have smuggled him out through the tunnel that runs underneath the plaza and comes out at the crime lab. There was a plan in play.

Halfway across the lobby, the group came to an abrupt stop. I had a better view now. Engel murmured something in Hiram's ear, but the old man was shaking his head at whatever the lieutenant offered. Finally Engel nodded and motioned for the uniforms to step aside. Hiram stood suddenly alone in the center of a small space. The overhead lights shone down on him like a consecration, and the room went quiet again.

Dressed in gray slacks, a white polo shirt, and a navy nylon rain jacket, the first impression Hiram Davenport gave was of a wealthy man making his way from the golf course to the private dining room at the club.

But a closer inspection stripped him of that veneer. The titanic energy that had powered his presence on the podium during yesterday's newscast had vanished; he looked like something tossed up on the beach by a storm and left to shrivel in the heat. He was gray under his tan, with a hollowness in his eyes that I recognized—the look of someone living through things no one should.

He cleared his throat. "Thank you for being here."

Even his voice was different—just a ragged whisper. Only the quiet of the crowd made it possible to hear him. "I will not take any questions at the moment."

A murmur rose, and Hiram raised his hands. He looked around the lobby as if measuring every man and woman there. The crowd quieted again, the faces earnest and willing. No matter his grief, Hiram could still manage a crowd.

"I am not at liberty to discuss my family's case. That is not why I asked you here."

I leaned in close to Mac. "He called the media?"

She shook her head. "Maybe a few. But the police would have made the first calls. The media is the best way to get people looking for Lucy and generating leads."

Hiram continued. "I stand before you, and through you the world, to offer a heartfelt plea for the return of my granddaughter."

Now the only sound was the rain.

"We have excellent police in Denver," he said. "Our men and women in blue are the very finest. And I know they're doing everything they can to find Lucy and bring her safely home. But—" His voice broke on the last word and moisture filmed his eyes. He blinked. A flash popped. "My little Lucy is only eight. She's small for her age. To look at her, you might think she's fragile. But . . . Lucy is tough. She's brave. She's just—she's just like her grandfather. She loves horses and books and she loves"—another blink—"*loved* playing with her brothers. Now my son, Ben, lies in a hospital bed close to death. The only thing that can save him is the return of his daughter. The only thing that can save *me* is Lucy's return."

He lifted his chin, picked a video camera, and spoke directly into it. "Please. Whoever has my granddaughter, please bring her home to me."

Lieutenant Engel laid a hand on Hiram's arm. He ignored it.

"I'm confident Denver won't let me down. I've given my entire life to this city, as some of you know. Now, I will give again. I'm offering a reward of ten million dollars for Lucy's safe return."

The crowd erupted. Clyde surged to his feet, unsure where to direct his focus. The uniforms closed in around Hiram as the reporters pushed forward, their mics lifted. Engel once again took point, shoving his way through the throng.

The media coordinator lifted her hands, waving to get attention. "Denver PD and the FBI will offer a joint press conference here in one hour. We ask that you please stand by for that so that we can get information out to the public."

Mac touched my elbow. "Let's get out of here."

We moved toward the elevators, passing Hiram's group. As we approached, my eyes met his, then his gaze dropped to my uniform.

"You," he said.

Everyone stopped. The uniforms jostled in place. The journalists close by looked at me.

"You're one of mine," Hiram said. His arctic eyes glittered. "You're the one who went after her this morning. After my Lucy."

Engel touched his elbow, but Hiram shrugged him off.

"Yes, sir," I said. The picture of the unknown woman and the article about the crossings seemed to burn in my duffel bag. I wanted to ask him about them. Wanted to ask him about his relationship with the Tates and how much Ben knew about MoMA and the land. But not here. Not in front of the journalists.

Hiram read the name tape on my uniform. "Special Agent Parnell." He cocked his head. "You saw my lawyers earlier today, I believe."

I lifted my chin. Here it came. "Yes, sir."

The reporters closed in around us, lifting microphones. The lieutenant and Mac waved them back.

A wild light shone suddenly in Hiram's eyes, like a match touched to a wick, a flame burning behind glass.

"Come see me," he said. "In two hours. We need to talk."

"You stepped in some shit," Mac observed as the two of us and Clyde rode up on the elevator.

I shrugged.

"Word is," she said, "the railroad wouldn't give the police permission to search Ben's office."

"That's right."

"But I'm guessing you went anyway."

"Fools rush in," I said casually. But inside I was wondering how I'd pay the bills if Hiram fired me. People talked about hiring vets. But outside of security and law enforcement, a lot of times it didn't go beyond the talking stage.

Mac nodded as if she knew what I was thinking. The composure was back in place, her body still except for her right foot, which tapped the floor with a life of its own.

"At least you've got a set of balls," she said.

"Standard Marine issue."

She laughed. "Look, if he wants to fire your ass for doing your job, we'll find a place for you."

I finally met her gaze. "For this investigation, you mean?"

"Sure. And more, if you're interested. As I said earlier, I read about that case you handled last February. It was great work. You should be looking at your options."

"And here I was thinking I didn't have a mom anymore."

"One reason they call me Mama Mac when they think I'm not listening. They also call me Mad Mac. I have the finesse of a bull in a china shop."

"Well, thanks, but I'd prefer it if you stayed away from my china."

Mac's voice turned soft. "You remind me of my daughter. Spine like a piece of rebar. And a sense of honor welded so strongly in place it will break you before you realize you're using it as a shield instead of for support."

"Maybe you should be having this conversation with your daughter instead of me."

The elevator came to a stop and the doors slid open.

"Wish I could," Mac said as she held the elevator door for a pair of uniforms getting on. "But it'd be at her gravesite. Honor makes a crappy shield."

Way to step in it, Parnell. "I'm so sorry," I murmured.

"So am I."

We stepped out into pandemonium. The main hallway was crammed with detectives, uniforms, FBI agents, and TSA officials, all hurrying somewhere or conferring in clumps or talking on the phone, a finger stuffed in one ear as they struggled to hear over the din. A hand-lettered sign taped to the wall with an arrow pointing toward the end of the hallway said simply, LUCY ROOM 2A. That would be the command center, where all the key players from every law enforcement agency involved would converge.

Mac and I walked in silence to the incident room, where I handed over Mauer's data. While she stayed in the room to check in with her team, Clyde and I went back out into the hall. I stopped one of the detectives hurrying past.

"Detective Cohen?"

"At his desk, I think. In the squad room." He sped past.

I threaded my way through a maze of offices and headed into the homicide warren. This place—with its disorder of desks, stacks of binders and old coffee cups, the smells of wet carpet, spilled sodas, sweat, ink, and overloaded wiring, with the television set rumbling a steady stream of news behind the hum of conversation and trilling phones—was the heartbeat of Cohen's life. When he came home at night, he still vibrated with its energy. Cohen's devotion to his job, when he could have been riding on family money, was part of what had persuaded me to allow him into my life.

As I walked in, I spotted Cohen standing by his desk, tapping his pen on a stack of papers while he talked on the phone. His expensive suit—one of a never-ending supply he received from a mother who'd been hoping for a trial lawyer instead of a cop—was wrinkled but clean; he must have stopped by the house to change. When he saw me, he kept talking but waved me forward.

I removed the evidence bags from my duffel and placed them on his desk—the photograph, the article, the MoMA folder, and the gun. I added the CD and the stills from the TIR video.

Cohen pointed to the evidence bags. "Ben's?" he mouthed, and I nodded. To whoever was on the other end of the phone he said, "Yeah, keep running it. I want to know what we've got."

He dropped his phone in his pocket and his butt in the chair and gave me a weary smile.

"Hey," he said.

"Hey. Any word on the blood test?"

"Not yet."

I sank into the chair next to his desk and gave Clyde the all clear. My partner once again greeted Cohen with a rapture usually reserved for a long-lost brother, then crawled under Cohen's desk and stretched out as much as he could in the confined space.

Cohen lifted his feet out of the way. "You big mutt." He picked up the CD and popped it into his computer. "Any surprises here?"

"Not really. Looks like she was hurt, as Deke said. And unable to move, as he also said."

Cohen watched the video in silence, then ran through it a second time. When he reached the part where the animal appeared, he hit pause.

"What is *that*?" he asked.

"That's the 'not really' part. I brought you some stills. Maybe you can get someone from the Fish and Wildlife Service to take a look."

He nodded and finished watching. After a third time through, he shut down the program and studied the stills. Then he picked up the clear evidence bag holding the photograph of the woman. "Any idea who this is?"

I shook my head. "It was locked in Ben's desk with the other things I brought, including that photo of Samantha and Jack Hurley. I'll see if Hiram Davenport knows who she is—he told me to stop by." I left out my fear that he'd likely fire me.

Cohen picked up the picture of Samantha and her assistant. "A day trip by two artists to an art museum. Why lock it up?"

"Why indeed? Unless you think there was more to their relationship."

"We just cut Hurley loose with a promise we'll be looking into those illegal sales he made. Like I told you, his alibi is so-so—his girl-friend swears he never left her side and she's got the used condoms to prove it. Not exactly an interview with the pope. But so far there's nothing that links him to any of the crime scenes. You find anything that DPC might want to hide?"

"Not really." I filled Cohen in on what I'd found in Ben's office. And what I hadn't. "No appointment calendar, no business cards, nothing to indicate who he might have seen lately or planned to see." I tapped the bag holding the newspaper article. "This piece suggests that the rivalry between Hiram Davenport and the Tates goes back at least thirty years, when Hiram bought out one of Alfred Tate's lines and got the cement factory as part of the deal. I'm guessing it was a hostile takeover. I'll look into that. But more immediately relevant is the fact that Hiram lured away Tate Enterprises' chief litigation lawyer six months ago and gave her a top spot at DPC."

Cohen's eyebrows shot up. "Veronica Stern?"

"None other. Has Stern said anything?"

"Not much. But she hasn't lawyered up, either." He picked up his pen, jiggled it between his thumb and forefinger. "They towed her car here and forensics is going over it. We've taken DNA swabs, and she gave us permission to search her home and garage and a tool shed, which has so far turned up zilch. She was adamant with the officer who brought her in that she knows Lucy by name only and that she has no idea how or why the clothes got in there, or who would have phoned in a false tip. But my spidey sense says she's sitting on something."

"Like what?"

He sucked in air, blew it out. "No idea. Bandoni and I will start the interview in about ten minutes. Anything strikes you as odd or off, I'd like to know."

"Of course. What else do you have?"

He tossed his pen on the desk. "We've got nothing. Half the civilized world is looking for that little girl, and the other half is telling us it was space aliens. Feds are working the terrorist angle, but they're pulling up empty lines. Neighbors didn't see anything. Hurley says Samantha mentioned a stalker, but he never saw anyone, and her friends never heard about it. We're working to track her movements during the last week, hoping CCTVs caught something. The tech guys are going through the family's social media accounts and e-mail, but they haven't picked up a lead with any legs. Could be Hurley's lying about a stalker in order to redirect the heat."

He picked up a paper coffee cup, stared into it, then crushed it. A trace of coffee dribbled onto his lap, and he swore and pulled a napkin out of his desk.

"What about the dead man who was shot outside the kiln?" I asked. "Any hits on the sketch?"

Cohen wiped at the coffee spill. "Not so far. We found enough of him to print, but the prints didn't match anything in the system. We also found a casing we hope is related to the case. Hard to be sure with the bomb blast, but ballistics says the large-caliber gun that killed him doesn't match the gun used on Ben and the twin boys. So either the shooter had more than one weapon, or we've got more than one shooter."

He dropped the napkin in the trash and picked up the clear evidence bag holding Ben's gun.

"That was locked in his desk with the photos and the article," I said. "There was a bottle of whiskey in there, too. And his military medals. Maybe that's what Hiram didn't want us to find."

Cohen frowned. "Says something to his state of mind, I guess. We'll run the gun. But a .40 cal? This won't match, either."

"And the bodies in the kiln?"

"Both male. We got an ID on one because we have his prints on file for trespassing and loitering. Frank Kaye. Been homeless since the time of Moses."

I found my hand reaching for the comfort of Clyde. "Trash Can."

"What?"

"Frank Kaye was known around the hobo camps as Trash Can. He was a harmless old man, never came out of his drunken stupor long enough to hurt a fly. He used to hang at Hogan's Alley when he was in Denver. He must have relocated to the cement factory."

"And stumbled on the killer," Cohen said. "Then maybe got whacked because he saw what he shouldn't."

I remembered the face I'd seen through the plastic before the bomb blew. "Could the ME tell if Kaye had been tortured?"

"It looks like it, Syd. I'm sorry. Bell said that, near as she can tell given the condition of the bodies, both Kaye and the other man in the kiln were tortured."

I laced my fingers around my bad knee, brought my chin up. Compartmentalize. It's how you survive.

Cohen set the gun back down on his desk. I swore he'd aged ten years since yesterday. I'd seen it before. The skin beneath his eyes went gray and he'd get a thousand-yard stare that said he knew trouble was out there, just waiting to jump him if he let down his guard. His shoulders would drop until I found myself looking for the weight of the world he seemed to be carrying.

Yet, each time he managed to bounce back. Right up until the next bad case.

He rolled his neck until it popped. "I can't get a read on Stern. She's about as warm as a deep freezer. But she pays her taxes, hasn't ever taken a sick day at work, dresses like she's got Grace Kelly as a wardrobe assistant. She donates time and money to the local art community. Doesn't even have a parking ticket. Bandoni's digging into her records, but if I put her in front of a profiler with what we've got so far, he'd laugh me out of the room. And we're still looking for a link between her and either Ben or Samantha."

"Maybe she crossed paths with them at an art event. Samantha's got work hanging in galleries—don't those places have openings and fund-raisers?"

"You're asking a murder cop about art?"

"It can't be all bullets and babes," I said. "As for Stern, she's completely by the book. No heart, according to those who work with her. But she's the best at what she does. Maybe that makes her appealing to a certain type of man. One more interested in conquest than occupation. If Ben is that type, she might have caught his eye."

"Occupation? Is that your word for a relationship?" He held up a hand. "Don't answer that. So you're thinking Ben might have relished the challenge? Former military man who's bored with the day job after leading troops into battle?"

It wasn't where I wanted to go, but I kept circling back to it. The photo I'd seen in Ben Davenport's employee file was that of a man who had bad days. Maybe a lot of bad days. I got that and I didn't want to hold it against him. But maybe persuading a woman like Veronica Stern into his bed had helped him make the transition from combat to corporate life.

"She's not bad looking," I said, going for understatement. "Pair that with the aloof, hard-to-get angle, and a man could get hooked. Even if she doesn't acquiesce, he could get possessive. Is Stern married?"

"Divorced. We're checking out the ex. Let's say she did decide to sleep with Ben. Then, once the challenge is gone, he moves on to the next target. Or maybe goes back to his wife. Stern's betrayed and enraged and decides to slaughter the family. She takes the little girl because—to her way of thinking—Lucy should be hers."

I stared out the window on the other side of his desk. His gaze followed mine. Outside, a gloomy landscape of clouds and skyscrapers brooded in the gray light. The din of horns sounded distantly through the glass.

"It doesn't work," I said.

"Because she's five feet five and a hundred pounds soaking wet?"

"Because the Davenport deaths were ugly. Hands-on and messy. I can barely put *Stern* and *messy* in the same sentence."

"So she had a partner. Someone else who slept with her or who wants to sleep with her."

"What about the person who called it in?" I asked.

"He didn't give a name. And he used a burner phone."

I raised an eyebrow. "And that's not a flag?"

"Of course it is. But it's not automatic proof of malice. People use prepaid phones when they're trying to sell something and want to remain anonymous, or if they have bad credit and can't get a phone plan. The Feds are trying to chase it down, but if the caller was setting up Stern, he will have used the phone once and ditched it. It'll be a dead end."

I rubbed Clyde's outstretched paw gently with my foot. "I guess you've considered the possibility that the killer might be someone she's rejected. He targets Ben for getting what he couldn't, then fingers her for the crime."

"First place Bandoni and I went. It fits with shooting the men and taking the women. And with the quotes. We'll see what she says. And if we believe her." He propped his feet on a half-open drawer of his desk and leaned back far enough I had to stop myself from grabbing his chair. He laced his fingers behind his head, elbows spread wide. A classic Cohen pose when he was thinking. To anyone who didn't know him well, he looked relaxed. But his freighted eyes betrayed him.

"Tell me about the crossing number," he said.

I told him about taking out the *X*s, and that the crossing had been converted to an overpass back in the eighties. That it was close to where Samantha had been murdered.

"No shit?" Cohen dropped his feet, and the front wheels of his chair slammed down on the carpet. Clyde shot out from under Cohen's desk, then gave him a dirty look when it was clear there weren't any bad guys around that needed chasing.

"Sorry, fur ball," Cohen said. Then to me, "Maybe he was signaling intent by writing that number in the kiln. Maybe he planned to kill Samantha when the hazmat train came through, but she fought back and he had to change his plans. So how would he know about an old crossing number?"

"Maybe he worked for the railroad years ago."

He picked up the article. "So, 1982. We'd be talking someone in their, what, fifties? Or older. Crime like this would be hard for someone that age to pull off."

Clyde had stretched out at my feet, safely away from Cohen's chair. But now he came up fast. Something blocked the lights, and I turned in my chair to face Cohen's partner, Len Bandoni.

"You two done making goo-goo eyes at each other, maybe we can get to work," he said. "We got Stern in Room 3."

Cohen's partner was not my number-one fan. I didn't think he ever fully accepted my version of events surrounding the skinhead shoot-out five months earlier. Cohen hadn't, either, for that matter. But they had different opinions as to whether what I'd done had been wrong or right. Bandoni fell so far on the side of the line that put me in the wrong that—until now—he'd managed to avoid me entirely. Which made things tough for Cohen. Which, in turn, made me dislike Bandoni even more.

"Jealous?" I asked him. "Cohen never gives you goo-goo eyes anymore?"

Bandoni snorted. "You haven't shot any of the witnesses yet, have you, Parnell? Flashed your little railroad badge and tried to arrest half of metro Denver?"

"This morning," I said. "While you were finishing your first donut."

He stuck a finger in one ear, dug around. "Something's making noise. Like a gnat, maybe."

Cohen rolled his eyes. "Let's get to work, partner." To me he said, "You know where the observation room is, right?"

I nodded.

As he and Bandoni walked off, Bandoni reached his hand up behind his back and gave me the finger. The last defense of the weak. Score one for the railroad cop.

CHAPTER 10

There are two main reasons we wage war: greed and revenge.

You can talk about dictators who've crossed a line, or about the need to defend the helpless. You can get on your soapbox and preach democracy and how it's your job to take it to the world.

But it all comes down to two things. Someone wants something. Or someone took something.

And now we're gonna kick a little ass.

—Sydney Parnell, ENGL 2008, Psychology of Combat.

When Clyde and I arrived at the observation room, the ten-by-ten space was packed with detectives and federal agents and reeked of coffee and sweat. The noise level was at a volume just above that of a squadron of F-16s at takeoff. Mac had found a spot to the left of the door, pressed against the wall. I wedged myself in beside her, while Clyde, miserable with the crowd, crawled into the gap between my feet and the baseboard.

A wall-mounted screen at the front of the room provided a direct view into the interview room, where a camera was already recording and transmitting. All of us could see Veronica Stern sitting alone at a metal table in a chamber consisting of peeling plaster, two metal-and-vinyl chairs, and a single window reinforced with black wire.

She didn't much resemble the Veronica Stern from earlier that day. Clearly, finding a child's bloody clothing in your car—assuming you didn't put it there—was enough to shock anyone. But Veronica didn't look so much shocked as simply . . . gone. As if the real Veronica Stern was off somewhere trying to strike a deal with the devil. Her lovely face was a static mask, her flat gaze fixed on an invisible spot six inches above the table. The fingers of her right hand clutched her necklace as if it were a lifeline.

She barely seemed to blink.

At the sound of the door opening, she moved like someone coming out of a dream. She released the necklace—a silver heart with a diamond-and-ruby center—straightened her shoulders, and lifted her chin. Her look was now one I recognized—the coldly competent litigation lawyer.

Cohen and Bandoni entered. Bandoni slapped a file folder onto the table and took a position behind Stern, arms folded and chin tucked. His gaze drilled into the back of her head. Cohen seated himself across from Stern. He opened his notebook and gave her a reassuring nod.

"I'm Detective Cohen. Behind you is Detective Bandoni."

Stern's glare was glacial. "I didn't put those clothes in my trunk."

"Then we'll get to the bottom of this," Cohen said, "and you'll be free to go."

He opened the file folder Bandoni had placed on the table. "We're recording this," he said, pointing to the camera in the corner.

"I am familiar with the process, Detective," Stern said.

"That because you've been arrested before?" Bandoni asked.

Stern arched a brow. "Did you not bother with your homework, Detective Bandoni? As DPC's chief litigator, I've conducted hundreds of interviews."

Cohen pulled his chair closer to the table. For the camera, he said, "Let's get started. Detectives Cohen and Bandoni, interviewing Veronica Stern. Ms. Stern, please say the date. Then state and spell your full name and address and your date of birth."

Stern complied. When she gave her street address, Mac and I exchanged glances. Wash Park. Where the Davenports lived.

Cohen went through a patter, recording for the camera that Stern was there of her own free will, that she wasn't under the influence of drugs or alcohol, and that she understood that she was not under arrest. Once through the formalities, he pulled the file folder toward him and picked up the pen.

"This must be a shock to you," Cohen said.

"Do you think?" The laser edge in her voice could have etched steel.

"You seem more angry than concerned."

"That is because I haven't murdered any children, Detective. I haven't even given one a nosebleed. This is clearly someone's idea of a sick joke."

"Who would want to play that kind of joke on you?"

She tucked a single loose strand of hair behind her ear. "My line of work places me against people who would prefer I not do my job. People looking for compensation from the railroad, whether they deserve it or not."

"You mean people hit by your trains. Can you think of anyone who's been particularly upset?"

She shook her head. "In instances where the railroad is at fault, we usually settle. When it's not—which is the majority of cases—we still do our best to settle. But this is a litigious country. People often refuse, then become angry when they realize they would have been better off taking our initial offer. So I've been mentally reviewing my cases. No one comes immediately to mind."

"You settle to avoid the publicity?"

"And the expense. But when the plaintiff refuses, we fight. And we usually win."

"Up until six months ago, you were fighting on behalf of a different railroad. Is that true?"

"SFCO. Yes."

"What made you switch to DPC?"

"They offered a better package."

"Higher salary?"

"And better benefits."

Bandoni cleared his throat. "Benefits like sleeping with the boss's son?"

Stern rolled her eyes. "Really."

"As a litigation attorney," Cohen said, "your pay is among the highest in the country, even for attorneys as a whole."

"Are you suggesting that's a crime? The work I do is difficult. Millions can be riding on the cases I handle. I was happy to accept DPC's offer."

"Were you driven by financial worries?"

In the observation room, a phone trilled. "Vibrate!" someone shouted.

"—merely pay commensurate with my work," Stern said.

"We will check your financials."

"Please do."

Cohen scribbled something in the notebook. "Let's talk about your car. Is it accessible at work?"

"When I park on the street. Usually I park in the adjacent garage, which is gated."

"But someone could walk in."

"Of course."

"What about this week?"

"I was in the garage yesterday. The street the day before."

"And what about at home?"

"I keep my car locked in the garage at night. I never leave it outside."

"What were you doing at Green Hills Park at four this morning?"

She blinked. "I wasn't."

"Bullshit," Bandoni muttered.

She didn't glance around. "I wasn't at *any* park this morning. I wasn't even out of bed then."

"And last night?" Cohen asked. "Where were you last night?"

"I picked up my usual Chinese dinner at Shanghai's right after work at six and then went home."

Cohen made a note. "And you are not married, is that correct?"

"Divorced."

"Did your husband cheat on you?"

She narrowed her eyes. "That is none of your business."

From his post against the wall, Bandoni said, "That's a yes. I bet that hurt—beautiful woman like you."

Her eyes glittered.

"Boyfriend?" Cohen asked.

"No."

"Roommate?"

"I live alone."

"Meaning no one can vouch for your whereabouts last night."

"After I left the restaurant, no."

"You make any phone calls, log on to the Internet, anything like that?"

"No."

"So how did you spend the evening?"

"I enjoyed a glass of wine with my dinner, turned on some Bach fugues, then settled in the living room to read."

"*Soldier of Fortune?*" said Bandoni. "I hear they got ads in there for people who want to make a hit."

She didn't respond, and Bandoni picked up the patter. "So you just sat in your chair and read. All by your lonesome."

She shrugged. "*Lonesome* isn't the word I would use."

"Sounds lonely to me. Just you and—who'd you say—Bach and some magazines. You ever get bored?"

"No."

"Ever try to alleviate the boredom by spending time with someone else's husband?"

A muscle jumped in her cheek. "That sounds more up your alley, Detective."

"Or maybe someone's wife? How do you swing, Ms. Stern?"

Cohen gently took the conversation back. "Give us a timeline of yesterday evening and last night, Ms. Stern. After dinner and reading."

"I read until nine o'clock. After that, I went to bed and read another thirty minutes, then slept until my alarm. At six thirty this morning, I went for a run around my neighborhood. I showered and arrived at work by eight. Half an hour later, I was called up on the Davenport case."

"You drove your car to the tracks?"

"Yes. And parked it alongside two police cruisers. Maybe you should check with them."

"What about after?"

"I went home to shower with the intent of returning to work immediately after. But your officer showed up on my doorstep."

"What is your relationship with the Davenports?"

A shadow passed over her face, a quick flick like a blind snapping closed. "I know them casually. Or rather, I knew Samantha Davenport casually. She and I sat together on the Board of Directors for MoMA."

"Must have been hard, seeing her under that train."

"It wasn't pleasant, no."

Bandoni snorted. Cohen and Stern both ignored him.

"MoMA," Cohen went on. "That's the Museum of Modern Art, is that right?"

For the first time, Stern looked guarded. "Could this have something to do with the museum?"

"You know anyone who has something against MoMA?"

"It's an *art* museum. Everyone has been behind it. The art community, the sponsors, the local government. Everyone."

"Anything questionable about it? The museum, the people working for it? Maybe the land it's on?"

Stern shook her head. "There is nothing improper or untoward. It's a good group of people and a good cause."

"Untoward," Bandoni said. "I'm gonna have to look that up."

She made the slightest inclination of her head in his direction. "I have no doubt of that, Detective. You'll find it next to *uncouth*."

"You sound pretty committed to the museum," Cohen said.

"I believe in the arts."

Cohen stood, stretched, his motions deliberately casual as he crossed to the window and looked out. Even through the video camera I could hear the rain hit the glass. There would be flooding—sewers and drains were already overwhelmed.

"Tell me more about your relationship with Samantha Davenport," he said.

"We met at an art show where her work was on display. The museum was her brainchild. Her father-in-law, Hiram Davenport, is quite wealthy, as of course you know. Sam got him to donate the land and provide some of the funding. Believing my legal background would be useful, she asked me to be on the board of directors. Naturally, I accepted."

"Did you donate any of your own money?"

"A few thousand."

"How much is a few?"

"Five. I donated five thousand of my own money."

"Was this before or after you took a job with DPC?"

She frowned. "Before. But if you're looking for a connection between my employment with DPC and the museum, you won't find anything."

"What kind of connection would I be looking for?"

"I don't know. You're the detective."

Cohen returned to the table and made a note. "How is it that Hiram Davenport was willing to give such a valuable piece of land to a museum? Riverfront property in a growing part of metro Denver. About as good as it gets."

"I'm sure it's because of Sam. And maybe he wanted the tax deduction. I can't claim to know what he was thinking or to know anything about DPC's finances—"

"Not even as DPC's chief litigator?"

"Not even then. I'm sure he also appreciated the press."

"Especially given his battle with the Tates for the bullet train."

"Perhaps. You would have to ask him."

"Who else is on the board? Aside from you and—I assume—Samantha."

"Wealthy art lovers and artists. It's a matter of public record."

"And what about Ben Davenport? Is he on the board?"

A tinge of pink rose in her neck. "No."

"But you know him."

Something glimmered on her face—a look like that of a child standing at the candy counter with empty pockets.

Beside me, Mac said, "Ah."

Stern looked down. "Not really."

Cohen gave the table a quick rap. "Ms. Stern? Can you look at me?"

She lifted her head. Her face was blank. "I met Ben exactly once. At a fund-raiser that his father insisted he attend. Or maybe it was Sam who wanted him to come. Either way, it was obvious that Ben was ill at ease."

"He told you that?"

She nodded. "He'd had a drink or two by then, I guess. He said he hated small talk because there wasn't anything he wanted to discuss except his family and the war. He said it wasn't fair to inflict either on a stranger."

"And yet he talked to you."

"Only that much. I knew more about him from Sam."

"What did she say?"

"That marriage could be tough. I thought maybe she meant his anger."

"He had a temper?"

Even Stern's shrug was graceful. "She said that Ben struggled after the war. Like a lot of veterans. Sometimes he'd get angry."

"She ever mention him getting violent?"

"Never. When Ben got angry, he retreated. What bothered her more was that sometimes he seemed sorry to be back home. She thought he missed the war."

"How's that?"

Stern began turning a ring on her finger, a simple silver band. "The excitement, I suppose."

"That your supposition, or Sam's?"

"Mine."

Cohen wrote a few more lines in his notebook.

In the observation room, I felt the sidelong glances from a couple of detectives who knew my past. I kept my eyes on the screen.

"You ever know Samantha or Ben to be involved with someone else?"

"You mean an affair? I never heard anything."

"What about Jack Hurley?"

"Who?"

"Samantha's assistant. You must have met him."

She shook her head. "No."

"Maybe at an art exhibit?"

"Not that I recall."

"And she never talked about him?"

"Not to me."

Cohen took the photo of the woman from Ben's office out of the file and placed it in front of Stern.

"Do you know this woman?"

She abandoned her ring and bent over the picture. "No."

"Never saw her with Ben?"

"No." She looked up. "Who is she?"

Cohen slid the picture back into the folder.

Bandoni scrubbed at his nose. "You don't seem exactly torn up over your friend's death."

"I am not public with my feelings."

Cohen went back to the window, leaving it to Bandoni to gauge Stern's reaction. "And what of Hiram Davenport? How well do you know him?"

"He hired me. Outside of that, I've had little interaction with him. We've met once or twice at fund-raisers."

"When you made your move to DPC, you didn't bring any information with you that might be of use to your new boss?"

"I'm offended by the suggestion."

Cohen's eyes met hers. "So, did you?"

"No."

"What is your impression of Hiram?"

"My *impression*? What does that have to do with anything?" Stern worried the ring again. "Is he somehow a suspect in this?"

"That upsets you," Cohen said.

"What upsets me is this waste of time while that little girl is still out there."

"Bear with us. What do you know about Hiram Davenport?"

She shrugged. "I know he's a railroad man, through and through. And I know he is passionate about art and is willing to put money into sharing that love with others. I know from Sam that, as a grandfather, he's big on gifts, less so on family events. Anything else comes from what I read in the papers."

Bandoni heaved himself off the wall, walked around the table, and splayed his hands on the metal surface, leaning in. "Oh, enough of this bullshit. Where is she?"

"If you're asking about Lucy, I don't know."

"You slept with Ben Davenport. You murdered his wife and sons." He was in her face now, shouting. "His daughter's *bloody clothing* was found in your car. What have you done with her?"

Stern didn't retreat. Her eyes flashed and sudden anger blotched her neck and cheeks. "I don't care what you think, or who you are, or what game you're trying to play to get me to confess to something I am innocent of. But that little girl is out there, no doubt suffering, and you are wasting time with me. I did not sleep with Ben Davenport. I did not—as you so crudely suggested—sleep with his wife. I did not hurt either them or their children. If you want to save Lucy Davenport, then for God's sake, put your energy where it might make a difference."

Silence in both rooms. Then someone in the observation room said, "That was righteous."

Bandoni stayed right where he was, his face still inches from Stern's. "I've seen the best liars the world has to offer, Ms. Stern. And you aren't anywhere near their league."

Cohen glanced at his phone. He passed it to Bandoni, who straightened and read whatever was on the screen. The detectives exchanged a look; Bandoni looked like he'd swallowed pins.

In the viewing room someone said, "They got the precipitin results. It's animal blood."

A murmur ran around the room. My knees sagged and I squeezed my hands together as relief spilled through me.

"Congratulations," Bandoni said to Stern. "It ain't Lucy's blood."

"I cannot pretend to be shocked by that." She shifted in her chair and crossed her ankles. "Perhaps you ought to be asking yourself who would want to frame me. You have yet to tell me who implicated me in this. Or what you're doing to locate him. Or her."

"You have some names?" Cohen asked. "People who might want to hurt you? Outside of your cases, I mean."

"I—no."

"People who might be jealous of your attention to Ben Davenport?"

"I didn't *pay* any attention to Ben."

"Someone at work with a grudge? Either at SFCO or DPC?"

She turned the ring again. "Popularity has never been my goal, but it is also true that no one has any complaints."

"What about would-be boyfriends? Someone particularly insistent?"

"Nothing I can't handle."

"Zach Vander," Bandoni said. "Can you handle him?"

Her eyes flashed hatred at him. "How do you—"

"You filed a restraining order against him. Did you think we wouldn't find out?"

She shook her head. "He was nothing but a nuisance. A railfan who overstepped."

"A what?"

"A train buff," Stern said. "I met him at a convention in Pennsylvania where I'd been asked to speak about crossing accidents. That was five months ago. For three months after that, he wouldn't leave me alone."

Bandoni threw up his hands. "Why didn't you bring him up twenty minutes ago?"

"Because I didn't even think of him. He moved away a long time ago. He's been out of my life."

"How was he a nuisance?" Cohen asked.

"He called me repeatedly at home and work. Sent e-mails. Photographs. I never took his calls or responded. But his messages were . . . rude."

"Rude in what way?"

"Sexual. Suggestive. That's why I called the police."

Bandoni kept at her. "What were the photographs of?"

"Me."

"Was he violent?"

"Only if you're opposed to sadism."

"What happened after you called the police?"

"An officer agreed to speak with him, based on his persistence and the level of distress he caused me. Two days later, the court issued a restraining order against Vander, barring him from contacting me or approaching within a hundred feet of me or my property. The officer told me Vander had agreed to stop all communication."

"And did he?"

"I've heard nothing from him since. A month ago, I looked him up online. He'd moved to Florida."

"Sadism," Bandoni said. "That sounds extreme."

"*Locker room talk* is how Vander referred to it. He told me I should be flattered, not offended." Stern sank back in her chair. The heat from her earlier outburst had faded; she looked drained.

"Are we done?" she asked.

"Just one final thing." Cohen pulled a second picture from his folder and set it on the table. It was an enlargement of the photo I'd taken of the dead man, shortly before the bomb went off.

Stern leaned forward, then jerked back.

"Sorry to have to show you this, Ms. Stern," Cohen said. "But we're trying to determine his identity. Have you seen him before?"

She shook her head, her hand over her mouth.

"Judging by your reaction, you know him."

She shook her head again. She'd gone a bad color.

"You think he looks bad here?" Bandoni pressed. "You should see him now. Parts everywhere. We're trying to identify him off one of the larger pieces. His thumb."

She sucked in air. "I'm going to be sick."

"We don't mind," Bandoni said. "We get that in here all the time."

Stern gave a low moan. I didn't know Bandoni could move so fast. He whipped out a paper bag from somewhere and shoved it into her hand. She did as she had promised and vomited.

Cohen left the room, came back with a damp paper towel and a glass of water. Stern wiped her mouth, drank the water.

"So you know him?" Bandoni asked.

She shook her head.

"You expect us to believe that? You all pale and throwing up?"

But Stern had regained her composure. "You show me a photo of a dead man and then act surprised when I'm affected?" She pushed back her chair, surged to her feet. Her suit jacket swirled around her in elegant pleats. "I've had enough. You want to ask any more questions, charge me, and then you can talk to my lawyer. And I'd like my car back."

"Your car will take a day or two, I'm afraid," Cohen said. "We'll notify you when it's available."

For a moment, Stern looked so miserable that even I felt bad about it.

"In the meantime," Cohen went on, "we will have an officer escort you home and stay with you while we locate Zach Vander."

Stern's hands flattened across her stomach. She suddenly looked very young. "You think he might have done this?"

"If you can wait here for a few more minutes, I'll arrange for that officer."

❖ ❖ ❖

With the interview over, Mac said good-bye and left quickly. She and her team had something to run with now. I wasn't sure how the Feds and Denver PD were splitting the work, but I figured everyone would be after Zach Vander. They'd put out a BOLO, check whether he was still in Florida, and talk to any family or friends in Denver. I found myself crossing my fingers. If it was Vander who'd set up Stern, the police and the feebs should make short work of finding him. And if he was the killer, then they would find Lucy as well.

I stayed behind in the room while everyone else filed out, gearing myself up to visit Hiram Davenport and mentally running through a list of questions I'd squeeze in before he sent me packing. But when I pulled out my phone, there was a text message from someone named Jeff, advising me that Hiram had suffered a minor medical setback and would see me the next morning at eight.

Relieved and disappointed both, I considered my options, then looked up the number for the Adams County sheriff. When a woman answered, I identified myself and asked to speak to anyone who could answer questions concerning railroad crossing accidents that had occurred in the county twenty-eight years ago.

"You want Rick Wolanski," the receptionist said. "He retired five years ago, but came back last month to start digitizing our old investigation reports."

"Perfect. Can you transfer me?"

"Not until tomorrow. Rick's at the end of a fishing trip in the middle of nowhere in Alaska. He flies home tomorrow morning. I can have him call you as soon as he's back."

"He have a cell?"

She laughed. "Rick's afraid of technology. I think the sheriff only asked him to digitize those files because Rick was always hanging out here anyway, distracting the deputies."

I bit down on the frustration. "Can I drive up there and go through the files myself?"

"I'm sorry, but they aren't here. Rick took them home to do an initial sorting."

"Is there someone at his house who can let me see them?"

"Rick's an old bachelor." She sounded impatient. "I'll have him call you just as soon as he gets in tomorrow."

I thanked her and hung up. For just a moment I debated breaking into Wolanski's house and helping myself to the files. But that wouldn't help us locate Lucy, and would render anything I found inadmissible in court. So with few options and fewer leads, I decided to check on Zolner again. A call to the Royal Tavern confirmed him as a no-show, and he still wasn't answering his phone. But my mind kept going back to the man the neighbor had seen. And Bull's truck. You don't leave a $100,000 vehicle in your driveway unless you've got no choice.

I didn't care about whatever hole Bull might have dug for himself. All I wanted was any information he had about that crossing—information that might explain the killer's interest in it. I decided on a drive-by. Maybe it had all been a miscommunication, and I'd find Bull supervising the installation of shiny new aluminum siding.

Cohen caught me as Clyde and I were coming out of the observation room. Clyde did his best impression of the Leaning Tower of Pisa against Cohen's leg, and Cohen buried his fingers in Clyde's fur. Therapy dog.

"What do you think?" he asked.

"I think that either she knows that guy . . ."

People jostled by us, and we stepped back against the wall.

"Yeah?" Cohen said.

"Or she's pregnant."

Cohen's mouth opened. Closed. I watched while he connected the dots. Another detective came down the hallway. "Meeting in five," he told Cohen.

Cohen nodded that he'd heard. "The suit jacket. It bells out. Isn't that the fashion?"

"Not for decades, I don't think, although I'm the wrong person to ask. But it was more her reaction to the photo. That's Stern's *job*. She sees people in far worse shape than that, and in person. Why would a photo of a dead man make her sick?"

Cohen palmed his forehead. "Okay. That's good. We'll let her recover, then have another go at her. Anything else?"

"I think she's lonely."

"I saw that, too." He tapped his notebook against his thigh. "It was something on her face when she talked about Ben. It was only there for a second. But if I had to give it a name, I'd be tempted to call it love."

CHAPTER 11

I was twelve when my grandmother brought the news about my mother. That she'd been diagnosed with cancer while serving a twenty-year sentence for murdering a drunken lowlife named Wallace Cooper, who'd assaulted her. And that by the time the doctors knew of the cancer, she already had one foot in the grave and was getting ready to step in with the other.

When my grandmother finally found the courage to break the news to me, there was nothing left to do but go to the funeral.

I was angrier than I'd ever been with my grams for telling me too late.

But I was even angrier with my mother. For landing herself in prison. And then for dying.

—Sydney Parnell. Personal journal.

A single light burned at the back of Zolner's house.

At four in the afternoon, a brand-new batch of storm clouds were bunched over the distant mountains, rushing the day toward dusk. The road still gleamed from the recent rain. Headlights swept shadows along the pavement, and the wind shook raindrops from leaves and telephone wires.

I pulled to the curb across the street from Bull's house. The place was even less appealing in the dying light. That morning it had been washed up and resigned. In the cloud-shot evening, it had jumped camp into malevolent. The upstairs windows brooded sightlessly out onto the street, while the red front door gave off a wet sheen, like a bloody mouth.

There wasn't a siding salesman anywhere around.

I raised my binoculars. A trace of light shone around the edges of the drapes covering the front window. I didn't think there'd been a light shining in Zolner's house earlier, but the day had been brighter then. The same red pickup sat in the driveway from that morning, still blocking the garage. Maybe I just hadn't noticed the light.

Or maybe Bull had lied to his neighbor, hidden his Dodge in the garage, and was now inside the house, keeping a low profile. In the neighborhood I grew up in, people got creative at hiding, whether they were avoiding a sheriff's deputy serving child-support papers or a bail bondsman looking to collect a debt.

Or siding salesmen who might be something else.

Clyde, sensing something important was going on, moved his gaze from the house to me and back again. I left my duty belt in the truck but removed the flashlight and clipped it to my belt loop.

"Let's go fishing," I said.

The instant I opened the door, Clyde's hackles went up. He leapt out of the truck with his ears pricked and his nose raised to catch a scent.

Alarmed, I said, "Boy?"

Clyde looked at me, waiting for my command before he took a single step. But he was on high alert. Not the death fear. Something else.

I frowned and my hand went to the butt of my gun. Silently, I signaled Clyde and we moved toward Zolner's house.

As we had that morning, we went up the weed-choked driveway to the front door. I kept my eyes on the house and yard and my hand near my gun. Clyde was all sinewy watchfulness, his head and ears swiveling. But whatever had caught his attention, he didn't deem it an immediate danger.

I knocked on the door. My hammering echoed, then died away, and the only sound was the wind rustling through poplar trees in the yard. I knocked again, then Clyde and I turned away and eased around the house to the gate we'd used that morning. I watched for a signal from Clyde that this was a bad idea. But he didn't escalate from hypervigilant to crazed, so I pushed the gate open and we slipped into the back.

On the concrete patio, light falling through a gap in the curtains at the sliding glass doors etched a faint white line on the ground. Clyde and I made our way past the piles of dog shit to the edge of the concrete slab. I leaned against the house, straining to hear. Far down the street, a dog began a frantic, high-pitched barking, and a man called to a kid named Joey to come inside now, goddammit. The dog yelped, a door slammed, and both the dog and the man fell quiet.

Clyde grew easier. Whatever he'd sensed seemed to have melted away into the gathering gloom. He wouldn't have reacted to another dog with such alarm. Maybe it had been coyotes or a bear—they wandered into the city now and again. I hoped Fido's yelp meant only that his owner had dragged him inside.

Clyde and I glided forward until we stood next to the patio doors. I peered through the opening where the curtain stopped short of the jamb.

I was looking into the kitchen. A battered table and two chairs sat in the center of the room, the table covered with half-crushed beer cans and two heaping ashtrays. Beyond the table I made out an old white stove, splotched with stains, and a section of countertop, also covered with beer cans.

The light came from a swing-arm floor lamp placed next to the table. A cord ran along the floor. By leaning back and angling my head,

I could just make out where the lamp plugged into a white-and-gray timer that sat in the electrical socket.

Deflated, I pulled back. Maybe this was what amounted—in Bull's alcohol-addled brain—to a theft deterrent. And probably it was sufficient. It was hard to imagine anyone being motivated to case this particular joint and break in, unless they were looking for aluminum cans to recycle.

I signaled Clyde, and we returned to the front of the house. I stopped at the single-car garage door.

"Achtung," I whispered. *Watch out.* I grabbed the garage-door handle and yanked up. The door groaned and creaked and came off the ground eight inches before refusing to budge any farther. I eased it back down and walked over to the pile of discarded cinder blocks I'd spotted near the edge of the driveway. Maybe Bull was planning some home improvements. I selected one and returned to the garage. This time when I wrestled the door up, I wedged the block into the gap, then lay down on the cement and shone my flashlight inside.

The light picked out a few rusty-looking garden tools against the back wall, a gas can, and a snowblower. The rest of the space echoed with emptiness. So Bull really had taken off in his black Dodge. And now I understood why he hadn't pulled the monster truck in. It wouldn't fit, even if he folded in the side mirrors and climbed out the back. It must have killed him to leave it behind. And the only reason I could think for him to do that was because he was on the run; the truck was way too flashy to serve as a getaway vehicle.

I stood, pushed the block free, and eased down the door. Clyde looked up at me and gave a small whine that sounded like the canine version of *Let's blow this Popsicle stand.*

"One more thing," I whispered. I walked to the F650, stepped onto the running board, and shone my light through the driver's window, bracing myself for an alarm to sound. But the world remained quiet. The truck was empty, as clean inside as out.

I gave Clyde a signal and we headed back toward my truck. We were halfway across the street when Clyde growled—a low, soft threat that upended a gallon of ice water down my back.

I stopped and pulled my weapon. Clyde's focus was firmly in the direction of my truck, but I couldn't see anything out of the ordinary. I backed up a few yards and directed Clyde across the remainder of the street. As soon as our feet hit the curb, I halted him and studied the truck from the other side.

I saw nothing other than a cracked and broken sidewalk, a neighbor's empty yard, and a mailbox that had been staved in by drive-by vandals.

Clyde's hindquarters relaxed a millimeter or two. He remained tense, but again, I got the sense that whatever had been here only seconds ago was gone. He and I continued our approach to the truck.

I hustled Clyde into the vehicle through the driver's door, threw myself in after him, and yanked the door closed. Once inside the cab, I took a few hard breaths.

"The hell was that, Clyde?" I said.

Clyde kept watch out the window. His hackles were coming down, but he wasn't happy.

I hit the lock and waited for something to show itself. A coyote, a bear, the abominable snowman. But the afternoon remained quiet.

My phone gave a soft buzz. I looked at the screen—a message from my boss.

Don't forget therapy in an hour. Job requirement so they don't fire your ass. Hang in there.

Trust Mauer to get straight to the point.

Furious at the strictures DPC had put on me for just doing my job, I considered blowing off the appointment. I was starting with a new therapist this week, and maybe he or she wouldn't report my absence—the VA wasn't exactly a model of efficiency. On the other hand, maybe I'd get suspended, assuming Hiram Davenport didn't fire me first. How much help would I be to Lucy then?

On it, I texted back.

I returned my attention to Zolner's house. The fading structure, the blasted yard, the $100,000 truck that said everything about Bull's priorities. I pictured the old man sitting at his kitchen table on other nights, hunched over his cigarettes and his beer, his dog whimpering in its sleep by the door. Maybe Bull wished for a wife or a daughter. Perhaps some friends to join for a night of bowling or poker.

Or maybe he didn't have any thoughts at all.

Maybe that was the point of the beer.

CHAPTER 12

*Aren't we all looking to be heroes? Right up until we get
our chance and realize the cost.*

—Sydney Parnell. Personal journal.

My mood was even darker because of my visit to Zolner's lonely house
and my upcoming counseling session. But I was determined to get one
more thing done before going to the VA. I drove fast through the city
and caught the northbound interstate, heading toward the cement factory. My goal wasn't the factory, but rather the overpass at Potters Road.
The bridge was part of the area searched by the police and volunteers,
but I wanted to see it for myself.

As I drove, I eyeballed the dark, distant clouds out my left window,
rolling in over the mountains with the regularity of bowling balls pop-
ping out at the ball return. With luck, we'd beat the next storm.

I exited the highway and turned east. The overpass was just outside
the extensive area cordoned off by the police. Beyond the bridge, a
police cruiser's blue-and-red lights strobed against the late-afternoon
sky. I pulled in behind a battered olive-drab Jeep Wrangler and killed
the engine. Except for the Jeep and the cruiser, the land lay open and
empty; all traffic to the east of the bridge had been rerouted north.

When Clyde and I got out of the truck, the soft cooing of doves floated toward us from across the fields.

A woman sat in the Jeep's passenger seat. She turned her head at the sound of our approach. She was young and thin, pretty in a starving-waif sort of way with chopped black hair, high cheekbones, and deep-set eyes. Her ears and nose were pierced, her pale skin tattooed on both arms with the vines and blooms of roses.

We nodded to each other and Clyde and I kept walking. Even before we got close to the bridge, I made out candles flickering in glass votives and a pile of flowers and toys left in the shelter of the bridge between the road and the concrete abutment. A man was crouched next to the candles, his head bowed. As we drew near, he stood and faced us.

He was in his midthirties, of average height with a lean build. He had a strikingly handsome face, green eyes, and bleached-blond hair pulled into a ponytail. I recognized him from Samantha Davenport's website—Jack Hurley, Samantha's assistant.

In his left hand he held a small hardcover book. He offered his other hand to me.

"Jack Hurley," he said as we shook. "I saw you on television. You work for the railroad."

"Sydney Parnell. This is my partner, Clyde."

"I came to pay my respects," Hurley said. Then he shrugged. "Or maybe . . . I don't know. I guess I came thinking I might find answers. But of course there's nothing here."

I gestured toward the book. "Is that for the shrine?"

He flushed. His smile was nothing like the cocksure grin I'd seen on Samantha's website. This one was tentative and it didn't reach his eyes.

"Yeah." He turned the cover so I could read the title. It was a collection of Shakespeare's sonnets.

"You're fond of Shakespeare?" I asked.

He shook his head. "I run more to Hunter S. Thompson. But Sam loved poetry. I thought—" His voice broke and he turned away.

While he collected himself, I studied the makeshift shrine. People had brought teddy bears and dolls. Bouquets of wildflowers. Sparkling pinwheels. A picture of Lucy photocopied onto a sheet of paper and placed in plastic with the words, "We love you, Lucy! Come home!" There were Mardi Gras beads and paper hearts pinned to cardboard and a DVD of the Disney movie *Mulan*.

Hurley cleared his throat. "I thought she'd like to have them. The poems."

"You worked with her every day," I said. "Did you see any sign this was coming?"

His faint smile turned wary. "Look, I told the police everything. The real police, I mean. I came out here to get some quiet. But since you asked, the answer is no. Other than Sam mentioning a stalker, there wasn't anything unusual. And, no, I never saw a stalker. Sam just told me she sensed something. Like ESP, or something. Now if you'll excuse me, I told Livvy I'd just be a moment."

"The girl in the Jeep, is she your girlfriend? She's what . . . sixteen? Seventeen?"

He narrowed his eyes. "Twenty-two. But she has an old soul. She's my muse. She got me into photography, which got me the job with Sam. It's a good job. *Was* a good job. I don't know what I'm going to do now. I'll keep running the business if Ben wants me to. But . . . I don't know. If it were me, I wouldn't want me around."

"Why not?"

"I'm just a reminder, right? Like the business. A reminder of everything he's lost."

"You and Ben get along?"

"Sure." Then he shook his head. "Mostly. Ben is a serious dude. Like everything is kind of a drag. I think he thought I was too flippant, too . . ."

"Frivolous?"

He laughed, a sharp, brief sound. "Frivolous. Exactly. I made Sam laugh, and sometimes I think Ben resented that."

"Should he have?"

"No. Man, the cops asked me that. There wasn't anything between Sam and me except a good business relationship."

"Well." I narrowed my eyes, studying him. "Maybe Ben will want a little frivolity now."

"You think?" Hurley's smile turned into a grin, transforming his face from sullen to guileless. He seemed ten years younger than what I suspected was his real age. "You know, you'd make a great subject, Sydney. You ever thought of modeling?"

This was the Jack I'd seen on Samantha's website—charming, boyish, flirtatious.

"Not a chance," I told him.

He sighed. "Well, call me if you change your mind. It's a good way to earn a little side money."

We shook hands again, and he walked past me and plodded along the road toward the Jeep. I watched until he'd gotten into his car and was headed toward the highway. Only then did I realize he'd left without placing the book of sonnets with the other offerings.

Clyde and I walked around the abutment so I could study the overpass. The bridge was nothing special. Concrete and iron rebar, a yellow sign indicating the bridge's height as thirteen feet, eight inches. But even this simple construction would have cost in the tens of thousands.

I tapped Clyde's lead and we climbed the hill to the tracks. From up top, the land undulated softly in all directions. The rains had turned everything green and filled the fields with wildflowers. Potters Road vanished over the eastern curve of hills. The silos of the cement factory were mere exclamation points against a distant sky.

From where we stood, the tracks curved to the north and south— Potters Road sat in the middle of a long, sweeping arc that resembled a single parenthesis. This was the curve that Deke had been coming out of when he spotted Samantha on the tracks. Thirty years ago, the curve would have meant that any drivers on Potters Road would lose sight of an oncoming train for a full minute before they reached the crossing.

Almost unbelievable, then, that according to what Mags Ackerman could find, there hadn't been any accidents.

I snapped my fingers. "Tate didn't report them."

Clyde stopped in his examination of rabbit spoor to give me a look.

"It's something he would have worried about," I explained to my partner. "The Feds would have shouldered the cost of an upgrade. But more accidents would mean more oversight and tighter safety rules. And more expense to the railroad."

As Veronica Stern had noted so coldly, a railroad's safety record is paramount.

Unimpressed with my thoughts, Clyde went back to sniffing for rabbits. He wasn't having much luck—I kept him on a short lead this near to the tracks.

But a trickle of excitement seeped through my gloom. If Alfred Tate's railroad really hadn't reported accidents at Potters Lane, maybe Hiram Davenport had learned of it and used this information to blackmail Tate into agreeing to the merger. Destroying the grade crossing and installing the overpass would have been an additional twist of the knife.

The sun slid behind clouds and a few drops of rain struck the ground. I glanced at my watch. We had to leave now to make my appointment.

We hurried back along the road toward the truck as the rain began to fall in earnest. A thick shard of lightning struck the ground nearby, and the world turned momentarily white. I blinked, bedazzled.

Had Samantha talked to the killer as they drove under the bridge? Had she begged for her life and that of her daughter?

What answer had the killer given?

Had he said anything at all?

Chapter 13

"You feel sick about it. Your first kill. Every night for weeks—hell, months—after my first, I had nightmares. I'd be just about to fire, but then the raghead would shoot first. When I woke up, I'd think about how the dreams were just some part of my brain, telling me it could have gone down bad. Telling me I was right to fire first.

Later though, I started thinking it was God telling me I was wrong. 'Cause I never knew if the guy really had a gun or if he was just some dumbass farmer with a hoe. I shot him, and we kept rolling.

And now the nightmares won't stop."

—*Kuwait, Conversation with a Marine.*

"The debris of war," someone said from behind me.

Linoleum squeaked under my boots as I turned. A man stood in the VA's hallway, the overhead fluorescents shining on his bald pate. He nodded toward the photograph I'd been studying. A blasted landscape of rubble-filled streets, downed power lines, and shattered buildings.

"Iraq, 2006," he said.

"Fallujah." I glanced at him. "Were you there?"

"Oh, yeah. But long after the two battles of 2004." He came to stand beside me and we both turned back to the photograph. "You?"

I nodded toward Clyde. "We both were. Operation Phantom Fury."

"You guys saw the heavy stuff."

"Yes."

The man, dressed in jeans and a white oxford shirt, the sleeves rolled to his elbows, offered a hand. "Peter Hayes, army major, 2nd Battalion, 7th Cavalry. The Garryowens."

"Corporal Sydney Parnell. Marine. Mortuary Affairs."

We shook. He introduced himself to Clyde, then turned back to me with a smile. "I believe you are my next patient."

I'd started therapy when I came home from Iraq. My mentor at the time, a man named Nik Lasko, had told me not to talk about the war or what I'd seen and done there. Talking was what made you come apart, what made people afraid of you. But I was desperate. Nightmares, flashbacks, visions of dead people—all of that had led first to alcohol and then to drugs as I tried to numb myself into detachment.

The therapy hadn't worked as well as the whiskey, and six weeks in, I quit. After that, I held myself together with liquor, pills, and a stubborn streak fifty miles wide.

Then after the murder investigation and the shootings last winter, DPC insisted I resume therapy. The bosses got twitchy at the idea that someone protecting property worth billions might be a few cars short of a full train. So, resentfully, I'd volunteered for a VA program studying the effectiveness of combining antianxiety drugs with a form of psychotherapy known as prolonged exposure. To participate, I'd agreed to meet with a therapist twice a week for sixty minutes.

I'd filled out a tower of paperwork—mostly surveys and consent forms—then sat down with a VA employee who administered a CAPS

Interview—the Clinician-Administered PTSD Scale. Big surprise—the test confirmed that I did, indeed, suffer from post-traumatic stress. I was assigned a therapist and began the twice-weekly sessions.

Everything went downhill from there.

Prolonged exposure required that I relive a bad memory over and over with the idea that eventually it would lose its potency. I'd no longer flash to it, dream about it, dwell on it. But in my case, therapy had made everything worse. In the last few weeks, along with increased nightmares and flashbacks, I'd had headaches, muscle tremors, anger-management issues. You couldn't call this progress no matter how loosely you defined it. But here I was, back for more because I'd promised. And while I have many faults, lack of commitment isn't one of them. Plus there was the little matter of my job being on the line—Mauer was watching me like a hawk.

"You don't want to be here," Hayes said as we walked to his office.

Mind reader. "Does anyone?"

"Not at first." He unlocked the door to his office and ushered me in. "I saw the news. You've had quite the day."

Fear for Lucy rose like bile. "You've been following the story?"

"As much as I can. Heartbreaking situation. I half expected you to cancel. I'm glad you didn't. That bomb—"

"I'm fine."

His eyes met mine, and I read something equivalent to all twenty volumes of the *Oxford English Dictionary* in his look. But all he said was, "All right."

Hayes had inherited my previous therapist's office, so I took my usual place in a chair that let me see both the door and the window, while Clyde settled himself on the floor as close to me as possible. I looked around. Hayes had added a few touches of his own—photos, a frayed flag. Most interesting was a wall of papier-mâché masks made by people who clearly had issues. The masks were bloodied, haunted, wrapped in barbed wire, or squeezed by vices.

"Cheery," I said.

"I know, right?" Hayes laughed. "They're all made by vets. Sometimes it's easier to make art than to talk about your feelings. It lets you express the invisible wounds."

Instead of retreating behind his desk, he dragged his chair out and placed it so it faced mine. I leaned back.

"Tell me how therapy has been going," he said.

I gestured toward the clipboard in his hand. "It's all there."

"I'd rather hear it from you."

"Is that therapist-speak for 'I haven't had time to read all this crap?'"

He laughed again. "No." He reached over and dropped the clipboard on his desk. "I've read it all. And I see that your symptoms have worsened. Sometimes things have to get bad before they can get better, but I'd like to try something different."

A bumpy mix of relief and wariness went through me. "Like what?"

"I'm going to be honest. The problem for a lot of vets is that prolonged exposure therapy flat-out doesn't work. The VA adopted it because it's the gold standard for people who've been raped or assaulted. But we're starting to realize that the trauma suffered in war is profoundly different from what a civilian might experience. And sometimes prolonged exposure is exactly the wrong approach to take. It can make bad memories more potent, not less."

As if someone had just unsnapped the handcuffs, I rose half out of my chair. "I'm out."

"Hold on, Corporal." Hayes rested his forearms on his thighs. "We'll pull you out of the study, if you decide that's what you want. But you can't walk away from therapy. We're just going to try a different approach. Not only because PE hasn't been working for you, but because after reading your file, I suspect PTSD isn't the worst thing on your plate. Have you heard of something called moral injury?"

I sank back down. I could almost hear the handcuffs click into place. "So now I'm a sinner?"

Hayes's laugh was easy. "No more than the rest of us. Here's the deal. What we know about post-traumatic stress is that it's an involuntary, biological response to a threat or a perceived threat. Clinically, it's described as fear-circuitry dysregulation. A person sees something that threatens them, experiences extreme fear and helplessness, and undergoes an automatic response to that fear. You with me?"

I folded my arms so that I could see my watch. "I've read the manuals."

"But moral injury is something different. It's a result of what the poet Peter Marin calls the terrible and demanding wisdom of war."

My gaze darted from the door to the window and back again. I'd read Marin's work—his theory that innocence wasn't so much lost in war as transformed into a heightened moral sensibility.

But my guilt went too deep. I leaned over the arm of my chair and kneaded my fingers into Clyde's fur, wanting his warmth. "Okay."

"The symptoms are similar to post-traumatic stress," Hayes went on. "Insomnia, flashbacks, memory issues. A startle reflex. But the root cause is different. And so is the treatment."

I pulled out my cigarettes, remembered where I was, put them back.

Hayes ran a thumb under his eye. A faint scar puckered the skin there.

"Moral injury is less about fear and more about grief and guilt," he said. "Maybe you feel bitter about your time in Iraq, fighting a war that no one at home seems to care about anymore. You might feel remorse for something you did or saw. Could even be simply the fact that you got to come home to the land of plenty while others stayed behind. So whereas PTS is about danger—'I almost lost my life'—moral injury is, well, a lot of times it's about seemingly immoral acts. Especially killing."

Killing. "Uh-huh." I kept my face light. Pleasant to the point of blankness.

Hayes leaned his elbows into his thighs and brought his hands together. "It's a pretty new concept. I'm no ivory-tower theorist, but it makes a lot of sense to me. I served two tours in Iraq, Sydney. I'm a chaplain and I earned a Bronze Star with the grunts over there. I have my own moral injuries."

We stared at each other. Hayes had an agreeable, open face. A ready smile, the easy laugh. He didn't look like a man who wrestled demons, even if he was a chaplain. But now, looking closer, I saw a flickering sadness in his eyes. And the scar under his eye had a twin at his temple.

My last counselor had been earnest and compassionate. But she'd never seen war. Never shot and killed anyone. Never watched a child die or handled a body blown apart by a bomb.

"I read in your file that you killed six men last February," Hayes said. "I looked up the newspaper accounts. Everyone called you a hero. How did that make you feel?"

I looked away and shook my head, unable to speak.

"Uncomfortable, I'm guessing," Hayes went on. "Sydney—can you look at me?"

Reluctantly, I meet his gaze.

"As a chaplain, I was prohibited from engaging in combat. I couldn't even carry a weapon. So killing was out of the question for me. I didn't have to deal with that moral quandary. But I had a lot of reason to think about it. Because everyone around me was fighting and killing. And after each skirmish, each battle, a lot of them came to me, to ask how they were supposed to feel about it."

"What did you tell them?"

"That I believe war and killing are sins. But I also believe that, sometimes, they are necessary. These men and women did what most people can't or won't, and we owe them our gratitude. Maybe our lives. So I listened to them, blessed them, then sent them on their way. But each time, I was left with the miserable feeling that most of what I offered didn't make any difference."

I looked up at the wall of masks. Row after row of mute pain.

"So given that," Hayes said, "will you talk about those six men?"

"I appreciate what you're saying. But—" I shook my head. "I'm not ready."

"Okay. Fair enough. What about today? What happened after the bomb went off? I know you lost two friends to an IED in Iraq."

I brought my palms together. "Don't link today with what happened in Iraq. It's not the same."

"I heard that the detective who was with you is in critical condition."

I threaded my fingers together. "Frank Wilson. He didn't get to shelter in time."

"How do you feel about that?"

"What do you think? I'm angry."

"At what?"

"The situation. The person who set the bomb." I sucked in air—it came as if through a straw. "At Wilson for being with me, even though I know that's not fair."

"Are you mad at yourself?"

"Of course."

"Because . . . ?"

"Because I failed to protect him."

"*Could* you have protected him?"

I looked at my ragged fingernails, the faint sunburn on my arms. "I should have told him to stay back. He *wanted* to stay back. Said the situation didn't feel right to him. Said he was getting too old for this sort of thing. I should have listened."

"He made his own decision."

"I might have encouraged him."

"What about in Iraq?"

"What about *what* in Iraq? I told you. It's not the same."

"Did you also feel guilty about your friends?"

I wanted to crawl under Hayes's desk and curl into a ball so small that no one could find me. "No."

"Because a lot of Marines and soldiers in your situation do. Survivor's guilt."

I glared. "I'm not them."

Hayes and I regarded each other like boxers in their respective corners. Clyde sat up and rested his chin on my thigh.

"What I want to know," I said, "is since you were clever enough to learn about moral injury, are you smart enough to fix it?"

Hayes palmed his bald crown. He picked up his clipboard again, an inch-thick stack of papers weighted with my story. "That, unfortunately, is the bad news. This is all so new that we don't really know yet how to treat it. But I will say that a couple of things look promising. Group therapy. And also doing some kind of service. Volunteering at a shelter, or helping disadvantaged kids. Any number of things."

I thought of the breakfast I took to the homeless every Saturday morning. The hours I volunteered in the women's shelter. The determination with which I cared for my partner and looked after my grandmother. The search I'd started for Malik.

But against the debts I owed, it was like trying to empty the ocean with a teaspoon.

"Atonement," I said, dully. "That's what you mean."

"In a manner of speaking. It's a part of a process that seems to help. And it's a long process, Sydney. There's no overnight cure."

"You're saying I really did do something wrong."

"No, not at all. But it doesn't matter what I think. As a chaplain, I could tell you that you're absolved of all guilt. Or you could go to a priest and confess your supposed sins and be forgiven. But it doesn't matter what others say. It only matters what you believe. The decision has to start inside of you. Your most important step is self-forgiveness."

"You have no idea what I've done."

"I know that nothing in war is clean. I know that we do things in the cauldron of battle that we would never do at home. And I know that most of us are too hard on ourselves." Again, he touched the scar beneath his eye. "Even a marathon requires a first step. Forgiveness could be yours."

I shrugged, as if what he had to say was of no great consequence. But I was remembering what my grams had said to me. That sometimes your best self was your worst self. That sometimes you couldn't separate the two. My lieutenant had told me that Marines were often called upon to do the unconscionable, and that it was all right, because ultimately the ends justified the means.

But damn. The day to day of living within those means . . .

Hayes leaned in, his hands on his knees. "None of your fellow Marines would say you've done anything wrong." He went on. "Neither would your family. But that's part of the problem. Their understanding or forgiveness means nothing to you, because you've convinced yourself that if they knew the real story, if they knew everything you've done, they would agree with your own silent judgment. They'd say you aren't worthy of forgiveness."

I caressed Clyde's ears and said nothing.

"In war," Hayes said, "we do all these things we find terrible and then we come home and people tell us we're heroes. So we wake up in the middle of the night and try to make those two things line up. But we can't. We don't know if we're sinners or heroes. We try to reconcile who we thought we were with the things we did. And when we can't, we think we're unworthy of forgiveness. But forgiving ourselves doesn't mean whitewashing our past. It just means we've decided to allow ourselves to move forward. To live without the guilt and the anger and the nightmares. To reengage with society. To let the past be nothing more than that—the past."

An alarm on Hayes's watch beeped.

"Ignore that," he said.

But I stood, trying to stay solid when I felt as untethered as a balloon. Clyde rose and shook himself.

"No, it's time," I said. "And I need to go anyway."

Hayes looked disappointed, like a man who'd almost managed to land a fish. But he stood and held out his hands, palms up in surrender. "Just think about what I've said. We'll talk more next time. I'm starting group sessions next week. Why don't you come?"

"Maybe." I forced a smile. "And thank you for what you've said. I'll think about it."

"That's a start." He handed me his business card. "And if you want to talk between now and our next meeting, just person-to-person over a beer or something, give me a call. Anytime."

◆ ◆ ◆

Downstairs, in the hospital bathroom, I locked myself and Clyde in the handicap stall. I squeezed my hands together until my knuckles and fingernails turned white and I stared down into the toilet. With a gut-twisting wrench, I leaned over and vomited. I stayed bent over for a while, the stench of my own vomit sharp in my nostrils. Then I wiped my mouth with toilet paper and flushed everything away.

"Let me find Lucy," I said, unsure if I was trying to strike a deal with God or the devil. "Let me find her and then I'll forgive myself."

When I walked out of the stall, the Six stood lined up by the sinks. Six dead men with their pale, tattooed skin, their shaven heads, the knife-edge glint in their watching eyes. They moved aside as I crossed to one of the sinks, then crowded close behind while I washed my hands.

"You deserved to die," I whispered. "All of you."

They watched me, unblinking, in the mirror. Then, one by one, they grinned and nodded, their bloody faces lean and satisfied, their dark, eager looks those of wolves who've run their prey to ground.

I glared at them.

"Fuck guilt," I said. "I'd do it again."

CHAPTER 14

If I stop having nightmares, if I stop living in the past,
how will I speak for those we left behind?

—Sydney Parnell. Personal journal.

Outside the VA building, the evening air was violet and balmy. The streetlamps cast warm puddles of light on the asphalt. There were only a few people around, and all of them were very much alive. I found a bench set in a small grove of trees and dropped onto it, needing a moment to sort through what Hayes had told me and to regain my equilibrium. Clyde pressed close against me and placed his head in my lap, his eyes locked on mine. I ruffled his ears. Dogs didn't believe in human guilt, only in love. Being with him was better than confession and a dozen Hail Marys.

To hell with the wisdom of war. What about the wisdom of dogs?

I reached into the side pocket on my pants and pulled out a wedge of dog sausage. Clyde came to his feet, his rear wiggling with excitement.

"Who's the Marine now?" I cooed in the high-pitched voice he loved. "Who's mama's big boy?"

Now his entire body quivered. I tossed the sausage high into the air. Clyde launched himself skyward, jaws wide. He snapped the sausage out of the air and landed nimbly, ready for more.

I tossed a few more treats for him, then dropped to my knees and gently pulled him with me to the relatively dry ground beneath the trees. I scratched his belly around his K9 vest until we both felt better.

"We've got one more thing we have to do before we go home," I told him.

His ears perked.

"It's a Marine thing."

◆　◆　◆

Ben Davenport's room was in post-surgery ICU on the ninth floor, on the far side of the nurse's station. The rooms on either side were empty, and a cop stood vigil just outside Ben's door so that he could see everyone who came by. I checked in with the unit clerk, then approached the officer and showed my badge. He nodded for me to go ahead, but the clerk called after me.

"Not your dog," she said. "The rooms are off-limits to animals. Risk of infection."

I looked at the cop. "Okay if he stays with you?"

A grin broke across the officer's face. "Of course."

"Clyde," I said, *"bleib."*

Clyde looked betrayed. He was a Marine, too. I promised I'd be quick.

Ben's room was standard ICU. The adjustable bed, the tray table, and the privacy curtain, now drawn back so that the nurse had a clear view of her patient. There was a TV bolted to the wall and a single chair. Because it was the ICU, there was also a vast array of monitors, bags, and tubing, accompanied by the steady, subdued beeps and clicks of the instruments. In the middle of it all, Davenport lay unconscious, his head bandaged, his face sunken and gray. A respirator had been forced through his open mouth, the tubes running along his chest.

Ben bore so little resemblance to the man whose picture I'd studied that morning, to the man he had been just twenty-four hours earlier, that something inside me cracked. How could it be right for him to have survived so much in war, only to come home and lose almost everything? How could one person be asked to carry so much?

I lifted my eyes to the window. Outside, the lights of Denver glowed. The clouds had cleared the mountains and now sat above the city, orange in the city lights. The sun burned in a sullen, western sky. I edged past the bed and leaned my head against the glass. Traffic streamed far below, but the sidewalks were empty of pedestrians. I closed my eyes for a moment, imagining the block where I stood replicated thousands of times across Denver. Thousands—millions—of garages and warehouses and condos; parks and fields and sewers; ditches and culverts and basements.

A hundred million places to hide a child.

A hundred million places to bury her.

A draft blew through the vent, chilling the room, and suddenly Samantha Davenport was there beside me. Her long hair whispered against her back, and the draft fluttered the hem of her dress. She pressed her ghostly fingers to the glass and traced the outline of her husband, his form reflected in the window. I stumbled back until I got caught up against the chair, trapped between pity and fear, wondering if it would always be my lot to carry the dead, certain I didn't have the strength.

How much, I wondered, had Ben told his wife about what had happened in Iraq? Most vets said nothing to their families, for all the reasons the chaplain had offered. But others found someone not only willing to listen, but also able to understand and accept what they heard. Samantha's photographs—the bleak ones—made me think she was strong enough to take whatever Ben had offered. And to give comfort in return.

The fan shut down, and the room went silent save for the machines keeping Ben alive. With a last glance at her husband, Samantha stepped through the window. She shimmered along the glass like sunlight rippling on water, then vanished.

"I'm sorry," I murmured, unsure if I was speaking to her or to Ben or to myself.

Outside Ben's room, a phone rang, and somewhere beyond the nurse's station a gurney rattled. I turned my back to the window and all the impossibilities beyond the glass and looked at Ben Davenport.

He hadn't stirred. I'd heard the newscast on the drive here—the surgery had successfully removed the pressure on his brain. But there had been damage to the brain itself, and the doctors didn't know how much of Ben would remain when he woke up.

My attention was caught by the only nonmedical thing in the room—a framed photograph of Ben and Samantha and their children. Maybe Ben's father had brought it. The five Davenports lay on their backs, the children smiling up at the camera. The boys looked goofy. Lucy—lying between her brothers—beamed. Their parents lay shoulder to shoulder. Samantha's hair spilled over Ben's chest and his hand clasped hers. Their gazes had locked just before the camera went off, their expressions both knowing and jubilant. Whatever complaint Samantha might have expressed about her husband to Stern, there was no hint of it here.

I looked from the photograph on the tray table to the man on the bed. Did Ben know what had happened to his family? He would have been down and presumably unconscious before the boys died, before Samantha and Lucy were taken away. In his artificially induced sleep, did he dream about them? And in his dreams, were they all still alive?

I reached out a hand, ready to turn the picture facedown so that it wouldn't be the first thing Ben saw when he opened his eyes. In case he knew. In case it broke his heart all over again. But then I stopped, my fingertips on the frame, unable to take away this last thing.

"We'll find her," I told him. "She's alive and we'll find her. When you wake up, she'll be here for you."

I left the picture where it was and walked out of the room to where Clyde waited.

CHAPTER 15

Hope is that thin gold line at the horizon on the far side
of a blasted landscape.

—*Sydney Parnell. Personal journal.*

By the time we reached Cohen's house, the day had settled into my
bones like wet sand.

I parked and retrieved my duffel bag while Clyde went about his
business. When he went sniffing for squirrels, I whistled for him to follow, then headed toward the stairs of the carriage house.

The nearby main house had belonged to Cohen's grandmother, and
he had inherited it from her. The place was over ten thousand square
feet, maintained by an invisible army of maids, gardeners, and handy-
men. But Cohen said living there would have made him feel like the last
man on earth, which was why he had decamped to the carriage house.
The only time he went back was when he wanted something from his
grandmother's library. Or to raid the wine cellar.

As soon as Clyde and I reached the bottom step, a motion-detector
light came on. I was so tired that for a moment the staircase looked like
the Swiss Alps. I saw the glittering soil where I'd scraped my boots clean
earlier that day and aimed for that. Once there, I kept going.

At the front door, I fumbled for my key. And noticed another scrape of dirt.

I hesitated.

The alarm was still armed. Clyde's casual demeanor said there was no one around. He sniffed the dirt, then paid it no more attention. But unease pressed a heavy hand against my neck. In the light from the porch, the dirt glittered faintly, just like the soil I'd scraped off my boots. Someone who'd been at the cement factory had also been here.

Cohen, I remembered. He'd come home to change.

Still, just because you were paranoid didn't mean they weren't out to get you. I punched in the code for the alarm, then rearmed it once Clyde and I were inside. I dropped my bag in the living room, dialed Mauer, then started a walk through of the house, pulling blinds and checking to see if someone had stashed a corpse anywhere.

"I'm working my way back from the most recent accident files," Mauer said. "Nothing yet. A couple of the Death and Dismemberment forms are either missing or misfiled, so it's possible we'll never find anything."

I paused in my survey of the master bedroom. "The crossing form for 025615P was missing from the Federal Railroad Administration files."

"Could be a coincidence."

"I don't believe in coincidences. But the good news is, someone put in a placeholder. Our crossing *is* the one at Potters Road, near where Samantha died. It's an overpass now. Margaret Ackerman at the FRA hasn't been able to find a record of any accidents there. But an article written in 1982 says there were several. Locals called it Deadman's Crossing."

"And you think the accidents are why the crossing is significant to the killer?"

"You have any better ideas?"

"I'll keep digging."

After we hung up, I finished my inspection of the house. Nothing more sinister than dirty laundry and a thick layer of dust.

In the kitchen, I stripped off Clyde's gear and gave him fresh food and water. I searched through the refrigerator and found last night's shrimp scampi, one of Cohen's favorite dishes. He made it every couple of weeks. I scooped half onto a plate and popped it in the microwave. Cohen would shoot me for treating his scampi so poorly. The least I could do was warm it up on the stove. But I didn't have the energy. And me being me, I'd probably burn it.

I poured myself a finger of Macallan and left it on the bar that separated the living room from the kitchen. I carried the scampi into the bedroom, eating as I walked. It was soggy. Mea culpa.

In the bedroom, I took a couple of Advils for my knee, yanked off my work boots, then stripped out of my uniform and showered. I smeared some antibiotic ointment on the cut on my forehead, added a bandage and called it good. At last, clean and comfortable in a pair of sweats and a tattered Mortuary Affairs T-shirt, I returned to the kitchen and sat at the bar. I used the remote to click on the TV.

". . . historic rainfall up and down the Front Range," a meteorologist was saying. "Creeks and rivers are swollen, and some dams—"

I clicked it off. Clyde wandered over to check on me.

"We're still good," I told him.

But it was a lie. The investigation was now nudging out of the first day of Lucy's disappearance and into the second, and we had precious little to show for it. Lucy's chances were diminishing with each passing hour, in direct correlation to the dread rising through me like an extra heartbeat.

Clyde kept watching me.

"Okay," I told him. "We're not so good. I made a promise, and what we've got so far is a whole lot of nothing."

His ears came up. "Then get on it," he was saying.

"Right. Let's see what we have. From the railroad perspective."

I opened up my laptop and started typing as a way to organize my thoughts.

First, a hazardous materials train that would never actually exist. The cops and the Feds would run down everyone associated with that train, from the railroad employees to the vendors and their employees through everyone involved from the regulatory agencies. It was a huge goddammit, as my grams would say, and likely to lead nowhere. The killer had to know that by writing down that number in the Davenports' home, he'd guaranteed the train would never exist. So what had he intended?

I paused in my typing. Maybe his only goal had been to create chaos, especially if he was pushing for some ideology—he didn't believe in drilling for oil, say.

But the up-close and personal nature of his crime suggested it was something else.

What, I typed, *is personal about a hazmat train?*

I stared at the blinking cursor. You hated hazmat trains on principle. They were dangerous, they were vulnerable to terrorism. Or, more personally, you'd been hurt by one. I made a note to look into chemical spills near Denver.

Next, we had the crossing number. Maybe there weren't any accidents listed because Alfred Tate's railroad had never reported them. But then why go after the Davenports? Hiram had actually eliminated the possibility of any accidents occurring at that crossing.

I needed to talk to the retired deputy, Rick Wolanski. He would be able to tell me definitively if there had been any accidents there. I typed, *Hazmat train and crossing at Potters Road? Linked? Need accident reports.*

Finally, we had the quotes about betrayed lovers. Back to the personal angle. I typed, *What does a hazmat train have to do with lovers?*

I stood and dug through the kitchen utility drawer until I found a box of thumbtacks, then picked up the whiskey on my way into the living room. On the far end of the vaulted space was an empty wall where normal people with time to think about normal things would have hung art. I stared at that blankness and thought about the hole that was left when a child went missing. About the emptiness created in a space where once a child breathed and laughed in a world that was a daily miracle to them—assuming they'd had a normal childhood.

I thought about what hole Lucy might be in now. In the ground or in a basement or on a mattress somewhere. Then I shook off the fear and opened my duffel. I removed the photos, books, and everything else I'd collected during the day.

Leaving the center of the wall open for the moment, I thumbtacked up the pictures of the Davenport family that I'd printed at my office— the ones of Lucy and the twins at the Edison Cement Works, the three of them standing like small ghosts in the falling snow. I placed a sticky note at the corner of one of the pictures: *Killer first sees Davenports here?*

Next I pinned up the article announcing DPC's takeover of Alfred Tate's T&W short line and added two more notes: *Hiram acquires Edison from Tate in 1982 and donates a portion of the property to MoMA in 2010. Questionable? Hiram turns 025615P into an overpass even though no accidents reported?*

And a third: *Tate stops fighting the merger. Why?*

I moved on to the stills from the train video, the woman's photo from Ben's desk which I'd made a copy of at police headquarters, and a photocopy of the deed transfer of part of the Edison Cement Works factory to MoMA. The fact that the article, the photo, and the MoMA file had all been together in a locked drawer made me hope Ben had found a link between the three. Something that I, too, could ferret out.

I added the photograph of Samantha and her assistant, Hurley. Back to the lover angle. It didn't matter if they'd been having an affair or not. It mattered only what Ben believed.

At the top of my collage, I placed the picture of Lucy on the swing. And in the very middle, I thumbtacked a piece of paper with the alphanumeric 02XX56XX15XP written on it, along with the hazmat train identification number, UNMACWAT21.

Below those two alphanumeric strings I wrote in red, *Find the killer, find Lucy.*

I picked up the Macallan and stepped back from the wall, wondering what, if anything, tied all of these together. My mind created imaginary lines from the land to the woman's photo to the Davenport children and back. Ghostly links traced themselves in my mind, then broke apart each time I looked more closely.

What had Ben found?

Frustrated, I drank down half the scotch and stared at the number. Why had the killer added all the *X*s?

In railroad terminology, an *X* represented one of two things: It was the universal symbol for a crossing. Or it meant a crossbuck sign. The crossbuck was the most basic type of crossing alert. It consisted of two slats of wood or metal crossed at the middle, and was posted at all so-called passive intersections—those without gates, bells, or flashing lights. It had been designed to resemble a skull and crossbones so that when people saw it, they'd think immediately of danger.

"You're playing with us, aren't you?" I said aloud to the killer. "Whoever you are, whyever you're doing this, you want see if we're smart enough to figure it out."

Maybe . . . an idea sparked. Maybe he'd played with the cops somewhere else, too. Killers like this one didn't usually go from zero to ninety. There were signs along the way.

I sat on the floor and opened my laptop again. Clyde wandered over and joined me, his weight a reassuring presence against my legs. I knew Cohen and the FBI would have checked their criminal databases for similar crimes. But I had access to something different.

I logged on to the DPC server and pulled up the folder containing the terrorism briefings and incident reports we received, along with the daily news bulletins. The bulletins included general train news from all across the country, covering all railroad lines, passenger and freight alike. In addition, there was a list, put together by and for railway police, of all crimes committed on or against railroad property.

I started with the newest files and worked backward to 2001, which was as far as I could go without accessing off-site storage. My search on keywords like *homicide, murder, unexplained deaths*, and the letter *X* led me down a macabre trail of trespass and demise. I scrolled through the myriad reports of fouled tracks and stalled cars and derailments. People who'd stumbled onto the tracks and died there. Or been trapped in boxcars or gotten sucked into a train's draft. College kids who goaded each other to jump a train and then lost a limb for their daring. Worst of all were the murders, many unsolved but likely perpetrated by members of the Freight Train Riders of America or one of the other gangs that preyed on their fellow rail riders.

Then a report popped up detailing a homicide on railroad property that had occurred last March—four months ago. As I read, a cold hand seemed to come and rest against my neck, as if the killer had walked into the room.

The incident had occurred in the city of Columbus, Ohio. A forty-year-old man had been found murdered in a boxcar, and the door of the boxcar had been spray-painted with a large black *X*. The bulletin offered little more, so I pulled up digital archives of the local newspaper, the *Columbus Dispatch*. The man had been beaten and tortured over a period of days. After death, his body had been wrapped in heavy plastic and left in the car. He'd been discovered by IPC railway agent Jim Norton.

The ghostly hand tightened around my neck. Hiram Davenport was from Ohio. Could there be a connection? I stood and looked at the clock—it was the middle of the night in Ohio. No help for it. I called the IPC dispatch, identified myself, then asked for Norton's phone number, assuming he still worked for the railroad.

"He's on call tonight," the dispatcher said. "Want me to patch you through?"

There was a God. "Please."

A minute later, a man came on the phone, his voice rough with sleep. "Special Agent Norton."

"Agent Norton, this is Agent Parnell with Denver Pacific Continental. Sorry to wake you. I'm calling about an incident that occurred on IPC property last March. You found the body of a man murdered in a boxcar. The death might be linked to a case I'm working in Denver. I've got the incident report, but I'm hoping to learn any additional details."

"Give me a sec." There came a long enough pause that I thought he'd put down the phone and gone back to sleep. Then he said, "I've pulled up my reports on the computer. Give me a minute to find it."

I waited, the seconds ticking on an imaginary clock.

Then, "Okay, I've got my report up. What do you want to know?"

"Was the man identified?"

"Yup. William King. He was an accountant in a previous life, but he'd been homeless for a couple of years. I'd seen him around, chased him off the property a few times. It was sad, him ending up like that. His mom used to work for your railroad. DPC."

I jumped to my feet, startling Clyde, and went to the counter for pen and paper. "You have a name and phone number for her?"

"It's here somewhere." A pause. "Here it is. Betsy King." He rattled off a phone number, and I wrote it down.

"Was the case solved?"

"Nah," he drawled, then yawned. "Police investigated, but there weren't any witnesses and there was nothing forensically useful on the body or at the crime scene. They finally decided it was gang related. I've been half waiting for something like it to show up again. You said you're in Denver?"

"That's right. Was there anything about the case that wasn't in the papers?"

"Yup." Another yawn. "There was one thing. Cops kept it quiet. I never did understand what it meant."

"What was it?"

"Killer wrote a number on the side of the car, above the body. I'll tell you what it was if you can hold on. I'm scrolling through the report now."

I paced the room with a sudden surge of energy. My mouth tasted of metal and the chill had spread from my neck across my shoulders.

"Here it is," Norton said. "02XX56XX15XP. You got something like that?"

Adrenaline flooded through me like I'd just been hooked up to an IV of the stuff.

"We do," I said. "We've got something exactly like that."

CHAPTER 16

Scientists say that when we recall something from our past,
it isn't as simple as taking out a photograph from an album.
Because it isn't the original memory we pull up. Rather, it's
a slightly different version of that memory—a memory of a
memory. With each retrieval, the memory is altered.
Our past is made up of unwitting deceits.

—*Sydney Parnell. Personal journal.*

Mac McConnell was wide awake when I called. She heard me out, then promised to alert the CARD team in Ohio and put three members of her own team on the next flight out to Columbus. I typed up my conversation with Jim Norton, attached it to the incident reports, and e-mailed everything to her and Cohen. I debated calling Betsy King but decided it would be too cruel to call a woman in the middle of the night about her dead son. It would have to wait until morning.

I continued scrolling through the incident reports but didn't find anything else with a connection to our case or the murder in Ohio. Then, assuming the FRA was wrong and that there had, in fact, been accidents at the crossing on Potters Road, I searched online for newspaper articles from the seventies and early eighties about Deadman's

Crossing. I especially wanted photographs of any victims, hoping to find a match to the woman in the photo in Ben's desk.

I came up empty-handed. Nothing had been digitized from that time. I decided that tomorrow, after my meeting with Hiram, I would head to Thornton. If I hadn't heard from the retired sheriff's deputy, Wolanski, I would check with someone at the *Thornton Chronicle*. Maybe they had an article morgue.

Defeated, I was glad when, twenty minutes later, the floor vibrated as the garage door rattled open below. When Cohen didn't appear after a couple of moments, Clyde and I went outside looking for him. We found him slouched on the top step, his head in his hands.

He looked up as we approached. His clothes and face and manner were as rumpled as a bedsheet, and the frown between his eyes looked carved with a knife. He had that narrow gaze he got whenever he was working his way through a problem. Like he'd opened the door to a room hiding a trap and was wondering how to take the first step.

He mustered up a smile. "Hey."

"Hey." I sat down next to him. The stairs were damp.

Clyde bumped his head against Cohen's back, then stretched out on the decking behind us. I handed Cohen the scotch. He drank it down in a single swig, so I went back inside for the bottle.

"I saw your report just before I left," he said when I returned. "Mac said she'd already spoken to you about it. This could be our first break. Good work."

I told him that Hiram was originally from Ohio. And that the victim's mother had worked for DPC.

Cohen was silent a moment. "You talk to the mother?"

"I'll call her in the morning. We'll find out then if she has any connection to Hiram." I rubbed Clyde's back; he let out a contented sigh. "What's the word on Veronica Stern's stalker?"

Cohen turned the glass in his hands but didn't drink.

"We know Vander is back in town. He's been living in his mother's basement and going back and forth between here and Florida for the last two months. We're looking now to see if he made a side trip to Ohio."

"Let me guess. He didn't come home last night."

"Hasn't come home the last two nights. And his boss at a comic book store in Aurora hasn't seen him for two days. We're working our way through a list of friends that his mother provided. Not that she's exactly falling over herself to cooperate."

"Why do stalkers always live in their mother's basements?"

"Their fathers have had enough of their bullshit." Cohen took a sip of the whiskey, then set the glass aside. "Carol Vander wouldn't let us in, so we got a warrant. Mama was right to try and keep us out. Vander's a railfan, all right. But not the kind that likes to take pictures of shiny new locomotives or shoot video of his kids on the California Zephyr."

"Let me guess. Railroad accidents?"

"His walls are plastered with pictures of smashed trains, smashed cars, smashed bodies. Most of the photos are in color. At least the ones of the bodies."

"Sounds like a great guy."

"No ties so far to the Davenports," Cohen went on. "But we found photos of Stern on Vander's bedside table. I can only imagine what he was thinking when he jerked himself off to sleep every night."

"What kind of photos?"

"The stalking kind. Stern getting in and out of her car. Stern shopping for her groceries. Stern going in and out of her office building—"

"Wait. Vander was near DPC headquarters?"

"Telephoto lens. We're working backward from the angle to figure out where he was when he took the shots. We're also checking the CCTVs at the stores where she shopped."

"No bedroom shots?"

"Lucky for Stern, she keeps her blinds drawn. The guys in the computer lab are chasing him on social media and working to get into his computer."

I stretched out my legs, rubbed my sore knee. "But no photos of the Davenports?"

"Not so far. Could just mean he's got a few brain cells rattling around in that ugly skull. Still . . ." Cohen shrugged out of his suit coat and laid it across his lap. "I'm not totally sold on this guy. Unless we can link him to Ohio, the only criminal charge we have against him is Stern's restraining order. And usually these guys do a lot of small shit before they decide to try the big time."

"Son of Sam didn't have a record before he killed six people," I said. "Neither did the BTK Strangler when he murdered ten."

Cohen gave me a strange look, then drank his Scotch and held out his glass. I poured more.

"The thing is," Cohen said, "if he's the killer, why risk making a false call against Stern? Even with a burner, he can't be sure we won't find him. What does he have to gain by trying to frame her?"

"She scorned him, and payback's a bitch?" But I knew that wasn't right. Our killer was deranged, not stupid. "His way of letting her know he's back in town?"

"Yeah, maybe." Cohen shook the glass as if there were ice cubes in there to rattle. "No fun doing bad things if no one knows you're doing it."

"BTK got caught because he bragged to the press about what he'd done."

"You know, Parnell, you sure keep a lot of garbage in your head."

"Mind like a sewer," I agreed. "You talk to Stern about a possible pregnancy?"

Cohen nodded. "She swears she's not. And she says if it will get us off her back, she's willing to pee on a stick."

I pulled my feet back in, hugged my knees. "You believe her?"

"I don't believe anybody. Present company excluded."

I pulled out my cigarettes. I apologized to Cohen just as I had earlier to Clyde and blew the smoke away from my two partners. The dark pressed in with suffocating closeness.

"You get anything else on that number?" Cohen asked.

"Not really. But I'm looking into the 1982 merger. Tate fought it hard for five years, then suddenly gave in."

"And you have a theory about that."

I pursed my lower lip and exhaled smoke. "If there were accidents at the crossing, Tate wasn't reporting them. Maybe Hiram found out and blackmailed him. Enmity could have been smoldering for years, then erupted when Stern jumped ship. I'll see what I can learn from Hiram in the morning." Assuming he didn't, as Mac put it, fire my ass.

"Some agency would have had to approve the merger, right? Wouldn't there be records?"

"The Interstate Commerce Commission approved the deal. But they don't exist anymore. They were replaced by the Surface Transportation Board in the midnineties, and I doubt if so much as a paper cup survived the transition. It wasn't a happy occasion." I tapped ash on the stair. "Still hate all the garbage in my head?"

Cohen leaned into me until our shoulders touched. "You seem angry."

"I'm always angry."

"There is that. But I mean about this case."

I sucked on the cigarette until it crackled, then held the smoke in my lungs while I thought. Finally, I spewed out smoke. "I *am* angry. Someone used my train, my tracks, to commit murder and to take away a child. That was my territory and my watch. It shouldn't have happened."

"Because your super railroad-cop powers let you be everywhere at once."

I glared at him.

"Sydney." He pressed his head to mine. "People like the man or woman who did this—they're not like us. They're a force of nature. Like . . ." He searched for words. "Like a natural disaster. We can't prevent them or even prepare for them. We can't know who they might go after or who they'll reach. The one thing we can do is not let them inside our heads."

"The other thing we can do is track them down and kill them."

"Always an option."

"She might already be dead, Mike."

If he was surprised by my use of his first name, he didn't show it. He leaned harder against me. "She might."

I smoked in silence for a time, calculating how much moral injury you would have to carry if you failed to find a stolen child. The memory of Malik burned a path down my spine.

Cohen leaned back on his elbows, stared up into the sky. Then suddenly he leaned over and kissed me.

But I pushed him away. "There's got to be something else we can do for Lucy tonight."

"What we can do is relax enough to let our subconscious minds work."

"That's bullshit."

"It's science. Try it."

I held my cigarette far away and kissed him back. "How long do you have?"

"Three hours. Then I'm heading back in."

I put out the cigarette and kissed him again. After a moment, he pulled away, a bemused look on his face.

"How was the shrimp scampi?"

"It was . . . soggy."

"You nuked it."

"I was hungry."

"Okay." He pulled me close. "Just so you know, that's a crime."

"Are you going to arrest me for crustacean abuse?"

"Crustacean? Who says *crustacean*?"

"Mind like a sewer," I told him.

"All I know, Parnell, is that I love you. And don't"—he touched a finger to my lips—"don't say anything back at all."

So I didn't, unsure what words I would offer him anyway.

Sometime later, I came awake with my heart in my throat.

Beside me, Cohen snored lightly. But next to our bed, Clyde was on his feet.

I slid out of bed and into the sweats and T-shirt I'd worn earlier, then grabbed my phone and gun from the nightstand. Clyde and I glided out of the bedroom and into the living area. In the milky light of the moon—filtered through the blinds—the photographs I'd thumbtacked to the wall stared down at us. I stood in the middle of the room, listening intently.

Clyde looked past me and whimpered, and I turned.

The Six stood against the far wall, watching me with eyes as deep and dark as graves. Clyde and I backed away from them until we came up against the windows.

My phone vibrated in my pocket. I pulled it out and glanced at the screen. The hospital.

"No." I started shaking my head. "Please, no."

I turned my back on the Six and—half-angry, half-fearful—I raised the phone to my ear.

"Special Agent Parnell, this is Amy Derose with Denver Health Medical Center. I have a note here to call you. I'm sorry to inform you that Frank Wilson passed away half an hour ago."

I slipped on my jacket, then picked up the bottle of Macallan and carried it outside to the second-floor deck. Clyde followed me, and we sat together beneath the awning, our backs against the wall, safe from the soft drizzle of rain and the faraway flicker of lightning. I swigged the Scotch then sucked the cool night air into lungs that seemed to have forgotten how to breathe.

The air in Cherry Hills was rarified. Rich people's air that smelled of freshly mown lawns and waxed Bentleys and just a whiff of corruption. I lit one of my last five cigarettes, giving the clean air the metaphorical finger, and stared out at the darkness. Then I pulled Malik's photo out of my coat pocket and held it between my fingers.

Photographs, like ghosts, are the persistence of memory. Over time, people fade from our recollection, or change. Their faces become kinder or more cruel, their hair less gray or more so.

But photographs carry the truth, if only one small piece of it.

Maybe the photos Samantha had taken were her way of holding back the inevitable tide of loss that sweeps down on us all. In the same way, I'd clung to the handful of photos I had of Malik, worried he was already fading from my mind. Now I worked to pull up a memory of one of my favorite images of him—a picture I'd taken on his birthday, only a couple of months after his mother was murdered. He looked stunned in the photo, the candles from the cake lighting his bewildered face. I hated the pain there, the loss in his eyes. But what I loved was how he had his arms wrapped around my waist. He'd counted on me to take care of him in a way no one ever had. And I *had* taken care of him, right up until I'd been redeployed and had to leave him behind. Then I'd failed him completely.

Moral injury. It was where I was at. I wondered if there was a limit to how much moral injury one person could suffer before they broke.

I slid the photo back into my pocket.

A breeze lifted and the trees murmured back and forth, their tops laced with stars.

Where were they? Malik and Lucy. Lying awake as I was? I hoped. Hoped with a vast, yawning need that felt like it would eat at me until I was nothing but a casing packed to the brim with rage and grief, ready to explode.

I startled when the door slid open. Cohen, carrying a sleeping bag.

"News?" I asked as he stepped outside.

"Nothing yet."

He settled next to me and spread the sleeping bag over the two of us, then pulled me close. I pressed my face into his shoulder, glad for the weight of his arm against my back.

"Frank Wilson died," I said.

He pulled me closer. His lips brushed my hair. "I'm sorry."

He laced his fingers through mine, and I squeezed back.

Eventually, I slid into sleep and dreamed that Lucy had fallen into a deep crevasse. I knelt at the edge of the abyss, holding tight to her hand, my fingers slick with sweat. But try as I might, I couldn't pull her up. My grip grew weak, and she slipped out of my grasp, crying out as she disappeared into the darkness.

Standing next to me, Hiram Davenport shook his head.

"You can't hack it," he said. "You can't do the job. You're fired."

I jerked awake, my face shined with sweat.

Five months ago, before I'd killed the Six, I'd had a choice to make between playing it safe and risking everything. I'd decided then that my lieutenant was right—sometimes the ends justified the means. Sometimes you had to let the monster out and damn the consequences.

If Hiram fired me, I'd keep working to solve this case and find Lucy. Outside the law, if need be. This was no time to worry about right and wrong, to worry about moral injury or whether working on this case would make my PTS worse.

It was time to monster up.

DAY TWO

DAY TWO.

CHAPTER 17

The hardest thing about having something to lose is that—inevitably—you do.

—Sydney Parnell. Personal journal.

When I awoke again, Clyde and I were alone on the deck.

An early morning rain had washed through and cleared out, leaving the world hazy and languid. To the east, the sun smeared a pearl line along the horizon. Birdsong and the sweet scent of damp grass filled the air.

I checked my watch. It was 5:40 a.m. Lucy had been missing for more than twenty-four hours. I dialed the number for Betsy King, the mother of the dead man in Ohio. An electronic voice message invited me to leave my name and to have a blessed day. I identified myself, told her it was urgent, and left my number.

In the kitchen, I fed Clyde and poured a cup of the coffee Cohen had made before he left. I leaned against the counter and flipped on the TV to see what the news stations were saying about Lucy and the Davenport case.

On Channel Nine, a reporter interviewed Lancing Tate. Tate was in his early fifties, handsome in a way that suggested health spas and golfing vacations, and was perfectly at ease in front of the camera. He wore his dark hair severely parted on one side, a style that—with the three-piece suit and bow tie—made him look like a railroader from the Vanderbilt days. According to the ticker running at the bottom, the station was running a playback of a studio interview done the day before.

"It's a terrible, terrible tragedy," Tate was saying. "Hard to understand this level of vindictiveness."

I set down my mug. Vindictiveness?

The reporter jumped on it. "That's an interesting choice of words, Mr. Tate. Do you think the murders and Lucy's kidnapping is about revenge against the Davenports?"

Tate fidgeted with his bow tie. Was he uneasy? Or did he just want people to think he was?

He forced his hand down, pressed his palm against his thigh. "Of course we have no idea what is in the mind of the person or persons who did this. I just know that in a business as competitive as the railroad industry, it's inevitable that you step on a few toes. Hiram Davenport is a hard-driving businessman. I imagine he's stepped on more toes than most. Some have called his business dealings . . . questionable."

"You're in direct competition with Hiram Davenport for the bullet train, is that right?"

Tate's hand strayed back to his tie, tugged on it. "That's true. Railroaders are notoriously competitive with each other."

"I understand he proposes running the train through land that was once owned by your company, Tate Enterprises."

"Many years ago, Hiram Davenport persuaded my father to sell him the short line that ran through that property, yes, along with the surrounding land."

"Persuaded?"

"Convinced him." Tate shifted in his chair. "That was a long time ago."

"Did Hiram Davenport step on your father's toes, Mr. Tate?"

I approached the television, inwardly applauding the reporter.

Tate's neck flushed red above the collar of his button-down shirt. "That merger is water under the bridge, Julie. These days, Tate Enterprises shares track and resources with Davenport's company. We are competitors, yes. But we are also allies. And we all want what's best for Denver. At the moment, that means one thing—getting Lucy Davenport home safe and sound."

The screen cut back to the morning show and the anchor moved on to other news.

I poured more coffee. I doubted Lancing Tate had created a trap for himself then stepped into it. I suspected he was too shrewd for that. He was opening up the possibility that Hiram's business practices were unethical, and that the murders and Lucy's abduction were in response to that. True or not, it was another shot fired in the ongoing battle between the titans.

After a quick shower, I forced down some toast while I checked in with dispatch. Outside of the Davenport case, there was nothing unusual going on at DPC. No jumpers. No train IDs painted on walls. The hazardous materials train had been indefinitely delayed. I called Fisher, who told me that even this early in the day, headquarters was swarming with every letter of the alphabet—JTTF, TSA, DHS, DPD, and probably anything else I could think of. He said he'd hold down the fort and be available for whatever I needed.

I tried Bull Zolner again—no answer—and my call to Margaret Ackerman confirmed only that she was still looking for any accidents related to our crossing.

I strapped Clyde's vest on him, poured coffee into a travel mug, and made sure the alarm was set when I went out the front door. Tom O'Hara from the *Denver Post* called as Clyde and I were heading down the stairs.

"You have made me cross-eyed," Tom said when I answered.

"You want violins?"

"Try a cello. You ready for a rundown of what I've learned?"

I threw my duffel in the back seat and gave Clyde permission to roam while I talked to Tom. "Give it to me."

"I went to the public library's western history department yesterday," O'Hara said. "Then last night I took a look in the *Denver Post's* archives."

Clyde disappeared around the corner of the house. I headed after him to see what had caught his attention.

"Go ahead," I said to Tom.

"The land now owned by Hiram Davenport and MoMA was originally Arapahoe territory. In 1867, a man named Ennis Parker spotted a bit of gold near the riverbed and staked a claim."

Clyde was sniffing intently at something he'd found in a copse of trees on Cohen's property. I walked toward him through the damp grass.

Tom went on. "According to what I can find, he never turned over so much as a single spade of dirt. He panned for gold on the river, then died in a gunfight in a Denver saloon."

Whatever Clyde had found, he didn't like. His hackles were up. I gestured him away and leaned over to see what he'd discovered. In the muddy ground beneath the pines was a single paw print. Canine. But huge. It was the biggest paw print I'd ever seen.

Tom's voice boomed in my ear. "Sydney? You still there?"

"Yeah. A gunfight."

I snapped a picture of the print, then glanced around. The homes of Cohen's neighbors were hidden behind strands of trees—the sound of people leaving for work echoed faintly. But nearer the Walker estate, nothing stirred. Even the greenway was empty of early-morning joggers. I thought of Clyde's unease at Zolner's house. And of the chain in Zolner's backyard.

"With six shooters," O'Hara was saying. "Those were some crazy times."

"You're making this up."

"You wound my journalistic soul."

I turned and looked back at the carriage house. Someone standing in the trees would have a view of the kitchen and bedroom windows. But Cohen kept the blinds drawn at night. It was a terrible surveillance spot.

The print simply belonged to someone's very large pet. It was that and nothing more.

I gestured to Clyde and we walked back to the truck.

"After Parker's death," Tom was saying, "a farmer named Wallace Walton claimed the land under the Homestead Act. He farmed it for a few years before he, too, met a bad end—got caught out in a blizzard and froze to death. The pioneering life, eh? His family pulled up stakes and returned east, and the land reverted back to the federal government. The government sold it to the T&W railroad a few years later."

I let Clyde in on the driver's side and followed him into the cab. "Alfred Tate's railroad."

"Well, it wasn't Alfred's then. It was his great-great-grandfather's, who leased the land to the Edison brothers so that they could take advantage of the local clay and limestone and try the cement business. But after a run of a few years, they went under, and the lease was never renewed—the land was too far out for anything but farming. There's nothing else in the news about it until the land transferred to Hiram Davenport with his acquisition of T&W. Back then, that acreage wouldn't have been worth a lot. It's a different story, now."

"What about any fraud regarding the land's value?"

"I can't find any evidence. The value claimed by DPC is inflated, but it's not beyond bounds. Property values are going up in Thornton, just like everywhere else in metro Denver."

"What else you got?"

"What makes you think I got anything?"

"My Marine superpowers. That, and the note of excitement in your voice."

"Which is why journalists make lousy poker players. I checked with a contact at Tate Enterprises. It was Alfred Tate who hired Clinefeld Engineering to do a site investigation at the cement factory. Strictly illegal since he doesn't own the land."

"Alfred Tate suffered a stroke six months ago. He's incapacitated."

"Or maybe not. He made the request only a few weeks ago. Or someone in his office did, anyway."

"You have any idea why?"

"Not yet. Maybe it's all just post-stroke disorientation. DPC had a survey conducted last April by a company named Geotech Engineering. They didn't find anything out of the ordinary, and it's their report that DPC used to state the value for the land."

"Did Clinefeld actually conduct the site investigation?"

"I'd love to know. I called the office a bunch of times yesterday, but all I get is a request to leave a message. So far, no one has called me back. But the day is young." A shrill of phones went off in the background. "Ah, crap. I gotta go."

"Wait—"

"Buy me coffee next time."

He hung up. I called Cohen and left a voice mail. It was a long shot, but worth pursuing. "If you don't have an ID on the dead man yet, try Clinefeld Engineering. Alfred Tate asked for a land survey a few weeks ago—the request is in that folder from Ben's desk. Maybe they only now got it scheduled, and the dead man is one of their engineers."

Hiram Davenport had homes in multiple locales, as one would expect of someone with his wealth. Island homes, mountain homes, a villa in Italy. But in his hometown, he'd opted to keep it simple—he lived in one of his own developments. Davenport Towers was a cluster of high-rises that had sprouted like weeds in a former industrial area near the railroad tracks close to downtown Denver. Before Transco United took over, the place had been a mix of small and medium-size businesses, low-income housing, and a homeless camp near the river. Hiram's company had no doubt promised to clean up an area gutted by the 2008 recession and, in exchange, been able to snap up the land for a song. He pushed the rezoning through and got the city to enforce an ordinance that said neither his trains nor anyone else's could sound their horns in that area between the hours of ten p.m. and eight a.m.

Once he had broken ground, the high-rises popped up like Legos in place of lost dreams and hardscrabble lives. The bottom floors were filled with coffee shops and boutiques and the remaining floors were made up of million-dollar apartments, the parking lots agleam with shiny new BMWs and Range Rovers. Never mind the water shortages or demolished homes or the displaced homeless. Never mind that per capita, Denver already had enough billionaires to make it hit the "most greedy" lists of cities in the United States without luring in more. Hiram had bet that people would jump at the convenience of quick downtown and highway access and the appeal of the brand spanking new, even with the gritty aesthetics of the railroad tracks. And he'd been right. People snapped up the leases like they were freebies on Black Friday.

"Takes money to make money," as my grams always said. Once Hiram married into it, he'd done well. I'm sure the views were spectacular.

Now as I exited the interstate, the high-rises, each one a glass-and-stone tower rising twenty stories or more, stood rosy in the morning light. Their windows were a gleaming reflection that caught the sunlight and tossed it back into the air in a shimmering halo.

How, I wondered, had Ben Davenport felt about his father's conspicuous wealth after the poverty of Iraq? His father's America was a two-edged sword that offered guilt as an ugly counterpoint to the good life. But maybe people like Hiram didn't worry much about moral injury.

I splashed through a gutter flowing with rainwater and pulled into a lot lined with media vans. A lone cop kept vigil, his job, presumably, to keep the journalistic mob from Hiram's door. Inside the building, I knew, would be other cops—detectives in plainclothes watching for anyone who might want to murder the family patriarch in order to finish what they'd started.

I found a twenty-minute parking space reserved for the coffee shop on the ground floor. As Clyde and I got out, I saw a man in a gray suit emerge from the towers and head toward a black BMW idling nearby.

Lancing Tate. No doubt come to pay his respects to Hiram only a day after suggesting it was Hiram's fault that members of his family had been murdered.

I signaled Clyde and we made a beeline across the parking lot toward Tate, cutting him off twenty feet from his vehicle.

"Mr. Tate," I said. "I need a word with you."

He didn't look at me. "If you want an interview, call my office."

He tried to move past, but I stepped with him.

"Sir." I flashed my badge. "We need to talk."

Behind me, a car door opened. Tate's driver. Who probably doubled as his bodyguard.

Tate took in the badge and then my uniform, and finally he looked at my face. His eyes flicked to Clyde. "I've nothing to say to you. Get out of my way."

A man who'd clearly created himself at a gym loomed into my field of view. Clyde lowered his head, ready to leap if I gave the word.

"Back off," the bodyguard said to me. Now the uniformed cop who'd been holding off the media was heading in our direction.

I ignored the muscle and said to Tate, "It's about that old merger between T&W and Davenport's railroad. I'd rather talk to you than the media."

"That wasn't a merger. That was a scalping."

The uniformed cop arrived. "You guys need help?"

The bodyguard and I both said no, and the cop retreated.

"I know there was something off about that merger," I said to Tate. "That's exactly why I want to know about it."

"You *work* for DPC."

"My concern goes beyond that."

His gaze dropped again to Clyde and he frowned.

The bodyguard puffed out his chest as if he thought that would scare me off. "Sir?"

"Five minutes," I said.

The look Tate gave me could have taken flesh. But he nodded. "Make it two. We can talk by your truck. If you lock up your dog."

"I was bitten by a stray dog when I was a kid," Tate explained after I'd settled Clyde in the passenger seat of my truck. "I had to go to the hospital for stitches and a rabies shot. We always had dogs when I was growing up. But now I try to avoid them."

"Understandable."

I leaned against the sun-warmed truck. Not even eight in the morning, and the day was already hot. Leaves hung listlessly and steam rose from nearby drainage vents. Tate stood on the sidewalk, in the shade cast by Hiram's high-rise. If he was roasting in the three-piece suit, he didn't show it.

"I know Hiram is a formidable rival," I said. "Losing T&W must have been hard on your father. I just wondered if he ever talks about it."

"You and that TV reporter," he said. "If you're looking for a way to link that old merger with the fight for the bullet train, you're barking up the wrong tree."

"How did your father feel about that takeover?"

Tate folded his arms. "It broke his heart, at least for a time. I was away at school when it happened, but my mother told me how much it hurt him." He shrugged. "But he's a businessman. And this is the business we're in. The history of railroads is all about mergers. Has been from the very beginning."

"Did you know that just a few weeks ago, your father asked Clinefeld Engineering to do a site investigation of the land that was part of that merger?"

"That's impossible. My father can barely remember his own name. Where did you get that idea?"

"Could someone else in your company have requested it?"

"Why would they? We've had nothing to do with that land for almost thirty years." He dropped his arms and drummed the fingers of his left hand against his thigh. "What are you getting at?"

"Could you confirm with your people, Mr. Tate, and let me know?"

"If you think it's important, I can check with our land office." He shrugged. "But if my father actually managed to request a survey, or got someone to do it for him, it was probably because he thought it was 1982 again."

"Thank you." I took out a business card and wrote *02XX56XX15XP* on the back, then showed it to Tate. "Does this number mean anything to you?"

"The police showed it to me yesterday. Sorry, it means absolutely nothing. What is this about?"

"What if you take out the *X*s?"

He looked at the number again, then shook his head. "No."

"The locals called it Deadman's Crossing."

His face cleared. "Wait. This is the crossing at Potters Road, isn't it? My dad mentioned that name years ago—Deadman's. It's the crossing that Hiram made such a big deal about upgrading after the merger." His wide eyes met mine. "Samantha Davenport was killed near that crossing. You think these deaths have something to do with that crossing."

"We're looking at everything."

"But how could the Davenport murders and Lucy's kidnapping have anything to do with that crossing?"

"Let's stick with the past. If mergers and takeovers are a regular part of business, why did the 1982 takeover upset your father so much?"

Tate gave a disgusted shake of his head. "You work for Hiram Davenport. What do you think?"

"There are a lot of layers between his office and mine. I'm afraid I don't understand."

"Hiram Davenport is the most rapacious man I have ever known. He went after my father's railroad using every legal tactic known. Which, as I've said, is business. I can at least understand that. But I suspect he used a few illegal tactics as well."

"Such as?"

Tate looked across the parking lot. I followed his gaze toward the media vans parked on the street, then looked back at him. I noticed a small cut near his ear where he must have nicked himself during his morning shave. Odd, for a man who seemed so meticulous. When he brought his eyes back, his expression had turned hard. He shoved his hands in his pockets and spread his feet, a gesture that looked like he'd watched too many *Great Gatsby* movies.

"All I know," he said, "is what my father told me when I came home from school that year. This was months after the fact. Dad called Hiram a lot of names. *Cheat* and *scoundrel* were some of the nicer ones. Then yesterday, after the detectives came to speak with me, I went to see my father. I wanted to try and explain to him what had happened to Hiram, to ask him if he had any ideas about it. Dad still lives in the house I grew up in. But it's more like a hospital now than a home. He's been bedridden since the stroke."

I nodded in sympathy.

"As soon as I mentioned Hiram's name," Tate said, "Dad started talking about the merger."

"What did he say?"

"Just that it was wrong. That what happened was all wrong. But I don't think he was talking only about the merger."

"What do you think he meant?"

He shook his head. "I don't know. He got agitated, and I changed the subject."

"Would your mother have a better idea what he might mean? Surely they spoke about it."

"My mother passed away years ago."

Again, I nodded my sympathy. "Have you ever heard of a man named William King? He lived in Columbus, Ohio."

Tate scratched his chin, thinking. "Sorry. No."

"Or maybe his mother, Betsy. She worked for DPC."

"I'm afraid not. Is this important?"

I decided to walk on the wild side. "The police are suggesting that if Hiram is distracted by a family tragedy, he might let go of his dream of a bullet train. Leaving you as the only one with the resources and infrastructure to pursue it."

Tate flushed. "You're suggesting that I had something to do with what happened to the Davenports? That's outrageous."

"Did you?"

Tate's spine went rigid. "Aside from how despicable that very suggestion is, if you knew anything about Hiram Davenport, you'd know that kind of strategy would never work."

"Why is that?"

"For Hiram, relationships are a game. He likes to figure out your vulnerabilities and your ambitions and then use them against you. I don't know if he's capable of caring about other human beings, including his own family. The only thing that matters to him is his empire. And the centerpiece of that empire is his railroad. He'd never let anything distract him from that."

"Not even his granddaughter?"

He gave me a contemptible look. "Depends on her value on the open market. I heard about the reward. Ten million is nothing to him. It just makes him look good." He freed his hands and glanced at his watch. "I have to go."

"One more question, Mr. Tate." I thought of MoMA and the fact that both Samantha and Veronica Stern were part of the art scene. And that Stern had abandoned Lancing's company for Hiram's. "Do you like art?"

"I don't . . . I don't understand."

"You know, sculpture, paintings. Photography."

"Sure, I guess."

"Would you say you're a patron of the arts?"

"No. What are you getting at, Agent Parnell?"

"Never mind. Thank you for your time, Mr. Tate. Here's my card. You'll let me know what you learn about the site investigation?"

"If it will help find Lucy. But I want you to leave my father out of this. His life has been nothing but struggle. Now that he's dying I'd like him to have some peace."

CHAPTER 18

*When I was very young, my mother took me to a fish
farm. She thought it would please me to see the artificial ponds
with their tiny fry. You could buy food from a machine for a
quarter, and when you tossed the pellets in, the water boiled
with gaping mouths as the fish fought for the food. That was
what stayed with me. The water roiling with openmouthed
fish. And the fighting.*

—Sydney Parnell. Personal journal.

After Tate left, Clyde and I made our way through the ground-floor
maze of shops and up to the second floor, where the residential area
began. The elevators opened onto a lushly carpeted lobby that swallowed all sound. Marble columns, gilt-framed mirrors, individually
lighted works of abstract art, and immense potted palms rounded out
a décor that suggested a five-star hotel lobby rather than a Denver high-
rise. Unlike the ground floor, up here there were no patrol cops or
members of the press. Too gauche for the clientele, I imagined. There
was a single security guard and one detective. I picked out the detective
by his cheap suit.

Clyde and I crossed to the guard's desk and I showed my badge. "I'm Special Agent Parnell with Denver Pacific Continental. Mr. Davenport is expecting me."

The guard studied my badge, phoned in to verify it, then called up to Hiram's penthouse and got the go-ahead to buzz me up. He escorted us to the elevator and pressed the call button. When the doors opened, he waved us in, then reached past me and inserted a passkey.

"You're good to go," he said.

Twenty-two floors up, the elevator doors opened onto an atrium filled with light from two banks of windows. The polished wood floors glowed serenely in the morning sun and the air smelled of flowers from an immense vase set on a glass table in the middle of the space.

All around the vase and piled on the floor were stuffed animals, cards, and more flowers. An outpouring of sympathy for Hiram.

A door straight ahead opened and a middle-aged man with a crew cut, arms big as tree trunks, and eyes like chipped glass emerged to check my credentials. He studied my badge, eyeballed Clyde, and asked if I had a gun.

I showed him.

"Empty it, please."

These guys were serious. I shrugged and popped out the magazine then cleared the chamber. Pick your battles.

"What's it like being the executive protection for a man like Davenport?" I asked by way of making conversation.

The muscle didn't respond. He opened the door he'd just come through and gestured me to follow. "This way, Agent Parnell."

He led me past spacious living areas and down a hallway filled with pictures of Hiram posing with a variety of dignitaries. Presidents and congressmen mainly, although there was the occasional Hollywood celebrity. I followed the muscle to a closed door near the end of the hall, where he stopped and knocked lightly. A voice from within told us to enter.

The first thing I saw as Clyde and I stepped through the doorway were the wraparound windows on three sides. I'd been right. The views were spectacular.

Hiram Davenport stood at the wall of windows that looked east, over the railroad tracks and into the heart of downtown Denver. Dressed casually in khaki pants and a polo shirt, he stood with his hands in his pockets, shoulders back, staring out the windows like an emperor surveying his realm. Which was appropriate enough, I supposed.

Except that the image was marred by the long green hose that ran from the plastic tubing hooked over his ears to an oxygen concentrator humming quietly next to the sofa. Two nubs were fitted into his nostrils. This was new. And the reason for last night's cancelled meeting, I assumed.

As Clyde and I crossed the floor to join him, I took in the rest of the room—the white-and-tan furniture, the tasteful objets d'art. Splashes of color in tribal-print rugs and a single piece of art over the white leather sofa—a painting of a man bending over to look at another man swimming in a pool. Green mountains rose in the background. I was sure it was original and expensive.

I couldn't help it—my first thought was that this wasn't a place where you brought the grandkids to play. What was it Samantha had said to Veronica Stern? That Hiram was big on gifts, less so on family events.

Hiram turned at my approach. He removed the oxygen leaders, turned off the machine, and beckoned for me to join him at the window. Clyde and I went to him and I ordered my partner to sit. Hiram gave Clyde a cold look but after a blink decided to accept my partner's presence. He turned to me.

I'd been bracing myself for the man I'd seen at the police station the day before—a grieving father and grandfather. A man brought to his knees by the level of tragedy that had struck his family. But Hiram was as calm as if the worst thing he'd heard that day was that his favorite dish was missing from the menu. I looked for signs that he was on antianxiety drugs or self-medicating with alcohol. But his pale blue eyes were sharp when they met mine.

Only the oxygen gave away his struggle.

We shook hands, Hiram's grip firm, his attention wholly on me. Of average height, Hiram wasn't an imposing man. But he had presence.

I gestured toward the oxygen machine. "How are you, sir? You seem quite—" I stopped myself.

"Composed?" His smile was without humor. "Years of training. What did you find in my son's office?"

I lifted my chin and braced myself. "Not much."

"Relax, Agent Parnell. I'm not going to fire you. I did consider it. But I believe you broke into Ben's office in order to help find my granddaughter. It would be harsh of me to punish you when your intent was honorable."

I let go my breath. "Why did you forbid the police access?"

"Let me guess what you found. Locked in his desk or maybe in a cabinet, was a bottle of scotch. Or cheap whiskey. Could have been either with Ben. His tastes aren't always the most discerning."

I said nothing.

"And a gun. And . . ." He shifted his gaze to some middle distance. "His medals. Because he couldn't decide if he was proud of them or ashamed." His gaze came back to me. "Is that about right? Is that what you found?"

"The police have their warrant now, sir. You can ask them."

"That is answer enough. I should have asked you to remove them. That's precisely what I didn't want the world knowing—that Ben could be weak. That he had considered taking his own life. Have you felt that way? Been tempted to end your life because of what you suffered in the war?"

I bit down on the response I wanted to offer. Something along the lines of, *None of your damn business.* Or maybe, *You have no fucking idea what war is like.*

I said, "I have a few questions for you."

"Of course. We'll get to that. You visited my son last night."

"Yes."

"When I heard you went to the hospital, I asked myself why. Was it because you're working this case and wanted to see one of the victims for yourself? Or was it because you're a former Marine and wanted to pay your respects? You served two tours in Iraq, I believe. Mortuary Affairs."

"How—?"

"I make it my business to learn at least a little about my employees. The important ones. And since you protect my property, that includes you. So. Mortuary Affairs. That couldn't have been pleasant. But look at you. None of this post-traumatic stress bullshit for you. You did your job and now you've returned to society, a healthy, contributing member."

Stiffly, I said, "Ben was investigating your 1982 takeover of the T&W short line." Maybe not too much of a stretch. "What can you tell me about it?"

"What?" Hiram barked a laugh. "I thought you were here to ask about my family. My granddaughter."

"Bear with me, sir. I'm trying to understand Ben's interest, and the details about that merger. Alfred Tate fought you for years. It looked like he would win. The ICC was poised to disapprove the merger. Then suddenly he capitulated."

"And you think I know why."

"Do you?"

A darkness stirred in his pale eyes, like ink leaching into paper. "You believe this might have something to do with what happened to my family?"

"It's possible, sir." I reached into my jacket pocket for the copy of the article. "This was locked in Ben's desk."

Hiram took the article, skimmed through it, then handed it back to me. His gaze went far away, presumably traveling back twenty-eight years, all the way to when he'd announced to the world that he would do his best to never let another person die on the T&W train tracks. The look in his eyes carried a nostalgic mix of satisfaction and melancholia.

Then a sudden fury edged out the other emotions, and his return to the present came with the suddenness of a steel-jaw trap snapping closed.

Interesting. Was the anger defensive? Had Lancing been right when he claimed Hiram used illegal tactics to persuade Tate?

Staring out the window, Hiram said, "I cannot pretend to understand why Tate suddenly chose to see things my way. Or to know what he was thinking at the time." The anger sparked off him like a blade against a whetstone. "Maybe he realized it was for the best."

"Why was that?"

"If I hadn't taken T&W off his hands, his entire company would have gone under. He was poised on the brink. He turned crybaby in public—poor SFCO, beaten up by the big bad bully next door. But secretly he was glad. I saved him from ruin. He was operating so far in the hole that I was his only glimpse of daylight."

"So there wasn't anything . . . questionable in his change of heart?"

"Are you asking if I put some sort of illegal pressure on him?"

"It's been suggested."

His sigh was exaggerated. "People assume the worst. But whatever pressure Tate might have felt to let go of the T&W, it came from him. Not me."

"You knew Tate well?" I asked.

He snorted. "Well enough to know he was a coward. If you offered him the brass ring, he'd say he needed to go home and think about it."

His gaze came back to me. "Tell me what you're thinking. If you suspect the Tates in what has happened to my family . . . surely that's ludicrous. What possible reason could they have to hurt me like this?"

"According to the article, after several fatal accidents at a crossing on Potters Road—a crossing owned by T&W—you promised you would upgrade the crossings if you won the merger."

"I remember."

"And you said it was because Tate's railroad put profits above safety."

"I might have said something like that. We were at war. Do you suspect him of murder because of that?"

"Was it true?"

"Knowing Tate, probably. He was as much a skinflint as a coward. Certainly, I had my suspicions. But I also admit to pandering to public fears. Teenagers had died there. So I vowed no one else would die at that crossing. And I decided to go one better than simply installing gates, which seem to be more of a temptation than a barrier. I wanted that crossing obliterated."

"But that wasn't your call to make. It was the state's."

"Your naïveté is showing, Agent Parnell." He crossed to a bar cart near the sofa and poured several inches of amber liquid from a decanter into a tumbler. "Care for a bourbon?"

Eight in the morning was too early for the hard stuff, even for me. I gave the obvious excuse. "I'm on duty."

"Of course." He came back to the window, took a sip of his drink, and held it in his mouth a moment before swallowing. "While upgrading that crossing wasn't something I could do on my own, that didn't mean I was without influence."

"Politics."

"It's how the world works."

"According to the FRA, there weren't any accidents at that crossing."

Hiram raised his eyebrows. "Now isn't that interesting. There most certainly were accidents there. I guess Alfred Tate is more of a skank than I realized."

"And you didn't know back then that the accidents weren't being reported?"

Amusement gleamed in his arctic eyes. "I did not."

I put the article back in my pocket and took out the photo. "I also found this locked in Ben's desk. With the article."

Hiram took the picture. He stared at it for a moment, unmoving, then set his drink down on a nearby table and stepped close to the wall of windows to tilt the photograph in the light.

"Do you know who she is?" I asked.

It was another minute before he turned around, and when he did, his expression was soft.

"Kids racing the train," he said. "I'm afraid I don't remember the details. It *has* been twenty-eight years. But I remember this woman. She's quite lovely, isn't she?"

I felt a flash of relief mixed with triumph. "So you recognize her?"

"I believe she might have been the last person to die at that crossing before I, as you so crudely put it, played politics and prevented anyone else from dying there."

"Do you remember her name?" I asked.

He handed the picture back to me. "Twenty-eight years," he said. "No."

"What about where she was from? Or if she had any family?"

The softness left his face. His eyes were now as sharp as a hawk's. "You are asking me these things because her picture was in my son's desk. Do you honestly think her death had something to do with my daughter-in-law's? With the deaths of my grandsons? Isn't it more likely that Ben intended to include that merger in his book about DPC, and she was a small part of that?" His voice turned as sharp as his gaze.

"Doesn't this seem like a colossal waste of time while someone is out there doing God knows what with my granddaughter?"

I held myself from flinching. "Bear with me, sir. As I said, we're looking at a lot of different things. Do you remember anything about this woman?"

He glared at me. "I went to the funeral. I remember there was talk that her death wasn't an accident at all, but suicide. I don't recall why. Maybe Tate started the rumor to downplay the danger of that crossing. That's as much as I can remember." He slammed down half of his drink. "Is that everything?"

"Just two more questions. Do you know a woman named Betsy King?"

Hiram crossed his free arm over his chest and looked down at his glass of bourbon. "Sorry, not that I can recall."

"What about William King?"

"No. Are they suspects?"

"No, sir. What about a railroad bull named Fred Zolner? Do you remember him?"

"Outside of seeing his name just now in that article? I'm afraid not."

"He was with DPC for decades. I've been trying to find him, to ask him if he remembers anything about the accidents. But he's disappeared."

Hiram drank the rest of the bourbon down in one swift motion. Something dark and cruel rose in his eyes. In that instant, I glimpsed the appetite behind the mask of the genial businessman; it was like finding a wolf among the guests at a dinner party. Hiram would be a dangerous foe, I realized. And your relationship with him would depend—always—on what you brought to the table. *Rapacious*, Lancing Tate had said. I found myself agreeing.

Then Hiram's face softened once more into bland pleasantness and the moment passed. I shook myself and blinked at the sunlight streaming across the polished wooden floors, at the artfully arranged rugs, at the old man with an oxygen tank and a shattered family. For a moment I wondered if I'd really seen it. And if it had been directed at me or Zolner.

Hiram said, "I'm sorry, I don't remember him. Maybe I spoke with him in the past. But at my age, memories pile up like stones in a cairn. I can't see them all."

"I understand," I said. "Thank you for your time."

I signaled Clyde and we headed toward the door. We'd almost reached it when Hiram spoke again. "Those who are the least guilty are the ones who feel most at fault."

I turned back. He was nodding as if to himself. He said, "And those who have sinned walk away clean."

"Is there some message here I should understand?" I asked.

"It's just advice, Agent Parnell. If you fail to find my granddaughter, then shed the guilt. It will only hold you back."

"Is that what you intend to do?"

"When it comes to Lucy . . . I don't know."

I couldn't believe what I was hearing. "Do you feel guilty about her disappearance?"

"It's always so with family."

"If there's something you should be telling me—"

"Only that I should have spent more time with her." Abruptly he grinned, a wide, bleak sneer. The wolf was back. "But with everything else? Oh, yes. I walk away without a glance back. Guilt is a useless emotion. It cuts you off at the knees and offers nothing in return."

"Sometimes guilt helps us grow," I said softly. "Could be it's the better way to live."

"We all make our own beds. Then our own graves." We both glanced at the oxygen machine. Then he inclined his head graciously. "Find my granddaughter, Agent Parnell. And save us both."

CHAPTER 19

War is not only the worst thing that will happen to you.
It is also the best.

—Sydney Parnell. Personal journal.

Riding down in the elevator with Clyde, I felt dirty. Like I'd stripped and rolled in horse manure.

"He knows something," I said to Clyde, who looked up at me with worried eyes. "About the past or about Lucy. If it turns out whatever he's holding back is something that would help his granddaughter, I will kill him myself."

Clyde and I crossed the residential lobby, heading for the next set of elevators. My headset buzzed just as we were getting on. I answered with "Special Agent Parnell."

"Agent Parnell, this is Rick Wolanski. I got a message this morning to call you."

"Yes! Thank you for calling me back, Deputy Wolanski. I'm very glad to hear from you."

"Wow, I haven't gotten a reception like that since I asked the class nerd to the senior prom. Hopefully our relationship will go better than that one did. And it's just *mister* now."

"Mr. Wolanski. I work for Denver Pacific Continental. I'm looking into some accidents that occurred at a railroad crossing that was in your jurisdiction when you were a deputy. A grade crossing at Potters Road in Thornton."

"You're talking a long time ago. That would have been the seventies."

"And early eighties. The sheriff's office says you're digitizing the old files. I thought you might have records of those accidents. If so, I'd love to see them."

"I probably do, although I haven't gone through everything. I agreed to do this for the sheriff, but it turns out I have less free time than I thought I did. Just got back from a fishing trip in Alaska. Incredible salmon. And moose. And the elk! I should have gotten a hunting license." He paused. "Where was I?"

"The grade crossing. People called it Deadman's Crossing."

"Oh, Deadman's Crossing, yes. I do remember those accidents. Four of them. Terrible. Just terrible. Flesh against metal. It never goes well. And it's always the worst kind of case when a life is snuffed out before it's gotten a proper start."

I cleared my throat. "Mr. Wolanski."

"Call me Rick. And sorry, I do run on. Yes, there were four accidents. I handled three of them. I'll tell you what, I'll go look for those files right now, while it's fresh on my mind. Then I can have them waiting for you whenever you get a chance to stop by."

Clyde and I walked past the gleaming shops and smooth-faced patrons on the bottom floor, past the discreetly placed plainclothes cops and out into the white heat of the day.

"Thank you, Rick." I turned to shade my watch with my body and looked at the time. "Would an hour and a half be good, sir?"

"Motivation. I like that." He chuckled. "I'll have the coffee on."

I thanked him and hung up, then phoned Cohen.

"I was just about to call you," he said. "They've located Fred Zolner's truck."

I straightened. Things were starting to break. But my excitement died with Cohen's next words.

"Just his truck. Not the man himself. A patrol cop found it parked at a hotel in Gillette, Wyoming, five hours north of here. Zolner never checked into the hotel, and there was nothing in his truck except an empty pack of chewing gum. No evidence that any crime occurred. But what his neighbor told you is correct. He's a gambler who's been on the edge of bankruptcy four times. The Feds found huge deposits in his bank accounts that can't be explained by his pension. The amount of the deposits went up recently. We've got people looking for him at the casinos in Cripple Creek and Black Hawk. And at the casino in Gillette."

"Where's the money coming from?"

"That's the question of the hour. The Feds are running a trace."

"Why Gillette?" I asked, wondering if he really did have a daughter.

"Its biggest claim to fame is some massive rock formation called Devils Tower, which was made famous by that sci-fi movie back in the seventies. *Close Encounters*. It's where the aliens land, or something. This is what Google will get you."

"Who's following up on the truck?"

"The local police. They'll let us know what they learn. And the Aurora police did a welfare check on Zolner. All they found were more cockroaches than a hound's got ticks. That's a direct quote. Quite an achievement in a place as dry as Colorado. Maybe he's hiding from those gambling debts. Might explain why his neighbor mentioned the mob when she brought up his visitor."

A hit man, she'd said. *Not Italian. Just bad.*

"Anything else?" I asked.

"The Feds are following up on what you found in Ohio. Nothing yet. Other than that, we're on the treadmill. Talking to the neighbors and friends of the family again. Nothing more on Vander, except the police in Columbus haven't been able to place him there at any time in the last six months. Which might mean he just didn't do anything to catch their attention."

Cohen sounded calm. But I knew what every hour was costing him. "You have anything for me?" he asked.

"I'm still trying to run down the accidents associated with our crossing. But Hiram Davenport recognized the woman's photo, the one from Ben's desk. He couldn't give me a name, but he said she was the last person killed at the crossing before it was changed to an overpass. I'm heading to Greeley now to talk to the deputy who handled that accident and two others. And to look at the paperwork for a fourth accident."

"You know, you're not too shabby," Cohen said. "For a railroad cop, I mean."

"Bite me. Hiram said the name William King didn't mean anything to him. Then I asked him if he remembered our missing railroad cop, Fred Zolner."

"And?"

"He said no. But he turned . . . dark. Almost frightening."

"You think Hiram has something to do with Zolner's disappearance?"

"Just thought I'd share. What's going on with McConnell and her team?"

"The CARD lead is here from LA. They're pounding the pavement with us. You want to see if McConnell can go with you to talk to the deputy? Might not hurt to have the backing of the Feds."

I doubted Wolanski needed any encouragement. But it couldn't hurt. "I'll give her a call."

"Let me know what you learn up there."

After we hung up, I dialed Mac's mobile and filled her in on what I knew so far.

"I'm heading up to Greeley right now to talk to Rick Wolanski."

"Can you pick me up at FBI headquarters?" Mac asked.

"Be there in twenty."

◆ ◆ ◆

Mac was waiting in the visitor parking lot when I pulled in. Cool and collected even in the heat, she waved away my apology for the dog hair and climbed in.

As I drove, I told her about my conversation with Hiram.

"My guess is that Hiram knew Tate wasn't reporting those accidents," I said. "When he found out, he used that to force Tate to not only agree to the merger, but publicly support it."

"Wasn't strictly legal," Mac said. "But I can't say I disagree with what he did."

We talked about other aspects of the case until we reached the highway, then fell silent for a time. From the back, Clyde's snores wafted over us.

A moment later, Mac cracked her window. Clyde's snores weren't the only thing he was sharing.

"Sorry," I said.

"It's all right. I have a chocolate lab. Goes with the territory." She pushed back her hair and cranked her head from side to side as if her neck hurt. "You sleep last night?"

"A little. You?"

"Some. It's always hard when I'm on a case."

"Thirty-six hours," I said. "That's how long she's been gone."

"I know." Mac's gaze on me was compassionate. "With each case, the hours race by. And yet there's a year in every hour. Just imagine how it feels for Lucy."

"Do you think she's still alive? Honestly, I mean."

"I'm sure you know the statistics. But I never lose hope. Not until we have no other choice."

I passed an RV. Through the window I spotted kids playing cards at a table. Laughing.

"Why do they call you Mad Mac? Are you really that much of a bull in a china shop?"

"Sometimes." Mac's gaze drifted to the window. Outside, corn fields shimmered in the heat. Two motorcycles blew past us, the roar of their engines rising then falling away.

"You feel like sharing?"

She kept looking out the window. A new tension had entered her body—her shoulders were up and she'd pressed a hand to the back of her neck.

"Hey," I said. "Just making conversation. We can talk baseball."

"No, it's all right." She dropped her hand. "There are three reasons. That I know of, anyway. People like to make stories."

"We've got another forty minutes. And the scenery isn't going to get any better."

Her laugh was soft. "Okay. If you're really interested. The first reason was because of how crazy I went after I lost my daughter. She was a cop."

I remembered what she'd said about honor making a crappy shield and I wondered what had happened. But it wasn't any of my business. "I'm sorry."

"It's been four years. I keep waiting for it to get easier."

"You've seen a counselor, I guess."

"Five of them." She laughed without humor. "I just keep waiting for a miracle, but of course there isn't one."

"I get that."

She shot me a look and nodded. "You probably do."

"How about the second reason?"

"Sword fighting."

"Say what?"

"I like medieval and Renaissance weapons. Once a week I practice sword fighting with a group known as the Society for Creative

Anachronism. The black eye came from a blow with a modern-day version of a two-handed broadsword."

I signaled and pulled around a pickup hauling a load of wood. "How's the other guy look?"

"You've seen liver pâté?"

"Remind me not to piss you off."

She laughed again, and this time it was genuine. "Don't piss me off."

Greeley was a town of ninety thousand people best known for two things: The University of Northern Colorado, famous for producing some of Colorado's best teachers. And, less fortunately, the odor wafting from the feedlots of JBS USA, a meatpacking company and the city's largest employer.

Former Deputy Rick Wolanski lived in an older neighborhood in the northwest section of town. I pulled to the curb in front of a small brick and stucco rancher with an environmentally conscious rock yard and a half-ton pickup parked in a gravel driveway. A man stepped out onto the small stoop as we walked up the driveway and introduced himself as Rick Wolanski. He was in his late sixties, a big-framed man dressed in Colorado's rural uniform of pressed jeans, button-down shirt, and cowboy boots. His mustache was robust; what remained of his hair formed a gray horseshoe around his suntanned pate.

I introduced myself and Mac and we shook hands.

"A railroad cop, her K9 partner, and a federal agent," Wolanski said. "You must be on the trail of something important. Come on in. I've got coffee on."

He led us inside and asked us to make ourselves comfortable in the front room, then excused himself. Mac and I sat on the plaid love seat with our backs to the window, leaving Wolanski his choice of the two recliners. I downed Clyde next to the love seat. A grandfather clock tick-tocked softly on our right. On the opposite wall stood a bookshelf filled with hunting and fishing guides, Cabela's catalogs, stacks of maps, and a sprinkling of framed photos, mostly shots of Wolanski holding trophy fish. An antelope head stared sightlessly down on us from above the recliners; two stuffed ducks flew over the gas fireplace.

Everything had a worn, patched look to it, but it was neat and clean. Precisely like its owner. Sunlight fell through the south-facing window, spilling over our backs and tossing stray strands of light onto a braided area rug.

We could hear Wolanski in the kitchen, opening and closing cupboards and rattling cutlery.

A thick stack of file folders sat on the coffee table. My fingers itched to go through them.

The minutes ticked by.

"Mr. Wolanski?" I called. "We really need to go through these files."

"Coming!"

Wolanski bustled back in with an urn of coffee in one hand and three mugs in the other, his fingers shoved through the handles. "Cream? Sugar?"

We declined, and he set the coffee and cups on the oak coffee table. He left and came back with a plate of warm Danish, napkins, and three plates and forks. He filled the mugs with coffee and handed us each one. Then he took a seat and gave us a friendly smile over his coffee. His mug said, I'D RATHER BE FISHING.

"The pastries come from Della's, down the street," he said. "You really should try them."

"It's very kind of you." I recognized the loneliness in him, a quiet space like a held breath. He wore no wedding band and the room had no family pictures. An old bachelor, the woman had said on the phone. I wondered if he carried his own burden of ghosts. And if so, what stories they would tell.

I drank some of the coffee and smiled at him. My mug said, I'D RATHER BE HUNTING.

Mac said, "We're here as part of an ongoing investigation." We had agreed that she would take the lead, figuring that would impress on Wolanski the seriousness of our search, should he need impressing. "We want as many details as you can provide pertaining to the accidents that took place at that crossing."

"Can I ask why?"

"It has to do with a current case," Mac said. "That's as much as we can say right now."

Wolanski gave a rueful shake of his head. "You Feds are always so secretive. But okay, I'll help however I can."

"Thank you," Mac said. "Why don't we go through the reports one by one?"

Wolanski pushed his coffee mug aside and reached over for the stack of files. They were thick, with multiple manila folders inside a green hanging file folder. Four of them. "I can summarize them for you, if you wish. Then you can look at the details."

"Please," Mac said.

He cleared his throat. "The first two deaths occurred together. October 1973. Tim Dalgren, age seventeen, and his sister Christine, age fourteen. They died when Dalgren's '65 Chevy was struck by a northbound train."

He picked up the top green file folder and handed it to Mac, who opened the folder up on the coffee table so she and I could both see.

"Autopsies are in there, too," Wolanski said. "Along with my report, the coroner's report, and any eyewitness statements."

Mac and I skimmed through the paperwork and photos together. According to witnesses, the driver, Tim Dalgren, had made a habit of racing the train. It was what kids did for fun in a rural town on Friday night when it wasn't football season. Crazy. Unless—like most teenagers—you thought you were invincible.

"I remember that family," Wolanski said. "Good people. Tim was a little wild, just like most teenage boys. But his sister was quiet. Into 4-H. She raised rabbits." He shook his head. "Seemed like I wasn't much past being a kid myself when we got that call."

As I flipped through the pages, I paused at the school portraits of the two victims. I tried to imagine what a priest or pastor must have said at their funerals. *Called home early, going to a better place, happy now as they looked down at their families and waited for the day when they would be reunited.* I didn't know if any of that was true. All I could think when I looked at the photos was how their deaths must have destroyed their parents.

"Parents broke up after that," Wolanski said, as if he could hear my thoughts. "I see it all the time. Nobody thinks when they say 'for worse' it's going to get this bad."

"Was there anything at all unusual about the accident that you recall?" Mac asked. "Or the aftermath?"

Wolanski rubbed his mustache again. "I suppose I was a little surprised when the railroad didn't install a gate. The railroad cop I talked to promised he'd look into it. But he said gates probably wouldn't have made a difference. People get impatient, don't want to wait, especially the kids. The railroads have to replace broken gates all the time, I guess. He said that at least having lights on the pole made it more than just a basic crossbuck, like they have at a lot of rural crossings."

"A crossbuck?" Mac asked.

"That's what the railroads call a passive crossing sign," he said. "The giant *X* you see at every crossing. Standard at rural crossings with low traffic. So in that sense, I guess, the cop was right. We were lucky to have the lights."

I closed the file and put it to the side. "What about the next accident?"

Wolanski handed us another folder off the stack.

"December 1975," he said. "Robert Spence, age forty-three, and Bobby Spence, age eleven. Spence drove smack into the train. The two of them died instantly. It was night, there was heavy fog, and Spence was deaf." Wolanski shook his head. "The fog that night was like pea soup. They shouldn't have been driving. I doubt they could even see the lights at the crossing."

My fingers were cold on the file. I didn't open it. I'd seen enough in two years on the job. I handed the file back to Wolanski.

Mac said, "What did the railroad say?"

"They sent out a maintenance guy to check the signal box. I was right there with him. That was, let's see, two or three days after the accident. He said everything was working fine."

"Did Mrs. Spence sue?"

Wolanski shrugged. "I don't know. That was the one incident I didn't handle."

"What about the first accident?" I asked. "Do you know if the Dalgren family sued?"

"Sorry. I don't have any idea." He looked back and forth between us. "You guys ready for the third accident?"

We nodded.

Wolanski picked up the next folder. Neither Mac nor I reached for it.

"Three months after the second one. Another teenager. Seventeen-year-old Melissa Webb. She'd gone on an errand for her dad. After the accident, her parents turned down the settlement offer from SFCO. They said the lights weren't working, and their lawyer sued. They lost, though. I heard that their lawyer and an independent expert checked the signal box and found everything in working order."

"So nothing more came of that?" Mac asked.

"Well, people got riled up this time. Usually these cases get a head-line for a day and then it's over for the rest of the world. But this time some folks started lobbying the city government to petition the state to get a gate installed."

"What was the response from the state?"

"More of the same," Wolanski said. "Which is to say, nothing. State transportation officials had been looking at that site for years. But they said they didn't have the funding to install gates. They were waiting on the Feds. You want the folder?"

"In a minute," I said. I was anxious to grab the file for the fourth and final accident so that I could look at the photograph of the victim. Or victims. See if one of them was the woman whose photo had been in Ben's desk. I was sure that somehow this accident held the key that would help us solve this case and find Lucy. But I wanted Wolanski to unspool the story for us so that nothing was left out. "Tell us about the fourth accident. That was the last one before the crossing was turned into an overpass, is that right?"

Wolanski set aside the folder for the third accident. "That's right. Raya Quinn. Hers was the only accident where I was first deputy on scene. I was out on patrol when I got the call. In a way, it was the saddest one of all." He picked up the final folder and set it in his lap. "Back in July, it was. Hottest damn month on record. We were all sniping at each other. The AC in the sheriff's office was on the blink, so all of us kept going outside to pour water over our heads from the hose, just to try and cool down. We'd have given anything for the kind of rain we're getting now."

"July?" I asked. "What was the date?"

He looked at his watch. "Why, tomorrow. It'll be twenty-eight years to the day. Now there's a coincidence for you."

It was also the day the hazmat train identified by the killer had been scheduled to roll through Denver. A buzz started up in my ears like the crackle of lightning. There were no coincidences.

"Who called it in?" I asked, half expecting to hear Bull Zolner's name.

"We got the first call from the railroad dispatcher, who'd been notified by the train engineer. Then we got a separate call from Alfred Tate. He was the owner and executive manager of SFCO. His railroad owned the T&W short line, which is where that crossing was located."

Mac said, "You're sure of that? Alfred Tate notified your office about the accident?"

Wolanski nodded. "It was a terrible night for him. He kept saying he blamed himself for letting Raya work late. Said he should have noticed when she left that she was upset."

My mind was shooting off in half a dozen different directions. "Raya Quinn worked for SFCO?"

"That's right. Had for a year or two, I think."

"So what did Tate say happened that night?"

Wolanski opened the file and looked down at a typewritten report. "He was heading home after doing paperwork at one of his branch offices. It was just after ten p.m. when he left. The railroad had a couple of rooms in a building in a tiny community called Grant, pretty far out east. Tate had investments in the sugar beet fields there. He told me he could manage both from that office. He was a real hands-on kind of guy, didn't like to delegate. Anyway, Raya had been working that night, too, but she left about an hour before her boss did."

"How far is the crossing from the office?" I asked.

"Maybe twenty minutes. Faster if you drive the way I imagine Raya was driving that night. So there was some unaccounted time. I'll get to that in a minute."

I nodded for him to go on.

"Tate was driving home when he came upon the scene. The train at a dead stop, blocking the intersection, the car knocked clear of the tracks. He said he knew from the condition of the car and all the blood that anyone in the vehicle was dead. It looked like it had just happened—no one else was on scene yet. He figured the engineer was still walking back from the head of the train. As you well know"—he gave me a nod—"it can take a mile or more for the train to stop. So anyway, Tate returned to his office and called it in. No cell phones back then. After he knew help was coming, he went back to the scene. I got there ten minutes after that. He was in bad shape. Just torn apart."

"Tate knew it was her?"

Wolanski nodded. "That's right. He recognized her car. I mean, she wasn't exactly identifiable. I ran the plates to be sure. And even then, we had to wait and get confirmation from the coroner the next day. You couldn't make anything out of that mess. Plus, it was dark, and the car had been crumpled up like a soda can."

"When you got there, was anyone else on the scene?" I asked.

"The engineer and the conductor had arrived. And DPC's cop was there. Even he was pretty shook up." He met my eyes. "I bet you've seen your share."

I said, "What was the name of the cop?"

"Fred Zolner. Everyone called him Bull. He was DPC's railroad cop. The track belonged to T&W at the time, but DPC leased the track from them. It was a DPC hazmat train that hit her."

My brain cells were colliding like bumper cars as the scattered pieces of this case seemed to be coming together. The date, the type of train, the crossing. I didn't understand what any of it had to do with the Davenports and Lucy. But it was there. I felt like a hunter whose dog has just gone into point. Something was in the bushes.

I exchanged a glance with Mac and saw my rising excitement mirrored in her eyes.

"Raya Quinn was struck by a hazmat train?" I said.

"Yup. Agricultural chemicals. I expected the Feds to show up. It's a big deal, right, the risk of a spill? But Bull and the engineer did a walk of the train. He told me that only the locomotive was damaged. A team from SFCO confirmed it the next day. No leaks or spills. Probably why it was kept local. If any Feds ever came, I didn't hear about it."

"You said Bull Zolner was upset?"

"Oh, he was torn up. First time I'd seen Bull bothered by anything other than trespassers and politics. Well, and religion. Bull was a mighty opinionated man."

"Do you know why this accident in particular bothered him?"

Wolanski splayed his hands. "Don't know that it *was* this one in particular. I figured it was every accident bothered him. It was just that night was the only time I worked an accident with him right after it happened. His reaction made me decide he wasn't a total asshole." He flushed. "Pardon my French."

"So who else was there?" Mac asked. "Any passersby?"

"Raya's friend, Jill Martin. She got notified by a friend in the sheriff's office. Jill and Raya worked together at SFCO. And let's see, Hiram Davenport was there, too."

Astonished, I said, "Hiram was at the scene?"

"Yeah. I'm not sure exactly when he showed up. He told me he was there because it was his train and because it was a hazmat."

Funny how Hiram hadn't mentioned that.

"Tell us what you know about the victim," I said. "Raya Quinn."

Wolanski rifled the pages in the file but didn't seem to be looking at them. His eyes were in some middle distance. "Raya Quinn. Young, twenty-one, I think. A real beauty."

"Did you know her personally?"

"No. I just felt like I got to know her some after the accident. Just like the other victims. But something about Raya stuck in my craw. Maybe because she was essentially an orphan. She grew up outside Brighton, over in Weld County. Her mom was a nutcase. Smart, I heard. But a—what do you call people who are scared to leave their homes?"

"Agoraphobic," Mac supplied.

"That's it. And a drug addict. Opiates. Friends said the drug abuse started getting bad around the time Raya was old enough to help out. Or maybe the old woman just leaned on her more then. Raya used to do all the shopping for Esta, soon as she was old enough to drive. No one could blame her when she took off for bigger and better soon as she turned eighteen. Went to Hollywood to try her hand at acting. She did have some talent."

Wolanski shuffled through the file and pulled out a sheet of paper. He passed it over to us.

"That's her in the lead in the high school musical, *Camelot*."

The paper was a photocopy of a newspaper article. The headline read LOCAL GIRL, BIG TALENT. The reporter gave the high school production a kind review—enthusiastic kids, great sets, an honest attempt at the musical score. But he saved his real applause for Raya Quinn as Guinevere: *Quinn eloquently captures the heartbreak of Arthur's queen, torn between the man she loves and the man she is wed to. With Quinn in the role, you believe Guinevere carries the weight of an entire kingdom on her shoulders. If we're fortunate, someday we'll see Quinn on the big screen.*

The article included a photograph of Raya Quinn in a long, medieval-style dress, staring pensively out over the audience with eyes that held a world of sorrow. And no question. She was the woman whose photograph had been in Ben's desk. I lifted the picture to the light spilling in from the window and stared into the eyes of a woman who, as a seventeen-year-old, had managed to convincingly portray someone both older and wiser.

I passed the picture to Mac, then took out the photo of the woman from Ben's desk so she could compare them.

"I'll be damned," Mac murmured. "It's her."

Wolanski said, "Raya Quinn is part of this case you're working on?"

I nodded. "It looks that way."

He finished his coffee and returned the mug to the table. "Then I'm sorry I can't offer very much. Just the little I pieced together after her death."

"What else did you learn?"

"She lived in LA for three years. Never saw her in anything. Not TV or movies. When she came home she went to work for SFCO. She'd worked there part-time in high school. Six months after that, she was dead." He gave a rueful shake of his head. "From what her friends said, she'd settled into her life. Liked her job, was thinking about college. She died a week before her twenty-second birthday."

I tapped the file. "What about the autopsy? Was there anything unusual?"

"There was no autopsy. Given the circumstances and the condition of the body, the coroner felt an external exam was sufficient." Wolanski tilted his head, smoothed his mustache. "But if you two are looking for a mystery, I don't think you'll find it. There's not much in that report other than a sad story. She was slightly intoxicated. Her car was on the tracks when the train struck it. The engineer said the car wasn't moving."

"Suggesting it wasn't an accident," I said.

"The coroner told me that, in his opinion, it was suicide. But because she was intoxicated and because she didn't leave a note, he ruled it accidental. For her sake, and her mother's."

Wolanski pulled out a sheaf of stapled papers. "You want me to give you the highlights?"

"Please," Mac said.

"Quinn was alone in the car. She died instantly when her vehicle was struck. Cause of death was multiple blunt-force injuries. Vehicle was in good working order, from what the mechanic could tell. No skid marks. I already mentioned the .04 blood alcohol level. There was an empty bottle of Rebel Yell bourbon on the passenger floor. Last act of defiance against the world, I figured. Or maybe a way to make death easier to contemplate. I found a fresh patch of oil on the road near the tracks. I figure she sat there drinking and thinking about her life before she drove onto the tracks. That would account for the missing time." He shrugged, a sad, helpless gesture. "Maybe she was more disappointed in Hollywood than she let on."

"I'd like to look at the report now," I said.

Wolanski handed the pages to me. I passed the photographs over to Mac and began skimming through the report.

"What did Tate say about why she was working late that night?" Mac asked.

"Just that she was finishing up for the day. She worked as a secretary—payroll department, I think. She'd had a doctor's appointment that morning and was trying to make up the hours. After she finished for the day, he said she went into the women's bathroom, changed into her going-out clothes, told him goodnight, and left. Next time he sees her she's—" Wolanski shook his head.

I flipped through the report until I found the list of Raya's clothing. She'd been wearing a black skirt and halter top, nylons, and black dress shoes, as if she'd been planning a night on the town. She had on silver earrings and a heart-shaped necklace with a single diamond. A sparkly sweater had been found on the seat next to her; the sweater was covered with a light distribution of animal hair. I thought of the black-and-white kitten she'd been holding in the photo.

"Did she have pets?" I asked. "A cat, maybe?"

He nodded. "Her mom had cats."

"The quality of the identifying photo in the autopsy is terrible," Mac said.

I leaned over and saw immediately what she meant. Instead of a straight-on shot of Raya's ruined face, the picture had been taken at an angle so that faint shadows were cast across the left side of her face. A slight blurriness suggested the photographer's hand wasn't entirely steady. I'd taken more than my share of photographs at Mortuary Affairs. I wouldn't have accepted this level of work.

"Is that unusual?" I asked Wolanski.

"Wish I could say it was. That was just Gerald Roper, the coroner at the time. He had way more ambition than work ethic. He didn't get reelected."

Mac paused over one of the photos. "That's startling."

She passed the photo to me. I found myself looking at the image of a heart etched on Raya's throat. Roper had noted it in his report as a "discrete impression abrasion."

"You talking about the necklace?" Wolanski asked. "Roper said it was pressed into the tissue by the force of the impact."

The image of the necklace was disquieting. But I moved on from the jewelry and studied Raya's neck, where bruising showed under the chin—blotchy purple hemorrhages that stood out against the more general bruising.

I went back to the report to see if Roper had made note of these. His only comment referenced the all-over florid distribution of the bruising.

"Are there other shots of her face and neck?" I asked Mac.

Mac handed over more photos.

I flipped through them quickly, hunting for a specific type of injury. And there it was.

Pinpoint burst blood vessels in the conjunctivae of her eyes. I looked again at Roper's report. He'd made note of the petechial hemorrhaging in the sclera and had also noted its presence in the inner lining of Raya's lips and mouth. But he'd written off the injuries as being caused by the accident.

I'd learned a lot about cause and manner of death while working in Mortuary Affairs. But Raya's photos took me back to a class I'd taken on domestic violence. Mauer had sent all of his railroad cops to the two-day course so we'd recognize the signs when we went through the homeless camps.

"Petechial hemorrhaging," I said, handing the photos back to Mac. "And look at the bruising under her chin."

Wolanski sat up. "She was strangled?"

"I'll be damned," Mac said, studying the photos. "Didn't Roper catch that?"

"He attributed the hemorrhaging to the accident," I said. "But with that bruising . . . there should have been an investigation."

Wolanski flushed. "All this time, and you're telling me it's murder?"

CHAPTER 20

We are hardwired to be afraid. It sucks. And it saves us.

—Sydney Parnell, ENGL 2008, Psychology of Combat.

I asked Wolanski if he had a fax machine. He said he had one of those fancy all-in-one printers that should do the trick. He led Clyde and me to his study, then went to make more coffee while Mac checked in with her team. I called the medical examiner, Emma Bell, and asked if she could look at a report I was faxing to her office, along with some photos I'd send with my phone.

"If they're linked to the Davenport case, of course," she said. "I'll look at them as they're coming in and call you right back."

It took fifteen minutes to send the relevant documents. Bell called a few minutes after that.

"You have the picture with the image of the heart in front of you?" she asked.

"Yes."

"You see the patchy bruising under her chin?"

"I do."

"That looks like injuries from external compression of her neck prior to the accident. Now look at the photograph you sent of her eyes. Petechial hemorrhaging. Another sign of strangulation. Even more damning are the photos of the oral mucosa. Not just the hemorrhaging you see there, but also the bruising of the submentum under the chin and along the jawline."

"Couldn't those injuries have been caused by the accident?"

"That's what the coroner ruled at the time. Given the damage there, I can't definitively say no. But I think it highly unlikely, especially given the location of the bruising. Plus there's something else. Look at the photographs of her arms."

I pulled it out. The inside of Raya's forearms were bruised and scraped. "Defense wounds?"

"Exactly. In my opinion, the coroner's exam was sloppy and incomplete. He should have asked a doctor to do an internal examination."

"So you're saying it's possible she was dead before the train struck her?"

"If this were my case, that's what I'd be looking at. Anything else I can help with?"

I looked at the photograph of Raya's clothes. Lancing Tate had mentioned growing up with dogs. Raya's top and skirt both had white hair on them, as if she'd been around animals. It was a look I was familiar with.

"The victim had animal hair on her clothing," I said. "Can you tell from a photograph if it's dog or cat hair?"

"I wouldn't be able to give you a definite answer without looking at samples under a microscope. But in general, dog hair is coarser than cat hair, if it's from the outer coat. Cat hair is finer even than human hair. You own a dog. How does the photo compare with your own clothing?"

I peered at the picture again. The quality of the photo was poor, but it looked like dog hair to me. "I can't be sure. I'll send you the picture, and if you can figure anything out from it, let me know."

"Will do."

"Thanks, Emma. You've been a huge help."

"Before you hang up, I have more news. I was just about to call Cohen. We got an ID on the second body from the kiln. A man named Zach Vander."

Well, shit. There went Cohen's top suspect, cleared by virtue of being dead. I figured this meant we could officially clear Vander of trying to frame Stern, too.

I sent Mac a text about Vander; she was in the next room, but I didn't want to say anything in front of Wolanski.

Where the hell, she texted back, does that leave us?

After agreeing to let us keep the files for the time being, Wolanski walked us to his front door.

"I still can't believe she was murdered," he said.

"What happened to the mother after Raya's death?" I asked.

Wolanski shrugged. "No idea. I never followed up. I don't even know if she's still alive."

"And no other family?"

"Raya was an only child. There was a nephew of Esta's who came to stay with her on and off for a few years. I heard that Esta had a sister back east somewhere. Sorry I can't tell you more."

"What about Raya's friend?" Mac asked. "Jill Martin. Do you know if she's still in the area?"

"She is. She left the railroad and took over her husband's taxidermy business. Ever After Taxidermy in Thornton. One of my friends took his elk there."

Mac offered Wolanski her hand. "Thanks for everything. You've been a great help."

We shook all around. Wolanski followed us outside. The day was warm but gloomy, with a high, thin scrim of clouds and pale shadows on the ground. When Clyde made use of one of the bushes in his front yard, Wolanski waved it off. He bade us farewell at the truck and trudged back toward his front door. His step was considerably heavier than it had been when we arrived.

I let Clyde in the back, then paused with my hand on the driver's door.

"We've just lost our main suspect," I said to Mac.

Her composure remained in place. Only the black eye suggested any weakness. *Weakness* being a relative term. She didn't look like liver pâté.

"We didn't lose him," she said. "He's just pointing us in a different direction."

"The dead speak," I murmured. Sometimes more than we might wish.

"Exactly. Look at the volumes Raya has just shared with us." She slapped the roof of the truck. "Come on, let's go see what we can learn from Jill Martin. Then we can track down Esta Quinn, if she's still around. I feel like the answer is just around the corner. And with the answer comes Lucy."

We got in the truck and I pulled away from the curb, merging with the traffic heading south. Toward Thornton. And hopefully some answers.

CHAPTER 21

The wisdom of war comes, over time, to resemble the wisdom of life. Stay calm. Aim well. Don't get attached to anything.
And always know who your enemies are.

—*Sydney Parnell. Personal journal.*

"Of course I remember Raya," Jill Martin said. "She and I were best friends from third grade. Right up until the night she died."

We were in the back room of Ever After Taxidermy, standing around a bobcat sprawled facedown on the table. All of us watched the cat like we were waiting for it to get back up. With its legs spread-eagled and its head propped to the side, the dead animal looked like it had gone down after an uppercut in a drunken brawl.

Jill lifted her gaze and frowned at us. "But I'm not going to talk about that night."

I'd left Clyde in his air-conditioned carrier, figuring this place would give him the willies. It gave me the willies. The dead watched us from every corner of the room. Deer and pronghorn and coyotes, and even a bear eternally trapped midgrowl. A large walk-in freezer suggested there were plenty more slated to join them.

My eyes kept returning to an enormous timber wolf near the front window. I was thinking about the animal on the TIR. Cohen had sent the tape to a wildlife expert, and the biologist said he thought we were looking at a hybrid animal—a wolf dog. He couldn't venture a guess as to what species or subspecies of dog or wolf had gone into the mix. But his expert opinion was that the animal was "damn big."

"We're sorry to dredge up bad memories," Mac said. "I'm sure it's painful. But Raya's death might be relevant to another case we're working."

"How could that be? Wrong place, wrong time. End of story."

"We only need to ask you a few questions about that night," I added. "Then we'll get out of your way."

Jill made a sound that might have been a derisive snort or even a sob and selected a whip-thin knife from a block on the table. She was fifty or so, her gray-streaked hair cut short, her freckled face lively and intelligent. Her rolled-up sleeves revealed strong forearms and hands ropy with tendons, the fingers knotted and callused. Her brisk motions conveyed a don't-mess-with-me vibe that I imagined kept a lot of people at arm's length.

She'd greeted us pleasantly when we first walked into her business. But as soon as we mentioned Raya Quinn's name, her eyes had gone round and wide, her hands had shot out to grip the counter, and she'd stared down at the cash register as if gathering herself. When her head came back up, a faint line of sweat glowed along her upper lip, and a look of worry had crept into her eyes beneath the calm efficiency. She asked for our credentials and verified them with phone calls before she finally waved us to the back of the store where she was working.

"That was almost thirty years ago," she said. She set down the knife and snapped on latex gloves from a box on a nearby workbench. "How can Raya's death be relevant to anything now?"

"It's just background for another case," Mac said soothingly.

Jill's eyes swept over my uniform. "Is it about the railroads?"

"I'm afraid we can't discuss it."

"Uh-huh."

Mac and I waited.

Jill sighed. "Look. There was a time when I felt intimidated by people like you. But not anymore. So if this is just some cover-your-ass maneuver by the railroads and the Feds and"—she sucked in air—"you somehow think Raya's death can help you with that, then both of you turn around right now and skedaddle your asses out of here."

She sounded so distressed I had to stifle the urge to hug her. "It's nothing like that."

Jill picked up the knife again. It was small, but her hand trembled as if even that slight weight was too much at the moment. "What *is* it like, then?"

"I'm sorry that we aren't at liberty to discuss our case," Mac said. "But we do need your help. And"—her eyes met mine across the table—"it might help Raya, too."

Tears shone unexpectedly in Jill's eyes. She swiped them away with her forearm, leaving a wet trail on her skin. "What do you know about Raya?"

"Not enough," I said gently. "That's why we're here."

She looked at us both through narrowed eyes, as if deciding whether we measured up to some invisible standard. But then she shook her head. We hadn't passed. "I told you. I've got nothing to say. Maybe you should talk to the sheriff's deputy who handled it. Rick Wolanski."

"We already did. He told us Raya's death was ruled an accident." I decided to try and goad her into defending her friend, to get her angry enough to speak out. "But he also told us that it was most likely suicide."

It worked. Jill seemed to regain her energy. She inserted the knife at the base of the bobcat's tail and began to slice along its spine. I watched, fascinated and horrified. I wasn't good at dead bodies anymore, whatever the species.

"That is such typical male bullcrap," she said. "A woman dies and everyone blames her."

"Her car was parked on the tracks," I pointed out.

Jill said nothing.

"And she'd been drinking," Mac added.

Jill's sawing grew more vicious. "So there you go. Step one in the blame game. Raya didn't drink. Not ever. She saw what drugs did to her mom. She saw all the booze and drugs out in LA. She swore she'd never be dependent on anything other than herself."

"You're saying the coroner falsified his report?" Mac asked.

A muscle jumped in Jill's cheek. "Is that why you're here, to bring up all that horrible stuff again? And somehow that's supposed to help Raya?"

"Is there something you know that we should know?" I asked.

The tears returned, spilling over this time. Angrily, she wiped her face against her shoulder. "What I know is that Raya—"

She stopped speaking but kept sawing away at the bobcat. I got the sense there was a battle going on, and it wasn't the one between the human and the dead predator.

"That Raya wouldn't have killed herself?" Mac asked softly.

But Jill shook her head. "I've got nothing to say."

Instinctively, my hand went into my pocket where I'd slid the picture of Lucy. I rubbed my thumb along the paper.

"Mrs. Martin," I said, "there's another life at stake."

"No kidding. Mine."

"What?"

In silence, Jill finished the incision along the cat's spine, then set down the knife and, with her gloved hands, gripped the skin on one side and began pulling on it. The skin separated reluctantly from the flesh underneath. Like peeling a particularly stubborn orange.

I swallowed and tasted Iraqi sand at the back of my throat. *Stay,* I told myself.

Mac moved around so she had a better view of the bobcat. I gladly stepped back.

"My father did some taxidermy," Mac said.

"Okay," Jill said with determined disinterest. She began working the skin down along the hips, like she was trying to help a woman shimmy out of pants two sizes too small.

"He tried to teach me," Mac went on. "But I was hopeless. I was a good hunter but a terrible taxidermist."

"It's more fun as a hobby than a business," Jill said, engaging reluctantly. "My damn arthritis. There's gotta be a better way to skin a cat. If you'll pardon the pun."

"How did you get into it?"

Mac's voice was intimate, coaxing. This was a side of her I hadn't seen.

Jill's eyes darted to Mac before she returned to her work. "My husband. He died in a car crash three summers ago. I was still with the railroad but decided to retire early and put everything into the business. This place mattered so much to him, you know? I couldn't let it go. But it was a bad decision. I've been working my ass off ever since, trying to help my daughter with her kids and keep the bank from taking my house." She gestured with her chin. "Since you know what they are, hand me that tail stripper. If I'd stayed with SFCO, I'd be a few short years from enjoying my pension."

Mac picked up something that looked like a fat pair of pliers and passed them over. "My dad used to say, 'You pays your money and you takes your chances. We never know how things will turn out.'"

"And my mom used to say, 'You made your bed, now sleep in it.'"

Mac's voice stayed soft as she looked around the room. "Seems to me you and your husband built something good here."

Jill's hands went still and she followed Mac's gaze. She puffed out a breath. "Yeah? Maybe."

Mac moved in for the kill. "It sounds like you know something, Mrs. Martin. That maybe there was more to Raya's death than a tragic accident or suicide. Special Agent Parnell and I aren't about defending the railroads. We're about *finding* the truth. This could be your chance to let the world know what happened."

Jill frowned. "You think I stayed quiet all this time because that's what I wanted?"

"Did someone threaten you?" Mac asked.

"Tell me why I should trust you." She glared at me. "You work for the railroad. I know who your boss is."

"I'm a cop, Jill. And a Marine. The only thing I'm interested in finding and protecting is the truth."

"And damn the consequences?"

She went back to work on the tail. The raw flesh glistened under the bright work lights. Shadows jumped and shifted on either side of the cat, creating an eerie sense of motion. I angled my head away and found myself looking into the black eyes of a badger standing on a shelf. He looked sad about the entire mess. I closed my eyes, but then all I saw was the video of Samantha staring into the TIR in the seconds before she died. And Lucy on the swing, smiling.

I opened my eyes. "Mrs. Martin—"

Jill said, "She called me that night, Raya did. Before she left work. She was scared."

"Of what?" Mac asked. "What was she afraid of?"

"I've spent twenty-eight years being scared, too. And I'll tell you something about fear. It'll wear at you until it takes you down to nothing."

The bobcat's naked tail popped free.

"That's excellent work," Mac said.

I locked sympathetic eyes with the badger.

Jill set the pliers down on the bloody tabletop. She said, "I'm the reason Raya died."

◆ ◆ ◆

At Jill's request and to my relief, we relocated to a family restaurant three doors down. Food, she said, would help calm her nerves. The hostess seated us in a corner, far from the restaurant's three other customers. A waitress brought Jill a bowl of green chili, a side of corn bread, and a soda. For Mac, she returned with a grilled cheese sandwich and iced tea, while I had black coffee and a ham sandwich. After asking my permission, the waitress also brought Clyde a small piece of steak, winning his immediate and undying devotion. Men and dogs—it's all about the food.

Jill pushed her chili around in the bowl for a time, took a single bite, then set the bowl aside. She drew in a deep breath. "I've sat on this story for almost thirty years. Now I have no idea where to start."

"Wherever feels right to you," Mac said.

Jill rubbed her upper arms as if she were cold. Her face grew pensive and her eyes went far away; whatever she was seeing wasn't in the restaurant with us.

"Raya and I were friends for most of our lives," she said. "She stayed at my house a lot when we were kids. Her home life was horrible. Her dad gone, her mom crazy as a loon. In some ways, I blame Raya's mom for what happened, because Esta was never anything like a mom should be. Raya had to grow up too fast."

Mac said, "How so?"

Jill picked up a piece of corn bread and shredded it. "Esta depended on Raya when it should have been the other way around. It was always like that. Raya had a lemonade stand when she was real little, then a paper route. In junior high she worked summers in the sugar beet fields. Most of that time, Esta was home lying on the couch, high out of her mind. And when she wasn't high she was . . . scary. There's no other word for it. As soon as Raya turned sixteen, she got a real job, working for SFCO. She got me a job there, too, but for me, it was just play money. Then after graduation, she went to Hollywood. We all hoped the next time we saw her, she'd be famous."

Mac nodded sympathetically. "What did she do at SFCO?"

"Before she went to LA, it was just clerical. Answering phones, typing memos, filing. When she came back, she worked payroll."

"What about you?"

Jill's eyes were dark. "I'll get to that."

Mac nodded. "Okay. Go on."

"When Raya came home from LA, she was a lot quieter. It's always hard, right, giving up your dream? But Raya wasn't one to cry over spilled milk. She moved on to the next dream pretty fast." Jill's smile was sad. "Raya always had a plan. And this was one of her crazier ones."

"What was that?"

"She said she wasn't ever going to be poor again and she decided the best way to make sure she always had enough money was to marry it. Or, if that didn't work, to sleep with it. Raya wanted a sugar daddy."

Mac's eyes met mine. "Did she have someone in mind?"

Jill nodded. "A man from Denver she'd known before she left for LA. He was kind of her only choice. I mean, the options were pretty limited, right? Not a lot of rich men in Adams and Weld Counties, especially back then. For sure, there were plenty of men falling over Raya. One creep we used to call Devil Eye—he sent her love notes all the time. But the only men we knew with money were the ones who worked high-level positions at the railroad."

"Someone like Alfred Tate?" Mac asked.

Jill laughed. The sound was girlish and almost merry. As if she and Raya had giggled about the idea in her bedroom a lifetime ago. "Alfred Tate was ug-ly. No, she wanted this man she'd met at a railroad conference in Denver when we were still in high school. She was only seventeen, but she begged to be allowed to go, and Tate finally agreed. Her job was to take minutes at the meetings. This guy was there. He was handsome, worldly. And rich. They flirted at the conference, he took her to dinner, and I think—I think there was more to it than that. Their relationship was one of the few things Raya never talked about. When she told him she was going to Hollywood to be an actress, he laughed and told her to look him up when she came home. So she did. He was still rich and still handsome and he found her beautiful and interesting. So that was that. She decided she was going to make Hiram Davenport fall in love with her."

CHAPTER 22

*Love is like falling off a cliff. It's good for a moment, but
it never ends well.*

—Sydney Parnell. Personal journal.

The waitress came by with more coffee. At my feet, Clyde snored.
Distantly, thunder bumped, and he lifted his head before resettling.
Another storm on the way. The world was getting water-logged.

"You're saying Hiram Davenport and Raya were lovers?" I dumped
sugar in my mug. "Wasn't he married then?"

"That was the sugar-daddy part," Jill answered. "Raya claimed she
didn't want to marry someone that old, anyway. So at first, I thought it
was just a game. A seduction, like in a movie. She'd get a few trinkets,
get taken care of for a few months or years, then move on to the next
guy. But over time I realized Raya was serious about Hiram, even if she
pretended otherwise. It wasn't the money. She actually loved him. She
wanted him to leave his wife."

"The naïveté of the young," Mac said.

Jill nodded miserably.

I frowned. "I read suggestions in the press that Hiram's wasn't a
happy marriage. But his wife was part of the key to his fortune. She

was heir to the lion's share of the railroad. What made Raya think she could get Hiram to leave her?"

"That's where I came in," Jill said in a voice so soft I had to lean forward to hear her. "She had a plan."

Raya's scheme to get Hiram to fall in love with her happened while Hiram was making his final push to take over T&W, Jill explained. Once Hiram bought the short line in and made it part of DPC, his success there would be unquestioned. He would no longer need his wife.

"So Raya and I decided if we could help Hiram win that case, he'd realize how much Raya loved him and that she was even more valuable to him than his wife."

"How did you plan to do that?" Mac asked.

I pushed aside my empty coffee cup as understanding dawned. "You knew Alfred Tate wasn't reporting the crossing accidents."

"That's right. But there was more. Alfred had a general policy for management: don't spend money maintaining crossings. If there was an accident, employees were to go in after the fact and cover up anything that made the railroad liable. I worked in Engineering, in the signal department, and it was my job to type up memos ordering employees to cut back overgrown vegetation or fix broken crossing equipment. But the memos went out *after* an accident occurred."

Mac and I swapped glances. We were both humming like piano wires now. I thought about all those reports that had never been filed. Reports that might have saved lives if the FRA had ever received them. Reports that would have forced Alfred Tate to maintain the crossings.

Six lives at Deadman's Crossing. God only knew how many elsewhere.

The waitress came by with a coffee refill. After she left, I said, "So you started collecting this evidence for Raya to give to Hiram?"

"That's right. I told Raya about it, asking her what I should do. It was wrong to know all this and do nothing. But if I went to a journalist with the evidence, I'd lose my job. And I couldn't afford to. My husband had gotten laid off, and I was pregnant with our first child."

"You figured if Hiram knew about the fraud, he'd use that information to blackmail Tate into agreeing to the merger."

"That's right. Hiram had already promised he wouldn't lay off any employees if he took over. So I'd have my job, the crossings would get fixed, and—"

"And Raya would have her man," Mac finished.

"But it didn't go according to plan," I said.

Outside, drops of rain spattered the glass, and a long, low roll of thunder rattled the windows. Clyde looked up at me. I dropped a hand to his head.

Jill said, "Hiram was thrilled with what Raya provided him to use against Alfred. He was building his case. But there was one key piece of information he wanted that I hadn't been able to get. A stupid list of serial numbers for the parts in the lights at Deadman's Crossing."

"Why was the parts list important?" Mac asked.

Jill began weeping, a silent, painful sobbing that shook her shoulders. Mac pulled napkins from the dispenser on the table and pressed them into her hands. Jill gave a short, harsh cry and covered her face.

"It's all right," Mac said. "We'll get to the parts list. Why don't you tell us about that night? The night Raya died. Tell us what happened."

After a few minutes, Jill lowered her hands. Her eyes were wet and red, the lids puffy.

"It was supposed to be a girls' night out. We'd been planning to meet up at a bar in Denver named the Saddle Up. Five of us, all friends from high school. It was a Monday, which was ladies' night at the Saddle Up. We were looking to put aside our troubles for a few hours.

"My plan was to drive down with two of the women, Carol Mackey and Ellen Yager. I was the designated driver since I was pregnant and couldn't drink. Raya and our other friend, Irene Nathan, were going to meet us there. We were planning a late night because Raya had to work and Irene had to wait for a babysitter. Since the band wouldn't start playing until ten, that was fine with us."

We'd ordered pie and more coffee as a way to help Jill settle in. Outside, the storm had caught up and it was black as pitch, the rain a sharp drumming on the sidewalks and street. The windows in the restaurant were filmed with mist, the dining room empty. In the kitchen, a Spanish-language radio station played mariachi music. The thunder had bowled past, and Clyde had put his head down again, dozing.

"Raya was working late to make up for a doctor's appointment?" Mac asked. "We learned that much from Wolanski."

Jill sniffed. "Well, Wolanski should have dug a little deeper. The appointment was fake. Raya just used it as an excuse to work late that night. At night, the whole office would be pretty much shut down. Not the operators, of course, but the admin people. The office would be almost empty. She figured that would be her chance to steal that parts list for Hiram."

Jill had her hands wrapped around her coffee mug as if she needed the warmth. Steam rose from the cup, and she breathed it in.

"A few days earlier, I'd found a memo from a vendor warning SFCO that parts for the lights at Deadman's Crossing and some of the other crossings were likely defective. They were causing what are known as short signals—lights that begin flashing too late to give a driver enough time to stop. The vendor said they needed to be replaced immediately." Jill sipped her coffee. "The memo was five years old. So I went digging."

My own coffee was cold. "You found evidence the parts hadn't been changed?"

"Oh, the parts had been changed. At least at Deadman's Crossing. But not until *after* a teenager named Melissa Webb died there. After Melissa's death, her family hired a lawyer. The lawyer inspected the signal lights with an expert and made a list of the serial numbers of the parts in the light. We had a copy of that in our files. Everything looked kosher. But then I found a second list. It was also a list of serial numbers for the parts in that light. But the numbers didn't match. These were the defective parts, the ones the vendor had warned us against. The list was attached to a repair report stating that a railroad employee named Robert Riley had gone out after the accident, yanked the defective parts, and replaced them with good ones."

"That's what Hiram wanted," I said. "If he had the two lists and the memo, he'd have concrete proof of SFCO's culpability."

"Exactly. I'd managed to sneak out the first list of serial numbers. But I'd only *seen* the second copy and the repair report. They were kept in my manager's office, and I never found a chance to take them. That's what Raya was going to do that Monday night. Get those reports for Hiram."

"She was caught?" Mac guessed.

"She called me from SFCO at eight thirty that night and said she had the intel. That's what she said. The intel. Like she was a spy. She said she was going to change her clothes there at work and leave in ten minutes. Then all of a sudden she whispered that Tate was still there, and she had to get off the phone. She sounded alarmed, but right after that she said everything was cool. That was the last time I ever talked to her. The next thing I know, I'm getting a call from a friend of mine who worked in the sheriff's office telling me Raya's dead."

In the kitchen, a dish shattered. Jill flinched.

Mac asked, "What do you think happened after Tate surprised her?"

Jill reached for more napkins. "I was so innocent. I didn't really think about her being in danger. If worse came to worse, I figured she'd lose her job. So I thought what happened was a horrible accident. That Raya was in a hurry and tried to beat the train. We did it all the time, you know. Raced the train. I knew she was going to give the paperwork to Hiram that night and I figured she was focused on that. On what he would say. I didn't suspect until later that she might have been murdered."

Remembering what Wolanski had told us I said, "You went to the accident."

She shuddered. "After all these years, I still dream about it. And to this day, I stop at every railroad crossing, whether it's got a gate or not. I told my kids I'd beat them to within an inch of their lives if I ever caught them racing a train."

"What did you see when you got there?" Mac said.

"Her car, knocked way out in the field. The train, of course. Tate was there. And Hiram Davenport had arrived."

"Did it surprise you that Tate and Hiram were there?"

She shook her head. "I knew Tate had called it in. And that Hiram was close by since he was supposed to meet Raya. He would have come to the scene regardless because a hazmat train was involved. He and Tate were off by the side of the road, talking about something. Davenport looked cool as a cucumber, the bastard. Tate was hysterical. I figured they were already discussing the merger. This last accident was the nail in the coffin for Tate."

The waitress returned with refills and an offer of a container for my sandwich. I shook my head. After she left, I turned back to Jill. "What happened after that?"

"That's it. My husband came and got me. I was too upset to drive."

"So." Mac pushed away her half-eaten pie. "When did you get suspicious that Raya's death wasn't an accident? Or suicide."

"At the funeral. Everyone was there. The whole town. I heard whispers that even though her death had been ruled accidental, some people thought she'd killed herself. That she was depressed because she hadn't become a big movie star. I was so angry. Then after a while, I noticed that Alfred Tate wasn't there. And as her boss, he should have been. For the first time, I started to wonder if Raya had only thought everything was cool that night. If Tate had caught her stealing those papers and realized what it would cost him if Hiram got them. What if, I wondered, he'd followed her in his car, killed her, then put her car on the tracks to cover it up?"

Mac and I were both nodding. But my mind was racing forward, trying to figure out how any of this linked to Ben Davenport's family, and especially his daughter.

"The service hadn't started," Jill said, "so I walked off by myself. I just needed to be alone for a minute." Her gaze turned inward. "It was rainy, like it is today. There'd been a lot of storms, and everything was soggy. I'd worn my good black pumps. I remember how my heels kept punching through the grass. I was standing under a tree, looking up at the leaves, not wanting to see them bring out her coffin. And suddenly he was there."

"Tate?" Mac asked.

"Hiram. He told me how sorry he was about Raya. Said he'd seen me at the accident, and that he knew Raya a little bit, and how sad it all was." Jill dropped the wad of napkins on the table and reached for more.

Mac nodded for her to continue.

"He went on like that for a bit, asking me how I knew Raya, if we were close. He was fishing, trying to find out how much I knew. Maybe Raya never mentioned me by name. She could have just told him she had 'a source.' But finally, I couldn't stand it anymore. I told him Raya was my best friend, and that I was the one who'd stolen most of the information. That we'd done it for him."

"Was he surprised?"

Jill nodded. "Shocked. Then I said I knew about the affair, that she'd done it out of love, and that it was his fault she was dead."

Mac said, "That was—"

"Stupid. It was stupid. I was already afraid of what Tate might know about me. Terrified that he really had killed Raya, and that before she died she'd told him I'd helped her. Now I'd just gone and told Hiram I knew things about him I shouldn't. Not just the things we'd stolen. But the affair."

"What did Hiram do?" Mac asked.

"He was cool as could be. Stood there for a while like we were just enjoying the day together. I started to move away, and that's when he told me that we should keep our friends close, but our enemies closer. I can't tell you how that made me feel. Like he'd just put a knife to my throat."

The lights flickered then went out, and the music from the kitchen fell silent. The restaurant was plunged into gloom. Beside me, Jill gasped.

Then the lights came back on. Jill took a shaky sip of her coffee and went on.

"He said that he appreciated what I'd done and that I could keep my job when he took over T&W. Then he leaned in close and said, 'Loose lips sink ships, Mrs. Martin. And when those ships go down, they take everyone with them.' He stared at me with those pale eyes of his, and it was like looking into the devil's eyes. He said, 'And I do mean *everyone*, Mrs. Martin. Guilty and innocent, alike.' He said it just like that. Then he asked me if he could trust my discretion. Of course I said yes, and he walked away. I was so scared that my legs gave out and I sat down right there in the wet grass. And I never talked about it to anyone. Not even my husband."

"What a terrible secret to live with," Mac said.

Jill's gaze went back and forth between Mac and me. "I still don't know the truth about what happened that night. But I'm sure Raya was murdered. I just don't know if it was Hiram or Alfred Tate who killed her."

"We can protect you until this is over," Mac said.

But Jill shook her head. "I'm leaving tonight anyway. Heading to Cancún for two weeks to hang out with a girlfriend. Maybe knowing I'll be out of the country is what gave me the courage to talk."

She stood as if she were sleepwalking and excused herself to use the restroom.

As soon as she was gone, I turned to Mac.

"Blackmail," I said. "It's the merger. *This* is what Ben Davenport found out."

"Explain."

"There are two possible scenarios. The first is exactly what Jill said. That Tate realized what Raya was stealing and killed her for it, and Hiram found out about it. Twenty-eight years later, Hiram threatens Lancing Tate that he'll go public with that information if Tate doesn't back off from the fight over the bullet train."

Mac shook her head. "Going public would make Hiram an accessory to murder after the fact."

"Maybe it was a risk Hiram was willing to take. There's no way Lancing would let Hiram go public—he'd be hanging out his own father for murder. Plus, Hiram could just leak the story to a journalist anonymously. No need for him to be involved." I thought of Tom O'Hara's business card locked in Ben's desk.

"Okay." Mac pushed away her empty coffee cup. "Lancing is enraged by the threat, freaks out, and goes after Hiram's family. It's possible. But not likely."

"Or," I went on, "it was Hiram who murdered Raya to guarantee her silence about the thefts and his plan to blackmail Tate. Or because of the affair."

"Or both."

"Then, years later, someone reenacts the crime with Samantha Davenport and uses it to send a message to Hiram. Maybe it's personal, an enemy—I'm sure he has plenty of those. Or it's for the money. Someone wants to blackmail him for that long-ago crime."

"And this person, he also took Lucy for the money?"

"If the motive is financial. Otherwise, to hold her in order to force Hiram to confess to the world that he's a killer."

"Who would that be? Who would have that kind of motivation?"

I shook my head. "I don't know."

I looked up and saw Jill making her slow way back to us across the restaurant. Wet strands of hair clung to her forehead and temples, and her cheeks were painfully pink, as if she'd scrubbed them. She stumbled on the edge of the carpet, caught herself.

"We don't have everything yet," I said. "But there's something here. I can feel it. We just can't see the entire picture. Damn it, Mac, we're running out of time."

She threw some bills on the table and stood. "Let's see if Esta Quinn is still around. Maybe she can shed some light."

CHAPTER 23

"The past is a leech. Digs its head into you and sucks your blood until it leaves you dry."

—*Nik Lasko. Personal conversation.*

Half an hour later, just outside of town and in a world washed fresh by the rain, I pulled in behind a cruiser belonging to Weld County Sheriff's Deputy Bill Phillips.

Jill had told us that, to the best of her knowledge, Esta Quinn was still alive. But she said Raya's childhood home was way out east, hidden in a tangle of dirt roads and vast fields, and that trying to find it on our own would be almost impossible. She had to close up her shop and get ready to leave for Cancún, so I called the sheriff and asked for help. Deputy Phillips agreed to lead us to Esta's.

Mac and I stepped out of the truck.

The deputy was a baby-faced twentysomething, with green eyes and a fresh-scrubbed look. When we shook, he gripped my hand with both of his.

"It's a pleasure," he said.

Next to me, Mac gave a soft snort. I tugged my hand free. Phillips flushed.

"I pulled up what we have on Esta Quinn," he said. "Single white female, aged seventy-one. Address is for a farmhouse forty miles east of here in the middle of what used to be acres of sugar beets before the farm went bust. Hell, I can remember driving those roads when I was a kid. Back of beyond if there ever was one. Esta is listed as the sole owner. A 2003 Jeep Grand Cherokee is registered in her name. And that's pretty much everything we know about her at the moment. No known family, other than a nephew who attended a month of public school in Weld County some twenty-five years ago. You mind telling me why you want to talk to her?"

"We're investigating her daughter's death," I said.

He cocked his head. "The only daughter on record died twenty-eight years ago."

"That's right."

Deputy Phillips caught his laugh before it fully escaped. "You guys must have a hell of a backlog."

"It's the Davenport case," I told him. "There might be a link between those deaths and the death of Mrs. Quinn's daughter."

His eyes lit up. "You're kidding, right?" He glanced west, toward the next row of thunderstorms. "Let's get this show on the road, then, before the next round of rains. Some of our low-lying roads have been flooding. We've got water running in creeks that have been dry since before my granddad was born."

As Mac and I were getting in my truck to follow the deputy, Cohen called. I filled him in on our conversations with Wolanski and Jill and offered our tentative theories about how Raya's death could be tied to those of the Davenports.

"Murderous railroad barons?" Cohen asked. "This just gets richer. We'll have another go at Hiram and Lancing. You're kicking ass on this, Parnell. Maybe you should be on the homicide squad."

"Bandoni would love that. I heard you lost your lead suspect."

"Word gets around. We're working to piece together his movements over the last week, trying to see where his path crossed the killer's. Right now, Bandoni and another detective are running through CCTV from the comic book store where Vander worked. But so far the guy's a ghost."

"Mac and I are on our way now to see Raya Quinn's mother," I said. "Maybe she can tell us more about her daughter's relationship with Hiram and Alfred Tate. And about the night she died."

"Stay in touch," he said and hung up.

As we followed Phillips onto the road, I dialed Veronica Stern. I wanted to ask her what SFCO's accident-reporting policy had been during her time there. And see if she could locate any of the documentation from the early eighties that Jill might have been working with.

When she didn't pick up, I left her a message, asking her to call me back.

Jill Martin had been right. Searching for Esta Quinn's home without a guide would have been like hunting for a white cat in a snowstorm. GPS was worthless out here. A maze of county roads crisscrossed through fields where sometimes the crops grew higher than the windows of the truck. The land was almost uniformly flat; we would have had to climb a tree to get perspective. If there were any trees.

The sun moved in and out as we drove, a fickle companion that shuttled light and shadow over the windshield. I thought about a young Raya Quinn; she must have been lonely out here with only a crazy mother for company. No wonder she'd longed for Hollywood. Or for a man who could take her away from it all.

Forty-five minutes later, Phillips turned down a single-lane road that, after a mile, narrowed into a rutted, muddy track. The track ran another two hundred yards, then petered out into what might have once been an expanse of green lawn but was now a gloopy mix of dirt and mud. I flashed my headlights at Phillips before he pulled into the circular drive, and he stopped. I pulled in behind him, killed the engine, and the three of us got out. I walked around to the back to let Clyde out. As soon as I opened the hatch, Clyde jumped down and lifted his nose, sampling the air. He wagged his tail and looked at me for permission to go check out whatever he'd found. But I snapped on the lead so he'd know this was strictly business.

"Sorry, pal," I told him.

Phillips grinned. "He sure is excited about something. We got a lot of coyotes and rabbits out here. Badgers and ground squirrels, too. Too bad you can't give him his head."

I watched Clyde for a few more seconds. But he didn't alert, and I turned to survey the house.

It was a two-story structure with a wraparound porch, the dark windows hung with lace drapes. The place was old and flagging and badly in need of paint on the south end, where the sun beat the hardest. The tiles on the roof had curled like tiny question marks, and the stairs leading up to the porch sagged from end to end.

The Jeep Cherokee Phillips had mentioned was parked on the south side of the house.

"Place sure doesn't look lively," the deputy said.

"Someone's been here." I pointed. A set of tire tracks ran along the length of the circular driveway. Someone had pulled in, swung around, and headed back out.

"Could be Quinn's," Phillips said.

"Could be," Mac said. "But it looks like she usually parks on the side."

As we drew near the house, I heard a faint metal pinging. On the north side of the house, a lazy wind fluttered through faded sheets, and floral-patterned dresses hung on a line to dry. The laundry was wrinkled and wet. The faint stink of mildew rode the wind.

The wind shifted and I smelled something else, a stench I knew all too well from my time in Mortuary Affairs. With the change in the wind, Clyde caught it, too. He dropped his tail.

Phillips wrinkled his nose. "You guys smell that? How long did you say since someone's seen Esta?"

"Unknown," Mac said.

The front of the house had three windows on the main floor, and two more upstairs. All were covered by curtains, and none showed any light. The porch, with its immense overhang, lay in shadow. The breeze kicked up again, and I saw something flutter in the darkness near the door before going flat again.

As we approached the steps, Clyde's manner changed. His ears pricked and again he sampled the air. This time he looked more agitated than excited—something more than the death fear. I raised a hand to stop Mac and Phillips.

Clearly visible in the mud were the imprints of bare feet. The prints were large, likely too big to be those of a seventy-one-year-old woman. They led off into the weeds and disappeared.

"Whoever was driving the car, maybe," Phillips said.

But something else had captured Clyde's interest. Running parallel to the footprints and a few feet closer to the house were animal tracks, each larger than my hand. They were exactly like the spoor Clyde had found under the trees outside Cohen's house.

I pointed them out to Mac and Phillips.

Phillips gave a soft whistle. "A dog of some sort." He stepped clear of the footprints and squatted by the tracks. He held his hand next to one. "A big one, too. Massive. Way too big to be a coyote. A mastiff, maybe. Or a Great Dane."

"There was a wolf dog near one of the crime scenes on the Davenport case," I said. "How fresh are these prints?"

Phillips stood. "Water has caught in them, and the edges are blurred. I'd say a day at least. Maybe more." He scratched his head.

"We get a lot of those wolf-dog hybrids out here in the county. People use 'em to run off the coyotes. But they give me the willies. Those animals can never decide if they're wild or tame. I've seen it go both ways. Had one take down its owner a couple of years back. Ugliest scene I've ever processed."

Clyde kept his ears up. But he wasn't going wild over the prints, so I was confident no predator watched from nearby.

Phillips was staring at the porch. "What *is* that?"

Mac and I squinted into the shadows. Now that we were closer, I could see something huddled in the gloom just beyond the top of the stairs. Tan fur shivered in the wind. My mind went to the bobcat on Jill Martin's table.

"The hell?" Mac said.

At the same time Phillips said, "It's rabbits."

Phillips was right. Heaped upon the porch was a mound of dead rabbits, their bodies piled atop each other like kindling in a funeral pyre. The bottom carcasses were well along in the decomposition process. The rabbits at the top of the pile looked relatively fresh. Intermixed with the rabbits were ground squirrels, prairie dogs, and a few woodrats.

None of them looked like they'd gone peacefully.

Phillips hitched up his belt. "It's like a . . . a damn offering."

Exactly, I thought. The way a cat left a bird or a mouse on the doorstep as a gift for its owner. Only the owner these were intended for never picked them up.

Phillips keyed his radio. "Dispatch, this is Unit Twelve. I'm on scene. Requesting assist. We have anyone in the area?"

"Roger that," dispatch said. "Deputy Armstrong is thirty minutes out from your location. I'll send a call-out."

We went on up the steps, the wood soft and spongy under our feet from the recent rains. We stepped around the dead rabbits and their unwanted guests—the rabbits near the bottom of the pile writhed with maggots, while flies worked the top. Phillips swallowed hard as he went by.

Clyde stayed close to me.

Esta Quinn's front door was old and scarred, the jamb splintered from years of heat and rain and cold. The doorbell dangled from a single wire. It looked like someone had taken a baseball bat to the porch light.

In the center of the door, someone had drawn a small *X*.

"The killer has been here," I said softly.

"What killer?" Phillips asked. "You mean the guy who got the Davenports?"

"You're up for this, right, Phillips?" Mac asked.

He took a step back. "Maybe we should wait for Armstrong."

But I shook my head. "Lucy might be in there."

Phillips swallowed again. "Shit."

He took another step back and all of us looked up and down the length of the porch, swept our eyes over the windows. I kept my hand on the butt of my gun, but the house appeared to offer no threat. No curtain twitched, no shadows passed the windows.

In silent agreement, Mac went to one side of the door, Clyde and I took the other, and the deputy—in his official capacity—knocked as if it were a perfectly normal visit. The sound echoed around the porch then died away.

Out in the yard, the wind rustled through a line of cottonwood trees and, far over the fields, a bird called. The clothesline kept up its metallic clang.

"Mrs. Quinn!" Phillips yelled through the door. "This is Deputy Phillips with the Weld County Sheriff's Office. I'm here to see if you need anything."

Clyde's ears came up. A second later, I heard it, too. A high, thin wail coming from somewhere deep inside the house—it sounded like the weak screech of an old woman.

"Let's go," I said to Phillips.

He tried the handle. The door was locked.

The wailing hiccupped into a cough and faded away.

Phillips stepped back, raised his booted foot, and slammed it into the door, just below the doorknob. The door groaned and a series of cracks appeared in the door's wooden frame. He kicked it twice more, the frame splintered, and the door burst inward.

As if the house had been holding its breath, a smell rolled out, a dark mix of urine and feces and another odor I knew from Iraq—the sickly sweet stench of rotting wounds. My eyes watered.

"Damn," Phillips said.

I touched Phillips's shoulder as he was about to step through the doorway. "Clyde and I will go first. Give us close backup. Once we've cleared the entrance, we can split up and clear every room until we find Esta. Keep an eye out for the little girl."

If an FBI agent and a sheriff's deputy had problems taking orders from a railroad cop, they didn't show it. Phillips moved aside, and Mac gave me a nod. Maybe it was because I had the dog.

I turned back to the house. A shadowy hallway disappeared into deep gloom. I reached around the doorframe and felt along the inside wall until I found a light switch. A single, dim bulb came on halfway down the hall.

Clyde and I moved through the shattered doorway. The hallway dead-ended fifteen feet down at a single doorway, which was closed. Just to the left of the door, a staircase led to the second floor. A small alcove on the left held hooks that brimmed with coats; a pile of women's shoes lay in a jumble below. Through an archway on our right, a living room stretched into the dimness beyond the reach of the light, the space crowded with mysterious lumps of furniture draped in dusty sheets. I stepped that way and found another light switch. Shadows scurried back. Stacks of magazines and newspapers filled the floor. Dirty dishes covered a coffee table. A dry rattling came from behind the walls—cockroaches or termites.

Then, from directly above, another long, thin wail.

Clyde and I went fast, winding our way through the furniture and thigh-high stacks of magazines as we cleared the room before we made our way back to where Mac and Phillips waited just inside the door.

"Clyde and I will check the rest of the lower floor," I said quietly. "You two head upstairs. Sounds like she's in a room right over the living room."

It took me only a few minutes to clear the downstairs. Kitchen, mudroom, a den. All filthy with dust and mouse droppings and old food. I heard the floors creak as Mac and Phillips walked through the rooms upstairs, shouting "clear" as they moved through each space.

Then Mac called out, "Found her! It's Esta."

I could tell by her voice that it was bad.

Esta Quinn had been stretched spread-eagled across her soiled bed and shackled to the bedposts. She was nude and gaunt and barely conscious, tied down in a painful stretch. Only her right hand remained free; a stack of dirty plates and water glasses on the nightstand suggested she'd been allowed to feed herself.

The longer she lived, I thought darkly, the longer the torment could continue.

I downed Clyde in the hallway and stepped into the room next to Phillips. In the confined space, the stench hit like a baseball bat to the knees.

Mac stood on the far side of the bed, her fingers on the woman's wrist to take a pulse. Mac was pale, and her black eye looked like a fresh wound in the sudden pallor of her face.

"I'll radio for an ambulance," Phillips said and went back out into the hall.

I forced myself to the bed and looked down at the ruin of what was now barely a human being. Esta had been tortured over a period of days, maybe weeks, and what had been done to her body revealed both the woman's astonishing determination to survive and her torturer's capacity for evil. Broken bones, knife wounds, burns. The room was chilly despite the July heat outside, and I retrieved a blanket tossed over a nearby chair. Mac helped me spread it gently over Esta's unmoving body. Esta moaned in pain.

I examined the shackles holding her in place. Chains and padlocks. Easy enough.

"I'll get my tools," I said to Mac.

◆ ◆ ◆

When I returned, Esta's eyes were open. They were overbright, blood-shot, the eyes of a woman who'd gone so far around the bend she wasn't even within shouting distance of sane. Rick Wolanski had called her a nutcase. But she was well beyond that offhand description, wandering in a faraway fever dream of despair and pain.

Her eyes tracked me as I moved around the bed, my pick and tensioner making quick work of the padlocks. She began a low keening as I worked, and Mac gathered the old woman's hands in hers.

"Sh, sh," she murmured. "You're safe. It's okay now."

Esta's mouth cranked open as if on rusty hinges, the teeth within long and yellow. Her tongue licked out, trying to moisten her cracked and bleeding lips, and Mac went into the bathroom, returned with a glass of water. She cradled Esta's head, cupping the fragile skull so she could dribble water down the woman's throat. Esta drank greedily, then coughed. Mac waited until she quieted, then lowered her head back to the pillow.

Clouds rolled over the sun, and such light as there was went to almost nothing. The old woman seemed to fade into the bed until she looked like nothing more than a rumpled blanket. Phillips came back into the room and turned on a lamp.

Esta's mouth opened. "He . . . he . . ."

We leaned closer. Her voice came from deep in her chest, a ghoulish rattle.

"Who?" Mac asked. "Who did this to you?"

Esta's fevered eyes turned bright as opals. "He . . . killed . . . them all."

"Who?" Mac asked again. "Who do you mean?"

The old woman began to thrash. Her body twisted, her back and neck arched, her head lashed back and forth.

"He's mad!" she screamed. "My wild child. Mad, mad, mad!"

Her hand shot out and clamped onto my wrist with surprising strength, biting down to the bone. Clyde barked until I quieted him.

"My grandson," Esta hissed, her fingers digging. "Roman. He will haunt me forever. You've got to get me out of here!"

"Raya had a child?" I asked. Stray threads began to weave into a picture.

"Raya's baby. Roman." Esta's gaze latched on to mine. She looked as feral and helpless as the rabbits on the porch. "He was hers, but I—I was the she-wolf who suckled the murderer."

Mac frowned. "You think she means the nephew that Rick Wolanski mentioned?"

Esta cackled. "Nephew. Everyone thought that. Raya's secret."

"Do you know where he is?" I asked. "Raya's son. Where is he?"

A crazy light shot into her eyes and she cackled. "He's in the ground now. Where he belongs. Deep in the ground, God rot his soul."

CHAPTER 24

A life lived selfishly is a heavy load.

—*Sydney Parnell. Personal journal.*

"You think he killed himself?" Phillips asked. "And took the little girl with him? You think that's what she means?"

"We're going to assume not," Mac said.

We were standing in the hallway, whispering. Esta groaned and muttered from the bedroom.

"She's pretty wacko," Phillips went on. "All that stuff about him being in the ground. You think it's true? That she has a grandson and he's the one who hurt her?"

I ignored him. "Lucy could be here."

Mac massaged her temples. "Sydney, you and Clyde search the house and grounds. Phillips, get tape up, secure the scene. I'll stay with Esta and get on the phone, see what I can find out about a grandson." She dropped her hands and looked at me. "No stone unturned."

While Mac returned to the bedroom and Phillips went outside, Clyde and I headed for the stairs. I phoned Cohen, left a quick summary on his voice mail of what we'd learned, and asked him to call me as soon as he could. Then Clyde and I went through another run of the house, this time peering into every small place where a child might be stashed. My heart gave a panicked heave each time I opened a cupboard or closet door or looked behind furniture and in shower stalls.

I found keys hanging in the kitchen and went outside and searched Esta's car. Nothing but a sweater and an empty plastic bag. In the rear of the house I found a root cellar, the dank musty air filling my nostrils as I left Clyde up top and descended a rotted ladder into the dark. My flashlight picked out only empty bottles and spiderwebs. But the image of Esta and her tortured body haunted me, and I realized I was whispering Lucy's name under my breath, like a prayer.

Phillips and the new deputy, Armstrong, met us at the front door. The ambulance was fifteen minutes out, Phillips said. While they began a more thorough search of the ground floor for any indication of Roman's identity or where he might be, Clyde and I returned upstairs. We looked into Esta's room, but the old woman appeared to be asleep.

Mac joined me in the hall.

"We're searching every database we've got for Roman Quinn," she said. "So far nothing. Maybe this asshole has lived so far off the grid that nothing would have landed him in a database. Or maybe Esta is just crazy. We'll keep digging, and once we have fingerprints from the crime scene guys, hopefully something will pop."

I pinched the bridge of my nose where a headache threatened. "If Hiram's the father, maybe that was why she was so determined to win his love. She wanted a father for her son."

"It would also give him a motive for killing her," Mac said. "It's one thing for a wife to forgive an affair. A child is more difficult. And it would give Roman, if he knew, a reason to destroy Hiram's family."

The house creaked around us while outside, wind rattled the trees. I rubbed my arms. "Maybe the answer is here."

I began my search upstairs with the room I assumed had belonged to Raya's son when he was a child.

The small space held a bunk bed and a child-size desk. A dresser sat in one corner, and opposite it rose a set of bookshelves filled with Colorado maps and rock-hounding books and Colorado-themed merchandise of the kind you could purchase at any mountain tourist shop. Chunks of pyrite and amazonite and gold ore. Tiny glass bottles holding even tinier flakes of gold. A belt buckle covered with rattlesnake skin. Miniature animal-skin tepees and plastic horses. Perched on the very top of the bookcase was a child's straw cowboy hat.

One shelf held books, including *The Odyssey* and the collected plays of Euripides—presumably the sources for the quotes Roman had left. The bottom shelf held a display of small animals, inexpertly taxidermied. A coiled rattlesnake, a hare on its hind legs, a squirrel locked— improbably—in mortal combat with a scorpion. I thought of the dead rabbits on the porch and tried to imagine what went on in a mind like that of Roman Quinn.

My wild child, Esta had called him. Was the wolf dog his? Had he been at Zolner's house last night? Maybe *he* was the man who had visited Zolner, claiming to be a salesman. He might have gone in search of everyone employed by the two railroads who'd been at the scene of his mother's death. He could still be trying to piece the story together.

I looked at my watch. By now, Jill Martin should be at the airport, safely out of Roman's reach. I called the number she'd given me. She answered, surprised, and confirmed that she had gone through security and was at her gate. I wished her a good trip and hung up.

My mind kept circling back to the question, *why now?* What had sent Roman to destroy Hiram's family after all this time?

In haste, I continued my circuit of the room while Clyde watched from the door, my anxiety mirrored in his eyes.

A dresser filled with a boy's toddler-size clothes; a pair of child's hockey skates in the closet. The walls were covered floor-to-ceiling with maps of Colorado and postcards of local tourist attractions like Estes Park and the Stanley Hotel, made famous in Stephen King's novel *The Shining*. There were street maps, topo maps, photographs of Colorado's famous peaks along with maps of mines and quarries and popular hikes.

On the desk was a photo of Raya Quinn and a boy I assumed was Roman. He looked maybe three or four, dressed in denim shorts and a plaid shirt, his smile wide. He wore the cowboy hat that now sat on his bookshelf. The photo couldn't have been taken long before his mother died.

What had it been like for him, I wondered, to grow up out here so far from other people, with a grandmother as drug-addled as Esta?

Clyde lifted his head, and a moment later Phillips appeared in the doorway.

"We haven't found anything useful about Roman so far," he said. "But I ran Esta Quinn again, digging deeper this time. Utilities, phone, property taxes, and a few other bills are paid through a lawyer who lives in Chicago, along with a monthly stipend. I called him, and he says a corporate trust was set up years ago to cover Esta Quinn's expenses. He doesn't know who set up the original trust, but it came from a third-party lawyer, so I doubt it was a settlement from the railroad for her daughter's death. No other visible means of support. She hasn't filed taxes in more than twenty years."

"The trust was set up by Roman's father, would be my guess," I said.

Or maybe it was blood money. Or both.

From outside came the sound of approaching sirens. "Cavalry's here," Phillips said and disappeared back into the hall.

The second room Clyde and I entered must have been Raya's. It held plain pine furniture—a single twin bed, dresser, nightstand, and a child-size desk. Movie posters were thumbtacked to the wall along with pictures of Meryl Streep, Jack Nicholson, and Jodie Foster. There was a framed photo of Raya as Guinevere in *Camelot*.

And on the desk was a single sheet of paper, once creased but now spread smooth, with a chunk of fool's gold glittering in the center.

A California birth certificate for Roman Quinn.

He had been born in February of 1979 in the city of Los Angeles to an eighteen-year-old Raya Quinn. The place for the father's name had been blank. But in slashing black ink, the pen pressing down hard enough on the paper to have punched through in places, someone had written in a name.

Hiram Davenport.

I should have been surprised. But by this point I was so desperate to find Lucy, I was more relieved than anything. The pieces were starting to collide.

The bastard, I thought. Pretending to know nothing of Raya. A picture began to form of a lost child realizing just how much he'd lost. A picture of grief and jealousy and rage. A father who wanted nothing to do with his son. A half brother who got all the love, a job, and a fancy office. Maybe that was why Roman had tried to destroy Ben—to punish him for having what Roman longed for.

I took out the gloves I'd grabbed from the truck when we first arrived and snapped them on. Underneath the birth certificate was a stack of five eight-by-ten photographs. I spread the pictures out on the desk.

All of the photos looked recent. They were casual, unposed. In all but two, the subject of the shot appeared unaware that he was having his picture taken.

The first showed Hiram Davenport in a suit, entering a bank or office building. The next was of Hiram and Ben together at a swank restaurant, the white-clothed table sparkling with silver and crystal, a dark-paneled wall beyond them. The third had been taken while Ben Davenport stood outside the door of the Colorado Historical Society, his tall body caught in a casual stretch, his eyes squinting into the sun, as if he'd just stepped outside to get some air.

In each picture, the subjects' eyes had been slashed with a razor.

The fourth picture showed Samantha Davenport in her studio. She sat cross-legged on the floor, surrounded by giant flower pots that I recognized from her website. She wore blue jeans and a sleeveless white blouse and was looking at someone who stood off-camera. The camera had caught her laughing, her mouth open wide, her head tilted back and her throat exposed. It was a gesture that was both confident and vulnerable. She had her right hand up, beckoning to someone. A child, maybe—Samantha's posture made me think she was showing her subject how she wanted him to pose.

An *X* had been slashed across her throat.

I flipped the picture over. At the top, someone had written, To Jack, you're the best. XO, Sam

Beneath that, written in a very different hand, were the words, If I cannot arouse love, I will destroy it.

The final picture was of a man standing in front of the kilns at the Edison Cement factory. He had dark hair and eyes as cold and pale blue as arctic ice. Hiram Davenport at thirty years old. Only it wasn't. Bleach the hair and add green contact lenses, and I'd seen this man just yesterday, standing near the overpass at Potters Road, holding a book of poetry.

"Jack Hurley," I said aloud. "Samantha's assistant."

Clyde heard the urgency in my voice and scrambled to his feet.

"Jack Hurley is our killer."

CHAPTER 25

All of us are bruised in places no one can see.

—Sydney Parnell. Personal journal.

I ran down the hall to Esta's room. The paramedics were tending to Esta, and Mac had stepped into the hall to give them room. Through the windows on the other side of the house, the lights of emergency vehicles strobed against the glass.

I touched Mac's arm as Clyde and I hurried past.

"Let's go!" I told her. "I'll explain on the way."

I punched in Cohen's number as we went down the stairs and left him a message to call me ASAP. He was out-of-pocket somewhere. My calls were piling up like cops on free-donut day.

Through the front door I saw an ambulance idling, its rear doors open. The yard was filled with Weld and Adams County law enforcement vehicles. Deputies from both counties worked around the house or talked on their radios. A crime scene van was just pulling in as Clyde and I ran outside, Mac right behind us. I found Phillips and told him that we had to head back to Denver, and asked him to be in touch with whatever he found.

"There are photographs and a birth certificate on the desk in the boy's room upstairs," I said. "I need to know as soon as you get those fingerprinted."

"Will do. Pleasure meeting you." He nodded at both of us. "Come back anytime. This is the most excitement we've had around here."

As I drove, I filled Mac in on what I'd found in Roman's bedroom. The birth certificate, the photographs of Hiram, Ben, Samantha, and Roman.

"The photo of Samantha was taken in her studio. I recognized it from her website. On the back, she'd signed it to Jack. Below that was another quote, written by someone else. 'If I cannot arouse love, I will destroy it.'"

"That sounds like our killer."

"There was another photograph. One of Roman at the cement factory. He looks just like his father, in case we still had doubts about his paternity. But here's the real knife to the heart. Roman is Samantha's assistant, Jack Hurley."

Mac grabbed the oh-shit bar as I went around a tight curve. "He was with them all that time?"

"Keep your enemies close. What I still don't understand is what made Roman decide to go after the Davenports now. What was the catalyst?"

"I think I can answer that one. Lancing Tate."

I braked as I entered another curve, then accelerated. "What?"

Mac shot me a triumphant look. "Esta told me a lot while I was sitting with her."

I was pushing the speed limit, the truck slopping through the mud. I kept a wary eye out for any deer or pronghorn that might come leaping out of the cornfields.

"Go on," I said.

"According to Esta, Lancing Tate visited her five months ago. He told her that after his father's stroke, he'd been going through Alfred's papers and found a journal."

"And?"

"And what Alfred wrote in his journal suggests that Hiram murdered Raya."

"What do you mean, 'suggests'?"

"From what Lancing told Esta, the journal wasn't definitive. Alfred was suspicious of Hiram, but not certain. He knew about Hiram and Raya's affair and he wrote that Hiram sent Raya to LA to have an abortion, which clearly she didn't do. Alfred claims that the night she died, he saw Hiram drive away from the scene just as he was approaching it. Then, forty-five minutes later, Hiram arrived again, pretending it was for the first time."

"Maybe Alfred Tate wrote that in case someone found his journal, hoping to put the blame on Hiram."

"I thought of that, too. Shame we can't ask him directly."

"So why did Lancing go to Esta with this news instead of the police?"

"She said he wanted her to be the one to report it. My guess is he thought it would look better if the request to open the case came from her, allowing him to stay above the fray. Lancing hadn't counted on Esta being quite so crazy. Nor could he have known that if Hiram has been paying her all these years, she likely already knew what he'd done. She'd stayed silent about her daughter's death and accepted Hiram's blood money twenty-eight years ago. Why would she suddenly agree to kill the goose that laid the golden egg?"

"So Lancing goes to her with this story, and maybe Roman overhears it. Did she say if Roman was there?"

"The three of them sat down together at the kitchen table. According to Esta, prior to Lancing's arrival, Roman didn't know that

Hiram was his father. It must have come as a terrible shock. All these years, and his father is living only fifty miles away. Then he hears that his father may well have killed his mother."

"And he goes a little crazy," I said.

"He must have decided to take Hiram's family away from him, just as Hiram had taken his. Once he realized that his grandmother has been accepting blood money all these years, he went after her, too."

My stomach rolled at the thought of the rage and rejection Hurley must have felt in order to extract such a brutal revenge. "He got to the Davenports by worming his way into the family and gaining their trust. Jack was hired only a few months ago. Maybe he tried to sleep with Samantha as part of Ben's punishment. But she didn't go for it. Another rejection on top of the news about his father."

"There's more," Mac said. "During the middle of this, I got a call back from my team in Ohio."

"They talked to the mother of the man murdered there?"

"They couldn't. Betsy King died two weeks ago. Natural causes. She had a heart attack at work. But they found a friend of her son's."

"And?"

"His mother never married his father. Nor did she tell him his father's name. Just that he was the son of railroad royalty. William King was an alcoholic, which is how he ended up homeless. But at some point, he was sober enough to put up a website. He called himself King of the Road and claimed that he was the son of a railroad magnate."

I tapped my brakes at a four-way stop, took a quick glance along the tall rows of corn, and powered through. "Roman assumed that William King was Hiram's son. He's killing off Hiram's family."

"Seems like he'd have more reason to commiserate with William than kill him. The two bastard sons."

I shook my head. "He wants to wipe out every trace of Hiram Davenport."

Mac sat calmly, but I sensed the pressure building in her. "And now," she said, "all we have left is Hiram himself. And Lucy."

My stomach made an ugly flip-flop. "Damn it. I was standing closer to him than I am to you right now. The guy turned on the aw-shucks show, and I fell for it. Mac, tell me that he didn't kill himself and Lucy last night."

"He didn't," Mac said. "When she said he was in the ground, she was speaking metaphorically. He lives in his own hell."

"She told you that?"

Mac remained silent.

"So he could be dead," I said.

"It's better to not think that way."

"So why did he take Lucy? Why not kill her the way he killed her mother and brothers?"

"I've wondered that from the beginning," Mac said. "My guess is that he wants to use her to lure out Hiram. I think he has something planned for them both."

"Something . . . like what?"

Mac shook her head. "God only knows."

I was working my way through a scalding, boiling stew of rage and grief when my phone buzzed. Cohen. I put him on speaker and breathed out his name.

"Sydney?" He heard the panic in my voice. "Are you all right? I just got your message to call."

I told him everything, the story spilling out in a toxic rush. The torture of Esta and the wolf dog prints and that Raya and Hiram had a son who'd grown up to be a killer—a man named Roman Quinn.

And the biggest news of all—that I was certain Roman was Jack Hurley.

There was a pause of two breaths while Cohen took that in, and I could imagine his expression—one of surprise shifting instantly to anger. I'd seen that expression on his face before, a look as close as he ever got to moving in for the kill.

"I'm sorry, Sydney. Hold on." His voice moved away from the phone while he talked to someone else. I heard Bandoni's rumbling voice in reply.

"We've got uniforms en route to Hurley's address," Cohen said, when he came back on. "But we've lost Veronica Stern. Our patrol car was still out front, keeping watch like we'd promised her. The uni knocked on the front door to let her know her stalker had turned up dead, but Stern was gone. She must have gone out the back, probably a couple of hours ago. The bathroom's been emptied of toiletries, and she rearmed her security system, so we're figuring she walked out of her own free will. There's an alley out back. She must have had a friend pick her up."

"So okay. She decided she'd be safer somewhere else."

"Here's the important part," Cohen said. "According to what we found on Vander's computer, Stern and Hiram have been in a relationship for more than two years. Vander had taken hundreds of photos of the two of them together, along with some shots of Stern going to see an ob-gyn. It's likely you were right about her being pregnant. And thanks to our stalker, Hiram looks like the only candidate for father."

"Hiram. Not Ben."

"Right."

"We missed it. We were so focused on Ben that we missed it." The panic surged to a crest. "Cohen, Roman tortured and killed that man in Ohio. And the man was probably Hiram's illegitimate son. Stern is in danger."

"We've already got a BOLO. We're talking to her neighbors and coworkers."

"What does Hiram say about his relationship with Stern?"

"We're having a little glitch there, too. Can you hold on again?"

More voices in the background; now they sounded alarmed. Cohen said, "Fuck all," and a bunch of other stuff, and a minute later he came back on the phone.

"Hiram's gone, too. They found one of his bodyguards outside the building's service entrance. His head was blown off with a large-caliber weapon. And—big surprise—Jack Hurley isn't home. Girlfriend says he's been gone all day."

Roman was very much alive. And on the move.

I pulled into FBI headquarters to drop off Mac so she could rejoin her team. We made plans to reconnect later.

"Stay above it all, Sydney," she said as she got out. "That's how you stay sane."

"I will if you will."

I let Clyde in the front seat, then headed toward DPC headquarters. If Stern had left home of her own free will, maybe there was something in her office that could point us in whatever direction she'd flown.

I was pulling into the parking lot when Dan Albers, the engineer who'd directed me to the Royal Tavern, called.

"I got damn taggers doing their dirty on my train," he said without preamble. "My train was sitting on the line for all of an hour, and some a-hole nails me."

The world slowed and contracted to a single point. "Tell me."

"It's some creepy shit. Not like our usual taggers."

"I know you wouldn't call unless it made you twitchy. What does it say?"

"It says, and I quote, 'Heaven has no rage like love to hatred turned.' Whatever the hell that's supposed to mean. The damn paint hasn't even dried."

"Where are you?" I backed out of the parking spot and headed toward the exit.

"I'm in the intermodal yard. My train's parked for the night. Walters and I had left and I was halfway home when I realized I'd left my damn phone in the rear DPU. When I went back, I spotted the tagging. Bastard had to have hit in the half hour I was gone."

"Did you see anything else?"

"I didn't see his skinny punk ass, if that's what you're asking. I've been walking all over trying to find him."

"You're still in the yard?" Adrenaline shot through my system. "You need to get out of there. Head east. I'll meet you at the overpass."

"Like hell. I'm gonna find the son of a bitch."

Albers would have no idea who he was dealing with—the graffiti found at the Davenports' home and in the kiln had been kept from the press.

"Not a chance," I said. "I'm pulling rank. You're not safe there. Get the hell out. Now."

On the way over, I called Cohen.

"Roman Quinn just tagged one of our trains in the intermodal yard within the last hour. I'm on my way there now."

"Sydney, hold on. I'll call some units and meet you there."

"Do that," I said. "But my engineer is in the yard. I'm going to pick him up. We'll wait for you there."

I hung up before he could protest.

I spotted Albers as I soon as I pulled into the yard. He'd leaned his six-foot-four, 250-pound frame against the bridge's concrete abutment and was enjoying a smoke as if he hadn't a care in the world. At least until I got close enough to see how pissed he was.

I pulled in, then hopped out with Clyde.

"Let's go," he said. "I'll show you."

I shook my head. "We're going to wait for the cops."

"You *are* the cops. He's just a tagger. C'mon. He could be off spraying some other part of my train. Let's nail his ass."

"We wait."

He gave me a funny look. "What's going on? Why'd you call the cops over a tagging?"

"It's part of a bigger pattern. We'll let them handle it."

He muttered something that sounded like *pussy*, but I ignored it. My nerves were on fire, but Cohen was right. Even though I doubted that Roman had waited around once he'd left his message, I couldn't risk getting Albers in his line of fire.

Albers held up something that flashed briefly in the light. "One good thing. I found this while I was looking for the tagger. I figure I'll give it to my girlfriend. Maybe she'll quit holding out on me."

I leaned in for a better glimpse.

It was a necklace. A silver heart with a solitaire diamond at the center and a ruby offset to the right. It was similar to the one Raya had been wearing when she died. But it was exactly like the one I'd seen around Stern's neck in the interview room.

Suddenly I was breathing hard. "Shit."

"Hey, Parnell? You okay?"

I pulled out my phone and dialed Stern's number again. Straight to voice mail.

I looked up at the engineer. He squinted down at me.

"I'm going in," I said. "Tell the cops when they get here."

"To hell with that. You go, I go."

I knew that unless I handcuffed him to my truck, Albers would follow me. I considered the fact that he was a civilian and weighed it against the sudden, urgent need to find Stern.

Albers was one of the toughest men I knew. He once single-hand-edly took down three members of a railroad gang who tried to hop his train. Albers coldcocked two of them before they knew he was there, and had the third cowering in a boxcar by the time the police arrived.

And that was just one of the stories I'd heard.

"You still carry a gun, Albers?" I asked.

"Do I still carry a gun?" He laughed and bent to pat his ankle. "Does a duck have wings?"

CHAPTER 26

"We've all been at least a little broken by the world. But the world only notices when we try to hurt it back."

—*Conversation with Special Agent Mac McConnell.*

"You're shitting me," Albers said in a loud whisper as we headed into the yard. "The punk's a killer?"

"He's murdered a lot of people, Albers," I said. "This isn't a lark. I have no idea if he's still nearby or not. You sure you don't want to wait for the cops?"

He rolled his eyes at me. "Fuck that. You go without me, I'll just follow you."

"You're more Marine than a Marine."

"I'm one better. I'm a redneck."

The next round of storms was rolling in over the Rocky Mountains as Albers, Clyde, and I walked west. Distantly, thunder boomed. Outside of that, the yard was quiet. The three of us seemed to be the only living creatures anywhere within shouting distance.

The vast, anonymous sprawl of boxes and railcars stretched silently around us. Intermodal traffic consists of goods transported in enclosed containers that are moved by ship, rail, or truck—usually a combination of all three. Electronics from Taiwan, machinery from China, furniture from Asia—they are all ferried around the world via intermodal containers. In the DPC intermodal yard, straddle lifts load and unload the containers, transferring them from one train to another.

Expedient. Efficient. Practical. But here in Denver, the intermodal system created a thousand different places where someone could hide a victim or stash a body. I pulled my gun and kept an eye on Clyde—he knew we were on the hunt, but he hadn't caught scent of anything yet.

"It's gonna start flooding any day now," Albers said, still whispering. "I seen enough of this kind of crap. You weren't even a gleam in your daddy's eyes when the Big Thompson Canyon flood happened. It was July then, too, back in 1976. That summer was just like this one. Everything dry as a bone until suddenly it wasn't. A hundred and forty-four people died."

I paused next to an idle train. "This one yours?"

"Nah. Mine's two lines over."

We crossed the tracks to Albers's train. As soon as we rounded the locomotive, Clyde's ears pricked and his nose came up. I was right there with him—a sudden chill lifted goose bumps on my skin. In addition to my fear for Stern, I now had that feeling of being watched that made every Marine and cop want to find a bunker and a .50 cal machine gun.

"My basement flooded once," Albers said.

I grabbed his arm and pulled him down to a crouch. "Albers, I love you, but you need to shut up."

My mind shot back to the schedule I'd reviewed that morning on my laptop. The intermodal yard was quiet today. A train had gone out at dawn, but nothing other than Albers's train was due to roll in or out until later that night. Distantly, traffic whizzed past on the interstate, while closer by, cars zipped along on local surface roads. But here, it was silent save for the wind rattling the chain-link fence and the continual rumble of distant thunder.

But Stern was here, I was sure of it. Maybe hurt. Maybe dying. Maybe dead.

She and her unborn child.

"Where's the graffiti?" I asked.

"Fifty cars down, maybe."

"Okay. Let's go. Stay right behind me. All eyes, all ears."

We rose and started walking again.

My gaze moved from the train to Clyde, then to the nearest train sitting two tracks over. The sense of being watched now registered as a shard of ice that pushed against the base of my brain, a raw warning I couldn't ignore. The reptilian part of me wanted to hide beneath the train—a potentially fatal urge.

Halfway down the train, Albers tapped my arm and pointed as we neared yet another stack of intermodal containers atop a flatbed car.

But Clyde and I were looking at the ground. Clyde had gone rigid.

Pressed into the mud was a line of animal tracks, just like we'd seen at Esta's house. The wolf dog. The ice at the base of my skull now spread along the channels of my brain, and the hair rose on my arms as my flesh tried to retract to somewhere safe.

Albers elbowed me. "You gonna look at the tagging?"

I tore my eyes from the paw prints and followed his gaze up. Add climbing to Roman's list of skills. The graffiti was on the top container, roughly fifteen feet up. The words were written in a dull reddish-brown, the color of dried blood. A perfect accompaniment to the message.

HEAV'N HAS NO RAGE LIKE LOVE TO HATRED TURN'D

Albers had a look of reluctant admiration on his face. "Fucker can climb."

"Albers," I said. "I need you to focus. There's a wolf dog somewhere nearby."

"Say what?" He looked at the tracks and grinned. "Target practice."

We made our way west along the train, while my sense of unease grew until it was as palpable as the storm making its steady way toward us. My gut—and Clyde—were telling me that everything was wrong.

That the killer hadn't left. That the wolf dog was nearby. Worst of all was the death fear—Clyde's drooping tail and unhappy expression had me convinced that Veronica Stern was past saving.

Clyde lowered his head and sniffed at some dark splotches in the dirt. His hackles rose.

I squatted to peer underneath the cars. Nothing. I raised an arm and pushed Albers against the train and placed my mouth near his ear.

"It's blood. Call for an ambulance. Then hunker down by the train and wait. We'll be right back."

He looked for a minute like he'd fight me, then reluctantly gave me a thumbs-up. Clyde and I moved forward.

Two units down, a well car sat empty in the soft light of the western sun—there had been a change in the lading, or a shipment that hadn't come through. The car looked like a gap in an otherwise full smile. As I drew closer, I saw another spatter of red along the car's bright-yellow side.

Clyde and I walked fast down the line, my eyes on Clyde for signs that we had company. His skin shuddered with the death fear. At the edge of the last intermodal container before the empty car, I signaled him to stop and peered around the immense box.

Veronica Stern was tied to a pair of wooden crossbeams, her arms and legs spread-eagled on the giant X. Roman had leaned the crossbeams at a steep angle against the containers sitting on the next car so that Stern's death looked like a crucifixion. Her head sagged against her chest, but I could see that her throat had been slashed—the amount of blood precluded any hope she was still alive. That, and the ruined flesh of her abdomen. Roman Quinn had made sure his half sibling would never enter the world.

I closed my eyes for just a moment, my hand to my heart.

Clyde stiffened. At the sound of footsteps behind me, I whirled, gun up.

Albers, looking sheepish.

"Can't cover you from two cars down," he said. He looked past me, caught a glimpse of Stern, and pulled back.

"Son of a bitch," he said in a harsh whisper. "Son of a motherfucking bitch."

◆　◆　◆

Knowing there was nothing we could do for Stern, I hurried us back in the direction of my truck.

"Shouldn't we, like, stay with her or something?" Albers whispered.

In the far distance, sirens shrieked.

"She won't be alone for long," I said.

We were still far from the truck when I heard a thin, high crack, and a hole appeared in the side of the nearest container.

"Get on the other side!" I shouted to Albers as a second shot rang out. "Go!"

Albers gave a soft grunt, but he moved fast.

The container cars sat too low on the tracks for us to crawl under them. Albers scrabbled over the drawbar as Clyde hopped up onto the narrow platform at the end of the car and I clambered after him. Vaguely, I registered the screeching of startled birds. We dropped down on the other side as a third shot echoed around the yard, and metal pinged nearby.

Then the world fell silent again save for Albers's harsh panting. I crouched and peered around the edge of the container. On the far side of the yard, just outside the fence, a flock of starlings was resettling on the limbs of a cottonwood tree.

"Damn," Albers said.

I dropped back down. "You okay?"

"Jackass got me," he said.

I looked over. He had a hand pressed to his shoulder. Blood leaked through his fingers.

"Let me see," I said, relieved that we'd already called for an ambulance.

"I'll be fine." At my look, he added, "He only clipped me. Find the shooter before he circles around."

"Stay down," I said. "I'll be right back."

I signaled Clyde to stay. Then, hoping Roman still had his sights on the drawbar we'd crawled over, I ran past four cars, my gun tight in my hand. At the fifth car, I stopped and leaned around the edge of the container.

No one tried to shoot my head off. I stretched on my stomach across the foot-wide platform next to the drawbar and surveyed the yard, trying to pinpoint where the shot had come from, looking first in the direction of the cottonwood tree.

Nothing moved.

We were near the south end of the yard. On my left, Albers's train stretched into the distance. To my right, in the direction the shots had come from, the yard lay flat across empty tracks. Far to the west, past the end of the intermodal train, was a line of lift trucks with their attached cranes. And beyond that rose an eight-foot-high chain-link fence.

On the other side of the fence, just visible in the distance, a wilderness of scrub oak and pine trees marked the end of DPC property.

Roman Quinn would have had to enter the yard on foot. Which meant there were only two places he could have parked his car that were within half a mile of the yard. Figuring he would have wanted to get as close as possible to the train with a struggling or unconscious Stern, I placed my bet on the nearer street, Carmen Avenue, a quiet stretch of road on the other side of the small woodland. With the approaching sirens, my guess was that he was either headed in that direction now, or still waiting near the lift trucks, hoping to take one last shot if we popped into view.

I returned to Clyde and Albers and crouched next to them. Albers was pale, his shirt soaked with blood. He was breathing like he'd run a marathon. But he was awake and alert, his gun on his lap. For a moment, I wanted to stop everything. Rewind the hour, the day. Squeeze my eyes shut, hunker down, and hide.

I shook it off.

"You doing okay?" I asked him.

To the east, the police cars were now visible as flashes of red and blue.

"I'm going to hurt the asshole who nailed me," he said.

I smiled. "Wait here," I told him. "I'm guessing the killer parked on Carmen Avenue. I'm heading that way. Tell the cops when they get here."

"I'm coming with."

"The hell you are. Stay here and let the cops know where I've gone."

An angry look flitted across his face, but then he grimaced and his hand went to his shoulder. "Yes'm, boss lady."

Clyde and I went west at a fast, crouching run, keeping the train between us and Roman. For Roman to make his way from the lift trucks to the fence, he'd have to go a longer distance than I would. I hoped I could head him off. If I was ahead of him, I'd have to decide whether to wait for him near the street or to circle back around to the line of lift trucks.

Briefly, I thought about the wolf dog, then pushed the image away. Clyde would let me know.

At the end of the train, Clyde and I halted and I peered around the last car, my gun up in both hands.

More silence.

The chain-link fence was several hundred yards ahead of us. Beyond was the stretch of trees, and somewhere beyond that, Carmen Avenue. With shadows thickening toward night, much of the yard lay in shadow. I strained my eyes for a glimpse of motion, first among the trees, then around the lift trucks.

There! A form slipped along the line of trucks, heading west, barely visible as night descended.

From far behind me came the sound of car doors slamming and the shouts of men. Roman had heard them, too. He was moving fast. I watched for any other motion in the yard, but he appeared to be alone. Whatever his relationship with the wolf dog, the animal didn't seem to be with him now.

I signaled Clyde and he and I darted for the fence. Once there, we cut north, heading toward the cars. Clyde was as quiet as any cat; I did my best to match his soft tread.

I lost Roman in the gloom, then heard the jangle of the chain-link fence. Clyde and I put on a final burst of speed. I flicked on my flashlight, and the beam captured a man straddling the top of the fence. I raised my gun, glad for the Glock's seventeen-round capacity. I couldn't kill Roman, because only he knew where he'd left Lucy. But I sure as hell could make him scream.

"Freeze!" I yelled. "Or I will shoot your ass right now."

The man went still. As I played the flashlight over him, he turned his head and peered down at us in a way that reminded me of a bird of prey. Our eyes locked, and a spark of terror arced down my spine at the casual cruelty in his eyes. The genial Jack Hurley I'd met yesterday—with his book of poetry and feigned grief—was gone. In his place was a man capable of unspeakable savagery. A broken man who broke everything around him.

I thought of the appetite I'd glimpsed in Hiram. Like father, like son—Roman Quinn was the wolf behind Jack Hurley's mask.

For a long moment, neither of us spoke. The man's heels were snugged into the links and he kept a casual hold on the top rail. He'd slung the rifle over his left shoulder. Lying on the ground on the other side of the fence was a backpack; he must have tossed it over before starting up the fence.

My adrenaline had spiked during the run, and now I shivered with it. "Roman Quinn," I said. "Or should I call you Jack?"

Roman looked eerily calm, even satisfied; another gratifying day in the killing fields.

"Clever cop." He nodded his head in acknowledgement. "Roman will do."

I thought of the paw print Clyde had found near Cohen's house. The knowledge that this man had been watching Clyde and me, maybe watching Cohen, made the anger rise in my blood like boiling sap. My finger twitched on the trigger. Beside me, Clyde growled.

"Congratulations on figuring out my true name," Roman said. "That was a tangled web to unweave. You've been busy."

"Not half as busy as you. Killing babies and torturing old women."

Atop the fence, he shifted ever so slightly. "I'd like to defend myself. But I have more pressing matters."

"You make one move to escape and I'll start with your kneecaps."

"It would be terrible if you missed. One stray bullet and Lucy will die alone. But not forgotten. I'm sure the entire city will turn out to mourn her."

Keep him talking. "But who will mourn you? Not your father."

Pain first, then rage. His face flushed with fury. "You want to swoop in and rescue her. Bring little Lucy home so you can live with yourself at night. Isn't that right, Corporal Parnell? Lucy is just another excuse for you to play the hero." He shook his head. "Cops and soldiers. How badly you wish to save the unsavable. And how often you fail."

My finger twitched against the trigger. But I'd noticed his word choice. *Lucy* will *die.* Which meant she was still alive. I focused on keeping my voice level. "I know exactly where to hit your spine to make sure you never walk again. And it's tempting. So get down before I change my mind."

His eyes narrowed to slits. In the gathering darkness, he looked both insubstantial and frighteningly real. Like a phantom only recently made corporeal.

Then the automatic lights popped on, a brilliant glow against the descending night. The wind shifted, rustling through the trees on the far side of the fence.

"Final warning, Quinn," I said. "Game over."

"You're right about one thing. It is a game. But it's far from over." Roman pursed his lips and gave a loud whistle, then grinned at me without humor. "And now the game is about to get interesting. Tell me, Agent Parnell, how fast can you run? And more importantly, which *way* will you run? I can't wait to learn who you choose. Will it be Lucy? Or your dog? We grow needlessly attached to our animals, don't we? Even when they're little more than tools."

A low growl rumbled out of the dark. The hair rose on the nape of my neck and my flesh went cold.

The wolf dog.

I aimed for Roman's left knee and fired just as Clyde darted around me, slamming against my legs and knocking me off balance. My shot went wild, and in that instant, Roman swung his other leg over and leapt from the fence. At the bottom he paused; there was a look on his face of rage mixed with grief before he grabbed his backpack and disappeared into the gloom.

I took a single step after him. But then Clyde growled, and the sound made my knees buckle. I'd never heard that odd cry from him, a snarl full of threat but also terrified. My bowels clenched and sweat popped on my skin.

As if in slow motion, I turned. Clyde was ten feet ahead of me, bouncing on his paws like a prizefighter, his lips slicked back from his teeth, his haunches tight. Seventy pounds of taut muscle and sinewy awareness.

Bounding toward us was a monster out of a children's tale.

The beast was nearly three feet at the shoulder and broad across the back, with an immense, barrel chest, long legs, and a large snout and ears. I figured it at a hundred pounds or more. Its fur was smoke-gray tipped with black and its eyes glowed green in the artificial lights. It moved in and out of the pools cast by the security lights, hurdling suddenly into sight then vanishing into the shadows.

My hands fumbled with the gun. I screamed at Clyde to get down so I could fire off a round. But no amount of training would make him obey an order to lie down in the face of so great a threat. He lowered his head and his bark was a harsh series of sharp challenges.

The wolf dog disappeared into shadow again, then emerged in midleap.

I screamed as Clyde—an arrow loosed from a string—hurtled forward to meet the animal. The two went down in a rolling tangle of fur and teeth and claws.

"Aus! Aus!" I yelled, racing toward them, trying to get Clyde to break free. "Out!"

The animals fell apart and I raised my gun.

Then they were at it again, a seething mass of fur and muscle so intimately wound I couldn't tell them apart.

"Damn it, Clyde!" I screamed, my entire body shaking. *"Out!"*

When the animals separated again, Clyde spun and rushed for the wolf dog's throat. But the beast skirted sideways, dodging Clyde's lunge and whirling to bite Clyde's exposed flank.

Just before the great jaws closed, I fired.

The beast's forward motion stopped. It turned its head, snapping at the unexpected pain. Clyde danced forward and then back, not closing in, sensing that the game had changed. I fired a second time.

The wolf dog sank to its haunches, then slumped onto its side. The immense eyes went blank.

I dropped to my knees. Clyde sniffed at the wolf dog, prancing in and out of the beast's range as if daring it to rise. I called him to me; he came, tail wagging. I ran my hands over his body, checking for injuries, my fingers coming back lightly stained with his blood. He licked the tears from my face.

I looked up when a shadow blocked the nearest security light. Albers squinted down at me.

"The fuck was that?" he asked. "A werewolf?"

DAY THREE

DAY THREE

CHAPTER 27

Home is where you stand on the front porch and wonder
which would be worse. To go inside. Or to walk away.

—*Sydney Parnell. Personal journal.*

I'd been to Joe's Tavern a lot when I was a kid. First my father, then later
my mother, had taken me there. My father to meet friends. My mother,
I think, just to get out of the house. I'd sit at the end of the bar with my
book, while a series of bartenders, none of them named Joe, gave me a
Coke with a straw and a maraschino cherry. My mom or dad would play
pool or darts or sit around one of the big tables with the half-sloshed
day drinkers who made up the bulk of Joe's clientele. I never thought
about the fact that a bar was no place for a child. Joe's Tavern was warm
and friendly, and if I didn't enjoy the company of my parents as much
on the way out as on the way in, it was better than being home alone,
or dropped off with a sitter.

I hadn't lived in the neighborhood for sixteen years. But Joe's Tavern
was a fixture from my childhood and, like a toddler to her mother, I
flew back there whenever I was distressed.

"You two sure that's all you want?" Ralph asked.

Mac and I were sitting in a booth near the front door, nursing our Cokes. I had a headache severe enough that half my face felt numb. The heartache was worse.

"You got burgers?" I asked. "Clyde's hungry."

Ralph grinned, pleased to be able to offer something. "Coming right up."

It had been hours since Roman disappeared. While the paramedics had taken care of Albers, and the ME arrived to deal with Veronica Stern, and Cohen and Bandoni started processing the scene, Clyde and I had joined the army of uniforms who were fanned out through the woods and along the streets, hunting for Roman. But we'd found nothing. Of course we hadn't. Roman had forced me to choose between running him down or protecting Clyde. He'd been gone within minutes.

At police headquarters, I'd repeated the entire sequence of events for the record. Then Mac and I sat with Cohen and Bandoni and the rest of the team, turning over every stone, following up on every lead, however remote. Finally, unable to think in the panicked bustle, Mac and I had walked out the door and ended up here, not long after midnight.

At my feet, Clyde huffed. He was willing to tolerate the bar as long as it made me happy. Or at least kept me from screaming. But I wasn't the only one who felt twitchy; he'd been up and down like a yo-yo all night. The vet who had come to see about the wolf dog had checked out Clyde's injuries, declared them minor, and given me some ointment. But the beast had sunk its metaphorical teeth into Clyde, just as it had with me.

Both Mac and I had our phones on the table, waiting for any news. Outside, across the city, searchers still crisscrossed Denver, looking for Roman and Hiram. Denver's crime lab people were running a DNA test on items taken from Jack Hurley's apartment to see if Roman Quinn was, in fact, Hiram's son. Whatever their actual relationship, no one looking for Hiram had much hope that he would be found alive.

Roman's goal seemed to be to eradicate every trace of Hiram's kin. Hiram—or maybe Lucy—would presumably be the last to go.

"That was a hell of a shot you made," Mac said. "A wolf. That must have been something to see."

"Wolf dog," I reminded her.

"Still."

"Clyde was terrified," I said. "But he didn't even pause."

We both leaned over and gave Clyde a respectful glance.

I hadn't been able to stop thinking about the animal since it first appeared out of the dark. The green glow of its eyes in the light and its eerie grace. The way my gut had clenched and the hair had gone up on my neck. The way I'd felt like prey caught way too far from the campfire.

"Let's hear it for electricity," I said.

Mac nodded as if she understood.

I looked down. Clyde had finally gone to sleep. But his paws kept twitching.

"I couldn't go after Roman," I said, for what was probably the thousandth time that night. "I couldn't leave Clyde."

"I know," Mac said. "I would have done the same."

In the dusty yellow light of the bar, she looked as though something deep inside had cracked. Nothing visible, exactly. She still appeared composed, if you overlooked the black eye and the way her blouse had worked its way free of her jeans. It was more a fragility in her posture, a sense that the only thing propping her up at the moment was some dimly registered sense that falling down in a bar like Joe's was something she couldn't allow herself to do.

"You need to come work for the Feds," she said. "You'd make a great agent."

My laugh was strung high. "Because I'd fit in so well? Me being a team player and all."

She leaned across the table, gave me her serious face. "You are wasting your talents. You should apply."

"Mac. No."

"Yes. It takes a year to run a background check. Do it now."

To distract her, I said, "Tell me the third reason."

She knew immediately what I meant. The brief animation in her face vanished. "It's not a good story."

"Then it will fit with the night."

Mac pushed her glass away and rested her chin on her clasped hands. Her eyes turned bright and she blinked and looked down. Tears, I realized.

"Hey," I said. "I'm sorry. Let's talk about something else."

But Mac said, "It was my second case. A child in Mobile was snatched on her way to school. She was raped and tortured for two months, then chopped into pieces, the body parts dropped in sewers across the city."

"Jesus." My fingers slipped into my pocket, touched the photos of Lucy and Malik.

"She was eight."

The headache exploded across the back of my skull and chewed down my neck like it had teeth. "Like Lucy."

Mac nodded. "We had no suspects, zero leads. So for two fucking months, this guy is torturing her, and we have no idea how to find her. We know she's still alive because he's sending notes and photos to the newspapers. I went a little crazy. Quit eating. Quit sleeping. My entire life became that case. I did everything I could, but in the end, I couldn't help her."

"It wasn't your fault."

"My marriage ended after that. Who wants to be with a fucked-up, crazy-obsessive woman? That was the worst part of it. Chris and I had survived so much together."

"He was a coward to leave you."

"It's a cautionary tale, Sydney. About not getting emotionally involved in our cases."

"You're emotionally involved with this one."

"And it's a mistake. It doesn't help Lucy. It only slows us down."

I drank down half my Coke, hoping the caffeine would take the edge off the headache. "What about later? Did you meet someone else?"

She gave a rueful laugh. "Ninety-five percent success rate, remember? I'm married to my work." She pushed free of the booth and stood. "Speaking of which, I'm heading back to the command center. You?"

"Five minutes behind you," I said. "Clyde's got a burger coming."

She pulled on her suit jacket, threw a five-dollar bill on the table. "Stop beating yourself up."

"Because you have."

"Don't think of me as a role model. Think of me as someone who's made mistakes so you don't have to."

I watched her head out the door. I could have gotten Clyde's food to go. But something was niggling at me and I decided to wait a little bit, see if it went anywhere. I'd done some of my best thinking in this place.

Ralph appeared with Clyde's burger on a paper plate. He set it on the floor, and Clyde woke and all but inhaled it. At least the wolf dog hadn't ruined his appetite.

"Dang, should I bring him another one?" Ralph asked.

I shook my head. "He needs to pace himself."

Ralph slid into the booth across the table from me where Mac had just been and set a bottle of brown liquid and two shot glasses on the table.

The bar was almost empty. A couple did a slow, drunk dance to Johnny Lee's "Lookin' for Love" playing on the corner jukebox. Two men sat at the bar, their gaze riveted to the muted television set as if they were lip readers. And an older woman was hunkered down in a back booth, nursing a glass of something clear. I'd bet my uniform it wasn't water. In the back kitchen, someone was banging pans around.

"You look like you could use some company," Ralph said. "And a drink."

"You ever get depressed working here?"

"All the time. That's what the whiskey is for."

The niggling continued. Whiskey. Bourbon. Something to do with bourbon.

"Actually, I love my job," he said. "You wouldn't believe the stories I hear."

He hoisted the bottle, but I shook my head. "None for me."

He raised an eyebrow, shrugged, then poured himself a glass and held it up to the light. "Nectar of the gods." He drank it down. "The gods sure know how to live."

There had been a bottle of Rebel Yell in Raya Quinn's car. My dad had drunk Rebel Yell. Called it the best of the bottom shelf.

Hiram had offered me bourbon when we talked.

"What do you know about Rebel Yell?" I asked Ralph.

He poured a second shot and cocked his head. "It's bourbon. Used to be cheap, but then they fancied up the bottle and the price. It looks different now, but it's the same stuff." He pulled his phone from his pocket and tapped on the screen. "It was introduced in Kentucky in 1936. Stayed in the South. Wasn't distributed nationally until 1984." He looked up at me and grinned. "So there you go. You want to try some?"

"No," I said, barely hearing him. The niggling became an itch I had to scratch. If only I could locate it.

I stood. "I'd better get going."

"Something I said?"

"I'm just restless." I pulled out my wallet. "What do I owe you?"

Ralph raised his hands, palms out. "It's on the house. I know you're working that case."

I thanked him and said goodnight, and Clyde and I pushed out the door, letting it fall closed behind us.

Outside, the night was mild, the air humid, and for once the sky was clear. I let Clyde off his lead, and while he explored whatever interesting scents he found nearby, I leaned against my truck and lit the last of Engel's cigarettes. The headache backed off a little; I no longer felt like someone had clamped my head in a vise.

I sucked in the deep, sweet burn and tilted my head back, looking for shapes in the stars. The North Star. Hercules, the hero. Another hero, Perseus. There was Cygnus the swan, the form Zeus had taken when he seduced Leda. After that seduction, Leda bore Helen of Troy, the most beautiful woman in the world. The woman whose face launched a thousand ships, whose kidnapping started a war.

I brought the cigarette to my lips. Watched the flare and fade of the ember. A car pulled in and parked nearby, a couple exited, and the door to Joe's opened. A spill of light and laughter fell into the night like a glimpse into another universe, then disappeared again when the door fell shut.

My eyes followed Clyde sniffing along the edge of the property in the faint moonlight. I would never regret my decision to stay with him instead of pursuing Roman. But I'd also never forgive myself for letting Roman get away.

A chill rose on my skin. The Six were here. I could sense them nearby in the dark, a palpable evil created out of my own scrambled brain. A moral injury, like the chaplain had said. Guilt as a harsh companion.

I tapped ash loose.

On the other side of town, Ben Davenport lay on the edge of death. Someday, maybe, he would wake up and learn anew what he'd lost, if that loss wasn't already with him on whatever silent paths he wandered. Maybe when he woke and found himself alone, he'd think about what he'd done and seen in Iraq, about whatever moral injury he'd suffered there. He'd consider the terrors he'd brought back with him and see the wreckage of his life here.

Then his thoughts would wander to the whiskey. And the gun.

Those who are the least guilty are the ones who feel most at fault, Hiram had said.

My mind was a tumble of contradictory thoughts. Raya's clothing had been covered with what was probably dog hair, even though her mother owned cats. Lancing grew up with dogs; maybe Hiram had kept dogs as well. There had been bourbon in her car, and Hiram drank bourbon. But maybe Alfred Tate did, too.

In his journal, Tate had written that he thought Hiram had killed Raya. But as Mac and I had speculated, maybe he'd lied. Or been confused about what he saw.

Bull had been there that night. He had to know something, if only I could find him. Was he missing of his own volition? Or had Roman killed him, too?

I watched the stars again, wondering what Bull lived for with his rundown house, his gambling, the stacks of empty beer cans, and a truck that he was afraid to use. What had sent him to Gillette, Wyoming? What was there, other than a shitload of pronghorn antelope and a giant rock formation that had once been the setting for a movie about extraterrestrials? For all I knew, Bull had gone there to commune with the aliens. Maybe he'd ascended from his truck into the mothership, never to be heard from again.

And never to be missed, presumably, by anyone other than Delia, his employer at the Royal. He didn't have a wife or children—I wondered if he had any family at all. Brothers or sisters, nieces or nephews. I remembered his southern accent, a softness that hadn't matched his brutality or the cold gaze of his good eye.

Rebel Yell. Raya had died in 1982. How had Raya—or her killer—gotten a bottle of liquor that wasn't sold in Colorado before 1984?

How, unless someone who'd recently been to the southern United States brought it to her?

I thought about the blood money Hiram had paid to Esta all these years. And then I considered the money regularly paid into Bull's bank account from an unknown source.

"Where are you, Bull Zolner?" I said aloud. "Because I'd sure like to talk to you."

At the sound of my voice, Clyde came trotting back. I slipped him a treat from my pocket, and he sat down next to me. I rested my hand on his head.

What if Bull wasn't actually in Gillette? What if he just wanted someone—and my money was on Roman—to think he was? If you needed to hide, be it from a hired gun or a psychopathic killer, what better way to disappear than to make them think you're somewhere else?

Denver to Gillette is a ten- or eleven-hour round-trip drive. Far enough away to keep people busy. But close enough to get there and back in a single night. And of course you'd take the old black pickup. Not the flashy red F650 super truck, which would attract a lot of notice.

Cohen's words about Gillette came back to me. *Its biggest claim to fame is some massive rock formation called Devils Tower,* he'd said. *Which was made famous by that sci-fi movie back in the seventies.*

The bartender at the Royal, Delia, had been wearing a T-shirt when I'd talked with her yesterday morning. A T-shirt with a little green alien and something about close encounters. And with a plastic sticker still on it, indicating the size—as if she hadn't bothered to wash the shirt before pulling it on. The shirt had been exactly the kind of cheap thing you'd pick up at a gift shop. Or an all-night gas station.

I dropped my cigarette on the gravel lot and ground it into the dirt. I touched Clyde's head.

"Let's go, boy. The fat lady hasn't sung yet."

CHAPTER 28

You get to the point where you're just empty. Empty of feelings and thoughts. Of bone and flesh and blood. Empty of hope and despair.
You aren't dead. But you aren't living, either.

—*Sydney Parnell. Personal journal.*

"You're hiding him, Delia," I said from across the bar.

Delia looked even more tired than she had two mornings ago. Her ponytail hung loose and her bangs lay flat with grease. The bags under her eyes had grown to the size of steam trunks. She'd swapped the *Close Encounters* T-shirt for one that read I HATE BEING SEXY, BUT SOMEBODY HAS TO DO IT.

The Royal wasn't any cheerier the second time around. The pool table was empty, and the handful of customers gathered on their stools at the far end of the bar looked like mourners at a wake. Outside, behind the tavern, a dog barked. I'd gone around back to check on it before I walked into the Royal. Figured it was probably the same dog I'd heard on my first visit.

Now, in the low haze of smoke, Clyde's tail flagged. Maybe he picked up on the desolate vibe, too. Or maybe it was the dog out back, barking, barking, barking.

Delia folded the bar rag she'd been using when Clyde and I walked in and shook her head at me. "You think I'd be working double shifts if I had Fred Zolner stashed somewhere like a backup bag of M&M's?"

"I think you're tired because you followed him to Gillette Friday night so he could leave his truck up there. Because that's the kind of person you are. Always ready to help a friend in need. Especially when that friend is single and comes with a pension."

She flushed and rubbed at an invisible bit of dirt. "You're talking crazy."

"Almost seven hundred miles, round-trip. I'm guessing you guys stopped for gas somewhere between here and there. Probably somewhere remote because Bull was worried about being followed. He wouldn't want to take a chance anywhere near Denver." I gave her a heavy look. "Am I going to have to pull every security camera at every gas station between Denver and Gillette?"

She licked her lips. "You want to give me a 'why' to go with your crazy story?"

"What 'why' did he give you, Delia? Did he let you know that by helping him, you might be putting yourself in danger? If he really wanted people to think he was in Gillette, he should have at least pretended to check into a room."

She was blinking rapidly now. "What kind of danger?"

"You familiar with the term *psychopathic killer*?"

She mustered up a derisive snort. "What I think is that you're crazier than he is. Now I need to get back to work."

All at once, I'd had enough. The exhaustion and anger came boiling up, a toxic sludge of fury and frustration. When Delia made a move to walk away, I reached across the bar, grabbed her by the arm, and held tight. Clyde barked, and outside the other dog howled in response.

"If you walk away from me," I said, "I will bust you on code violations. The cigarette smoking. That pool table blocking the back exit.

I'm sure I can find a lot more. The city will shut you down so fast you'll get whiplash."

Her face paled. "You wouldn't."

"Maybe they'll only shut you down until you clean everything up," I said. "But that might turn into forever because you won't be able to make payments without any money coming in. After that, I'll find a reason for the police to search your home. Maybe for some recreational drugs, or a notice of unpaid taxes. I'm sure there's something in your past I can work with, Delia. This is a matter of life and death. Do not," I finished, "fuck with me."

The stricken look on her face almost made me ashamed. But I got over it.

One of the zombies down the bar stirred and blinked in our direction. I leaned in close to Delia in case he had his hearing aids in. "You've seen the news reports about the missing child."

Some life came back into her eyes. "Lucy Davenport? What's that got to do with Bull?"

I released her. "He's got information that might help. Maybe something he doesn't even know he has." It was probably a lie, but I wasn't feeling particular. "So it could be he's hiding from his gambling debts, or from whoever killed the Davenports. I don't care. I just need to ask him some questions."

Down at the other end of the bar, one of the zombies opened his mouth. I was sure I could hear it creaking.

"Delia!" the zombie called. "Another beer if you're done yapping."

"Be right back," she said to me.

I forced myself not to grab her by the throat. I watched as she headed down to refill the guy's glass. Clyde looked up at me to see if we were ready to go. I'm sure he found the stink of the smoke almost unbearable.

"Hang in there, pal," I said.

Delia had finished pouring. Now she slipped her phone out of her pocket. Bingo. Speed dial to Zolner, no doubt. Maybe she'd talk him into meeting with me. If not, I'd start breaking the place apart until she told me where he was.

The conversation was a hot and heavy one, it looked like, with Bull doing most of the talking. But after five or six minutes, she slid the phone back in her pocket and returned to me.

"He's awful pissed," she said.

"Then everything's normal."

"He's in a room in the back."

CHAPTER 29

We all have our price. If we're lucky, we never learn what it is.

—*Sydney Parnell. Personal journal.*

Bull sat on a cot in a storage room behind a makeshift screen of stacked beer cases. The room consisted of a concrete floor and walls, with metal rafters high overhead, all weakly illuminated by the light of a gooseneck lamp. Set high in the wall behind him was a narrow rectangle of window, which even during the day probably let in almost no light.

Bull was fat and fleshy with that gone-to-seed look you find in ex-cops who have no desire to keep up with the physical. His hair was close-cropped, his nose red with broken capillaries. His good eye watched me coldly; he wore a patch over the other. He looked like an immense, bloated spider sitting at the center of a web that was empty of all but the wreckage of dreams.

His head swiveled to follow me as Clyde and I entered the room. He wore shorts and a wife-beater shirt. The room reeked of beer and the overpowering stench of days-old sweat. Beneath that was the sharp tang of Bull's fear, like electrical current running behind a wall.

Beyond the cot was a desk, and on top of that were piles of food wrappers and a small fan laboring to circulate the stale air. Outside the weak halo of the lamp, the room was black as pitch.

Bull's eyes stayed on mine. "You're Jake Parnell's daughter."

"Yes."

I downed Clyde next to the boxes of Pabst and Budweiser. I was carrying a bottle of Rebel Yell and a glass. I walked past Bull to the desk, set down the glass, and opened the bottle.

I showed him the booze. "Am I right in guessing this is your poison of choice? Beer and Rebel Yell?"

"Only liquor I drink. Your dad tell you that?" His eyes followed my hands. He licked his lips. "I remember when you weren't much taller than my knee. You were a spitfire. Heard you stayed that way when you grew up."

Bull chattered, but his uncovered eye remained flat. His accent was as long and drawled as I remembered it. The only thing gentle about him.

I handed him a glass with a finger of bourbon in it.

"Go on," I said. "Drink up."

He gulped the liquor and held the glass up to me. I poured more. He drank that, too. I poured a third glass, but held it out of reach, then snagged the bottle. I spotted a folding chair leaning against the wall, popped it open, and sat down. I put the bottle and the glass of bourbon on the floor.

"Let's consider that a warm-up," I said.

"I don't know what you think I have to do with that little girl." His eye made a sticky click when he lowered and raised the lid. Like a snake's third eyelid. "But I swear I don't know anything about her. I'm not so far gone I wouldn't tell you if I knew."

He struck me as a man who was as far gone as it was possible to go. But still, I believed him.

"How long you been on Hiram's payroll, Bull?"

The change in topic didn't throw him.

"I retired eight years ago," he said.

"Not that payroll. I mean the one that covers your gambling debts. The one that has you doing things that fall a little too far on the wrong side of the line."

He eyeballed the bourbon. I passed him the glass, and he tilted his head back and drank it down in one gulp.

"I don't know what you mean," he said.

"What I think, Bull, is that you're not a bad man. Sure, you've got a bit of a gambling problem, but who doesn't have some sort of addiction? Pills, alcohol, sex. Television or solitaire. There's something that gets to all of us. It's not our fault. We're just wired that way."

He was nodding as I spoke. He'd probably told himself this story a million times. And from what I knew about addiction, it was at least partially true.

"So I can understand your wanting to pick up a little extra work," I said. "A railroad cop's pension doesn't go very far, does it? I mean, I would know."

"It's not enough to support a rat," Bull agreed. "Not if the rat has any ambition."

"And you want more. Of course you do. Hiram's money gives you that chance."

I watched a bead of sweat make its way through the hair on his right leg, the one he'd stretched out in front of him. His scalp shone through the buzz cut.

"What addictions do you think a man like Hiram has?" I asked. "A man who can have whatever he wants? What are his weaknesses?"

Bull smiled. The grin stretched his cheeks and flattened his face into the kind of visage you'd see in a fun house mirror.

"Power and pussy," he said. His good eye glittered. "What any man would take if he could."

I thought of Raya Quinn and Betsy King and Veronica Stern and wondered how many other women Hiram had been with. It was appallingly easy for a man in power to get what he wanted—from other men as well as from women. I wondered about Bull's relationship with Delia. For a single woman with nothing but Medicaid in front of her, even a man like Bull had power. Queasily, I pushed the image out of my mind.

I offered more bourbon, and Bull held out his glass.

I said, "So Hiram's sitting up there in his gold tower, commanding the world. And here you are, hiding like a mouse in a hole, waiting for the cat to find you. You did things for Hiram, followed his orders. And where has it gotten you?"

Bull watched me in silence. I could hear the second hand on my watch tick steadily. Noise from the television set in the bar filtered faintly through the walls. A ball game.

"I'm guessing at heart you're a good man, Bull. And it eats at you, the things Hiram has had you do all these years. Unsavory things. Illegal things. Like sabotaging Lancing Tate's trains."

"I'm not confessing to anything."

"Maybe some of the things he's had you do even led to his family getting hurt and killed. And Lucy going missing. But here's the deal." I leaned forward, resting my forearms on my thighs, projecting an image of caring concern and hoping he wouldn't see through it. "The thing I want you to know, right from the get-go, is that the only person in trouble is Hiram. Not you. Not anyone else he hired to do his dirty work. Hiram gave you orders, paid you a lot of money, and you did what you had to do. And that means I can protect you."

He snorted, swiped at his nose with the bottom of his filthy T-shirt. "I'm not that naive."

"It's not men like you the FBI wants. It's men like Hiram. You're just the means to get to the really big guys, the trophy animals. You testify, and the Feds make all your troubles go away. Gambling debts. Killers like Roman Quinn—" Bull twitched at the mention of Roman.

"Anything that's a problem for you. The Feds can make it go away. Then, if you want, you can start somewhere new. Somewhere fresh."

"Why are you telling me all this? What is it you want? I told you, I don't know anything about the kid."

"I know, Bull. I know you've got nothing to do with what happened to the Davenports. But the money Hiram's been paying you went up recently—the Feds have already looked at your bank account. I think Hiram knew trouble was coming and he paid you to watch his son and his family. You'd done security work for him in the past, right? Now maybe you've lost your edge. Samantha must have seen you or sensed you—she thought you were a stalker." I shrugged. "But so what? Watching out for someone isn't a crime. I'm just wondering if you saw something you don't even know is important."

Bull shrugged. "Hiram got some threatening letters from the guy you just mentioned. Roman Quinn. Hiram said the guy's story was a bunch of bullshit, but he was worried about his family."

"Did he call the police?" I asked, knowing damn well Hiram hadn't. Calling the police would lead to Roman, which would lead to the whole story getting out. Bad timing, when you were competing for billions in federal funding.

"He likes to handle things himself."

"So were you watching the family last Friday? The day this started?"

Bull nodded. "It was a pain in the ass watching them, with everyone all over the place. I kind of moved around, rotated who I was watching. On Friday, I was watching Samantha. Beautiful woman, Samantha."

I'll bet you were watching her. "Where was she?"

"At her studio. I was about to leave, go check on the boys—they were at summer camp. Then Sam up and left by herself, without her assistant, so I followed her."

"Where did she go?"

"That place near where she ended up dying. That old cement factory."

A spatter of rain hit the window high up in the wall. Clyde lifted his head.

"What did she do there?" I asked.

"She just took a lot of pictures. I don't know why. She already had a lot of photos of that place. It's uglier than I am—why would anyone want to look at pictures of it?"

"Where, exactly, did she go in the factory?"

"She parked at the gate, walked in. There's a gap there between the fence and the gate. She went by the beehive things—"

"The kilns?"

He shrugged. "Whatever. I followed her that far, but when she wandered in deeper with her camera, I decided to wait. I was afraid she'd see me. After half an hour or so, she came back out. She went right by me without seeing me, then got in her car and left. I was finishing up my cigarette, so I didn't leave right away. I should have, though."

"A man came," I said, remembering the body outside the kiln and what Cohen had said about the ballistics not matching. "He surprised you."

"You know about that?"

"The gun used on the Davenports was different from the one that killed the man at the factory." I narrowed my eyes at him. "What kind of weapon you have, Bull? Man like you, it'll be high-caliber. When the police find it—"

"It wasn't my fault," Bull said quickly. "Asshole came out of nowhere, running at me. I was already spooked as shit. I had my gun since I was on duty, watching out for that crazy Roman Quinn. I thought it was him. So I brought the gun up fast and shot him."

"In the stomach."

"Right. In the stomach. I didn't have time to get my gun up more than that."

"Did you call an ambulance?"

"Why bother? The guy was dead."

"You have any idea who he was?"

Bull shrugged. "I checked his wallet. Dave something-or-other. He worked for some engineering firm."

Alfred Tate's surveyor. "Clinefeld Engineering?"

"Yeah, maybe."

"Okay, Bull. Not your fault." I kept my hands fisted tight together so I wouldn't choke the life out of him. My heart was racing now. The threads of this case were so knotted I wasn't sure we'd ever unravel all of them. But Bull was pulling at least a few of the threads free.

"What happened after that?"

"I snapped a photo, sent it to Hiram. He said it wasn't him. Wasn't Roman. I started freaking out, figuring I'd just killed some innocent guy. I went home to clean up. But there was a note on my door."

"Go on."

"It said, 'I'm coming for you.' It was signed with an *X*, which is how the letters to Hiram had been signed."

"So you left town," I said.

"Damn straight. I was supposed to wait around for some guy to break in and kill me in my sleep? Hiram didn't pay me that much. Plus there was the guy I shot on accident. I had to figure out what to do about that. I needed time to think."

The disappointment bit deep. I'd been hoping he'd seen Roman go into the Davenports' home, maybe followed Roman and Samantha and Lucy when they left in Samantha's car. I'd been hoping he'd have some clue to Lucy's whereabouts.

I got to my feet and signaled Clyde that he was free to get up. I poured Bull another round. Why not? It might be his last. And we weren't done yet. Not by a long shot.

While Bull had been talking, I'd been doing some mental fact-checking, running down what I knew about the night of Raya's death. And what I knew about Bull.

"Deadman's Crossing," I said. "Does that ring a bell?"

"I remember it. It's an overpass now, but it used to be a grade crossing."

"Do you remember the last accident that occurred there?"

"Not in particular."

"July 1982. A woman named Raya Quinn."

Bull set down the empty glass and pushed the trash around on the desk until he found a metal nail file. He placed the tip beneath his thumbnail and scraped out a wedge of dirt. "I don't remember."

"Young. Beautiful. Had an affair with Hiram and bore him a son. *That* Raya Quinn."

"Oh." A smiled played around his lips. "*That* Raya Quinn."

"You knew about the affair."

He nodded slowly, the eye patch black in the dim light, like an empty socket. "I was the one set things up for him after she caught his eye. She was just a high school kid when it started. Sometimes I picked her up, drove her to a hotel. I'd watch out for them while they were inside doing the nasty. Then I'd drive her back home. Get her something to eat if she was hungry. I did a lot of things for Hiram Davenport back then, just like now. If he needed something, I took care of it."

"But that isn't why you took care of Raya Quinn. You did that for yourself."

Something dark and cold slithered into his eye. "What do you mean? Her death was an accident. You just said so yourself."

"No, Bull, it was definitely murder. At first we—the police and the FBI and I—we thought Raya's killer was either Hiram or Alfred Tate. Hiram because of the affair and the child. He's been paying Raya's mother all this time. I figured it was blood money, but what if it was child support? Hiram's way of absolving himself of any guilt over abandoning his son. He may not be able to pass through the eye of a needle, but he can certainly afford to buy off people here on earth. You with me so far, Bull?"

Bull had gone very still while I spoke. But I sensed the fury building in him, like distant flares of lightning. Clyde sensed it, too. He kept his eyes on Bull.

Bull sneered. "Okay, so maybe Hiram killed her. First and last time he did his own dirty work."

I went on. "We also wondered if it might have been Alfred who killed her because she stole something valuable from him. Something that cost him part of his railroad. That seemed likely, too. But then I got to thinking."

Bull folded his arms, rotated his head back and forth.

"I asked myself who else was there that night. There was the sheriff. Raya's friend, Jill. Hiram and Alfred. And you."

"I was a cop. I was supposed to be there."

"The little I know of Alfred Tate made me think he was too mild mannered to be a killer, so my money was on Hiram. I thought maybe he hired you. As you said, he doesn't like to do his own dirty work."

Bull began tapping his knee with the nail file.

"But I've been thinking while you and I have been having this little conversation."

"You think a lot, don't you?"

"My boss said something to me a couple of days ago. That people used to say you were such an asshole because some woman broke your heart."

He snorted.

"Then I remembered how you used to raise pit bulls. I saw the stake and chain at your house. And tonight, before I came in, I walked around to the back of the bar. And what did I see?"

"So what?"

"A pit bull. There was dog hair on Raya's clothes the night she died. But she didn't own a dog." I was going out on a limb with the hair. But Bull wouldn't know. "Now, I agree that none of that makes you much of a suspect. But there are two things that do."

"Can't wait to hear."

"One is a comment made by one of Raya's friends. She said there was a man who'd taken a fancy to Raya. Used to send her love notes. They called this man Devil Eye. Not *eyes*, Bull. *Eye*. So I know, that's a minor point, too. But then, while I was thinking about all of this, I got to the alcohol they found in her car. An empty bottle of Rebel Yell."

"A lot of people drink it," Bull said.

"Raya didn't drink at all, so that made it odd. Where are you from, Bull?"

"What?"

"What state? I know you're from the South. But what state are you from?"

He spoke before he saw the trap. "Kentucky."

"Did you go home and visit your family that summer, Bull? Or maybe over Christmas? You would have brought back as much Rebel Yell as you could fit in your car, I imagine. Because you couldn't buy that bourbon in Colorado. Not back then."

He threw the nail file at me. I dodged it, heard it clang on the concrete wall. Clyde growled.

"That's what I figured," I said. "You must have gotten tired of driving a beautiful woman around at the beck and call of a man you knew would drop her like a used tissue as soon as he tired of her. What happened that night, Bull? Did you follow her from work? Could you just not take it anymore? Did you offer her love? Marriage? Security?"

Fury swept across Bull's face. He leapt to his feet. "You don't know anything about it."

Clyde gave another growl and shot in front of me. Bull looked at him, then sank back onto the cot.

"Did she laugh at you, Bull? Did she call you ugly, tell you she'd rather die? She would say something like that. Because Raya had big plans. Bigger than anything you could offer her. It's why she named her son Roman. She wanted him to own an empire."

"She was a bitch!" Bull shouted. "A cold, icy bitch. She had it coming. Laughing at me when all I did . . ." He buried his face in his hands. "All I did was offer her everything I had."

"How'd you get her to drink, Bull? Did you tell her you'd hurt her if she refused? But even after the bourbon, she still said no. All the alcohol in the world couldn't make her fall for a man like you. So you wrapped your hands around her neck and choked the life out of her."

Bull was sobbing now.

"Then you took the papers she'd stolen from SFCO and gave them to Hiram. He was probably a little sad about Raya. But it was the papers that mattered. He forgave you."

The door into the storage room clicked open. Delia.

"What's going on in here?" she asked.

Rain began to pound the roof.

I stood, crossed over to Bull, and snapped a pair of handcuffs on him. Then I pulled out my phone and called the Aurora police, told them they'd find a killer handcuffed in the storage room at the Royal Tavern.

"Enjoy that T-shirt," I said to Delia as I walked by. "I think that's all you're ever going to get from Fred Zolner."

CHAPTER 30

I'd been raised on excuses. But the Marine Corps taught
me that excuses don't matter. That excuses—even when pret-
tied up as reasons—are just a way to avoid doing what needs
doing.

—Sydney Parnell. Personal journal.

I sat in my truck with Clyde, thinking of greed and lust and murder
while rain pounded the roof and the interior of the cab grew warm and
moist with our breathing.

To the west, lightning flashed. The storm, coming on hard.

How could we have come so far, learned so much, and still not
know where Roman had hidden Lucy? What were we missing? How
had all of Hiram's gold failed to protect him?

"Gold," I said aloud. All the gold in Roman's room. The gold mining map pinned on his wall.

He's in the ground now. Where he belongs, Esta had said.

I thought of Ennis Parker, the man who'd staked a mining claim
on land now occupied by the cement factory. According to what Tom
O'Hara had learned, Parker had never found much of anything—he'd
been focused on panning for gold, not digging it up.

Parker had died in a gunfight—what if the man who shot him had wanted his claim? What if, after Parker's death, he'd mined that land for gold?

Mines meant tunnels.

With rising excitement, I started the truck. I turned on the defroster and the wipers. Outside, the branches of the ailing poplars flung about in the wind. The neon ROYAL TAVERN sign bled in the rain.

Alfred's family had owned that land long before Hiram bought it. Maybe—I sat up straight—maybe the land was riddled with tunnels, and Alfred Tate knew it. Once he realized Hiram planned to use part of the land as access for his bullet train, the news might have been enough—even after the stroke—for him to order the survey. It wasn't uncommon in Colorado for undocumented mines to open up suddenly beneath structures—buckling roads and swallowing homes. No one could build high-speed tracks on land like that. The results of Alfred's survey would be one more weapon to use against Hiram in their ongoing war.

A gust caught the truck, rocking it. In the seat next to me, Clyde panted.

Hiram would have also ordered a survey—a requirement before he could donate any land to MoMA. No doubt, that survey would have revealed the risk. But Hiram would have done what he always did—used gold. He would have bought off the engineering firm, donated part of the land to MoMA, and gotten a huge tax write-off. It must have seemed like a reasonable risk. The cement factory had remained stable for a century. Who would expect a five-hundred-year flood to occur in one's lifetime?

My hands were shaking as I opened my laptop and pulled up the status reports I'd been receiving on the Davenport case. I found the name and phone number of the specialist the Thornton detectives had brought in to run a GPR scan—a survey of the area using ground-penetrating radar. I dialed. After a few rings, a sleepy voice came on the line.

"This is Special Agent Parnell with Denver Pacific Continental. I'm looking for Jeff Bittman."

A pause. "Speaking."

"Mr. Bittman, I have a couple of questions about when you used the GPR at the Edison Cement factory."

"Your name again?" More alert now.

"Parnell. Sydney Parnell. I'm on the task force searching for Lucy Davenport."

"Okay." There came the faint rustling of sheets. "What do you want to know?"

"You didn't find any anomalies, is that right? No evidence of structures or bodies underground."

"That's right. It's all in my report."

"It's possible that the land was mined for gold many years ago. Wouldn't that have shown up during your scan?"

"It depends. Like I told the Thornton detectives, clay-laden soil is a poor conductor. Add all the rain we've been having, and I got very little ground penetration. In places, no more than a few centimeters. They eventually had me stop. I wasn't hitting anything. But I only covered a small area."

"The area near the kilns, right?" Which were at the opposite end of the complex from the gate someone had cut into the fence. A gate seemingly next to nothing.

"Right," Bittman said. "I was led to believe the killer had been tracked to that location. I did fan out a few hundred feet from there, but the results I got weren't any better. My understanding is they were relying on the K9s through most of the complex."

I thanked him and started to hang up.

"If you really think there are tunnels," he said, "don't go looking for them now. The ground will be saturated from all this rain. If there really is a mine, the tunnels could collapse at any moment."

"Got it," I said, and we disconnected.

I whooped as I put the car in gear and sped out of the parking lot, the rear tires fishtailing as I turned hard onto the street. I refused to think about flooded tunnels and waterlogged earth. We'd come too far for that. "Hang on, Lucy. We're coming."

Clyde's eyes were bright on mine. He'd picked up on my excitement and now he gave a single joyous bark, his ears up and head lifted.

"Game *on*, boy."

I punched Cohen's number. "She's at the cement factory," I said when he picked up. "Lucy is. I'm on my way now."

Cohen didn't ask me how I knew this. "I'll call for backup and meet you there."

"She's in a mine shaft underneath the factory. On the west side, I think. Remember that gate the killer cut? We need engineers in there. We need lights and equipment. The tunnels will be flooding. She doesn't have much time."

"I'm on it," he said. "Meet me at the front gate."

Outside, the night was dark as pitch. I glanced at the clock on the dash. Dawn was still a couple of hours away.

I tried Mac next. When she picked up, the connection crackled with the coming storm, dropping our voices in and out as I tried to explain what I'd learned and where I was going. In the end, I wasn't sure what I managed to communicate before the call dropped and I couldn't raise her again.

Talk to Cohen, I'd told her, hoping at least that much would get through.

By the time I got off the highway and headed toward Potters Road, the rain was coming down hard enough that the wipers couldn't keep up. I had to slow to a crawl to make sure we stayed on the road. Traffic on the highway, heavy no matter the day or time, had been reduced to twenty miles an hour, and most of the time I got through by hitting my lights and siren and driving on the shoulder, weaving in and out of the slowed cars.

Now, on Potters Road, there was no traffic. But we were driving through an ocean.

I imagined it had been this way two nights ago, when Samantha and Lucy Davenport had come this way with Roman Quinn. I pictured Samantha driving, Roman in the seat next to her with a gun, Lucy in the back clutching her sock monkey. Samantha knew where they were going. She had been there just that afternoon. She knew all about the empty, echoing silence of the cement factory, the many places where someone could be held and hurt. The fact that no one would be around to hear or see anything at all.

And so she had driven hard off the road, slamming the Lexus to a stop, screaming at Lucy to run, throwing her keys into the field so that Roman couldn't force them to drive anywhere else. Maybe she thought she could keep the killer busy while her daughter escaped into the darkness.

The lights from the police barricade pulsed in the rain. I eased to a stop, rolled down the window, and showed my badge to the officer. I explained what I was doing, told him that more police were on their way, and asked him to direct them to the cement factory.

"It'll be flooding out there near the river," he said, water dripping off the brim of his cap.

"Why I'm in a hurry."

He nodded and pulled one of the sawhorses out of the way. A few minutes later, I went past the place where Samantha had driven off the road. The pullout was awash in mud, the crime scene tape snapping hard in the lashing wind. As I went by, a piece of tape broke free and slapped into the windshield, startling me and obscuring my vision before the wind lifted it free again.

Clyde barked when the tape hit, a hard, savage sound.

The gate into the factory was open when we got there, the chain and padlock hanging free. The gate swung in the wind, its metal bars banging repeatedly against the fence with a stiff clang. I braked and we eased through, the tires bouncing as the asphalt ended and the mud and weeds began. I skewed the steering wheel right, heading toward the gate Roman had cut into the fence. I drove fast, the rear tires fishtailing, weeds slapping into the headlights and disappearing under the wheels.

For the first time, I allowed myself to wonder what the tunnels looked like. Was rainwater seeping in, turning the clay walls into a slick slime?

The rain backed off a bit, and I thought I saw a light ahead. I slowed and tried to raise Cohen on my phone, but the storm must have knocked out a tower or maybe the base station—I had no service at all. I picked up speed again, the truck bouncing violently on the rough ground. There was no question of waiting for the police. Roman had brought Lucy here, I was sure of it. And probably Hiram, too, for whatever ugly thing Roman had planned for them.

I turned between warehouses. There it was again, a faint light at the far end of the building on my left. I killed my own lights and rolled forward, confident that the roar of the storm would drown our approach should anyone be listening.

A black Mercedes SUV was parked in the alley formed by the buildings, blocking any further progress. The headlights were off, and I could see no movement inside. I parked my vehicle at the mouth of the alley where it would be visible to the arriving cops and killed the engine. I went to try Cohen a final time but couldn't get a signal. I dropped my phone into an inside pocket of my rain jacket.

I climbed over my truck's console and planted my knees in the back seat, reaching into the rear of the car where I kept a locked metal box filled with extra equipment. I opened it and selected a pair of night-vision goggles, a headlamp, a knife, and a can of Silly String. The knife, headlamp, and goggles were standard-issue for a railway cop. The Silly String was not.

I hung the goggles and a headlamp around my neck and tucked them in my jacket, and put the knife and the Silly String in a cargo pocket of my uniform pants.

Back in the front seat, I clipped Clyde's lead onto his harness. A flare of lightning revealed him staring out the front window. He was as tense and eager as I was.

"Let's go find Lucy," I said.

I turned off the Ford's interior light and opened the door as a gust of wind rocked the truck.

"And forget embracing the suck, Clyde. We're going to kick its ass."

CHAPTER 31

—Listen up, recruits. Some of you are hardwired to be heroes. Dump that. In Iraq, trying to play hero will get you killed so fast you'll pass your coffin going out almost before you're in-country.

—Sir, this recruit would like to know what to do if he's the only thing standing between his platoon and the bad guys.

—In that case, you put yourself forward. That's not being a hero. That's being a Marine.

—Classroom, USMC Leadership, Parris Island.

Hail mixed with the rain. It hammered the cars and stung my exposed skin like a thousand tiny whips. The heart of the storm seemed to be right above us. Lightning flashed and sizzled all around, each bolt followed almost instantly by the deafening crack of thunder.

I held tight to Clyde's lead as he and I darted between the buildings and came to a stop by the Mercedes SUV. I recognized the plate number—the vehicle belonged to Hiram. A BOLO had gone out hours earlier when Hiram's guard had been found shot dead. Clyde and I crouched next to the Mercedes and I turned a careful eye on my partner, worried about his reaction to the noise of the storm. He glanced at me, then leaned forward again—ears up, head erect, focused on the mission.

"What are we waiting on?" he seemed to ask.

Good boy.

A faint light shone through the windows set high on the building on our left. I strained to hear anything above the storm, but the roar of the hail drowned out everything else. I rose high enough to shine my headlamp into the vehicle. The front seat was empty save for a litter of fast-food wrappers on the floor. The rear driver's side door was slightly ajar, and my light picked out the slackened features of another one of Hiram's bodyguards. Jeff, I remembered. He sat as if napping, his shoulders relaxed, his head tilted back against the seat. A small round hole showed darkly between his blank eyes. I touched my hand briefly to my heart, as I did for all the dead, and was about to turn away when I spotted a man's necktie on the seat next to him. Hoping it belonged to Hiram, and that Jeff's presence meant Roman had brought Hiram here, I eased open the door and grabbed it, tucking it inside my jacket to keep it dry. Clyde would be able to catch Hiram's scent from it.

Another blaze of lightning, then more darkness. The light was gone from the building, which meant either we'd been detected, or we weren't far behind Roman and Hiram. I signaled Clyde with a touch to his shoulder and we maneuvered past the SUV and pressed against the ancient bricks of the warehouse, watching for movement. When nothing stirred, we moved along the wall, looking for an opening.

Fifteen feet on, we reached a doorway, and I halted Clyde. The door itself was long gone. I snugged the night-vision goggles into place and peered around the concrete jamb.

Beyond the doorway, a vast, empty room—made green by the goggles—stretched ahead of us and to the right. A stone-paved floor and high windows gave the place the feel of an ancient prison. I signaled Clyde and we eased through the doorway and hunkered down just inside. I took another look around, straining my ears for any sound. In here, the rain was a muffled thrumming, like distant drums. Nothing moved.

Hoping that somewhere nearby lay an entrance to a mining shaft, I pulled out the necktie and gave Clyde a hit.

"Seek!" I said softly.

Clyde took off, with me right behind. Forty feet into the room, he slowed and then stopped, his nose to the floor where a slight disturbance turned it uneven—a stone slab lay askew from the others. Beneath it, the goggles revealed a darker shade of green, as if the stone concealed an opening. Clyde's nostrils flared as he breathed in the scent, then he raised his head and looked to me for guidance.

I squatted next to him, listened for a moment, then knelt and pressed one eye to the crack. The goggles showed a long shaft that dropped into the ground before making a ninety-degree turn. An aluminum ladder, affixed to wooden rails, led downward. I rose back to a squat and lifted the thin slab away from the opening, careful not to let the stone scrape against the floor.

With the stone gone, cool, moist air wafted upward. It smelled of dirt and rotting vegetation and old roots. And another smell—the sludge and stir of the dark depths of the Platte River.

I closed my eyes. Darkness and cramped spaces and rising water. I swallowed the bile that rose in my throat and opened my eyes. I gave Clyde another hit on the tie. He drew in a deep breath and circled the opening, wagging his tail.

"Okay, boy," I whispered. "Hold on."

I removed the can of Silly String and sprayed a large cluster of brightly colored strands near the entrance to mark our passage. Then I unclipped Clyde's lead, rolled onto my stomach, and lowered myself until my feet hit the first rung of the ladder. I went down two more rungs, then signaled for Clyde to follow. This was a routine he knew well. He dropped onto his own belly and shimmied his rear over the edge.

When I was a kid, my neighbor had a German shepherd that could climb up and down ladders. Going up was easy. Coming down, the dog always put me in mind of an old man, gingerly feeling his way back to earth, his rear paws sliding on the aluminum rungs, his head swiveling from side to side as he picked his way down.

Clyde was more sure-footed. He'd practiced this maneuver with his new trainer many times, starting with a nearly horizontal ladder that Avi had gradually made steeper. Now, as Clyde made his way down, I stayed right below him, guiding his feet, ready to catch him if he slipped.

The ladder ended in a cramped space. A man-height tunnel led off to the left and the right, in opposite directions. Clyde jumped from the final rung, and I clipped on his lead, then gave him another hit on Hiram's tie.

In the dark, guided only by scent, Clyde turned into the western tunnel, heading away from the cement factory. I marked our path with more Silly String and followed.

The tunnel was an engineering marvel. Maybe it had begun as nothing more than a narrow passage carved out by Ennis Parker or another man in the search for gold. But at some point someone, presumably Roman, had improved upon it.

The tunnel was four feet wide, more than five feet high, and buttressed every ten feet by wooden support beams. The path was flat and well groomed. Lanterns hung at regular intervals, although none were lit. Despite the dark, Clyde walked fast, with confidence. The only sounds were his breathing and mine. And a faint, faraway whisper—the distant murmur of water.

My goggles picked out walls that shone with damp. Patches of moisture gleamed on the floor.

Three minutes deeper into the tunnel, Clyde stopped, his ears up, his posture rigid. Then he lay down. Behind him, I froze, my breath trapped as my heart tried to rise into my throat.

Only three things would make Clyde alert in this manner: contraband, trespassers, and explosives. Since we were alone in the tunnel and we weren't searching a train for contraband, that left only one option.

A bomb.

I took an involuntary step backward as my mind ran down a list in a flash, like a flame licking along a fuse. Pipe bombs, suitcase bombs, barrel bombs, land mines. Bouncing bombs, pressure-cooker bombs, IEDs. All the different explosives that had torn humans apart since the invention of gunpowder.

A gibbering part of my brain begged me to turn and run. Away from bombs and water-weakened tunnels and a psychopathic killer. To get myself and my partner out of there and back up to solid ground and the sweet, life-giving rush of fresh air.

Behind me, the Six stirred, a rustling felt rather than heard. Here to witness my end.

Then a voice in my ear. The Sir.

Steady, he said. *We're still good.*

I took a deep breath and forced myself to study the tunnel, looking for signs of explosives. Ten feet along, on the right-hand side of the path, a small heap of dirt and rock disrupted the otherwise clean space. The debris looked innocent—a normal by-product of clearing and maintaining the tunnel.

I swallowed. My mouth was dry and my heart felt like it was trying to flee without me.

But I'd expected this. More than expected it. I'd known Roman would protect his tunnels in the same way he'd guarded the kiln. And since bomb makers tend to specialize, I'd also known he'd probably use the same kind of detonator. I pulled the can of Silly String from my pocket and sprayed a long stream into the seemingly empty space ahead of us.

In Iraq, soldiers had come to rely on this child's toy as an effective way to find a bomb's trip wire. As it fell to the ground, the sticky material would cling to the wire and show its location. A perfect reveal without being heavy enough to trigger the bomb.

But now, the plastic strands fell uselessly to the ground. I inched forward and sprayed again. This time the ten-foot-long strands caught on an invisible wire a foot above the ground. The threads hung like Christmas tree tinsel, swaying gently in a faint draft.

I heard a moan, realized it was mine.

Beside me in the tunnel the Sir said, *You're scared. That's okay. Keeps you sharp.*

I stared at the trip wire then set my jaw and drew back my shoulders. In Iraq, I'd handled dead bodies until my fingers stopped working and my legs gave way and the stench of the dead stayed with me like my own skin. I'd been spit on, shot at, blown up. I'd brought the dead back with me from Iraq and added a few more. I'd done so because I'd sworn to protect my country.

And so what? Marines were tough. First in, last out. America's conscience and its might.

"What do you say, partner?" I whispered.

Clyde lay still, waiting for a signal from me that he could rise. Waiting for me to get my act together.

His tail thumped. "Game on," he was saying.

I signaled him to stand, then I squatted next to him, slid my hands under his belly like a forklift, and hugged him tight. Clyde stayed quiet. I lifted my right foot high over the trip wire, brought it down on the other side, followed through with my left.

Nothing went boom. The world stayed in place. The Silly String still swayed softly, a warning for anyone who followed.

I set Clyde back on the ground and released my breath.

"Seek," I said softly, and off he went.

◆ ◆ ◆

At some point, the tunnel narrowed and the ceiling lowered, reducing me to a hunched walk. The patches of moisture on the ground turned into puddles; my boots became tacky with wet clay, and Clyde's paws built up a scrim of mud. Whenever we passed other tunnels that yawned into the dark, I marked our route. As we went along, the trail we followed began to glow in my mind—I recalled one of the maps Roman had pinned in his room and recognized the route. The turns were leading us toward the river.

By now, up above, Cohen and other police would have arrived. They would have found my truck and the Mercedes, and were probably making their way into the building.

But down in this tomb, I could hear nothing except my own breath and Clyde's, and the persistent murmur of water.

The tunnel made an almost-ninety-degree turn to the right. I halted Clyde, cleared the corner, then motioned him forward. As soon as we rounded the corner, the sound of voices drifted toward us from the tunnel ahead.

I halted Clyde again and lowered my goggles. Up ahead, a light shone. The tunnel widened before it made another ninety-degree turn, this one thirty feet ahead and to the left. Clyde and I were in a blind pocket between the two ninety-degree turns. I looked around for a camera or motion detector, but the passageway lay empty. The double-blind was a dubious defense strategy on Roman's part. There was no way for us to see him—but also no way for him to see us. I signaled Clyde to sit, then hunkered down beside him, weapon drawn, working to sort out the voices.

Water pooled around our feet.

"I set up a trust for your expenses," said a man. "And every month I sent enough money to your grandmother to take care of you. To pay for your college, to buy you whatever you needed."

Hiram. His voice was steady—neither defeated nor defiant. The voice of a man negotiating a deal in the boardroom. "You had everything that you could—"

"Blood money!" The second voice came harsh. "She's an *addict*. A *junkie*. We barely had enough to live on. It was like a fucking *prison* being out there with her. She snorted your blood money. Injected it. Swallowed it."

Jack Hurley, aka Roman Quinn.

"All these years you've had to tell me," he went on. "To claim me as your son. All these goddamn years, and you never once acknowledged me."

Clyde and I crept closer. Two feet. Three feet. My boots made a splashing sound, and I looked down. There was an inch of water on the ground.

"Your grandmother didn't want me to—"

"Shut up."

Four feet. Six. Ten. Somewhere there was a faint clanging, like metal on metal. But I couldn't tell if the sound came from ahead or behind.

"None of that matters," Roman said. "I survived. But you murdered my *mother*."

"No, Roman. I swear. I didn't hurt her."

Clyde stopped. His nose came up as he sampled the air. Then he alerted by sitting down.

Another bomb. Sweet Jesus.

"She was helping me," Hiram said. "Why would I hurt her? She was—"

There came the ugly wet slap of something hard striking flesh, and Hiram went silent. Then another sound, both gut-wrenching and sweeter than anything I'd ever heard.

A child. Crying.

I reached with my left hand for the Silly String, my eyes flicking from the tunnel for an instant. I swore softly when the can caught against the pocket flap.

Clyde growled, and I whipped my head up.

"Freeze," said Roman, "or I will blow out your fucking brains."

I stopped. Clyde came half out of his alert.

"Stay," I said to him. *"Bleib."*

He sank back down.

Leaving my left hand on the can of spray, I raised my eyes.

Roman stood at the corner. He had his left eye closed and was watching me down the barrel of a .45.

"You are persistent," he said.

"The cops are right behind me."

He shrugged and lowered the pistol slightly. "It doesn't matter. I'm almost done here."

"Give me Lucy."

"Move and I'll shoot the dog first. Payback. Then you."

My own weapon was pointed down and to the right, where I'd let my hand drift as I reached for the spray. And yet, I considered.

"Put your gun on the ground," he said. "And let me see your hands."

"Roman," I said, softly. "I'm just here for the girl."

"Now!" he shouted.

I dropped it. It made a small splash when it landed.

"Kick it toward me." When I gave it a small nudge, he said, "Farther."

The gun skidded along the ground and landed near Roman's feet.

"Let me take Lucy," I said.

He shook his head. "When I am finished, there will be nothing left in this world that is his."

"Except you."

"I'll die with them. One big, unhappy family, finally all together. That's why I took her. So Hiram can watch her die."

"If that's what you want, why didn't you go back and finish the job with Ben? I can't imagine you'd let a single cop stop you."

"No need. If he survives, he'll know what his family suffered." Roman's smile didn't come within shouting distance of his eyes. "And by now, I suspect you know a little about Ben Davenport. He'll finish the job himself. And then we'll all be in hell together."

Behind me, in the tunnel, came another faint noise. I coughed, hoping to cover the sound of any approaching cavalry. Clyde was wound as tight as a compressed spring, but he didn't even twitch an ear.

"Hiram didn't kill your mother, Roman. I have a confession from the murderer."

He grinned at me. "Nice try."

"Your mother was murdered by a railway cop," I said. "Fred Zolner. You know Zolner. You paid him a visit, hoping he could tell you something about what happened that night. He was there at the start of the affair. He was the one who drove your mother to see your father. All those hours together in the car. He fell in love with her."

"Not bad," Roman said. "How long did it take you to think up that story?"

"The night she died was the night Zolner decided to tell her how he felt. He thought she'd give up your father for a man who truly loved her. But after he poured out his heart to her, she rejected him. Laughed at him. Called him Devil Eye. And he strangled her for it."

Roman's eyes flicked toward the room on his right, maybe looking to read something in Hiram's face.

I dropped my hand to reach for the Silly String.

His gaze snapped back. "Don't."

I lifted my hand again. "I just talked to him an hour ago. He's been hiding from you at the Royal Tavern. Do you remember him from when you were a child? He sent your mother love letters."

The first glint of uncertainty showed in Roman's eyes.

Far away, the earth groaned. Closer by, a wooden timber creaked. My heartbeat was so loud in my ears I was amazed I could hear anything else.

"Your mother and her friend used to laugh about that," I said, my words racing out in a rapid staccato. "They called him Devil Eye because he has only one good eye."

Roman shook his head. "Thin, Parnell."

"He confessed."

"So you say."

"He drank Rebel Yell," I went on. I inched to my left as if I were jittery, drawing his gaze, trying to leave room for whoever was coming up behind us. "He forced your mom to drink some that night. Hoping if she was drunk she'd change her mind. He left the bottle in her car. You can look at the autopsy report."

"I read the page from Alfred Tate's journal," Roman said. "He saw Hiram there."

I had him. He was listening because he wanted to believe. *Needed* to believe that his father hadn't killed his mother.

"Alfred was suspicious," I said. "But only that. He knew about the affair and he knew about you. He thought your father wanted your mother out of the way. But in fact, she was helping him. She was the one who gave him what he needed to take away part of Alfred's railroad. It was much more than an affair." Just like when talking to the press, it was okay to lie to murderers. "They loved each other, Roman."

From the tunnel behind me came a faint splash.

"You went after the wrong man," I said. "The wrong family. Let's get out of here before the tunnels collapse. Before you have more blood on your hands."

A shadow loomed behind Roman. Hiram, pale and wide-eyed, blood pouring from a wound on his head. He held a hammer, and now he swung it at Roman.

I didn't wait to see what happened. I jerked the can free of my pocket and sprayed, looking for the trip wire. Clyde was quivering in frustration.

Up ahead, there came sounds of a struggle, and someone shouted in rage. I didn't know if it was Hiram or Roman.

The string caught on the wire, and it popped into view.

I looked up and saw that Roman was half-turned away from me, standing over a prone Hiram. Hiram's face was slicked with blood and his lips were drawn back in a grimace.

I kept my gaze on the trip wire as I lifted Clyde and we stepped over. I was muttering, "Please God, please God," under my breath, praying that Hiram would keep Roman's attention long enough for Clyde and me to reach them.

But as I brought my second foot down, Roman spun in our direction, the .45 up.

"Bad mistake," he said.

And then, behind me, Mac said, "Get down."

I dropped, still clutching Clyde. Water soaked my clothes, his fur.

Mac's shot caught Roman high in his left shoulder. He shrieked—a cry that rattled my eardrums—and dropped his gun. It skimmed away in the rising water and fetched up against the wall as Roman sank to one knee.

Mac stepped fully into the corridor behind me.

"Hands up!" she yelled.

Roman lifted his head. His face was spattered with blood—his or Hiram's or both. Beyond him, Hiram lay unmoving.

Somewhere deep in the earth, a great rumbling built. From far away came a series of cracks that sounded like tree trunks snapping, then an oddly muffled *whump*.

Roman sank to all fours, his elbows bent, his good hand grappling for support. "Can't . . . ," he said weakly. "Hurts."

I eased off Clyde. *"Fass!"*

But even as Clyde leapt, Roman's groping hand found my gun where it lay near his knee. Clyde was in midair when the gun went off. The sound boomed in the small space.

Then Clyde slammed into Roman, and the two of them tumbled backward.

I ran after Clyde. He had his jaws clamped around Roman's arm. Roman was awake, but he didn't move or make a single sound. His eyes followed me as I kicked the .45 farther out of his reach and grabbed my gun where he'd dropped it.

"Don't move," I told him. "The more you struggle, the harder he'll bite."

I wanted to check Clyde. I wanted to fall on my knees and run my hands over him, see if Roman's shot had struck him.

Instead, I ran past him and Roman and Hiram, rounded the corner, and skidded to a halt in a small room.

Light came from a lantern set on a barrel. There were two cots. A shelf stacked with food. A pair of shovels propped in the corner. A table covered with the makings of bombs. On the other side of the room, a small opening led to what appeared to be another tunnel, this one narrow and maybe five feet off the ground.

Nothing of Lucy.

"Lucy? Where are you, honey? You're safe now."

The ground shook for a second or two. One of the shovels teetered and crashed. Then everything went very, very quiet.

My eyes scanned the room again. On one of the cots, the huddle of blankets gave a slight twitch.

"Lucy!"

I dropped next to the cot and, terrified at what I might find, drew back the blanket.

I knew her face. Had held it constantly in my mind, seen it in my dreams. The lively brown eyes, the soft brown hair.

But now Lucy's face was rigid with terror, her eyes wide and vacant. When I reached a hand toward her, she flinched.

"Lucy," I said. "My name is Sydney. I'm going to take you to your dad."

She blinked. "My daddy is dead."

"No, Lucy, he's very much alive." Willing it to still be true. "He was hurt, but now he's waiting for you."

She shook her head. "I saw him."

I remembered the picture she'd drawn, the one in Ben's desk. "He told me to tell you something. He said, 'You have to be brave, Lucy Goose.'"

Her eyes came into focus, met mine. A small bit of the horror there was replaced with hope. "He told you that?"

"Cross my heart."

"It's wrong to lie. My mommy said so."

"No lie, Lucy. Let's go see him."

She held out her arms and I scooped her up and carried her back toward the tunnel. I paused next to Hiram, took one look at his wide, staring eyes, and stepped over him and out of the room.

Clyde had released Roman's arm but sat close. My partner looked unhurt. Roman had fallen onto his back when Clyde hit him, and now he lay in an unmoving, broken sprawl. His eyes were wide and empty, his mouth open. Maybe Mac's shot had nicked his heart and he'd bled out. One could always hope.

"Mac!" I called.

Silence.

I set Lucy down next to Clyde and turned her away from the body of her half uncle.

"Lucy, this is my partner, Clyde. I want you to wait with him. I have to go back down the tunnel and get one more person. Wait here, okay? There's a bomb, so you have to stay very, very still. Wait with Clyde and don't move. Can you be brave again?"

Her eyes widened in her pale face, but she nodded.

"*Pass auf,*" I said to Clyde. Guard.

I hurried down the tunnel, stepping over the trip wire. The light was faint here, and I pulled my goggles back over my eyes. The world came greenly into view.

Mac sat with her back to the wall, her legs stretched in front of her. Her face was white and still. A chunk of flesh was missing out of her right leg, halfway between her knee and her hip. She'd removed her belt and yanked it tight around her thigh as a tourniquet.

Beyond her, the tunnel ended in a pile of rubble. And from beyond that came the sound of water rushing.

"Mac?" I crouched next to her. "Mac!"

She opened her eyes. "Lucy?"

"She's waiting. We have to get out of here."

She smiled. "Roman?"

"Dead. Now get on your feet!"

"We're trapped," she said. "The water . . ."

"There's another tunnel. Get up!"

She pressed her palms against the ground, bent her good leg, and pushed. I grabbed her beneath her arms and hauled her to her feet.

She screamed when her bad leg touched the ground.

I slung her arm across my shoulders, and we hobbled along the tunnel. At the trip wire, I lifted her over and we shuffled on toward Lucy and Clyde. I helped Mac lean against the wall, then bent to pick up Lucy.

The four of us rounded the corner past Hiram's body, which was already half-submerged by the rising water. We sloshed our way across the room to the mouth of the tunnel. I shone my light down the passageway—it disappeared into the distance, but a faint breeze trickled my face. Of course Roman would have another way out.

"It leads to air," I said to the others. "But it's narrow. We'll have to crawl." I looked at Mac. "Can you manage?"

"I'm not liver pâté," she said.

"No," I said. "You most definitely are not."

I fitted my headlamp on Lucy, then hoisted Clyde into the tunnel, followed by Lucy. Mac insisted on going last.

"If you stop, you'll force me to come back for you," I said.

"I won't stop."

I scrabbled after Lucy, then heard Mac's sharp intake of breath as she lifted herself in after me.

I tried to determine if we were moving toward or away from the river, tried to picture where the tunnel would emerge into the dawning day—if indeed it did. I tried not to think of the four of us getting trapped here as the water rose; tried not to think of Cohen or anyone else who might have been caught in the tunnel behind us when it gave way.

Every ten yards or so, Lucy would stop, and then Clyde would stop as well. I could hear him waiting up ahead, panting in the moist coolness. Behind me, Mac's breaths came in ragged gasps.

Each time Lucy stopped, I urged her on. "Follow the dog, Lucy Goose. He'll take you home."

And each time, after a minute or two, she'd start up again.

I don't know how much time passed—minutes or hours. But then Lucy stopped again, and before I could urge her forward, she said, "There's daylight."

I pushed off my goggles and squinted past her. Wan, gray light trickled into the passageway, and with it came the faint scents of rain and grass.

"Keep going, Lucy. Keep going. We're almost there."

The tunnel widened, then ended sharply in a small space that led to a vertical shaft. Clyde squirmed free of the tunnel, and Lucy followed him. The smells of rain and grass grew stronger, overriding the stink of wet earth. A ladder, a twin to the tunnel beneath the cement factory, led to the surface.

And, high above, through the round opening, a pearl-gray disc shone—the coming dawn.

TWO WEEKS LATER

CHAPTER 32

Every person's life is a struggle against a world filled with resistance. That resistance may defeat us or warp us or crush us.

But sometimes, we find a strength we didn't know we had. And with that newly recognized strength, we move past the hard times. And we become a little stronger for the next round.

—Sydney Parnell. Personal journal.

The funeral for Samantha Davenport and her two sons was held on a brilliant Colorado afternoon in August—a day that was sunny, dry, and warm. The only clouds were high and thin—wisps of cotton stretched across the azure blue. The rains, after causing record flooding across Colorado, had moved on. The ground had responded to the unprecedented moisture with a luxurious tide of green that spread across lawns and parks and open spaces. Denver looked like a city reborn.

At the service, Clyde and I stood close together in the shade of a copse of trees, watching from a distance as the mourners gathered by the graves. Neither of us were ready to be so near the dead. I'd already said what I needed to say to Ben. And to Lucy. We'd come to pay our respects, but no one needed to know we were there.

Even across the roll of green lawn, I could make out the tall figure of Ben Davenport, his face pale but his bearing military erect. He wore his army dress blues uniform and held a cane he refused to lean on.

The nurses told me that he had awoken in the early morning hours while we were hunting for Lucy. It was as if her need for him had reached the place where he dreamed. As if he knew how much she would need him when she returned home.

As if God knew exactly what the two of them could handle and had given them that much and no more.

The doctors said it would take months of therapy for Ben to relearn skills he'd once taken for granted. But the brain was amazingly elastic, and he was expected to make a good recovery. Probably he would never be quite as he had been, the doctors said. He needed to be prepared for that. But he'd been a different man since the war, anyway. I was confident that Ben wasn't someone you should underestimate. Whatever the future held, he would adapt.

And maybe the same could be said for Lucy, who, while physically unharmed, had memories no one should carry. But I didn't underestimate her, either.

She stood beside him now, dressed in a pink dress and white sweater, her hair neatly braided. Her hand was in his, and their eyes sought each other continually during the service. At some point, Ben loosed her hand to wrap his arm around her shoulders. She leaned into him.

They had each other.

My hand slipped into my pocket and—as I had done so many times—I ran my thumb across the photo of the Iraqi boy, Malik. We should never quit fighting for what we believe in. Or what we love.

Beside me, Clyde wagged his tail, and I turned to see Mac McConnell approaching across the grass. The bullet from Roman's gun had taken out a chunk of muscle and resulted in copious blood loss from a lacerated femoral vein. The wound had then become infected after being dragged through the mud. Mac had undergone immediate surgery and was still in physical therapy. But she'd discharged herself early from the hospital and refused the wheelchair ride to the car, insisting that recovery would come faster if she didn't baby the leg. The doctors told her she was apt to do more harm than good if she wasn't careful. She waved them off and laughed, and now there was another reason for people to call her Mad Mac.

"It's good to finally see the sky again," she said.

"I wasn't sure we would."

We'd talked about those hours we'd spent under the ground. Mac had gotten my message loud and clear, but it had taken her a while to get to the cement factory. She still beat Cohen and most of the police there. The young officer who arrived before she did had been content to stand guard at the entrance to the mining shaft while she descended. *Officer Ketz*, she'd told me later, *is a boy who needs to grow bigger britches.*

Ketz was the officer who'd arrived at the accident when all of this started. Maybe getting knocked down a peg or two wouldn't be all bad. He'd rebound.

Mac's story was straightforward. She'd followed the trail I'd marked with the Silly String and been—she noted drily—particularly appreciative of the strands hanging off the trip wires. But the water had been rising fast as she went through the tunnel, and she'd known we had little chance of returning that way. She'd come after me anyway. *You really are crazy,* I'd told her. *Crazy enough,* she'd responded, *that God has learned not to argue.*

When the earth collapsed, only one cop had been in the tunnel. Detective Michael Cohen. He'd descended the ladder and was thirty feet in when the walls started to buckle. He'd scrambled back to the ladder and barely made it out, then spent the next two hours yelling at the engineers to find another way in. When we finally emerged, Cohen's level of enthusiasm for us was as great as Clyde's at seeing him—it was like being around a pair of two-year-olds.

Now I smiled at Mac as she propped herself against a tree and removed her sunglasses. The black eye was a faded yellow, almost gone.

"Smart move," she said, "filing your application. You'll make a great FBI agent."

"I started the process, Mac. But I'm still not sure."

She waved a dismissive hand. "It'll be great."

I didn't tell her that I'd also been approached by Cohen's boss, Lieutenant Engel, who thought I'd make a solid addition to Major Crimes. He wanted me to make a lateral move from railroads to Denver PD. Six months with a training officer would teach me everything I needed to know about rules and forms and regulations. Then I'd be invited to join the Homicide/Robbery Bureau because of my "talent and experience." The golden girl on the fast track.

Mauer and Cohen thought it was a great idea. I'd told Cohen he'd be sick of me by the end of the first day. But I promised to think about it.

"I'm meeting a few people at Joe's Tavern," Mac said. "Why don't you join us there?"

"You claiming territory on my turf?"

"Why not, when it's good turf? Meet us there in thirty."

But I shook my head. "I'm heading over to the cement factory."

"Why the hell would you want to do that?"

"You aren't the only crazy one. I feel a need to say my good-byes."

She nodded as if she understood. But neither of us made a move to leave.

At the graveside, a winch was lowering Samantha's casket. Ben and Lucy watched stoically, but even at this distance I could see their tears.

"We have a duty to others," Mac said.

I nodded.

"But we also," she went on, "have a responsibility to ourselves."

"You going to lecture me about something?"

"No lecture. Just a piece of advice."

I shot her a look. "Is this about honor making a crappy shield?"

"Forgive yourself, Sydney. I know you think you should have found Lucy sooner. That you should have saved Hiram."

"I don't. I know I couldn't have—"

"Don't bullshit me."

I fell silent because she was right. I'd talked to the chaplain about it at my counseling sessions. As Hayes had said, self-forgiveness was the first step on my marathon. But it was a struggle. I'd been blaming myself for pretty much everything since my father left and my mother started drinking. It's what kids do. And even once you grow up, it's hard to sell yourself a different line.

"I'm working on it," I said finally. Because I had a plan. A way to mitigate at least some of the guilt.

"That's good then," Mac said. "I'll look for you at Joe's Tavern."

"Sure," I said.

After Mac left, Clyde and I made our way to the truck. Clyde hopped in beside me and I drove slowly through the parking lot and away from the cemetery, my mind on the last two weeks and all the fallout from the Davenport case.

Fred "Bull" Zolner had been arrested and charged with the murder of Raya Quinn. He faced a second charge in the death of David Monroe, the engineer from Clinefeld. He'd also been accused of committing acts of sabotage against SFCO. In regard to the latter charge, the prosecuting attorneys had opened an investigation looking into other questionable activities related to Zolner, Hiram, and DPC.

From what I'd read in the paper, it looked to be a long list.

Lancing Tate never admitted to his role in igniting the fire in Roman Quinn that resulted in the deaths of eleven people, including Veronica Stern's unborn child. Lancing publicly expressed his dismay over the terrible fate that had befallen his fellow railroad titan, then went silent on the entire affair. But three days after the story broke, he announced he was starting a charity to support orphanages and provide for foster care in rural communities.

His form of atonement, I guessed. Not for me to decide if it was enough.

As for the bullet train, after all the feuding between the Tates and Hiram Davenport, the funding fell to a congressional axe. White elephant or savior, there would be no Gold Mine Express to make the West great again. Not in the foreseeable future.

How the mighty had fallen.

Esta never fully recovered from the torture she'd endured at the hands of her grandson. Or maybe the drugs had already done so much damage that the torture was just the final straw. She was institutionalized at a home in Thornton for the mentally disturbed, not far from where her grandson murdered Samantha.

Roman's body was never recovered. Hundreds of man-hours unearthed Hiram's corpse. But Roman had disappeared under tons of mud and sludge. Or maybe his body had been swept into the South Platte and would emerge someday in the future, like a ghastly Jack-in-the-box.

My feelings about him were complicated. He'd murdered nine people that we knew about. And he'd done so in horrific ways. There could be no earthly forgiveness for him—at least, not on my part. But I couldn't help but wonder what kind of man he might have been if he'd grown up in a stable home, surrounded by family and friends and classmates. All the energy he'd put into assuming a false identity, into worming his way into the Davenports' lives just so he could destroy them, all of that could have gone into his photography, which showed real talent. Or into his relationship with the woman who'd been sitting in his Jeep. Maybe instead of Roman Quinn, he would have been the congenial, buoyant Jack Hurley he'd pretended to be.

We would, of course, never know. The chaplain, Hayes, told me that some forms of mental illness lie hidden like bombs—they can remain forever dormant or be detonated by a single wrong step.

The sun was lowering when I parked at the gate leading to the Edison Cement factory. Clyde and I got out and slid through the gap between the fence and the gate. We picked our way to the wall where we'd stood after the bomb went off that first morning. I glanced around, half expecting to see the Sir or to catch a glimpse of the Six. But the only sound was the wind through the ruins, and only the grasses moved, stirring in the breeze.

After the flooding in the tunnels, the earth had collapsed under many of the structures. An edifice that had lasted for decades and been fought over by titans had been brought to ruin by nature. The warehouses were falling, the surviving kilns crumbling, two of the three silos showed immense fissures. Every structure would have to be brought down, the bricks and cement and other debris carted away. Then, maybe, someone would fill in the tunnels and turn the area into an art museum.

Or—without Hiram and Veronica Stern and Samantha—maybe the land would remain empty.

Gravel crunched behind us as a car pulled up and parked. I turned to see Cohen emerge and place a hand above his eyes, scanning for me. I waved, and he started across the field toward us.

Clyde took off like a shot. I watched the two of them greet each other. When Cohen regained his feet and started walking again, Clyde raced back to me.

"Hey," Cohen said when he reached the tumbled wall where I stood.

"Hey."

"Nice place for a date."

"It's gothic," I said.

"Fitting." He looked around, then his eyes came back to me. "I don't have a lot of time. Bandoni and I just caught a new case. No trains in this one. No children."

I said, "Good."

I turned so that I was facing Potters Road. I could just make out the overpass near where Samantha Davenport had died. In my mind, I followed the tracks north. Out of Colorado and through Wyoming. On up into Montana and the Powder River Basin with its millions of tons of coal, which had helped make DPC a success. Which had helped make Hiram Davenport a success. Then I kept moving north, through Montana and into Canada, where DPC had extended its reach.

While Cohen watched me, I spun southward, mentally following the train tracks down through New Mexico and across the border, into the often dangerous state of Chihuahua and on through the rest of the country, down to the federal district of Mexico City.

My fingers went to the photograph of Malik in my pocket.

Two days earlier, David Fuller with the Hope Project had sent me a photo. A boy who looked like Malik had been seen with a Caucasian man in Mexico City. It was our first lead.

I rested a hand on Cohen's arm.

"I have to go away for a while first," I said. "There's something I have to take care of."

He faced me. "Is this about that phone call? The one that made you sit on the floor for twenty minutes?"

I nodded. "It's about a child, Cohen. About something that happened in Iraq." *It's about moral injury,* I thought but did not say.

"And it's one of those things you said you can't talk about."

"Not yet."

I expected him to argue. To be angry. But instead he slipped his fingers through mine. Maybe it was because in the week after we'd found

Lucy, I had started to talk. To tell him about what had happened in Iraq. Not the stuff that could get him killed. But the other things. The IED that had killed Gonzo. The bodies I'd processed. The little boy we'd found, although not how we'd found him or that he'd gone missing. Maybe this was my first step in that marathon. Maybe talking would allow self-forgiveness. Already, I thought, bringing those things into the light had loosened some of their hold.

"How long?" Cohen asked now.

"I don't know. Maybe a long time. Maybe no time at all."

He nodded, turned away again. He leaned his elbows on the wall, and I leaned next to him. We were silent for a while, watching the sun sink, watching the red shafts of light turn the eerie ruins into something both frightening and fragile.

I thought about my love for a dead man, then leaned against the living man standing next to me. There was a lot to be said for the living.

"Will you still be here when I get back?" I asked.

He gave me a smile. It was sad. But then he nodded.

"It's like I hear you tell Clyde, sometimes."

At the sound of his name, Clyde looked up at Cohen, and Cohen ruffled his ears.

"What's that?" I asked.

"We're still good." He squeezed my hand. "We're still good."

ACKNOWLEDGMENTS

Writing my first novel took a village. This one took a city.

I want to thank the members of my critique group and my beta readers: Donnell Bell, Ronald Cree, Kirk Farber, Robert Spiller, and Riley Walker. For going above and beyond, my deepest thanks to Michael Bateman, Michael Shepherd, and Chris Mandeville. A special thanks to Deborah Coonts for being willing to help every step of the way—at times, that must have been excruciating. Also to Kyle and Amanda Nickless, Cathy Noakes, Lori Dominguez, Patricia Coleman, Maria Faulconer, and always—first and last—to my husband, Steve.

This book would not have been possible without the knowledge and insight of retired Denver K9 officer Dan Boyle, Senior Special Agent Scott Anthony, Foreman General Edward Pettinger, and Career Intelligence Officer Steve Pease. Also, Harding Rome, retired senior trial counsel at Union Pacific Railroad; Meredith Frank, medical examiner, Denver Office of the Medical Examiner; Candy Muscari-Erdos, CEO of Mountain High Service Dogs, and her trusted companion, a German shepherd named Count Nathaneal Athos (Nate to his friends); Pete Klismet, retired FBI Profiler and Special Agent; Deborah Sherman, public affairs and community outreach specialist, FBI Denver Division; and FBI Special Agent Phil Niedringhaus. To Britta Lietke for her help with Clyde's German commands. Ever and always, a special thank you to retired Denver detective Ron Gabel for his patience, knowledge, and wealth of stories. The help I received from the people listed here was invaluable; any mistakes in this book are entirely my own.

Some of the incidents in *Dead Stop* were ripped from the headlines. I refer to a series of articles in the *New York Times* written by Walt Bogdanich. If you're interested in knowing just how dangerous railroad crossings can be, then you'll find these articles fascinating. Just remember, there are two sides to every story.

If you're curious about the great titans of railroad—past and present—and how railroads are created and sometimes destroyed, you will enjoy *The Well-Dressed Hobo* by Rush Loving Jr.

For more information about moral injury, I highly recommend *What Have We Done: The Moral Injury of Our Longest Wars* by David Wood, which looks at the impossible moral dilemmas created by war.

Finally, if you'd like to know more about the USMC's Mortuary Affairs unit, please read Jessica Goodell's heartrending book, *Shade It Black: Death and After in Iraq.*

Special thanks to my agent, Bob Diforio of the D4EO Literary Agency, and to the incredible Liz Pearsons, Charlotte Herscher, and the team at Thomas & Mercer. I am so very fortunate to work with all of you.

Author's Note

A modern freight railroad is an immense and complex entity. To avoid bogging the story down in detail, I present a simplified management structure in *Dead Stop*.

I also took certain liberties in how I portrayed some of the counties, cities, railroad tracks, military bases, and institutions described in this book. The world presented here, along with its characters and events, is entirely fictitious. Denver Pacific Continental (DPC), T&W, and SFCO are wholly fictional railways. Any resemblance to actual incidents and corporations, or to actual persons living or dead, is entirely coincidental.

ABOUT THE AUTHOR

Barbara Nickless lives in Colorado, where she loves to snowshoe, hike, and drink single-malt Scotch—usually not at the same time. Her first novel, *Blood on the Tracks*, won the Daphne du Maurier Award of Excellence and the Colorado Book Award and was a Suspense Magazine Best of 2016 selection. Barbara is a member of Mystery Writers of America, Sisters in Crime, and International Thriller Writers. Her essays and short stories have appeared in *Writer's Digest* and *Criminal Element*, among other markets. Connect with her at www.barbaranickless.com.